The Mists of Time

SACRIFICE

Linda Coleman

Copyright © 2019 Linda Coleman

ISBN: 9781074313890

This book is sold subject to the condition that it shall not, by way of trade or otherwise, be lent, resold, hired out, or otherwise circulated without the publisher's prior consent in any form of binding or cover other than that in which it is published and without a similar condition including this condition being imposed on the subsequent purchaser.

The scanning, uploading and distribution of this book via the internet or via any other means without the permission of the publisher is illegal and punishable by law. Please purchase only authorized electronic editions and do not participate in or encourage electronic piracy of copyrighted materials. Your support of the author's rights is appreciated.

This is a work of fiction. Names, characters, businesses, places, events and incidents are either the products of the author's imagination or used in a fictitious manner.

*For Richard
With love*

Marcus Antonius

83 – 30 BCE

veritatem dies aperit

Prologue
Bay of Actium, Greece -31B.C.

"The plan is a sound one, for the navy, but what of our army? We do not have enough ships to safely carry nineteen legions and their supplies by sea."

It was a fair point, and one well made, by Publius Canidius Crassus, the most senior officer remaining in Mark Antony's beleaguered army. All but surrounded, low on supplies, riddled with malaria, their forces desperately needed a way out of the swampy lagoon which had long been their home, before there was no one left to save.

When his battle strategy first came under criticism, Mark Antony's cruelty in response had reached new heights. Decimation was no longer a sufficient punishment for the doubters. One of the senators was physically torn limb from limb. Her royal highness, Cleopatra VII, queen of Egypt, delighted in such 'entertainments', but the remaining officers were sickened by her sadism. The trickle of desertions became a torrent, until only a few officers were left. Defections to the enemy were now a daily occurrence, although efforts to stop the outward flow of men had long since waned.

Canidius sometimes felt as if he was the only one trying to keep the legions in check. He wished he knew what was in his commander's mind, but Mark Antony no longer kept counsel with his officers in the way he once had. The only counsel he accepted, or was allowed to accept, was that of the queen.

Canidius was the last man standing, so to speak, in Mark Antony's trusted retinue. Of the others, Lepidus had become the first casualty of the new order, deposed many years earlier. Ventidius died in mysterious circumstances. Pollio retired, possibly before he too was disposed of. Plancus turned traitor, selling off the secrets of Cleopatra's court, along with Mark Antony's will. Each of this generation of great men – Caesar's men – had been carefully removed from Mark Antony's inner circle by the underhand actions of one Gaius Octavius Caesar, or Octavian as he was more commonly known, and his agents.

At least, that was what Canidius chose to believe. He and Ahenobarbus were all that remained of the old guard, but, when Ahenobarbus succumbed to dysentery, the latest plague to hit their marshland location, Mark Antony gave permission for the sick man to leave in order that he might return home to die. That left Canidius as the last Roman general to remain loyal to the world's most infamous pair of lovers.

How they had come to be trapped in such avoidable circumstances was equally tragic. A year before, when Octavian declared war on the queen, Canidius supported the plan for an immediate invasion of Italy. They had enough men to make the ground quake as they marched, whilst the queen had more than enough ships to carry them. A lightning attack, straight to the heart of Rome, would have proved decisive. Even the mighty Marcus Agrippa, Octavian's most skilled general, could not have withstood the sheer force that Mark Antony was then capable of mustering to his side. Yet Mark Antony dithered, apparently unwilling to shed blood on home soil, while the queen whispered suggestions of far greater schemes. Her plan was for a slower, more grandiose advance towards the western shores of Greece, a stage-managed display, designed to broadcast a message of unequivocal power – her power.

The plan failed dismally. Spread out in pockets along the coast, Mark Antony's forces were nibbled away one encampment at a time by the brilliant counter-moves of Agrippa. All that remained of their army was trapped in this disease-ridden, mosquito-infested hell-hole that the gods had long ago forsaken.

Even though Canidius' question was aimed at his commander, it was the queen who gave the reply.

"Let the army do what it does best. March them back to Egypt. When we engage Agrippa's fleet, it will provide enough of a distraction to allow their withdrawal from the camps."

"Our army will fight given the chance," Canidius growled. His patience was wearing increasingly thin with Mark Antony's eastern harpy, who merely shook her head in uninterested disagreement.

He tried again. "If they are to retire, who does your majesty suggest lead them?"

"We are told you are the most competent *man* here. You do it!" Her tone was deliberately insulting, and it pushed Canidius to the brink.

He clenched his fists as he fought to keep his temper in check. "I think it would look better if the general led them himself. He has a solid reputation for turning such a defeat into a triumph by leading from the front."

His mistake was in using the word defeat. Cleopatra exploded with the speed of a cobra, aiming all her venom at him.

"Ridiculous! A general is required to lead a battle, not cower in the retreat like some frightened dog. The front is where Mark Antony is required, and that front will be at sea. If your beloved legions must have an officer to hold their hands while they limp away to safety, you will do it. You have our complete confidence in this matter."

Cleopatra could not care less what happened to the Roman army, regardless of its strategic value to her cause. All she cared about was keeping Mark Antony within easy reach. If she allowed him to leave her side, Canidius would poison his mind against her. If Mark Antony could be persuaded to lead the army to safety, he might well be persuaded to lead them directly into Octavian's arms. If that happened, all she had achieved would be lost. Any alliance between Mark Antony and Octavian had always posed the greatest threat to her sovereignty. She had worked too hard, and for too long, to destroy the accord between them. She could never allow such arrangements to become a reality again.

Canidius wanted to strike her for her insolence, but to raise a hand to the queen meant an instant death. He knew he had lost the argument, but he gave one last, valiant plea in an attempt to change the outcome. Canidius' loyalty was to Mark Antony, not the evil witch standing at his side.

"General Antony, what do you think? Those legions have stuck by you through thick and thin." He was pointing now, towards the leather walls of the Praetorium to remind his general that the men were out there, waiting for their orders, yet Mark Antony appeared to ignore the gesture.

"They have shed blood for you more times than I dare to remember. They have held when lesser men have run. Show them you still have faith in them." Canidius slammed his open palm on the table in front of him in a last-ditch effort to get some kind of reaction.

Everyone in the room jumped, except for Mark Antony. He did not even blink.

"Walk out with me and lead your men to safety," Canidius begged. "I swear to you, this is our best course of action."

Mark Antony slowly turned away from his officers, closing his eyes as a wave of doubt overcame him. His preference had always been to stay with his army. At Mutina, he had withdrawn across hostile terrain with the enemy snapping at his heels, yet he had returned more powerful than before. In Parthia, he had faced seemingly insurmountable odds, yet still he led the bulk of his troops to safety. Could he do it again? Should he follow his heart and stay with his men? Or should he listen to his head, and stay close to the woman who paid for everything? Without her, he was broke, washed up, bankrupt.

He had no idea what to do. In truth, his judgement had been clouded for many years. He was no longer the phoenix, raised from the ashes of defeat at Mutina to crush Caesar's assassins, Brutus and Cassius, at Philippi. His formidable powerbase, earned with the spilt blood of good Roman citizens, had all but slipped from his grasp, lost to both the mists of time, and the constant demands of the queen of Egypt. She called the shots now, as she had for so many years. It was her navy that transported his forces from country to country and her armies who shed blood for him: hers because she paid them. These days, he was little more than a pawn in her grand plan for world domination: a Roman figurehead behind which she could rally what was left of her Roman troops. And she made sure he knew it.

He wondered briefly if it had been the same for Caesar, though he doubted it. For ten years now, Mark Antony had done her bidding. Caesar had only suffered four years of her constant nagging, before being saved by the assassins' blades. Oh, how he wished he had shared his mentor's fate on that day. To die a heroic death meant passing into legend. Instead, he felt destined to fall into obscurity, nothing more than a historical footnote at best. It was his own fault - he knew that. He allowed himself to be led along by the considerable hold she had on his cock. Both her hands were firmly wrapped around it, jerking it along to whatever tune she chose to play.

The queen's considerable sexual cravings were once a blessing to a man well known for sharing an equally voracious appetite. Now, their relationship hung around his neck like a curse. The hero of Philippi was better known as a hopeless, lovelorn sap, bewitched by Egyptian mysticism. He was regarded as little more than a fool, and an old one at that. It was far too late to extricate his self-esteem, or his balls, from the queen's vice-like grip.

His thoughts turned again to Melissa, as they always did in times of the greatest despair. *Why did I have to lose you? Why could I not have kept the one woman who made me truly happy? Where are you when I most need your counsel?*

Without thinking, his hand went to his chest and lay over Melissa's locket hidden beneath his uniform. He had worn it next to his heart every day since Ventidius had given it to him. Even when he learnt the truth about who Melissa really was and where her visions came from, it did not change his feelings. That she was a liar and a charlatan made no difference to the stomach-wrenching love he felt for the woman he would never see again. For the past twelve years he had regretted his decision to let her leave. He should have gone with her, regardless of the consequences. His soul screamed in pain to the gods - he would willingly give his life, if only he could hold her one last time.

"General?"

Canidius dragged him back to his present predicament. He opened his eyes to find himself looking straight into those of Cleopatra's. They were full of hate as she stared at his hand, knowing what lay beneath it. That locket had been the cause of many an argument between them.

She gave the slightest nod. It was a subtle gesture, but it was there, instructing him how to proceed. He had no choice but to comply with her demands as her metaphorical hand once again jerked his member to the beat of her chosen drum.

He shook himself, briefly forcing his thoughts of Melissa, and happier times, to the back of his mind. This was not the moment to give in to his melancholy. He was far too sober for that. He pushed past Cleopatra, reaching for the flask of wine sitting behind her on a side table.

Cleopatra glanced at it, before raising her eyes to the sky, disgusted that he intended to drink himself into oblivion yet again. He glared in response, though he made sure only she saw it.

He made a half-hearted attempt to bark out the orders as if he meant them.

"Cleopatra's fleet is the priority. It must be saved at all costs. Make arrangement as the queen suggests. Burn whatever ships we cannot hope to take."

Mark Antony stormed from the Praetorium, carrying only the flask, intent on leaving his bemused officers, Cleopatra, and all of his troubles behind him for a few hours, whilst he sought solace from the bottom of a wine glass.

Chapter 1
Bay of Aktion, Greece – Present Day

Melissa Marcus stood on the prow of her husband's yacht, *Selene*, staring across the still waters of the bay. It was early, but she had been awake for some time. Restless, she had left Anthony sleeping below, coming on deck to watch the inky-black of night fade through its pale blue-grey hues to the initial blood-red rising of the golden sun as it breached the horizon.

It had been a swelteringly hot night, but there was an unusual coolness about the early morning that was making her uncomfortable. Normally, she would hear the first sound of birdsong to accompany the brightening skies. Today, it was eerily quiet. The only sound was the gentle lapping of the water against the hull of the yacht. For some reason, the silence made the hairs on the back of her neck stand on end. There was an odd smell in the air too, adding to her discomfort. It was damp and earthy, and it brought back painful memories of a past that she was desperate to forget.

Anthony and Melissa Marcus lived an idyllic life on Anthony's estate in northern Italy. The land had been turned over to traditional Roman farming methods, with the help of Henry, their estate manager and long-time family friend. Archaeologists by profession, their project was recognised as a real-life historical study and was used by numerous universities as a base for their students' fieldwork. There had even been a TV deal, providing a substantial income. Life was good for both of them, and their growing brood of children.

The estate also held a dark secret. Melissa had time-travelled in the woods by the small stream, recently identified as the Rubicon, on two separate occasions. Both times she had found herself in the Roman era, where she was forced to use her academic knowledge to ensure her survival. She was also forced into a torrid affair with the infamous Roman general, Mark Antony. Whilst his patronage had kept her alive, her infidelity was a constant source of consternation to her otherwise exuberant husband.

Anthony had also travelled in time, having been born in the more decadent surroundings of ancient Rome. He was raised by a Roman, to Roman standards and with Roman morals, which made his attitude to the modern world somewhat lax. His genes did not help either. Being descended from one of history's most notorious philanderers certainly played a part in his shaping his outlook on life. Anthony's father was none other than the same drunken, licentious womaniser who had once been Melissa's lover – Mark Antony.

It made for an unconventional marriage, being more 1st century B.C. than 21st century A.D. Anthony was headstrong and reckless. He drank too much and he gambled far more than Melissa liked. He also had an 'arrangement' with a high-class escort service in Bologna – it was perfectly acceptable for Roman men to entertain mistresses, but they expected their wives to be chaste. Melissa meanwhile acted the part of the virtuous matron, holding the family together and pretending not to care about her husband's infidelities.

The Marcuses had three beautiful children. Vicky was

the eldest and fast approaching the turbulent teens. Alex, four years her junior, and Jack, two years younger again, were the image of their father. All three were complete tearaways, following in Anthony's reckless footsteps. Melissa often despaired at their antics, and at her husband, who never punished them, regardless of the seriousness of their misdemeanours.

Despite their odd marital arrangements, theirs had been a happy and relaxed household for many years, until Jack was taken from them. Melissa knew few details of the tragedy, other than that it was a result of a farming incident. She badgered Anthony constantly, desperate for him to tell her what had happened, but he flatly refused to answer her questions.

The last thing Anthony wanted to do was talk about it. When he found his son's bloodied body in the mists beside the Rubicon, he knew immediately that the boy had been cut down by a sword. It meant the past was catching up with them once more, as no one from their own time could have got into those woods to harm their son in such a savage way. Anthony lied in a moment of panic, saying Jack had fallen under the plough, believing the truth would scare his wife. Once that first lie had been told, there was another, and another, until it became impossible to retrieve the situation. He dragged both Henry and his closest friend, the local doctor, into the tale, thus making them accomplices in his crime. They had all lied – to Melissa and to the authorities – because the truth raised too many questions that could not be answered.

Anthony chose to grieve in his own way, choosing to lose himself in a whisky bottle for many days before relieving his frustrations in the comforting arms of a woman – any woman – eventually burying any remaining pain so deep it could never again surface. Melissa could not cope with his attitude, or constant advances, and pushed him away. Tempers flared daily. Both seemed oblivious to the pain they were causing to their remaining children who were also grieving the loss of their brother. Eventually, Henry was forced to step in, sobering up Anthony enough to persuade him to take Melissa away sailing. Henry hoped that spending time alone in a confined space would force the pair to work through their problems. Reluctant to leave her children, Melissa had refused until Vicky screamed at her mother to 'sort out your shit!' Sometimes, it takes a child's bluntness to put things in perspective.

Anthony loved his yacht almost as much as he loved his family, and often took the children sailing when the weather was good. She was an old, wooden-hulled craft, built to a design so simple that it had not changed in centuries. Ever the romantic, Anthony wanted to preserve the traditional look of the yacht and had spent years renovating her by hand, re-teaking the decks and woodwork himself. The interior was more modern, having been stripped and refitted to his specific designs, cleverly concealing the luxuries of a toilet and navigational equipment behind wooden facades that could only be released by someone who knew how they worked: secret panels designed to entertain the children. The final change was to fit a junk-rig to make her easier to sail single-handed, an idea inspired by the story of Lt-Colonel Blondie Hasler and his yacht *Jester*. While Anthony had no intention of emulating Hasler and sailing *Selene* single handed across the Atlantic, he was an experienced yachtsman and confident enough to brave the unpredictable waters of the Adriatic.

The trip had taken them down the coast from Rimini to Brindisi, across to Corfu and then south. They moored in the bay of Aktion for the night as it was too late to continue any farther. Aktion, or Actium as it had been known in Roman times, had played a significant part in history. The naval battle fought there, when the combined forces of Mark Antony and Cleopatra clashed with Octavian's Republican army, marked the beginning of end for the infamous lovers. It seemed a fitting place for two archaeologists to moor overnight, especially two on whom Mark Antony's influence had been so great.

The sound of the hatch opening made Melissa jump. She turned slightly to see the back of Anthony's head appear above the deck. He turned until her saw her, staring for what seemed like an age before slowly climbing on deck and moving towards her. He was half asleep and a little unsteady on his feet as he moved along the side, rubbing his heavy eyes. Wearing shorts and a white shirt that he had not bothered to button up, his tanned and muscular physique looked as impressive as it had in his twenties. Despite his many foibles, Anthony was still a man to be admired and Melissa often wondered how a plain Jane like her had ever landed such a catch.

Moving up behind Melissa, Anthony slid one arm around her waist, pulling her back towards him so she could feel his warm, muscular chest pressing against the coolness of her back. His other hand moved her hair to the side and he gently began to kiss her neck.

"Come back to bed," he murmured softly, "you'll catch a chill up here."

"It's too hot down there," she sighed.

"Is that the only reason, or is there something else?" he asked. In the months since Jack's death there had been very little intimacy between them. There had been the occasional cuddle, but nothing more. Melissa always seemed too tense and frosty in the house, but she had been relaxing more every day since they had been on the yacht and their relationship was improving as a result.

Melissa wriggled slightly against his chest and bent her head sideways. He glanced across and saw her eyes were closed and there was a hint of a smile on her face. He pressed his luck, sliding his hand under her blouse. "You're freezing. Come back to bed and let me warm you up."

The warmth of his palm against her cold stomach was comforting, yet sensual at the same time. Being in his arms had always made her feel safe and she began to relax. "I can't breathe down there. It's stifling," she teased.

He pressed his body into hers, leaving her in no doubt of his intentions. Whether they went below or not, he wanted to make love to her and, for the first time in many months, she did not pull away. It had been too long for both of them, and at that moment the timing felt right.

"Then we'll stay up here. I'll grab a blanket and we can lie on the deck and see what happens."

She turned around and wrapped her hands around his neck, sliding her fingers into his short, dark hair.

"Someone might see us," she whispered before brushing her lips against his.

"Who?" he groaned in desperation. "It's not like the kids are gonna . . ."

She froze.

Mentioning the children was the wrong thing to do. Melissa stifled a sob and began to shake. She turned away quickly, not wanting Anthony to see her tears.

Anthony knew immediately that the romance of the

moment was gone. His chance was lost yet again, as it had been so many times on this journey. As much as he wanted to force her to make love to him, he could not bring himself to do it. All he could do was hold her as they stared towards the shore, watching the mist rise slowly from the water and roll towards them. Eventually Melissa closed her eyes and slumped back against his body, allowing his warmth to transfer to her as she quietly sobbed for her lost son.

The mist thickened as it continued to move towards them, eventually enveloping the boat. It was getting colder and Melissa was shivering badly. Anthony noticed a familiar musty smell in the air. He was starting to get a bad feeling about this mist. He kept thinking back to their experiences at the Rubicon.

Surely it could not be happening again here? Surely time was not shifting again?

He could not afford to take the chance. He decided it was time to leave.

"You're freezing, we should go below," he said as calmly as he could. He had no intention of sharing his suspicions and frightening his already emotional wife if at all possible.

Melissa nodded and opened her eyes. Anthony let go of her gently, moving away, until she began to turn to follow him along the side.

It was then that she saw it. A dark, ghostly shape was moving through the mist alongside them. It had to be another boat, but where had it come from?

Suddenly, the mist began to clear and Melissa got a good look at what was in front of her. She gasped as she lurched forward towards the safety rail.

"*ANTONY! NO!*" she screamed into the mist. Melissa

knew only too well what was happening. They were being dragged into the past, and it was a point in history they should avoid at all costs.

Anthony turned his head back towards the prow, almost in slow motion. Something in the way she had shrieked the words made him realise that she was not addressing him. A sickening feeling lodged in the pit of his stomach as he looked desperately into the clearing in the mist.

What he saw made his blood run cold.

There in front of him was a Roman warship. With five banks of oars on each side, its deck towered above their yacht as it moved past them silently, its ghostly form moving in and out of view.

And on deck, staring back at them in disbelief was a man so similar in looks and stature to Anthony that he could have been looking into a mirror at an older version of himself. He was looking straight into the eyes of his father, Mark Antony.

Melissa stood rigid, staring across the water. She watched as Mark Antony began to remove his battle armour as the ship continued to float away.

Anthony knew only too well what was coming next.

"He's coming for you. He's going to jump," he said. There was a lump growing in his throat as he said the words. Fear was now swelling within him. All his instincts were telling him to run, to get them as far away as possible, but he was rooted to the spot, unable to move. His heart began to beat faster as the panic inside grew. Beads of sweat formed on his temple and trickled down his face. His mouth was dry, as if it was full of ash. His usual bravado failed him. He felt desperate and completely unsure of his next move.

Dressed in only his tunic, Mark Antony dived into

the waters and began to swim towards the *Selene*, while his men looked on in horror from the deck above. As he jumped, Melissa caught a glimpse of something golden hanging around his neck. At that distance it looked like a medallion, but somehow Melissa knew it was her locket. He must have kept it with him since the day their good friend, Ventidius Bassus, handed it to him. The fact that he was still wearing it gave her a new cause for concern. If he still valued it, it meant he still had feelings for her and that left her husband in a precarious position. Mark Antony was a man prone to jealousy, especially where she was concerned, and had once sworn an oath to kill any man who touched her. The situation was becoming more dangerous by the second.

She swung round to face her husband, her eyes full of fear.

"We have to go – NOW!"

The response was so sharp that it took Anthony by surprise for a moment.

"Anthony! *DO SOMETHING!*" Melissa screamed again, jolting him into action. He moved aft and jumped into the well. The quickest escape would be to use the engine, as unfurling the sails would take too long. He stuck his head through the hatch, grabbed the key from its hook and rammed it into the ignition. As Melissa reached the well, he turned the key, but nothing happened. It was completely silent, as if the engine was not even there. Obviously modern technology did not work when time slipped backwards.

He had to swallow hard to force the next words from his lips. "Get below, and cover up anything technical," he called frantically as he tried the key again. Still nothing happened.

"Why? Don't we need it to sail?" Melissa asked as she passed him, heading below.

Anthony glanced over her head and saw one of Mark Antony's hands appear on the fore deck. He had used the anchor chain to pull himself far enough out of the water to get a grip on the deck.

"It's too late," he shouted in reply, throwing the ignition key at her before running along the deck again. It took strength and determination to make a climb like that after such a frantic swim. Anthony could only hope that such exertions had taken their toll on their unwelcome visitor.

Melissa turned her head in time to see Mark Antony pulling himself aboard. She went below, her hands shaking as she replaced the wooden panelling to hide the radio and navigation systems. She stuffed the ignition keys in the pocket of a pair of jeans and shoved them to the back of the clothing locker. She could only hope it would be good enough to keep them from being found.

Above deck, Anthony reached his father, who was already halfway over the guard rail. He punched him on the jaw in the hope of knocking him back into the water, but the experienced soldier was more than a match for his son. Holding tight to the rail, the older man waited for the next blow to fall, dodging it with ease.

Mark Antony now had the advantage. As Anthony's blow sailed past his father's jaw, Mark Antony head-butted his son's shoulder with enough force to knock Anthony sideways. Anthony lost his footing briefly and slid along the deck, giving Mark Antony enough time to make it on board.

Anthony steadied himself and turned in time to receive a punch to the jaw so powerful, it floored him. As he sprawled across the deck, Mark Antony dived on him, his hands around his throat. Fighting for his life, Anthony hit hard into the stomach of his attacker, once, twice, three times, until Mark Antony was too winded to hold on any longer and fell to one side, trying to catch his breath. He was tired from the swim and now the exertion began to take its toll as his arms began to cramp.

Anthony took his chance. Younger and fitter, and with his father's greater combat experience nullified by a lack of air, he pummelled his victim over and over with short, sharp blows. Mark Antony raised his arms to protect his face from the beating, but it made no difference. His vision blurred and he began to lose consciousness.

Anthony's fists flew at such a rate there was no defence. He was winning and he knew it. More worryingly, he was revelling in the satisfaction of besting the man he had long regarded as his rival. Melissa may have chosen to live with him, but it was not enough. He had lived for too long in the shadow of his infamous father. He had a point to prove: that he was the better man. Unfortunately, he was not behaving like the better man in that moment.

Melissa arrived back on deck to witness the final flash of Anthony's triumph. She was horrified and screamed at him to stop, but he ignored her.

At that moment, another pair of hands gripped the guard rail, and then another. Two more men, both brutishly large, were now aboard the *Selene* and going to Mark Antony's aid. One of the men pulled a whip from his belt. He let it fly with a great crack, lashing Anthony's arm and preventing him from delivering the next punch. As Anthony turned around, the second man punched him in the jaw and he was knocked sideways, away from his victim. Now fighting on three fronts, it was no longer a fight he could hope to win.

Both Antony's pulled themselves to their feet. Mark Antony punched his son in the kidneys. Anthony turned and landed a hard kick in his father's groin, dropping the older man to his knees. The whip cracked a second time across Anthony's back, and then a third as he cried out from the pain now searing through his flesh. As one of the other men grabbed Anthony by his arms, wrenching them backwards and pinning them behind his back, the other discarded the whip and landed a number of punches to Anthony's solar plexus. He tried to kick out, but he could not fight both men.

Melissa tried to go to her husband's aid, but she did not make it. As she tried to clamber over the roof of the cabin, the man delivering the blows hit her with the back of his hand, knocking her to the deck. She hit her knee hard, splitting the skin to the bone. She shrieked, holding her stinging knee until the initial shock subsided.

As she tried to get up, a strong hand gripped her shoulder, holding her down. She turned her head upwards to find herself staring into the almost demonic stare of a rapidly-recovering Mark Antony.

Terrified, she pleaded with him to save her husband. "Please stop this. We surrender. I beg you, please, stop them hurting my husband."

Mark Antony gripped her shoulder harder and wrenched her to her feet. He forced her in front of him and held her facing her beaten and now well-bloodied husband who could no longer stand unaided.

As Anthony slumped in the arms of the man holding him, the other gripped his chin and forced his face upwards. Melissa could see the defiance still in his eyes as he mumbled, "I love you." It was clear that he thought he was going to die.

"You wish to take his place?" Mark Antony hissed in Melissa's ear.

She shook her head.

"I thought not," he continued. "Perhaps I will stop. Or, perhaps I will tie him to the rigging and scuttle this craft. You can watch your beloved husband succumb to Neptune's will."

Melissa sobbed, but she knew better than to plead any longer. Mark Antony was a man capable of anything at the best of times, and this was, perhaps, one of the worst. Agreeing with him was all she could do and hope for the best.

"If it pleases you, my master," she whispered, "As your servant, I always obey your wishes."

Mark Antony had always hated Melissa referring to herself as his slave. Her use of the words 'master' and 'servant' were enough to make him pause. He squeezed her arms against her sides painfully, before he threw her forwards into the arms of one of his henchmen.

"Take her aboard," he ordered, jerking his head behind him towards the warship that was once again looming large above them.

Melissa was dragged towards a rope ladder dangling from the deck of the larger vessel. When she reached it, she looked over her shoulder to see Anthony fall in a heap onto the deck of the *Selene*, and then watched in horror as his own father kicked him repeatedly in the head and chest.

As she was forced to climb, she had no idea whether her husband was alive, or dead.

Chapter 2

Melissa was dragged to the prow of the warship *Antonia* – the flagship of Queen Cleopatra's fleet. Her hands were tightly bound with a length of rope, before her guard tied the loose end to a mooring ring. He threw a rag at her before forcing her to sit down on the deck to await Mark Antony's arrival. She tried in vain to look aft to see if her husband was being brought on board, but her line of sight was blocked. She strained against her bonds in an attempt to get a better view, but was forced back every time she tried to move. Giving up, she clutched the rag across her knee to stem the flow of blood and waited, occasionally biting at one of her fingernails as her nerves got the better of her.

For once, she knew exactly when and where she was. The mists had brought her to Actium in the September of 31 B.C. Cleopatra's fleet was in the process of forcing its way out of the bay and through Octavian's blockade, so skilfully arranged by the formidable Marcus Agrippa. Melissa had met him once, as a young man. Even then, he had displayed the tactical abilities that had undermined Mark Antony's forces time and again. He was the real military brain behind Octavian's advance, but he had always been happy with being second-in-command, and would remain so all his life.

As the remnants of the queen's navy sailed for

Egypt, Mark Antony's army, now under the command of Canidius Crassus, had been left to find its own way to safety. Melissa knew only too well that this was also a mission destined to fail as the men would soon desert. As she waited on the deck, she began to wonder how different her world would be if those legions did reach Egypt. Mark Antony had always been more tolerant of the old ways, preferring the old Republican methods of governance and, of course, rampant corruption, rather than aiming for the autocracy pursued by the Caesars. The Roman world might have remained more egalitarian under his leadership, and she had always wondered why he had thrown it all away. Now, it appeared, she was about to find out first-hand.

Eventually, Mark Antony walked past her. Ignoring her completely, he sat down in the prow of the ship, staring towards the horizon. Melissa knew he was despondent after the battle, broken by his failure to extricate more of his fleet. Less than half of it was intact. Many ships had been destroyed and many more were trapped, unable to disengage from the fight and follow their commander to safety. In military terms, it was a disaster. The Egyptian navy was far superior to that of Octavian in terms of power, but his ships were lighter and more manoeuvrable. The tactics of Agrippa had won the day yet again. Not only was this battle over for Mark Antony and Cleopatra, the war was effectively lost.

Plutarch recorded that Mark Antony spent three days sitting like this, in complete silence. For Melissa, the prospect of spending three days staring at a man's back was mortifying. She knew he was prone to depression, both from the details recorded by ancient historians, and from her own personal experiences at Mutina. She believed he would be reliving the battle in his head, analysing every detail to try to find the fatal flaw in his plans and, in doing so, he would hear again the screams of the drowning men and smell the burning flesh of those trapped on the fiery hulls. These memories would overwhelm any man, but especially one in Mark Antony's delicate mental state.

There was a brief respite from the silence when a shout went up from the watch. There were other, smaller vessels in pursuit. Faster and more agile than the *Antonia*, they posed a significant threat to her intended escape. Immediately, the soldier resurfaced from inside the defeated shell slumped in the prow. Mark Antony jumped into action, shouting orders for the defence of their vessel. Whatever the cost, the flagship and her valuable cargo must break free. Cleopatra had placed on board the remains of the expedition funds: her war chest. It was a substantial amount of money that he could not afford to lose to either Octavian, or to the sea.

Within the hour, the threat was gone. Mark Antony was back in his slumped position. An hour more, and Melissa decided he had wallowed in self-pity for long enough. The time had come to force him into a dialogue. That had to be why she had been brought there and even if it was not, she needed to know what had happened to her husband.

"General Antony," she began softly. "Will you not speak with me? Can I not offer you some form of counsel in your hour of need?"

Mark Antony remained silent.

"All is not lost – not yet. In three days we will make land. More ships will come. They will bring news that Octavian does not follow by sea."

Still he said nothing.

"At least put me out of my misery and tell me the fate of my husband," she grumbled, half to herself.

Mark Antony shifted his position slightly, but did not turn to look at the woman who had long haunted his dreams. When he had first seen her, he believed her to be a mirage - nothing more than a trick played on a desperate man by his equally desperate imagination. When he heard her call out to him, his heart leapt with joy, believing the gods had answered his prayers, returning their divine messenger to his side. His hopes were dashed seconds later when he saw a man with her. She had not come to help him, but to taunt him, flaunting her lover in full sight. Consumed by rage and jealousy, he had dived into the water, intent on retrieving the woman he considered rightfully his. Imagine his surprise at coming face-to-face with his twin. In the space of a few minutes he had experienced every extreme of emotion possible – panic then relief, desperation then hope, love then hatred. He wanted desperately to take her in his arms and declare his undying love, but, if he did, he was just as likely to crush the very breath from her lungs in his rage.

"Why . . . are . . . you . . . here?" he asked slowly, and a little too calmly for Melissa's liking. She knew him well enough to know a lack of an emotional outburst was a very dangerous sign. This was the calm before the storm. Only time would tell how badly it would blow.

"I am not here by my choosing. It is by accident," Melissa replied with honesty, but with caution, not wanting to inflame the situation any further than necessary.

"An accident you say?" He paused. "I say not. You have a habit of arriving at the most inconvenient of moments, and always when you want something done. A war in Rome, or in Mutina, for example, neither of which were the choosing of their commanders, though both directed by your hand." Again, he paused. "Today lady, your timing is a little off. The battle is long over."

His words were tinged with bitterness, but Melissa failed to spot it. Now she had him talking, she was simply too desperate to maintain momentum and keep the conversation going to spot the danger signs of a man about to lose control.

She straightened her back and began again. "Yet the war is not. There is still time for you to recover your position. Do not continue with the fleet to Egypt. You should return to the head of your army to lead them to safer shores." This statement was the exact opposite of what was recorded in history, but it could become fact if he would only try. "If you do not, you will lose control of every man in those legions to your enemy."

"Lies! All you ever speak is lies." He spat the words out with venom as he flexed his hands, balling them into fists before stretching them out again. It was a last, desperate attempt to keep his temper in check.

Unperturbed, Melissa pressed ahead, leaving the subject of her husband alone for the time being. "If you travel overland you can join with the legions in Macedonia. It will give them heart to know their general has not deserted them."

Mark Antony winced at the thought he had deserted his men, but she could not see his reaction with his back turned towards her. "Canidius is more than capable of leading the army across the mountains. I trust his abilities far more than I trust the advice of a lying whore." He shifted his position slightly. "Your advice is false and I will listen no longer. You have told your last lie, Lissa."

"I have never lied to you," Melissa replied defiantly.

"It is all you have ever done, witch."

Slowly, he turned around to face her. Raising his hand, he tapped the locket hanging around his neck. "Ventidius told me everything. You 'see' nothing."

Melissa looked away. Many years earlier, she had taken Ventidius Bassus, one of Mark Antony's most loyal friends, fully into her confidence. He had her locket. He had opened it and seen the photographs it contained. She had to give him some form of explanation, so she told him the truth: that she was no seer, but had come to them from the future. She fully expected to die, but to her surprise, he had taken the news rather well, keeping her secret for as long as she had known him. She always hoped Ventidius would find a way to explain that the little girl in the picture was Mark Antony's daughter, but she was shocked that he had chosen to divulge everything else that he knew.

"You wonder why he told your tale, when you asked him to show more discretion," Mark Antony hissed.

She nodded without looking at him.

"Loyalty, Lissa. A concept you should try to understand." He tapped the locket again, "When he first showed me this, I was afraid. Mark Antony, the hero of Philippi, terrified by an image!" He shook his head; half in disgust, half in disbelief at what he was saying. "I refused to look upon it. Ventidius had little choice but to explain every detail given to him by you and that farmer I found you with." He meant Henry, the estate manager. On Melissa's second foray into the past, Henry was with her, posing as a farmer. "It proved a most interesting tale – how a woman from the future came into the past to bewitch me. You told your lies and deception with such eloquence for so many years, and all for your own purpose."

Shocked, she turned to face him again. "That is untrue. I cared for you," she exclaimed.

"You cared only for maintaining the stories written in your books, whilst I loved you in ways I had never loved any woman, before or since. Your feelings for me were nothing more than a lie. You belonged to that . . ." he paused, searching for an appropriately damming word to describe his rival ". . . that abomination you married. I vowed I would kill him if I ever had the misfortune to meet him, yet it appears another tale you told Ventidius may be true. He believed that, if I killed the wretch now resident in the hold, I would cause the death of one of my own." He eyed her with suspicion as he waited for a response.

Melissa's heart leapt. Anthony was alive at least. She smiled as the relief washed over her like one of the many waves lapping against the hull.

"Is it true?" Mark Antony pointed towards the deck. "Is the man below Antonius? Is he my eldest son?" His voice shook as he spoke the words. He could hardly believe what he was saying.

"He is," she blurted out with sudden joy.

Her outburst was met with a scowl.

It was Melissa's turn to pause. "What will you do to him?" she asked more calmly.

It felt like an age passed before he answered.

"I do not know. I need time to consider." He crossed his arms as he continued to stare at her. "Do you love him?" he suddenly asked.

Melissa looked down at the deck as she considered her options. To tell the truth could completely destroy what little was left of her relationship with the man standing in front of her, whereas to lie might put Anthony's life in even greater danger.

She hesitated too long. With lightning speed, Mark Antony crossed the deck and grabbed her by the neck with one hand.

"Do you love him?" He hissed, pulling her upwards.

Melissa gasped and gargled as he squeezed her throat. "Yes," she squeaked.

He let go of her, throwing her backwards with such force that she sprawled across the deck. She stayed where she was. She knew better than to try to move when he was in such a towering rage.

He resumed his seat in the prow of the boat, staring at the deck. Minutes ticked by before Melissa dared to look up.

"How much of this is known to Cleopatra?" she asked nervously. She needed to know exactly how much danger they were in. She had no love for Egypt's last pharaoh, whom she had met years before, and she knew the feeling was mutual. Cleopatra would need no encouragement to execute her on any pretext whatsoever.

As he replied, Mark Antony raised his head to look at her. "You think me such a fool? That I could bear to hear her laugh as I regaled her with tales of your deceptions? First you dupe Caesar, and then me?" He shook his head slowly. "She knows nothing and, if you value your head, I would advise it remains that way. My humiliation would be complete, and your position would quickly become . . ." he paused, searching for an appropriate phrase ". . . untenable."

When their eyes met, Melissa could see how bloodshot his were. He had been weeping, but she did not know if it was for her or for his men languishing in the seas behind them. Not daring to ask, she nodded her agreement and he turned away once more.

They both stared out to sea for some while, listening to the creaking of the oars followed by their gentle splashing as they slipped beneath the waves. Eventually he shouted a half-hearted order to one of the guards stationed further down the deck.

"Take her below. I find her company is no longer as enjoyable as it once was."

Below decks meanwhile, a petite woman stood in the shadows watching the semi-conscious form of Anthony Marcus through the open door of the storeroom now doubling as a brig. Wearing a plain knee-length tunic, and no shoes or jewellery, she had the appearance of a low-ranking slave. Only her eyes revealed a hint of her true status. Peering from beneath the scarf which covered her head and face, they were heavily made up and cat-like.

In her hands she carried an open jar of ointment. Nodding her intention to the guard, she slipped through the doorway of the makeshift cell and silently approached the curled body lying on its side. He was no threat to her with his wrists and ankles both tightly bound.

Dropping to her knees in front of him and placing the jar on the floor beside her, she made a visual assessment of the prisoner. A trickle of blood had dried on his chin, having seeped from the split on his lip. His eyes were closed. One eye socket was swelling, the result of a well-aimed blow to the cheekbone. There were other marks appearing too but, despite this bruising to his face, she could see his handsome features. The tales she had heard were true. The man forcibly brought on board at Actium was indeed a double for Mark Antony or, to be more precise, for the man Mark Antony had been some ten years earlier. This man was toned and muscular, lacking the developed paunch of middle age. She reasoned this man was far closer to her own age than the one moping in self-pity above decks. This man was strong, and virile, and still willing to fight for his freedom, unlike his ageing double.

She could see weals on one arm where the whip had cut across his flesh, though it had not broken the skin. There would be more marks on his back to match. Gingerly she lifted the front of his open shirt and inspected his torso. Again, she could see the reddened marks on his ribs, which were developing a bluer hue. It had taken three strong men to subdue him. He would suffer greatly for it if she did nothing to tend his wounds.

She let go of the shirt and turned her attention to the jar on the floor. Steadying it briefly with one hand, she dipped her fingers into the top and withdrew a liberal amount of the ointment. Lifting the shirt again, she moved to apply the salve across Anthony's ribs.

At the first touch of her fingers on his skin, he grabbed for her wrist with his bound hands, but she was too quick for him. She pulled back and stared into his one open eye. There was no fear in it, only defiance.

She smiled, not that he could see it. "That is most rude," she said in perfect Latin.

"What is that?" he replied, pointing shakily at the jar in her hands.

"An ointment used for bruising. It will help to ease your pain."

"Why would you do that?" She could hear suspicion in his voice.

"The queen wishes it," she said soothingly.

"Where am I?" he queried.

"You are aboard the *Antonia*, flagship of her royal

majesty, Cleopatra VII, Thea Philopator, Queen of Egypt."

He closed his eye and groaned in anguish, though she mistook it for pain. He and Melissa had gone back in time, as he feared, but he did not understand how it had happened. They were nowhere near the Rubicon, which was the only place he believed these mists could form. For years he had refused to move from his Italian estate, thinking he had a duty to protect its secret, but it may have been in vain. If the mists over the Bay of Actium had the same frightening ability to move a person through time, it meant it could happen anywhere in the world. The possibilities were terrifying.

He relaxed slightly, allowing her to dab the ointment on him. He winced initially, so she lessened the pressure of her fingers until her touch was featherlike.

As she worked, Anthony continued to ask questions. To his surprise he received answers.

"Why does the queen want to help me?"

"Your capture was not her wish. She did not order it. General Antony did."

"But she sent you to spy on me?"

"She has concerns for your welfare."

He opened his good eye again. "If she is so concerned, why not order my release?"

The woman shook her head. "The queen cannot be seen to undermine the general so openly. They are partners in this endeavour. If it is his wish you remain here, then here is where you will remain. And yet, it is within her power to make your imprisonment as comfortable as she can."

Despite his pain, Anthony's mind was as quick as ever. Something about this situation did not add up. Her voice seemed vaguely familiar, as if he had heard it before, but a long time ago. Perhaps he was confused. His mind wandered to Melissa. He had no idea where she was, or if she was safe. He needed to find a way to get to her if he could, not that he was much use to her in his current state.

The woman's touch became more sensuous as her hand wandered across his chest to areas that were not bruised. Despite his pain, he found her kindness strangely arousing. One possible way out of his current predicament was to lavish attention on this interesting woman. Never one to miss an opportunity to flirt, he decided to chance his luck and see where it took him.

"How comfortable will she make me? Will she remove these bonds?" He raised his wrists slightly. "As you can see I am no threat to her in this state."

"Bruises heal. When they do, you may become a threat."

"Why would I want to threaten the most beautiful woman alive?"

She paused. "You think the queen a great beauty?"

He knew from that pause, he had struck a chord. He pressed on. "I have not had the pleasure of seeing her myself, but I have heard she is the most stunning creature to have ever walked this earth."

The woman smiled again. This time, Anthony could see it in the way her eyes lifted at the corners. "You will meet her in time, in Alexandria I imagine. When you do, show loyalty and your bonds will be cut. I guarantee it."

"A guarantee from a slave has no meaning, unless of course . . ." Anthony reached up suddenly and pulled on the loose corner of the headscarf. It fell away enough to reveal a glimpse of her face. She had flawless skin, strong cheekbones and, unfortunately, a rather large nose. Not a beauty in the strictest sense, but striking nonetheless and, again, strangely familiar.

"It is not permitted for you to touch," she snapped harshly, glaring at him as she hurriedly adjusted the scarf in order to cover her face once more.

Now he saw the superiority in her heavily kohl-lined eyes. She was more than a slave, but how much more he did not yet know. She could be one of Cleopatra's hand maidens, but his gut was telling him that she was even more than that. He had met Cleopatra once when he was a small boy. He barely remembered it. In fact, all he really remembered was a coin given to him at the time. But there was something familiar about that voice that made him wonder if this woman was Cleopatra herself.

His godfather, Victor, had taught him both Latin and ancient Greek as a boy. His Greek was rusty, but he knew it was Cleopatra's preferred language. He gave it a try.

"Not a slave, but a 'malakh' sent to watch over me," he mused, deliberately throwing in the Hebrew word for angel. He knew Cleopatra spoke six languages, including Hebrew, Latin and Greek. It was unlikely one of her slaves would speak all of the three he had now used. If she understood him, he felt certain it would confirm his suspicions.

She dabbed more salve on the weals on his arm, far less gently than before. She spoke again, in equally fluent Greek. "I am no 'malakh'; no angel. I am flesh, not some other worldly being intent on mischief."

"Shame," Anthony replied. He could only remember the present tense, so his phrasing was less than ideal, but it would make the point. "I enjoy the thought of the mischief we can make."

Her eyes shot to his, surprised at his remark. He gave a weak smile and the best attempt at a wink he could manage with one eye partially shut.

Behind her, the guard coughed. It was her signal to leave. The other prisoner was being brought below.

"Your back may need attention," she said with a hint of disappointment. "I will leave the jar. Have your woman apply the ointment tonight and then again to all your wounds in the morning. Do this until the jar is empty."

As she stood up and turned away, Anthony acknowledged her last remark in Latin once more. "I will give my wife your message, and give thanks for your kindness . . ." adding quietly, ". . . your majesty."

The woman hesitated for a split second, as if wondering whether she had heard him correctly, but she made no attempt either to acknowledge or to correct his statement.

Then Cleopatra VII, Queen of Egypt, melted into the shadows, leaving Anthony to wonder if she had been real, or nothing more than a dream.

Chapter 3

Alexandria was nothing like Rome, but then ancient Rome was not what most modern people would expect. At this point of time, the Eternal City bore no resemblance to the orderly towns, laid out with military precision, that are so familiar from later Romano-British settlements. Republican Rome was built on a marshy, mosquito-infested swamp, drained and developed over the centuries more by luck than by sound judgement. It was not laid out on any plan, but had evolved in much the same way as any other settlement, growing street by street, in line with the demands of its increasing population. The rich lived on their spacious hills, while the poor crammed into the valleys. Randomly arranged streets and dark alleys were in plentiful supply.

Alexandria, on the other hand, was laid out to a plan, and a grand one at that: one that Rome would later adopt. The city had been founded by Alexander the Great some three hundred years earlier, and the Greek influence was more than apparent. This was a city that was ordered, structured, spacious and beautiful, visibly glistening from a distance beneath its white marble coat. Her crowning glory was, of course, the famous Pharos, or lighthouse, standing tall at the entrance to the harbour where it burnt day and night to guide weary travellers home.

This was a city of culture and learning to rival Athens. Its library and museum were the repository for almost all the written knowledge of the time, gained by both fair means and foul, until it caught alight during the siege of 48 B.C. Although low on both men and supplies, even the mighty Caesar understood what a catastrophe its loss would have been, and organised his troops to save what he could. Mark Antony added to its volumes, when he bestowed upon Cleopatra the library of Pergamum - a wedding present some said, though Melissa preferred to doubt that suggestion. Despite the damage from the flames, the brightest scientists and most accomplished teachers could still be found pacing its hallowed halls: a seat of learning to rival its modern counterparts of Oxford and Cambridge, or Harvard and Yale.

All of the buildings in this part of the city appeared ostentatious to say the least, with their tall columns and carved facades. There were no doubt rougher areas on the outskirts where the poorest members of the population lived, but not here on the grandiose boulevards of the royal quarter. The Canopic Way, the main thoroughfare, was the width of a race track and twice as long. Even the side streets were wide enough to put their modern equivalents to shame.

Melissa wondered if Alexandria was the model followed by later Roman architects. One thing the Romans excelled at was 'borrowing' the best ideas from the societies it conquered. After all, why invent when you could simply assimilate? And assimilation was something the Romans managed with chilling effectiveness. For centuries they took the best, and worst, aspects from the civilizations they conquered and bent them to Rome's will.

Less attractive was the heat. Even in the autumn, Egypt was far hotter than Rome ever was. The gentle onshore breeze made little difference to the sweltering temperatures coming off the land. If anything, it merely gave the sultry air a salty tang. And then there was the sand, a fine layer of which reminded any visitor that the vast Saharan desert was, quite literally, on the doorstep of this expansive metropolis. Alexandria was indeed an oasis nestling in an inhospitable landscape.

By the time their cavalcade passed by the famous library, which appeared to be undergoing a full refurbishment, Melissa found her usual fascination for new places had somewhat waned. In fact, she could hardly wait to enter the cool interior of the palace and end the journey, even though this meant internment at the whim of Egypt's petulant pharaoh.

Anthony, on the other hand, was wildly gesticulating at the opulence of the various buildings they passed. The beating he had received in his initial struggle for freedom no longer troubled him. A couple of weeks at sea had healed his wounds. He looked like any other tourist, unless you glanced at his wrists, which were still tightly bound. Whereas Melissa's slight form posed no threat to Cleopatra's hulking guards, her husband's muscular physique was a different matter, although his uncanny likeness to Mark Antony saved him from the worst treatment. It seemed the guards were either confused by his presence, or simply scared of him. At times it almost seemed that they thought he *was* Mark Antony.

As for the great man himself, Melissa had not seen him since the day they had first been captured. History told her he had spent much of the remaining journey exactly where she left him – sitting in silence in the prow of the ship – a fact confirmed by the mutterings of the crew. Some said he was lost in thought, planning his next move. They spoke of plans for a counter-attack worthy of Caesar himself. Others felt he had lost his mind. Melissa felt the truth was somewhere between the two. She knew only too well that, at times of such heartfelt despair, the attitudes of those closest to Mark Antony were of vital importance. What he needed was to be supported and encouraged, not vilified or ridiculed. What she felt he really needed was her counsel, but he had clearly rejected her intervention. Other than her first brief encounter with him, Melissa spent the rest of the voyage below decks, nursing her battered husband.

They had stopped twice on the journey. The first time was in Greece, where the remnants of the fleet caught up with them. Less than a hundred ships made it out of the bay of Actium. The remainder had either been sunk or surrendered. Both Egypt's queen and her Roman consort now blamed each other for the debacle that was the battle of Actium. Mark Antony raided the queen's coffers to provide many of his loyal followers with the means to escape from what was now a hopeless cause. The queen railed against his actions, proclaiming her dissatisfaction to everyone around her. For days they refused to speak to each other, until Cleopatra's determined handmaidens coaxed the pair back together. Their alliance had to remain in place if there was to be any hope of survival; to separate now would mean annihilation for both of them.

The second stop had been a few days earlier at the port of Paraetonium, where Mark Antony disembarked with a small entourage. His new-found determination to survive took him to Cyrenaica and Libya, to gather the remaining Roman troops left in North Africa. Despite his mood swings, he seemed determined to make a stand with whatever forces he had left.

Since then, the fleet had turned eastwards and headed directly towards the Egyptian capital. Within the harbour was a designated area for the royal barges, next to the royal residence but, ever the showman, Cleopatra disembarked on the far side of the harbour in order to parade along the Canopic Way, allowing her subjects to celebrate the triumphant return of their monarch. She had actually sent word ahead that she and Mark Antony had won – a fact that amazed Melissa, but made sense given the politics of the time. Cleopatra was not exactly popular with all her subjects. While the general populace loved her, the Alexandrian elite were less keen on her willingness to collaborate with not one, but two successive Roman generals. They believed that Egypt should be allowed to rule itself without interference from any other nation. It was an ironic position to hold, considering that most of the city elite were, in fact, Greek by birth rather than Egyptian.

Their journey through the royal quarter came to an end at the entrance to the palace. Anthony and Melissa were held back until the royal party had disappeared through the great entrance, after which there seemed to be a free-for-all to get inside. They were jostled and shoved from every direction by people who had appeared from nowhere to unload goods from the wagons that had transported them from the docks.

"Don't let go," Anthony shouted. As hard as Melissa tried to hold on to his arm, it felt as if the crowd was deliberately trying to separate them. She lost her grip as they were pushed apart by two men carrying a large chest. Desperate to keep sight of his wife, Anthony strained to see over the heads in the courtyard. He could see she was just in front of him looking back. Their eyes met and he smiled at her, hoping to keep her calm. Then someone kicked him in the back of the knee and he stumbled forwards, knocking into one of the porters who began protesting in a language Anthony did not understand.

"My apologies," he said humbly in Greek, attempting to pacify the man. The porter glared at him before turning away.

When Anthony looked around again, Melissa had vanished, along with most of the crowd, which had mysteriously melted away as quickly as it had first arrived.

As Anthony fell, Melissa was dragged into the palace. She tried to call out to him, but a hand was slammed firmly across her mouth. Orders had obviously been given to separate them, but as yet she did not understand why.

She was half dragged, half carried by her guard through a large hallway with impressive marble columns, whose Corinthian capitals were coated with gold leaf and strips of ivory. The mosaic floor was laid in a geometric design which was simple yet beautiful. A grand staircase took her to the upper levels of the palace. As she climbed, Melissa noted the ceilings, studded with cut agate and lapis. This building made a statement about the wealth of its owners. No expense had been spared in its design or maintenance.

Eventually, she was taken through a pair of huge cedar doors inlaid with mother-of-pearl. She was pushed to her knees in what appeared to be the queen's boudoir, waiting for an audience. Behind a screen, Cleopatra was being helped from her robes by her maid and, when she finally appeared, she ignored Melissa, brushing past her to sit at her dressing table, where another maid began to remove the pins holding her ceremonial wig in place. Only when her own hair had been unpinned and brushed did she turn on the stool to face her prisoner.

With a flick of her eye, she gave the signal for the guard to retreat to the doorway, and then Egypt's queen gave a cruel smile as she addressed Melissa in Latin.

"How our circumstances have changed. Once, your opinion was well-regarded. Now it is ignored. At last, the woman they once called Caesar's witch, exposed for what she truly is – a liar and a whore!"

"Takes one to know one," Melissa muttered under her breath. Her knees were killing her and she was desperately worried about where Anthony had been taken.

"Your counsel is not heeded. My husband is no longer swayed by your words," Cleopatra continued, relishing the change in their circumstances. The last time they had met, Melissa had been Mark Antony's lover. Now, under Egyptian law, he was regarded as Cleopatra's husband.

"Or by yours, it seems," Melissa replied calmly. She was referring to the fact that neither of them had had much of an impact on his mental state or behaviour, which had continued to be erratic up until he left for Cyrenaica. "It appears he prefers his own company to either of us."

Cleopatra remained unmoved by Melissa's dig. "It is his right to do so, although he at least shares the warmth of my bed." She glanced at the pots on the dressing table, picking one up and idly opening the top while she changed the subject. "What of your husband? Are his wounds much healed?"

Melissa was not comfortable talking about Anthony. "He is well, thanks to the ointment given to him by your servant." She hated having to thank Cleopatra for anything, but she had to do it. "I am grateful for your kindness."

Cleopatra smiled, revelling in every moment of Melissa's discomfort. "It is of no consequence," she replied, in a tone which obviously meant it did. "I can afford to be generous to any woman, even if she was not so courteous when the situation was reversed."

Her eyes shot up from the pot to stare at her prisoner. "When we last met, you told me Caesar would kill my son. Did you really believe it to be true?"

Melissa knew she was on dangerous ground. With a snap of royal fingers, Cleopatra could order her death. For once she erred on the side of caution. "I cannot say. I lost the ability to see the future along with my virtue."

"I do not see how," the queen scoffed. "My husband has spoken of your good advice, given to him on the battlefields of Mutina. He had parted your legs on many occasions by then." Her eyes narrowed. "Your false modesty is wasted on me. I know you have a gift to rival the Oracle of Delphi itself. I do not question your abilities, only their current application. Tell me, what do you know of the whereabouts of my husband?"

"I know he has travelled west to the legions in Cyrenaica. He hopes to rally them to your cause." Melissa spoke quietly in an attempt to appear meek, but without giving too much away.

"Will he succeed?" Cleopatra asked.

"I do not know," Melissa lied.

"Should I send assistance?" the queen persisted.

"I cannot tell you what to do." Melissa held firm to her decision to remain silent.

Cleopatra laughed lightly, but to Melissa its falseness was apparent. "Come now. Do not play coy with me. We both know you want to impart your knowledge. I am sure you realise it is in your best interests to speak. You will find my terms more favourable than those of either Caesar or Mark Antony. I can provide you with accommodation that is more than adequate for your needs. If you agree to my request, you shall dine on the finest produce, be dressed in the finest linens and bathe in the most sumptuous of surroundings. I will grant you every freedom imaginable within this city. I assure you, witch, you and your lapdog husband will want for nothing." She threw the pot back on the side in disinterest.

Melissa did not answer. She dare not. Cleopatra's offer was too tempting. Gaining her trust might even provide a means of escape in time, but it was simply too dangerous to consider. On both her previous sojourns in the past, Melissa had been able to predict successes for those she looked to for protection. All that Cleopatra would have from this point forward were failures. Melissa found the risks outweighed the benefits on offer.

"I cannot help you," she stated firmly.

"Cannot or will not? Cleopatra snapped. "If you think you have a choice in the matter, you are sorely mistaken. Mark Antony is not here to indulge your insolence. Speak to me in such a tone again and I will slit your husband's throat before your eyes."

Melissa did not answer to begin with. On the one hand, she thought it better that she and Anthony both die than change the events unfolding around them but, on the other, she knew she could not bear to watch him being tortured. She had done many things in the past that she was not proud of, and many that deserved punishment, but Anthony was an innocent in this situation. He did not deserve to suffer for her prior mistakes. She was caught.

She had to say something so she went for something close to the truth.

"I cannot help you to save Mark Antony. His path is set. There is nothing I can say to change it. As for my husband, I would rather he die now in innocence than be corrupted by the vices of your court."

Inadvertently, Melissa's statement gave Cleopatra all the information she needed to wreak utter havoc. It seemed to the queen that what Melissa feared most was not how her husband might die, but how he might live. It gave her pause for thought. Perhaps the two men who shared such similar looks also had the same penchant for excess. If so, Cleopatra knew she had the greatest bargaining chip imaginable. She would use Anthony to get what she needed, but through kindness rather than violence. She was, after all, a talented seductress. Melissa's husband stood little chance against the charms she would offer.

Cleopatra smiled once more. "I admire a fellow woman with intellect and bravery beyond that expected of her sex, though a woman in such a position cannot afford to bluff. Your husband's presence here weakens your position, yet I have no more wish to hurt an innocent man than you do to bear witness to such intolerable pain as my agents can inflict. It presents us with an opportunity for negotiation, but I believe you need time to reconsider my offer."

Cleopatra turned her back and opened another pot of cream, sniffing it before barking an order at the bodyguard by the door. "Take her to the Alexandrian jail. A few days in solitude will help her decide what is best."

"What?" Melissa exclaimed. She realised she had made a serious error of judgement, but it was too late. The guard grabbed her arm and pulled her backwards.

"No, please, wait," she begged, but her words fell on the deaf ears of a woman who appeared more interested in the contents of her dressing table.

Cleopatra discarded the pot she was holding and opened a third one that proved more in tune with her mood. She began applying the moisturiser to her arms with cold efficiency, as Melissa's pleading gradually faded into silence.

Chapter 4

Anthony stood in the hall outside the throne room, wondering if his decision had been a wise one. For two days he had asked for a private audience with Cleopatra in the hope of learning where his wife had been taken. Instead, he was standing in line for a very public one.

While waiting, he studied the beautiful mosaic floor. The pattern was a simple repeating geometric shape, but the quality of the workmanship was such that the pattern seemed to jump out three-dimensionally. It had to have been laid by a Roman artist, and a very talented one at that. The pattern became quite mesmerising, taking on a life of its own and appearing to move by itself, which was when he decided it would be best to stop looking at it.

There had been a number of other petitioners waiting with him. Each had taken their turn to enter the throne room and detail their complaint. Each one had come out, some looking happy, some looking more distressed than when they went in. Anthony was dreading which category he would fall into, if he was ever seen.

The person before him left some time earlier, but he had not been called. He twisted the rose he was holding between his fingers, having pulled it from the vase in his room before he had come on this mission. He thought it best to offer the queen something in return for seeing him, but the only possessions that he had were the clothes on his back. He could hardly afford to hand over any of those plus, even though he had rinsed them in some of the water brought to him the day before, they were not particularly fresh.

Finally, the great cedar doors were pulled inwards and the fat little eunuch calling himself Diomedes came out. Anthony knew from memory that he was Cleopatra's secretary: not a man to cross.

The eunuch looked at Anthony disdainfully.

"You there," he sneered, "Her royal majesty, Queen Cleopatra, deigns to see you, though I do not understand why she ever agreed to your pitiable request." There was a loud tut before he began barking instructions for how Anthony was to behave. "Show respect. Kneel at her feet. Never make eye contact. Speak only when spoken to. Be quick and direct with your question. She has little enough time to spare as it is. She cannot afford to waste it on the likes of you."

Anthony followed Diomedes inside the throne room, which was an awe-inspiring sight. Agate columns supported roof beams coated in gold leaf. Inlaid marble, glittering with semi-precious stones, surrounded the trompe l'œil panels depicting beautiful vistas and garden scenes. The floor mosaics were also more outlandish than those in the hall, portraying mythological tales.

Cleopatra sat on a golden throne directly opposite the door. She was dressed in the traditional robes of Isis: a white linen shift dress covered with a diaphanous layer in black. She wore a wig shaped in the triangular style often seen in wall paintings. On top of her head sat the red and white crowns of Upper and Lower Egypt, set with the uraeus, or rearing cobra. In her hands she held the trappings of her office, the crook and flail, crossed in front of her chest in the way Anthony had seen on so many carvings, tomb walls and, most famously, on the sarcophagus of Tutankhamun. The overall spectacle was designed to leave the petitioners awestruck. It did not fall short.

Never one to be overawed and always determined to make an impression of his own, Anthony completely ignored everything Diomedes had said. He walked boldly up to the throne and looked straight at Cleopatra. Diomedes gasped in horror, but was too slow to restrain him.

"Your Majesty," Anthony began. "May I say how grateful I am for your generosity? I am well fed and watered and my accommodation is excellent."

She did not alter her gaze, continuing to stare over his head. "And you show your gratitude with a flower stolen from our garden?" she barked briskly.

He leant forwards and placed the rose at Cleopatra's feet before kneeling in front of her. After his initial arrogance, he intended to show contrition.

"Your Majesty, I do not mean to cause offence, but I have stolen nothing. This flower was given to me by way of the vase placed in my quarters this morning. It is my deepest regret that I have no gift of value to offer you. It was simply the most beautiful item available to a man who stands before you stripped of all his worldly possessions. It seemed apt to give this beautiful flower to the most beautiful woman alive."

Her eyes flickered slightly as she listened to him, but she recovered quickly. "An arrangement has many flowers. Why choose this particular bloom?"

Anthony was more than ready for that question. "It was the aroma. It reminded me of the vision of loveliness you sent to tend to my wounds while I lay in agony in the bowels of the *Antonia*. Yet another act of your kindness I must give thanks for." He retrieved the rose and waved it lightly in the air. "If it pleases your majesty, may I show you what I mean?"

Finally, Cleopatra dropped her gaze to meet his. She was immediately taken aback by the man kneeling at her feet. His likeness to Mark Antony had been obvious from their first meeting, but now she could see just how alike they were. With his olive skin and strong jawline, the resemblance was uncanny, but it was his dark brown eyes, twinkling with mischief, that sent a shiver down Cleopatra's spine. They were undeniably Mark Antony's eyes and it felt as if it were his soul she could see shining from within. It was as if the gods had taken back the sad wretch her husband had become, and returned to her the self-assured man she had bewitched at Tarsus some ten years earlier.

He winked cheekily.

At first, her eyes widened at his sheer audacity, but then nostalgia softened her stance. This was exactly the kind of gesture she had come to expect from her husband. On his return from a campaign, he would walk up to her throne, kneel at her feet and then wink at her, daring her to smile. When she did, he would jump up and kiss her. She smiled, but this man made no effort to rise. Instead, he merely winked again.

"Rise and approach the throne," she commanded.

Anthony got to his feet and stepped forwards until he was face to face with her. He presented the rose, just beneath her nose. She tilted her head slightly and sniffed, knowing already that the perfume matched exactly the one she wore onboard the flagship. It was the same one she was wearing today.

"As your majesty will remember, her scent was most bewitching that night . . ." he murmured, and then added in a near whisper, ". . . as was her touch."

"Your sight was impaired. You are mistaken," she replied coolly.

Anthony took a step backwards. "If it pleases your majesty, then I will say it is so, though it means I shall always be mistaken in your presence."

They stared at each other, neither blinking. Eventually, Cleopatra lowered the crook and flail. Immediately, a servant stepped forwards with a cushion to take them from her. She placed them on the cushion and stood up.

"Walk with us," she commanded, and floated across the room towards the open doors.

Anthony followed her outside and found himself at the top of a small flight of steps leading into the gardens. He stopped the moment the sun hit his face. He closed his eyes, deeply inhaling the stunning aromas enveloping him.

At the bottom of the steps the queen coughed lightly, encouraging him to join her. As he trotted down the stairs, she signalled for the guards to remain at a distance. Once they were out of earshot, she became more relaxed, dropping her use of the plural in referring to herself.

"The rose is a common scent. How can you be sure it belonged to me?"

"I recognised your eyes, which are as exquisite as this flower." Once again, Anthony offered the rose to her. This time she took it, graciously.

"I doubt that. You could hardly see anything in the dark of the hold, especially with one eye shut," she countered.

"Then it was your voice, which sings joyfully of the beauty of its mistress." Anthony was overdoing the flattery and Cleopatra knew it.

"Rubbish," she scoffed. She took a few more steps, before continuing in a coyer manner. "Your attempts at flattery are not unwelcome. You are correct, I tended your wounds."

Anthony nodded to acknowledge her statement. "May I ask why? Surely such a task was beneath you."

"I heard rumours of a Herculean beast being brought aboard my flagship, one requiring ten men to subdue it." She smiled. "You aroused my . . . curiosity."

Anthony grinned. "I too found your presence arousing," he quipped. It was enough to make Cleopatra falter between steps, surprised at his audacity. He continued quickly, "I must have been quite a disappointment. I did not fight ten men. It can have been no more than two."

"I would not say you are in anyway disappointing. It is a strong man who can best *three* seasoned warriors," she corrected, "especially when one of those men was Mark Antony."

Anthony made no comment, but she saw his fist clench at the mention of her husband's name. He was clearly jealous. She surmised the younger man knew of the relationship between Melissa and the Roman who shared his face. It was a subject he obviously found uncomfortable. She chose to change it, for the time being.

"Onboard ship, you referred to me as a 'malakh'. I have read of such creatures in Jewish texts. Are they not beings sent by the Jewish god to deliver justice? Do they not hurl fire and brimstone down upon the unworthy in such places as Sodom and Gomorrah? Do they not turn those who do not heed their words into pillars of salt?"

"Your majesty is well read indeed," Anthony complimented her knowledge of the Bible. "That is one of their duties, but they also watch over his people and show kindness. Above all, they are meant to strike awe into the people they meet. Your kindness most certainly left me in awe."

"You must have a good memory to have retained so much information from one brief and dark encounter," she replied, with a light laugh.

Anthony smiled. "If I am truthful it was not our first meeting. We met once before, in Rome."

"Rome?" Cleopatra prided herself on having an excellent memory, storing details on every person she met for future use. She did not remember meeting a double for Mark Antony on her trip to Rome, only the man himself who had the audacity to appear before her naked. "I am sure I would have remembered such a meeting."

"I was a very different person back then," Anthony said with a smile. He had, of course, been a four-year-old boy, but he could never mention that. "It was nothing more than a brief passing. You hardly noticed me, but as a younger, more impressionable male, I remembered you. Your servant gave me a coin. It was my most treasured possession for many hours, until it was taken from me."

Cleopatra nodded graciously, assuming she had given money to a poor soul in need of alms, who had then treasured that coin until hunger got the better of him. "And now your fortunes have changed. You are here, and I have once again been benevolent."

"And I am again thankful for your generosity."

Cleopatra tutted. "Your wife does not share your appreciation."

"Liss . . ." Anthony corrected himself, using the name Cleopatra was more familiar with, ". . . Lissa finds it hard to be pleasant, especially now."

"Why so?" Her interest was piqued.

He was playing the sympathy card. "Our son died a few weeks ago. She is both grieving for him and angry at me for taking her away from our home."

"How old was the child?" Cleopatra showed genuine interest, storing each fact away for later use.

"He was six." Anthony's voice faltered and tears formed in his eyes. Speaking about Jack's death was proving too much for him. He stopped walking and turned away from the queen.

She paused, watching him as he wiped the tears from his eyes. She wondered briefly if it was nothing more than an attempt to gain her sympathy by appealing to her maternal instincts. When he did not turn around, she knew his emotions were genuine and that he was attempting to keep them hidden; yet another similarity with his lookalike. She took a step towards him and placed her hand on his arm.

"I am sorry for your loss. As a mother myself, I understand the pain of it," she said with sympathy.

He nodded his thanks and wiped his eyes once more. "For us to be taken captive by a man who regards my wife as his slave has all been too much for her to bear. Now Mark Antony has taken her from me, I fear for what he has done with her." He turned to look at the queen and dropped to his knees again, taking her hands in his. "Please, your majesty, I have come here to beg for your help."

Finally they had come to the crux of the matter. As with every other man who came before her, this one wanted something. He had flattered her, appealed to her better nature and now expected her to return the favour. Except, this situation was different. She could see the depth of his fears in his pleading eyes and, in that moment, she knew the power she held over the cold-hearted seer languishing in her prison cells. By using the man at her feet, she could get all the information she wanted and something more. She could have her revenge on Melissa for her insolence. Caesar's witch would know her place at last.

"What is it you wish me to do?"

"Mark Antony has taken my wife from me. Please, I beg you to intercede and return her to me. I will do anything you ask in return."

He still had hold of her hands. She should have pulled them away, but even his touch felt familiar. Everything about this man reminded her of a younger version of the man who shared her bed. As his thumbs began to gently caress her skin, she began to wonder exactly what 'anything' meant. He had nothing of interest to offer, except perhaps his lean, muscular body. Was he offering to prostitute himself for the life of his wife, or was her imagination getting the better of her? As he lifted her fingers to his lips to kiss them, she felt her face flush. Quickly, she withdrew her hands from his grasp.

"Mark Antony does not have your wife. She is in the city jail."

The look of horror on Anthony's face was apparent. He visibly recoiled, dropping backwards to rest his buttocks on his ankles. "Why?" he asked. "What has she done?"

"Your wife's abilities are well known to the general, yet when he needs her counsel the most, she has chosen silence. It was felt a few days of suffering would loosen her tongue, but she has not spoken, nor do I believe she will."

Anthony shook his head. "She can be stubborn. You will get nothing from her if she does not wish to talk."

"The death of your son was not known. Her pain was mistaken for impertinence, resulting in this unfortunate situation. It is a mistake that could be rectified, if she can be made to see it is in her best interests to use her knowledge to assist the defence of Egypt."

Anthony nodded, slowly.

"If I arrange for her return, can you persuade her of this?"

"I can try," Anthony offered.

Cleopatra gave a loud tut of disapproval. "You will need to do much better than that. I have no love for your wife, or her visions. I am more than happy with her current location."

Anthony knew damned well that Melissa had no intention of ever giving Cleopatra information, but he did not need her to. He knew as much as Melissa did. All he had to do was convince Cleopatra the information was coming from his wife and he could keep both women happy. It was a dangerous game to play, but it was the only chance he had to get Melissa back.

"She will be persuaded. You have my word on it," he promised.

Cleopatra smiled. "Then she shall be returned. I give you two days to convince her to yield her knowledge freely. If she still does not speak, she will be returned to the jail to await the general's justice. I offer no more than that."

"Two days will be enough. I will not fail you." Again Anthony was making quick promises, believing he could front it out. He gave no thought to what might happen if his deceit was uncovered.

"See that you do not. I believe crucifixion is the appropriate Roman punishment for an escaped slave. I have not witnessed the event myself, but I understand it is one of the most painful deaths imaginable."

Anthony shifted nervously. Cleopatra was correct. If Mark Antony wished to claim Melissa was an escaped slave, he could nail her up on a cross in the blink of an eye.

Cleopatra noted his discomfort, knowing this was something she could use to her advantage. "Remember, loyalty in my court is well rewarded. Failure is equally punished."

With a wave of her hand, she signalled to the guards behind her that the audience was over. They immediately stepped forwards, pulled Anthony to his feet and began to lead him away.

"Wait!" Cleopatra called out suddenly. "You have not told me your name. I cannot refer to you as husband of the seer. What would you have me call you?"

Melissa had begged him not to reveal his real name, but Anthony did not see any point in telling a lie that could be so easily be unearthed. "My given name was Antonius, but my wife prefers to call me Anthony. You may use either."

Cleopatra could not hide her surprise this time. The man Melissa had married was not only the visual double for the man she herself called husband, they also shared the same mannerisms and the same name. She wondered if there was anything about these two men that was different beyond their age. Had the gods answered her prayers and returned to her the strong, arrogant leader of men she had first encountered some fourteen years earlier, albeit in the body of another? Clearly there was more to the whole situation than she presently understood.

As the guards removed this younger Anthony from her presence, she resolved to get to the bottom of the mystery by any means possible.

Chapter 5

Back in his room, Anthony paced around like a caged tiger. It had been hours since his audience with the queen, where she had given her word that Melissa would be returned. He was beginning to doubt whether Cleopatra could be trusted when the door opened and Melissa was thrown through it. She was dishevelled and dirty, but otherwise appeared unscathed.

The first thing she spotted was the half-eaten tray of food on the side table. She had not eaten in almost three days and was starving. She ran to the table and grabbed a fig, cramming it into her mouth whole before reaching for another.

When she reached for the wine, Anthony spoke.

"I missed you too, Liss," he said almost choking on the words. He was so happy to see her alive.

She spun around. As soon as she saw him, she ran into his arms.

He held her tightly for some time, brushing his hand over her matted hair as she clung to him.

"You OK?" he finally asked.

Melissa pulled away slightly and smiled weakly. "I am now. I thought I'd never see you again."

Anthony kissed her gently. "You're here and you're safe. We just have to keep you that way."

Melissa looked around at the unmade bed and then

back at the food. It was obvious Anthony had not been kept in another cell in the jail.

"Been here long?" she asked, with a hint of sarcasm.

He briefly considered dodging the question, but decided it was best to be honest. "I've been here since we arrived. When you didn't show, I went to the queen and asked for her help. I thought *he* had you."

From the emphasis on 'he', Melissa knew who her husband meant. It seemed, after all these years, he was still jealous of her former lover. Now they had met, and he had seen for himself how alike they were, Melissa feared Anthony's jealousies would reach fever pitch. That usually meant he would do something reckless: drinking, gambling, prostitutes. To act recklessly here could get them both killed.

"Mark Antony isn't here – as you well know," she countered. "That bitch he calls his wife is the one who threw me in jail."

Anthony nodded. "Yeah, I know that now. Hey, I got you back, didn't I?"

"How?" She questioned.

He shrugged. "Easy - it's called bartering. You want something, you offer something in return."

"Bartering with what? What did you offer to get me out?" She had to know what he had done to be rewarded with such luxury while she had spent days locked up in a dark cell.

"Nothing ... yet," he hesitated.

Melissa knew immediately there was a catch. "What have you done?" she demanded.

"Cleopatra wants information. We just have to work out what to tell her."

She stepped back from him in amazement. "That woman is an evil viper. I'm giving her nothing. She's too damned dangerous. She tried to have me disgraced and Victor castrated within half an hour of meeting us! Had it not been for your father, we'd probably all have been dead."

"Oh, right, so you'd trust him, but not her?" Anthony's sarcasm was more than evident in his tone.

Melissa straightened her back defiantly. This argument was old ground that had been covered far too many times. "Yes, damn it, I would. I know where I stand with him. He would never hurt me."

"Really?" The sarcasm was now tinged with bitterness. "He'll happily kick his own son half to death, but hey, who cares, coz he won't hurt you. Cheers, Liss. It's taken long enough, but at least I finally know where your loyalties lie."

Melissa wanted to cry. Two and a half days alone in a stinking, dark cell, listening to the wails of terror and pain from the other inmates, and she had come back to this. All she wanted was to be held and to be told that everything would work out alright, even if it was a lie. She wanted to hear how much he loved her, not how much he hated his father. All he wanted to do was reopen old wounds that it seemed would never heal.

She tried again, her voice faltering as the tears welled. "We can't trust her. I'd rather die in that pit she threw me in, than be reliant on her for anything."

"And where would that leave me? I'm already a lousy father so let's add inept husband to the list, shall we?" He shook his head. "How the hell do I explain to the kids that I let you die? Isn't it bad enough they think I killed their brother?"

Anthony's voice faltered too as he collapsed onto the bed, his head in his hands. In the last two days all he had thought about was the prospect of losing his wife, and of losing his remaining children. His thoughts had turned to Jack, and to the lies he had told to cover up the truth of his son's death. He hated himself more every day for what had happened, believing it was his fault for making Melissa stay on the estate all those years. She had wanted to leave and return to England, but he had charmed her into staying. Now it felt like he was being punished by some unseen hand. He needed to forget these problems, and for that he desperately needed a whisky. There was none available to him here, and the wine on offer did not quite have the same dulling affect. He choked back a sob.

"I lost him, Liss. It's my fault. My kids hate me because of it – Vicky told me so. They'll never forgive me if I lose you too."

Melissa stared at him, unable to move. Suddenly his odd behaviour in the weeks since Jack's death made more sense. Anthony had never been good at dealing with problems head on. Usually he avoided issues until they went away by themselves, but Jack's loss was a problem that could not be avoided. On the few occasions Anthony had tried to carry on as normally as possible, the children had reacted badly. They could not understand how he could continue to laugh and joke as if nothing had happened. They were both too young to understand that different people experienced grief in different ways. At one point Vicky told her father she never wanted to see him again, but it was just one of those things kids say. Ever since she first learnt the word 'hate', Vicky had told her mother she hated her at least twice a week, though Melissa knew it was purely out of frustration rather than real hatred. Anthony had never experienced such emotional outbursts from any of his children before. He was their hero and they all loved him unconditionally. He must have been devastated by Vicky's remark.

She sat down beside him and wrapped her arms around his shoulders. "Oh Anthony, I never realised how much Vicky hurt you. She didn't mean it. They don't hate you. Your kids love you . . . and so do I."

He leant his forehead against hers. "Prove it," he whispered.

She kissed his cheek gently, prompting him to turn his head slightly to return the kiss, gently at first, but with growing passion. Sliding his arms around her waist, he pushed her backwards onto the bed and slid his hand inside her blouse.

She tried to protest. "Anthony, I'm filthy. I haven't washed in days,"

"I don't care," came his breathless reply, before he silenced her with another kiss. Within seconds he was unbuttoning her blouse, his mouth following his hands downwards across her chest until her objections were replaced by moans of pleasure.

They had nearly lost each other twice already since that fateful day at Actium. Cleopatra had given Anthony two days to persuade Melissa to cooperate and, despite his assurances to the queen, he suspected it was a mission doomed to failure.

If these were to be their last two days together, Anthony was determined not to waste another moment.

The night passed all too swiftly, along with the following day. They spent their time making love and discussing whether they had any options for escape. They were no further forward by the morning of the second day.

Lying in bed, with his arm around his wife and eating a breakfast of fruit left over from the night before, Anthony knew time was running out. His time was almost up, and he had no idea how long they had before he was summoned to report his progress to the Egyptian queen. If he failed to impress, it would be the last time he ever saw his wife. Whatever the outcome of the day ahead, he would not admit to Melissa just how desperate their situation was. Instead, as he stroked her hair, he made one last ditch attempt at persuading her that his plan was sound.

"I still think we have a good chance of finding a way home, if we can just buy some time. Alexandria has some of the greatest minds of this age in terms of scientists and . . ."

"None of whom we can trust," Melissa interjected as she lifted her head to stare at him. She felt any escape attempt was too risky to try until Mark Antony returned, especially considering their current surroundings were so pleasant. For two days they had been together in the palace and nothing had happened to them. She felt they were safer staying where they were. She had no idea their happiness could be ending at any second.

Anthony frowned at his wife. "I never said we had to trust them, just use the information they have access to. If anything like this has ever happened before, it'll be recorded in the library. The entire knowledge of the world is at our fingertips. We just have to access it."

"How?" Melissa sighed. "We couldn't get to the library if we tried."

Anthony could see his powers of verbal persuasion were getting nowhere, but he had no intention of giving up. Dropping the stone from the peach he had eaten onto the small table beside the bed, he rolled Melissa onto her back.

"Leave that to me. I'll work on her royal high and mightiness to see what I can get. Cleopatra stands no chance against the famous Anthony Marcus charm!" He winked and ran the tip of his finger down between her breasts.

Melissa wriggled beneath him. "It doesn't work that way. We're prisoners and Romans do not negotiate with prisoners."

Anthony's lips were now covering her breasts with kisses. "Cleopatra's not Roman, she's Egyptian."

"Actually, she's Greek," Melissa corrected, trying to play hard to get.

"Semantics," he murmured past a mouthful of nipple.

"Yeah well, you know what they say - beware of Greeks bearing gifts."

Anthony rewarded her cheeky remark with a sharp nip with his teeth, making her squeal. Hard to get was failing dismally.

He brought his head back up to hers. "I've done OK so far."

"Have you?" She could feel his erection against her leg. Reaching down to his waist, she tried to nudge him to lie on top of her.

"I got you out of jail didn't I?" He moved slowly, teasingly, in response. He began kissing her neck and nibbling her earlobe while his hand moved between them to position himself to make love to her again.

Melissa had to think, but it was difficult with his tongue in her ear and his penis rubbing teasingly against her. Maybe he was right. Cleopatra was intelligent, devious and completely untrustworthy, but she did like intelligent men and Anthony Marcus was certainly intelligent. Having to deal with a man who looked like Mark Antony might unnerve her enough to give them the opportunity they needed, but equally Melissa feared Anthony's resolve. He was so weak when it came to women that she was worried he might fall victim to Cleopatra's powers of seduction.

"What if she makes a play for you?" she whispered.

Anthony was determined to get them home regardless of what he had to do, even if it meant bedding one of the most famous women in history. "That's the point, Liss – I make her want me and keep her dangling. You know I'm capable of screwing with any woman's head, or any other part of her for that matter. And you know they mean nothing to me. You're the only woman I have ever loved or ever will."

This much was true. Anthony was a schemer. Melissa had spent many years watching Anthony's 'love them and leave them' philosophy, stealing women's hearts long before she stole his. He had a way of getting a woman to do just about anything he wanted, but he had never before tried to seduce a woman like Cleopatra. Egypt's queen had successfully seduced Caesar, the conqueror of Gaul. She had successfully seduced Mark Antony, the hero of Philippi. By the next summer, she would try to seduce Octavian, the man destined to become Rome's first Emperor. Cleopatra set her sights high, and she usually got her way. What chance did her husband have against a woman with that track record?

"C'mon, Liss, let me try and get under her skin. I promise not to sleep with her." Anthony meant only half of that statement, but there was no need for Melissa to know that. He was prepared to do anything to get his wife out of Alexandria before Mark Antony returned. The mere thought of Mark Antony touching his wife brought out the worst in him. He wanted to tear his illustrious father limb from limb merely for looking in her direction.

"Just you remember, that one bites!" Melissa forced the words out with difficulty. His teasing had won and her mind was now firmly on sex. She wrapped her legs around his waist. She was not prepared to wait any longer.

Anthony winked. "So do I, sweetheart! So do I." He sank his teeth into her shoulder as he slipped swiftly inside her, making her gasp with pleasure.

Neither of them knew they had an audience. The bedroom door had been opened and Cleopatra now stood watching their every move, listening to their every word. Her secretary, Diomedes, stood beside her. They were flanked by three of the palace guard.

Anthony's movements intensified. Melissa continued to gasp and moan. As he brought them both closer to their climax, they were interrupted by slow clapping. Realising they had an audience, he shot out of the bed with the speed and agility of a leopard. He was looking for some form of weapon, but was quickly overcome by two of the guards who held him by his arms, forcing him onto his knees before the queen.

She looked down to his erect member before commenting sarcastically, "We do so like a man who rises in our presence."

"What do you want at this hour?" Anthony demanded in Greek, putting on a show for Melissa. He knew only too well why the queen was there, though he had expected a summons. He never imagined she would come to them.

Ignoring him, she made eye contact with Diomedes. He said something to the guards in a language Anthony did not understand. Immediately they dragged him from the room, with Diomedes trotting along behind them.

Melissa too was out of bed and struggling into a robe. "Where are you taking him?" she asked in Latin, as the queen walked over to the window. "What has he done?"

Cleopatra stared out into the garden, obviously looking for some sign of activity. Eventually, she smiled and turned to nod to the other guard. A second later, Melissa was kneeling at the feet of the queen.

"Where is my husband?" she asked again.

"Your husband promised information for us today. Failure to comply will result in his punishment."

Again, Cleopatra gave a signal with her eyes to the guard. He dragged Melissa to her feet and over to the window. She looked down in horror at the sight before her. Below them in the garden was a large granite sphinx. Anthony had been dragged to it and spread across its hind quarters. The two guards were holding an arm each, keeping him pinned against the stone surface. He was trying to pull himself free from their grasp, but failing dismally. One of the gargantuan oafs was more than a match for him, two were simply impossible to beat. Melissa found herself left with no choice. She had to tell the queen whatever she wanted to know, or watch her husband die.

Melissa was dragged back to kneel in front of Cleopatra once again, who began her interrogation. "Tell us where Mark Antony is and what he has been doing."

Melissa glared up in defiance, but she spoke. "Mark Antony has failed in his mission to gather the troops from Cyrenaica. Their commander, Pinarius Scarpus, declared for Octavian. The strain has taken its toll. Mark Antony has attempted suicide, though his colleagues have prevented it. He rides for Alexandria."

"How long until he arrives?"

"A week, maybe two – prediction is not an exact science."

Cleopatra looked a little disappointed. Her tone became hushed as she spoke her thoughts aloud and to herself rather than to Melissa. "A shame, I wanted to prepare a great feast for his return."

Melissa answered, regardless of whether the comment was aimed at her or not. "That would be unwise. His failure to win over the troops has deeply troubled his mind. Upon his arrival he will shun the fineries of the palace, choosing abstinence and solitude."

"Ridiculous! Mark Antony will expect a great banquet in his honour and I shall not fail him." The harsh tone had returned with a vengeance.

Melissa ploughed on, desperate to save her Anthony's life. "He will choose to live in an old house in the harbour which he will name his Timoneum, after the hermit from Athens. He will not be swayed from this course."

Cleopatra said nothing. She returned to the window and looked down at her prisoner, spread-eagled over the sphinx, but still fighting against his captors. This one had spirit, as well as a considerable intellect and a lithe body. She suspected she could get hours of pleasure from his company and she found herself hoping she would not have to give the order to put him to death.

"Your husband – does he know these details?" she finally asked.

"He knows everything I do," Melissa answered truthfully, fearing they were about to be tested.

A moment later, Melissa's fears were confirmed.

"Let us see what story he tells." Cleopatra looked up at the guard. "Bring her!" she barked.

The remaining guard took Melissa by the upper arm, dragging her behind Cleopatra as the queen glided through the palace and down into the gardens. They paused a short distance from the sphinx.

"Speak one word and he dies." There was more than a hint of cruelty in Cleopatra's tone as she continued towards the statue alone.

Another man had joined the group since Melissa had witnessed the scene from the window of her room. He was standing on the far side of the sphinx with a whip in his hand. As the queen approached he cracked it in the air in front of Anthony, who immediately stopped struggling as he strained his neck to watch the whip master warming up. The man cracked the whip a few more times to loosen his arm before walking slowly around the sphinx, swapping places with Cleopatra until all Anthony could see of him was his shadow ominously stretched out on the ground to his side.

Now Anthony faced Cleopatra. She was smiling at him, but he was in no doubt that her smile was false.

Her harsh tone did nothing to allay his fears. "We commend you for the pleasing entertainment this morning. We were most reluctant to interrupt your energetic display." She looked over to the whip master who cracked the whip in the air once more.

Anthony strained against his captors again. Cleopatra did not need words to explain her intentions. What he did not yet understand was what he had done to deserve this treatment. She had not given him an opportunity to tell her whether he had persuaded Melissa into giving any information on the future.

As if she read his mind, she answered his question. "You seemed to have forgotten our appointment. You should know that we do not tolerate lateness."

There was the accusation and, although Anthony did not remember any agreement on a specific time for them to meet, he did not dare to argue. He was too busy wondering how many lashes he was due to receive.

"We believe your wife speaks of her visions to you and that you are told all that she knows," the queen continued.

When he said nothing, she demanded his reply. "Answer, or suffer the consequences. The choice is yours."

"She does," he replied somewhat nervously. Now was not a moment for his usual bravado.

"Then we will see how much you remember. We will ask questions, you will provide answers. If they are correct, you are free to return to your morning's activities. If your answers differ to those given by your wife, you will feel the leather of our whip caress your rather striking backside."

Anthony tried to pull his arms loose again. This time Cleopatra nodded to the whip-master, who let one lash fly directly above Anthony's back. He winced even though no contact was made. Behind him, he heard Melissa gasp. He knew she was there, being made to watch this cruel spectacle. He would answer whatever questions were asked. All he could hope was that Melissa had told Cleopatra the truth.

"What was the outcome of Mark Antony's mission?" Cleopatra barked her request sharply.

Anthony continued to pull against his captors as he answered. "He failed. The troops declared for Octavian."

"What are his plans?" The queen's questioning was quick and relentless.

"He is coming here."

"When will he arrive?"

"I don't fucking know." In his panic, Anthony reverted to English.

"In Latin please, so your wife may understand."

He took a breath and repeated himself in the correct language. "I am unsure – a few weeks perhaps."

"What welcome will he want?"

"None. His dark mood makes him shun palace life. He wishes to live like a Greek hermit."

"Which hermit?"

Shit, Anthony thought. Panic was clouding his memory. He strained against his captors again, but his situation was hopeless. He looked around him in desperation until he glimpsed Melissa, who was being held by an equally large brute. She looked terrified. He had to get this right. He had to concentrate and clear his mind. *What the fuck was the guy's name?*

"Which hermit?" Cleopatra repeated impatiently.

Anthony looked at the ground where he saw the shadow of the whip master raise his arm. He closed his eyes and gritted his teeth, steeling himself for the pain.

And then the name came to him.

"TIMON," he shouted. "TIMON OF ATHENS."

He waited, but the whip never fell against his back. The grip on his arms was released, and he was left clinging to the statue. Slowly he opened his eyes to see Cleopatra smiling at him once more. Carefully, he pushed himself away from the sphinx and took a step backwards from it. He rubbed his arms which stung from where he had strained against the guards. He had a wary look on his face.

"We are pleased. You listen well and remember much. Your services will be of great use, as messenger for your wife."

She looked towards Melissa and gave a nod to the man holding her. As soon as the guard relaxed his grip, Cleopatra returned her attention to Anthony, who now stood directly before her, rubbing his wrists. Her eyes wandered down the length of his muscular body, but he made no attempt at modesty. Instead, he took a deep breath and drew himself up to his full height in defiance. Despite his close shave with the whip, the adrenalin pumping through his veins meant he was still showing some signs of his earlier arousal.

Cleopatra's smile widened, impressed with what she saw. Walking up to him, she allowed her hand to brush delicately across his groin. Her touch was as light as a feather and, despite his better judgement, continued until she got the firming reaction she wanted. She whispered so only he could hear. "Your performance today has been more than adequate. You will be rewarded accordingly." She walked away into the gardens, with her secretary following in her wake.

Once the queen and her henchmen were out of earshot, Melissa ran into her husband's arms sobbing in English, "I'm sorry. I'm so, so sorry."

"I'm OK, Liss. I'm not hurt," Anthony soothed as he kissed the top of her head. His eyes were following the departing Egyptians, making sure they did not return.

"This time," Melissa whimpered, clinging to him.

"Let's get back inside," Anthony suggested. "I'm a little exposed out here." When he felt Melissa nod against him, he turned her towards the palace and they began walking back.

"How could you let her touch you like that?" Melissa asked after a few steps.

"You think I could stop her? I lay so much as a finger

on her without an invitation and I'm dead. If she wants to feel me up, she can, just so long as she leaves you alone."

"Well, you don't have to enjoy it," Melissa said with a slight tut.

"I'm a man. An attractive woman touches my dick, I get hard. It's how it works," he grumbled.

Melissa stopped. "You think she's attractive?" she asked sharply, refusing to move.

Anthony knew immediately it was the wrong thing to have said, but he was not about to justify his remark. He spread his arms out in despair. "For fuck's sake, Liss, I'm in the buff. Can we do this when we are inside?"

Melissa looked sheepish and nodded, following him into the palace. She would let his remark go, temporarily, but it would nag at her until she had an answer.

Cleopatra returned to her chambers to attend to the rest of the morning's business. Once seated at her desk, Diomedes dared to ask what her intentions for the foreigners were.

"What do you really want done with them?"

She pulled one of the pieces of papyrus from the pile awaiting her attention and began studying it. "Make the following arrangements. Move them to the lower guest quarters where they can have free run of the inner palace and gardens. Arrange clothes for both of them and a personal retinue to see to their needs. Treat them as if they were visiting dignitaries from one of our allies."

"You do not want them placed under guard?"

Cleopatra dropped the papyrus and stared at him in disgust. "Did they remove your brains along with your balls?" she snapped. "Of course I want them guarded, you fool."

"Yes your Majesty, I understand," he simpered. It was clear he did not.

She sighed in despair. She should not have to explain herself to her underlings, but these days it was all she ever seemed to do. "No, you do not understand, but you will. I will teach you the greatest lesson I ever learnt from Caesar. You must understand your enemy and learn from their behaviour. It is like training a dog: you let it run on its leash until it misbehaves, when you snap the leash tight. Only then will it learn to obey your commands."

A glimmer of understanding appeared on Diomedes' face, encouraging her to continue. "Of course we guard them, but with subtlety. I want them watched, not harassed. Give them freedoms to wander the public areas of the palace complex. Allow them to visit the waterfront, if they desire. Let them explore, but never let them out of your sight. To know their every move will provide me with the most valuable commodity there is — information. The seer will eventually set her own trap, before falling into it."

A rather sadistic leer appeared on the eunuch's face. "And the husband? What of him?"

"He may yet prove more useful than the alleged visions of his wife," Cleopatra snapped, returning her attention to the papyrus before adding in a murmur, "If he can give me that which is most desired,"

"And that is?" Diomedes still appeared uncertain what the end result was to be.

The queen raised her eyes from the papyrus again, staring coldly at her adviser for some moments. "That is the freedom to rule without the influence of Rome. I have negotiated with the greatest men in Rome. Octavian is a coward compared to them — a man who claims the achievements of his Marcus Agrippa to be his own. Yet I know what it is this latest Roman despot truly wants, and may soon be in a position to offer it to him, with the assistance of our latest houseguest."

Octavian wanted Mark Antony, dead or alive. Cleopatra knew this, but she also knew she needed Mark Antony as the commander and figurehead for her army. And yet, this once great general was all but lost to her – nothing more than a drunken, depressive dog, too busy licking his wounds to have any thought for her or their children. Her eyes wandered to the window as she formulated a plan for entrapment of the younger Anthony, knowing this duplicate for her husband could prove a useful pawn in the deadly games that were to be played. The future of her family, her throne, and, most importantly, her country were all that mattered now. It was up to her to secure all three by any means possible.

"If this new 'Anthony' asks for an audience, grant it. We must indulge his every request, for he will repay each favour in kind."

"And if he fails to meet up to your majesty's expectations? What then?"

Cleopatra's eyes shot to her secretary again. She said nothing, but gave a low hiss before her mouth twisted into a cruel smile.

Diomedes backed away without showing any sign of the fear now welling inside his chest. He knew she was thinking of the reptile farm, a place Diomedes hated and one he would be happy never to enter again. For some time Cleopatra had been experimenting with the venoms from different snakes, learning their effectiveness by testing them on those who displeased her. Some of the men died such horrible deaths, writhing in agony for many hours as the poisons they had ingested ate slowly away at their insides. It made Diomedes sick to think of their lifeless, twisted corpses with their faces forever frozen in the final agonies of death. No one deserved to die like that.

If the newcomer did not prove useful, it appeared he was destined to become the queen's latest test subject.

Chapter 6

The next few weeks passed in relative peace. Melissa and Anthony were relocated to a suite of rooms in what was termed the guest quarters. This appeared to be an older residence now annexed to the main palace. It benefitted from direct access onto the gardens, which they seemed to have free use of. They were given a plentiful supply of food and clothing. It appeared Cleopatra had kept to her word, and their new freedoms were their reward for the provision of information. Melissa found the whole situation suspicious, but Anthony felt she was overreacting as usual.

Anthony spent the early mornings running in the gardens. He was always followed by a guard, but not one who seemed particularly bright. He made sure he followed the same circuit each day, seemingly uninterested in any of the other available paths. Occasionally, he would stop to study the carving of a statue, or to smell a flower. In fact, he was looking at something else that had caught his interest, a gate in the wall perhaps, but he always did it furtively to ensure his 'shadow' was none the wiser. He was looking for a way out, but found their situation was hopeless: there was no escape. Any gates he could see were locked and guarded, and the walls were too high to climb. Even if he could push Melissa up onto one, there was no chance he could follow her. And he could never let her out onto the streets of Alexandria alone. She might be the cleverest woman he had ever met, but she lacked what he termed 'street smarts'. A clever woman would not last long among the pimps and thieves he knew to be resident in downtown Alexandria, especially if she did not have the sense to know when to talk and when to kick someone in the balls.

They discussed finding a way to access the famous library. Neither of them knew how the mists worked. They did not know if the mist from Actium was the same as the one from the Rubicon. If so, their only chance to get home was to return to the same place from where they had left their own time. Without a boat of some description it could take months, if not years, to return to that part of Greece, especially at a time when Octavian's growing army stood between them and their destination.

Perhaps there were other mists in other places? If there was any record of a similar event happening elsewhere, it would be recorded in that library. They needed time to explore its many halls at length to see if any of its thousands of volumes held any answers to their predicament, but it was time they simply did not have. Octavian was coming. In less than a year his arrival in Egypt would mark the end of Cleopatra's reign and the end for anyone resident in the palace at that time. Anthony had to find a way out of Alexandria before the following summer arrived, but first he had to find a way out of the palace.

When the summons eventually came from Cleopatra, it was for Anthony alone.

"What does she want with you? I'm supposed to be the bloody seer."

Melissa was dumbstruck at the single invitation, but also scared by its possibilities. She still harboured doubts over the queen's intentions for Anthony, following their last meeting. Cleopatra was a skilled seductress, who had already succeeded in perverting the intentions of two of Rome's most powerful men. Her husband had a roving eye and a voracious sexual appetite. He would be 'easy meat' for a predator like Cleopatra.

In the years they had been together, Melissa had learnt to turn a blind eye to his infidelities, which she always blamed on his Roman upbringing. Even though he lived in the twenty-first century AD, Anthony's attitudes towards sex were from the first century BC. He had a wife whom he loved deeply and who bore his children, but he saw nothing wrong with using prostitutes, as and when the need arose. She knew he had an account with a local brothel – she had seen the direct debit on their bank statements.

"Yeah, well, you two don't exactly see eye to eye, do you?" Anthony countered. He regarded himself as a skilled seducer and more than capable of playing the long game. He knew Cleopatra was interested in him and he fully intended to flirt with her, if it provided an opportunity to improve their situation. Whether or not he would bed her was a question as yet unanswered, but anything was possible provided the 'price' was right.

The guard took a step forward. If Anthony did not go willingly, it was obvious he would be taken by force.

"I will come," he said in Greek, and the guard backed off. Giving Melissa a quick hug, he whispered to her, "I'll be OK. I won't tell her anything we didn't agree to."

"Be sure you don't." Melissa was not certain he would keep to their agreed course of action: Anthony had an unpredictable streak and, as adorable as it could be, it was just as likely to get them killed.

Cleopatra was sitting in the rose garden once again. As Anthony approached, she held out her hand for him to kiss. Dutifully, he pressed his lips to it.

"Your majesty is well, I trust?" he asked, with sincerity.

"Well indeed, and well pleased with the delights my garden offers me each morning." Slowly her eyes wandered down the length of Anthony's body, leaving him in no doubt of her meaning. This woman seemed to be mentally undressing him whenever she saw him, something he fully intended to exploit. When it came to playing with the emotions of women, his acting abilities rivalled those of Olivier or Burton.

He straightened up, puffing out his chest and tensing the muscles in his arms for effect.

"It is indeed beautiful," he declared, with a theatrical gesture. Closing his eyes, he took a long, deep breath, savouring the scent before slowly exhaling. "I enjoy it most in the morning, when the aromas are the sweetest."

Cleopatra studied his face. Everything about him reminded her of Mark Antony, from his muscular physique to his facial expressions. He both confused and intrigued her. Her original intention to use him purely to force information from Melissa had been replaced with something more sinister. Mark Antony was past his prime, whereas his younger 'twin' was fit, and agile. His mind was not yet dulled from imbibing the fruits of the vine. If she could tempt him away from the seer, she could have both her revenge on the woman she loathed and replace the old drunk with a new commanding officer for her armies. All she needed was a strong figurehead to lead her men, with one of her own generals standing at his shoulder to give the orders. If he refused, she could always kill him and send his corpse to Octavian, dressed as Mark Antony. It might be enough to allow her to keep her throne.

When he opened his eyes, she looked around her at the flowers. "Ah, roses and sea salt – a heady mixture with fond memories perhaps?" she teased, but he simply stared at her in an unnerving fashion. His unwavering gaze drilled into her. It felt as if he knew exactly what she was thinking. When his eyebrow twitched slightly, she found herself blushing.

Standing, she gave a slight gesture with her hand to the guards, instructing them to stay where they were. Then she beckoned Anthony to follow as she walked deeper into the gardens.

"Your new quarters are comfortable?" she asked politely, once they were alone.

"More than comfortable, Anthony responded. "I have never before stayed in such luxury."

"And the food and clothing? They are adequate for your needs?"

"Absolutely," he nodded.

"And your wife? How does she feel about her situation?"

"Lissa is more than happy in her own company." He smiled at the queen and added, "Of course, the peace and quiet helps her to think and understand her visions."

"And has she had any visions lately?"

He tilted his head sideways, as if thinking. "Perhaps."

"Yet you do not speak of them." There was a hint of impatience in Cleopatra's reply. She was enjoying the flirting, but was not accustomed to being kept waiting. "Your purpose here is to provide me with information," she chided.

He laughed briefly, and with a hint of nervousness.

"Forgive my hesitancy. The last time we met, you threatened to have me whipped."

She nodded briefly. "There will be no repeat today, I assure you. Although, if memory serves, I believe you found the experience somewhat stimulating."

Anthony ignored her suggestive remark, but looked relieved. "Thank you, your majesty. I have no desire to face the whip again." He stopped walking. "Forgive me, but I am unclear why I am here and my wife is not. Surely she is of more use to you than I?"

It appeared they were at last getting down to business, so she turned to face him and gave an honest answer. "I make no secret of the fact that I dislike your wife. Spending time with her displeases me. Your presence is more enjoyable. Our last encounter proved she trusts you enough to tell you all she knows."

"Lissa and I have no secrets from each other," Anthony agreed, although he made sure he looked less than certain of his remark. He was hoping Cleopatra would know more about Melissa's relationship with Mark Antony than he did.

Cleopatra took the bait. "I doubt that. Every woman has secrets that they keep. For example, I find it hard to believe you knew how similar you are to her former lover until you saw him with your own eyes."

Anthony looked away and smiled to himself. Of course, he knew how similar they were – he had seen his father when he was small – but the queen had no idea of this. He was feeling more confident by the second. It appeared a decade of marriage had not dulled his ability to toy with a woman mentally. He clenched his fists as if controlling his anger, but said nothing.

As Cleopatra's eyes flicked to his fists, she believed her statement to be true. She moved to calm the situation, or so she thought. "It is my wish that you act as our intermediary. She will tell you of her visions and you will bring the information to me. Your agreement will give me great . . ." she waved her hand for dramatic effect ". . . pleasure."

Anthony pretended to consider his options. It did not take long. He only had one. He turned slowly to face her again. "Whilst I would be more than happy to oblige your request, to stand between two strong-minded women is not a task any sane man would willingly accept. My wife will remain mistrustful of your motives and you will challenge every vision I report. My position will be tenuous and, if you do not like what I have to say, short-lived. I must ask you, what do I get for being placed in such a precarious position?"

Cleopatra turned her head away a fraction and he could see a hint of a playful smile on her lips. "Why, my gratitude, of course."

Anthony wondered what form that gratitude would take. Years spent playing poker meant he felt confident in reading other people, especially women, but he had not yet got the measure of Egypt's legendary queen. Her expressions changed in a heartbeat, so quickly that he knew she was toying with him in the same way he was toying with her. She would be a tough nut to crack, but he was nevertheless confident. Needing to negotiate further, he looked less than impressed, remaining silent and holding out for more.

Cleopatra laughed. "You believe you have a talent for negotiation, Anthony, especially when you have nothing to negotiate with."

He shrugged. "Having nothing, means I have nothing to lose and everything to gain."

She shook her head. "That is not true. You stand to lose a great deal."

"Such as?" He looked genuinely baffled.

"Your life."

Cleopatra's answer had come so quietly that Anthony knew she meant it. She turned away to smell a rose, giving him time to digest her words. She would not think twice about killing him, if it suited her purpose, but for the moment he believed he was more valuable alive. On each of their encounters he had sensed her sexual interest in him. Regardless of the risk, or the promises made to his wife, now was the time to use his greatest talents to seduce history's greatest seductress.

Moving close behind her, but not touching her, he bent slightly to whisper in her ear, his hot breath falling on her earlobe. "Kill me and you would have to deal with my wife, which would displease you." He dared to run a fingertip down her arm, despite the danger. Although he could not see them, he knew the guards were within easy reach. Unsanctioned bodily contact with a woman believed by her people to be a living goddess would bring them running from every direction.

She gasped in surprise at his boldness, but made no attempt to move away or even to chastise him. Instead, she replied calmly and without any hint of fear at his proximity.

"Indulge me and I will grant certain liberties,"

"What kind of liberties?" Anthony brushed his lip against her earlobe.

She straightened her back, deliberately leaning against him. She waited for him to move away, but he did not. Instead, he dared to run his whole hand across her arm, gripping her elbow and pulling her closer, before stroking her arm again. This foreigner was as arrogant as Mark Antony had been on their first meeting in Rome. It was another similarity between the pair that unnerved her. Cleopatra felt confident that she was winning this game of seduction, and far quicker than she had anticipated.

"That depends on what you tell me," she half-whispered, turning her face towards his.

Anthony spoke in the same hushed tones. "Octavian will come, but not until the spring. He will come by land as well as by sea. There are many client kings whose realms lie between you and Octavian. You must cultivate their friendships to ensure they do not become your enemies." His free hand found its way onto her hip.

This time, she tried to conceal her gasp. "Which of these kings do you have in mind?"

Lissa believes your best options lie with those best placed to stand against Octavian. Armenia, for instance …"

"Armenia is a Roman province with a Roman governor," Cleopatra interrupted.

"Mark Antony is a Roman general and a good friend of the governor, who has not yet declared his intentions. It is a relationship worth fostering," Anthony countered. He continued to stroke her arm, and she continued to allow it. "If not Armenia, then Nabatea is an option. Their king has helped your family in the past. He will honour past allegiances, despite your recent disagreements over the bitumen deposits." Bitumen was used in the waterproofing of naval vessels. Mark Antony had granted Cleopatra the revenues from the Nabatean king's bitumen fields to furnish himself with the fleet he needed. The Nabateans had not been best pleased and petitioned Mark Antony to change his decision. They failed.

"It is true, the Nabateans were good allies once," she muttered, as she began shifting her weight from one foot to the other, gently rubbing her rear against Anthony's groin while considering the possibilities under discussion. She noted that he had not mentioned anyone by name and wondered if this was an oversight, or whether he simply did not have those details.

"Judea has plentiful resources at its disposal, as well as a strong army," he added, in a deliberate attempt at provoking her to take the sexual heat out of the situation.

Cleopatra spat her response in respect of the king of Judea. "Herod! He is an uncouth lout who does not deserve to sit upon a throne. I would not ask that psychopath for aid if my life depended on it! I would sooner die than beg for his assistance."

Anthony immediately stepped away. "As you wish, your majesty, I am merely passing on the information as it was given to me. I have no knowledge of the personalities involved."

Cleopatra's frustration was immediate and confusing. He was getting under her skin in a way that only Mark Antony had previously managed. When she turned around, she saw a man whose face was a mask of indifference. He immediately dropped to his knees and stared at her feet as if begging for her forgiveness for his indiscretion. Was he playing her or was he merely concerned by the prospect of the lash? Whatever the answer, their encounter for the morning was over.

She calmed herself. "There is no need for apologies." She extended her hand. Anthony took it warily as he rose to his feet. "I had hoped for better news. For example, I would like the names of those whose loyalty is assured rather than of those who may be persuaded by the wealth of my treasury."

Anthony shook his head. "My wife's visions do not work that way. When Caesar came to Egypt, Lissa could not tell him which Ptolemy to support, only that he must choose one. It was his decision to choose you. Had he chosen your brother, I have no doubt the world would be very different."

Anthony paused nervously, hoping Cleopatra would accept what he had said, but when he received no confirmation he decided to press the issue. "My wife is fearful you will return her to the prison if you do not like the news she offers."

"I still may," Cleopatra replied coolly, struggling to suppress her yearnings further. She turned her head to face him.

"If you do that I will have no excuse to spend time in these beautiful gardens with their beautiful owner." The smile was back, but she was unsure if it was genuine or sheer bravado. "And I would be loath to lose such a great honour. It is not often I meet such a fascinating and stimulating woman."

There it was again; the flattery. Cleopatra's lips parted in anticipation. She found herself hoping his arrogance would lead him to try to kiss her. She wanted to feel his lips on hers to see if they too were reminiscent of the other Antony in her life.

Instead of a kiss, it was another suggestion that parted his lips. "Lissa believes you have a prisoner of interest to the king of Media, and that their loss will not cause any drain on your finances."

Cleopatra replied politely, not wanting any disappointment to show. "You are referring to Artavasdes, the former king of Armenia."

Anthony continued to pretend ignorance. "If he is the king of Media's sworn enemy, then yes, he is the man to whom Lissa refers."

She smiled slightly, and Anthony knew she was formulating the best way to dispatch her prisoner and gain favour with the Medians. He also knew he had just proposed a death sentence for Artavasdes, but that was what his history recorded. The king of Armenia would soon be embarking on a long trip to Media, or at least his head would.

Cleopatra's smile became a wide grin.

"This information is pleasing and deserving of reward. Ask for whatever you desire, and it shall be yours."

Anthony pretended to look surprised at her generosity. He thought for a moment and even went as far as to start to speak and then shook his head as if she would never agree. It helped to raise her anticipation of what his demand would be.

Her impatience grew, making her hasty in her response. "Make your demands before I change your mind. Tell me, what you want. I assure you, I will deny you nothing." *Except your freedom*, she thought.

He had the decency to look embarrassed. "I am a simple man, your majesty, and require little. I run every morning in your gardens, but at home I use our local gymnasium where I enjoy the company of like-minded men whilst I exercise. I wondered if perhaps I could use the gymnasium in the town. I hear it is the finest in the world."

Cleopatra's face fell. This was not what she expected, and she did not want to give her newest prize the chance to escape. And yet she had given her word. To retract it so quickly would destroy any trust she hoped to build with this intriguing man, and she needed him to trust her. She had to say yes.

"What assurance would I have that you would not try to escape?" she asked bluntly.

"Where would I go? You hold my wife. I have no knowledge of the region, nor do I know any person who would agree to help me. I am completely at your mercy, and if I am honest ..." he leant closer and whispered in her ear again "... I am rather enjoying it."

As he pulled away he winked at her. The fear was gone and the arrogance was back, but Cleopatra believed it was a thin line dividing the two personas. Was this purely an act to gain favour, or did he really like to live life on the edge?

Understanding that he was trying to return to the earlier ease that had been between them, she continued to play the coy woman. "What of your wife? Will she not be jealous of such an arrangement?"

"Not at all – she is far happier reading a book than spending time with people, including me. Perhaps you would be willing to let her examine your exceptional library? I cannot believe Caesar allowed the entire collection to burn."

Cleopatra shook her head. "You have more impertinence than I have come to expect from any man . . . except for one perhaps," she mused. "I will grant your request to use the gymnasium, if for no other reason than you had the gall to ask for it, though your wife may not visit my library. She remains in the palace at all times. She will never leave it."

The queen's last sentence was delivered with such spite that Anthony could not fail to notice, though he made no visible acknowledgement of her hatred. He bowed slightly in acceptance of her generosity. He had no real interest in going to the Gymnasium, but it did give him a chance to explore the town more. It would do for now.

"Thank you, your majesty. In return I promise I will be your willing servant." He winked at her again, emphasising the innuendo.

If seduction was a game, Cleopatra knew this man was as gifted a player as herself. She would need to raise her game significantly, if she wanted to steal him from the seer's grasp. She wanted revenge on Melissa for owning her husband's heart, and she wanted that revenge even more than she wanted Anthony's body. It might take longer than she had hoped, but she would take this strong-willed individual and turn him into her puppet, whilst extracting the maximum pleasure from him. She would eventually find his weakness and exploit it.

Her response was regal in its tone. "I look forward to that day, Anthony. I will expect a great deal in return for granting such a freedom. When the time comes for you to repay me, be sure you do not disappoint."

She gave a wave of her hand to dismiss him but, as he bowed and turned away, she had an inkling of an idea – a way to strike the first blow in her private war with Melissa.

She called him back.

"I am feeling particularly generous today. Though I cannot grant your wife access to the library, I will send a selection of scrolls to her. She deserves some reward for her visions, which have proved most accurate to date."

She beamed, unable to hide her pleasure at her own idea.

And then Cleopatra delivered the one piece of news that Anthony dreaded more than anything.

"As your wife predicted, my husband shuns palace life. Mark Antony seeks solace in a deserted building in the harbour."

Anthony bowed again, partly from respect, partly so she would not see the colour draining from his face, but he failed to hide the quiver of fear in his voice.

"Thank you, your majesty. Lissa will be most grateful for your generosity."

If Mark Antony was back, it meant Anthony Marcus' problems were just beginning.

Chapter 7

Melissa stood at the end of the causeway linking the royal quarter to the small island that housed the Timoneum. She had come here every day since Anthony told her of Mark Antony's return. It had been the single event that had finally dragged her out of her self-imposed imprisonment.

Until that moment, she had refused to enjoy the limited freedoms the palace complex had to offer, but no longer. As soon as Anthony left for the gymnasium, she would walk in the gardens and stroll along the quays in the royal harbour. She had a guard who followed her, but she never made any attempt to board a ship. Nor did she walk too close to any of the palace gates. She had no interest in finding a way to get out of the palace, rather the opposite. As the weeks went by, she became desperate to find a way in to one of the most secure locations within the complex.

Although there were no guards on the causeway, she never dared cross it. She assumed that was where her freedoms would be cut short, so she only ever ventured onto the end of the narrow jetty, where she could sit down on the edge and pretend to watch the sailors as they undertook their daily tasks. The main trade took place beyond the palace harbour, but ships docked every day bringing an assortment of luxury goods direct to the palace. Amphorae of oils and wines from Greece and Italy jostled for space alongside expensive perfumes, silks and exotic spices from the east. Melissa would try to guess the cargo of each ship before it was unloaded, with little success.

As she watched the Alexandrians at work, she would glance along that causeway in the hope that Mark Antony would appear. He did not. In fact, there was very little going on at the opposite end of this narrow length of stonework, beyond a few sea birds loitering in the hope of picking up scraps from the fishing boats.

From the moment her husband told her of Mark Antony's return, Melissa's spirits lifted. She always knew he would return, but not when, as Plutarch had never mentioned the exact date. Their last meeting had been frustrating: she had been angry, believing it was his fault she had been dragged back into the past; he was unable to overcome his jealousy at seeing her with another man. She knew he was still in love with her and, although his mental state was delicate, to say the least, Mark Antony was still Melissa's best hope for survival. If she could only find a way to speak to him, she felt certain her fortunes would improve dramatically. She would far rather take her chances with him than with Cleopatra, whom she had detested from their first brief meeting some thirteen years earlier in Rome. Melissa did not share her husband's liking for the woman she still regarded as Caesar's whore, and she most definitely did not trust her.

She had to be careful. Anthony Marcus could prove to be just as jealous as his famous father. If he felt Melissa was too keen to see her old lover, his jealousy would erupt with the force of a volcano. The first time he had been forced to accept that Melissa had shared his father's bed, he had gone off the rails, drinking and sleeping with any number of women. Here, the only women available were the queen and her flunkies. Neglecting Anthony could drive him into Cleopatra's arms, so Melissa was doing her utmost to appear disinterested in the tiny island and its newest inhabitant. It was why she only visited the causeway when Anthony was at the gymnasium.

The Timoneum fascinated her. It was hardly the one-roomed structure she had imagined from the historical descriptions she had read. The island contained a mansion built by one of Cleopatra's ancestors next to a sizeable temple dedicated to Poseidon, though neither appeared to be in regular use. From what little information Melissa had ascertained, the palace was shabby and in need of renovation, but it was not the wooden hut described in some ancient sources. It made sense: the Mark Antony she knew would not lightly discard his customary luxuries. He might have withdrawn from palace life, but not from palatial living.

At times she wondered if there was anyone out there. Mark Antony was a soldier at heart and more than capable of taking care of his own needs, but, given the opportunity, he happily let others wait on him. His tendency towards excess had grown over the years, if the ancient sources could be believed. He and Cleopatra had formed the Amimetobi, or The Society for Inimitable Livers. There were stories of eight wild boars being roasted at different intervals across the same day just so that one would be ready at the precise moment they demanded it, or of guests at dinner parties in Alexandria being gifted the entire gold dinner service to take home. On one occasion, Mark Antony had been so impressed with his meal that he had given the chef a house. His behaviour had spiralled out of control and was way beyond excess. It had certainly helped Octavian to continue Cicero's defamation of his character and to label him as a waster with low morals.

There should have been at least some movement of slaves to tend to the needs of such a demanding master, but there was nothing. Day after day it was the same. Melissa even wondered if her husband had been mistaken and the Timoneum's most illustrious inhabitant was not yet in residence. It would explain the lack of people. Yet she did not give up hope of catching sight of him. She knew if she were invited to visit, even Cleopatra would not dare to stop her.

Today felt different. There had been a flurry of activity in the halls of the palace all morning. As Melissa understood it, Canidius Crassus had reached Egypt the night before and, while the news he brought was less than favourable, his arrival had certainly lightened the mood. He had led the legions from Egypt as ordered, but as they crossed the mountains of Macedonia, Octavian's forces intercepted them. The legions held firm for a week, though neither from loyalty to Mark Antony nor to Canidius. They held their ground only as long as it took their centurions to negotiate acceptable terms for surrender. The officers were given a choice: to give up along with their men, thus betraying Mark Antony, or to leave to re-join his cause. Many stayed. Canidius and a few others decided to leave. Their journey by land through increasingly hostile territory had been long and arduous, but perhaps the greatest test of Canidius' loyalty was still to come. He had to deliver the news to Mark Antony that the last of the Roman legions were gone.

Melissa did not sit on the quayside today. She paced nervously; hoping that at some point Canidius might appear. Her intention was to use him to send a message to Mark Antony, but she had no idea what he looked like. She had seen a few men in Roman uniform pass by, but these had been ordinary legionaries carrying baskets of food and a rather plentiful supply of amphorae. No doubt these were here at Canidius' request. Any Roman officer worth his salt would want his own men to guard his beleaguered general, rather than trust local troops, who might be harbouring resentment towards the Roman occupying force.

Eventually, a middle-aged man in a well-polished uniform walked towards her. He was the most likely candidate that she had so far seen. With his stocky frame and weather-worn face, he had the appearance of a seasoned soldier. Something in the way he carried himself implied he was of senatorial rank. That made him an officer, and one of some standing.

As he approached the end of the causeway, she calmly stepped forwards to address him, but the guard had other ideas and tried to prevent her, forcing her to shout.

"Canidius Crassus. I must speak with you. I have an urgent message for your commander."

The Roman stopped and pulled the Egyptian guard away from Melissa roughly. Although he had no idea who she was, he could tell she was a stranger to the court, both from her lack of jewellery, and her exceptional command of Latin. Most of the women here only spoke Greek and it was a pleasure to hear his native tongue coming from a pretty face, rather than a scarred legionary.

"Lady, do I know you?" he inquired, once Melissa was standing freely in front of him.

He had not denied being Canidius, so Melissa assumed she had the right man. "We have not met, sir, but I have knowledge of you by reputation. We both had the honour of calling Ventidius Bassus friend."

Canidius smiled. "Now there is a name I have not heard in many years." He folded his arms casually. "How did that wily old dog get to know such a pretty thing as you?"

Melissa did her best to look embarrassed at the compliment. "Ventidius regarded me as he would a daughter, though I doubt he ever made mention of me to you. My name is Lissa, sir."

Canidius' smile vanished, to be replaced by a look of astonishment. "Lissa, you say? Can it be true? Does the woman known as Caesar's witch truly stand before me?"

Caesar's witch! It was a term that Melissa had not heard in years, but one she had herself used to describe her position to Caesar's mistress, Servilia.

She nodded.

The smile returned to Canidius' face. "Then, lady, I do know of you. Ventidius spoke of you often. He held you in the highest regard. But tell me, how do you come to be in Alexandria?"

Melissa moved her head sideways slightly towards the guard. "Let us say, I was actively encouraged to try the climate. It is far drier here than in the marshes surrounding Actium."

Canidius' eyes widened. Had the seer really been at Actium? Was she the reason the general had left so suddenly? Was everything Ventidius had said about her true? These were questions he wanted answers to, but not within earshot of one of Cleopatra's henchmen.

He put a hand on Melissa's shoulder. "Why not join me? I am sure the general will be pleased to see you."

The guard immediately stepped forward and Canidius sensed that he would not be allowed to take Melissa without resistance. His hand went to his sword, but Melissa shook her head slightly.

"No sir, you will find my counsel is no longer welcomed by the general. As you will see, he is not himself. My only wish is to pass on the message that I am available to *any* Roman officer who has need of my services." She ran her hand down his arm, hoping he would understand she wanted to talk privately.

Despite her act, all Canidius could see in Melissa's eyes was fear, but he did pick up on her intimation.

He played along. "That is a most generous offer to make. We will indeed speak again. I would welcome seeing your pretty face in my quarters." He reached out and stroked her face, giving the impression to the guard that he believed her to be little more than a whore. "I have spent many weeks without the attentions of a decent woman."

"And I would welcome the invitation, sir. I prefer the attentions of a Roman any day. I find the conversation more . . . intellectual."

He nodded. "Then I will send for you when I next seek the services of a woman. In the meantime, forgive me but I have an appointment to keep." Without another word he turned and walked away up the causeway.

Canidius knew only too well that if the woman he had just met was who she claimed to be, he was in the presence of the greatest possible ally. He remembered the stories, told in hushed whispers by his compatriots Ventidius and Pollio. They spoke with admiration of a seer who travelled with both Caesar and Mark Antony on many campaigns before vanishing in mysterious circumstances. Even the traitor, Plancus, had spoken highly of her abilities, but all of them warned him to never mention her name in Mark

Antony's presence, for fear of the general's reaction. Ventidius said her loss after the treaty of Bononia had changed their leader, bringing out the very worst aspects of his personality.

For the first time in many weeks Canidius Crassus felt there might be some improvement in their situation. The arrival of the seer could make all the difference to their fight. All he had to do was find a way to mention it to Mark Antony, without losing his head in the process.

A little over two hours later, Melissa was sitting in her quarters waiting for Anthony to return from the gymnasium. It seemed to her that he was spending longer there every day. Little did she know that Anthony was touring the city, memorising the layout of every road and alley so that, when the time eventually came to run, he would know the quickest way to get to the outer walls. She had no idea he was doing this, because he had chosen not to tell her.

The windows to the gardens were wide open in the hope of providing some air, but there was little. Winter in Alexandria was as warm as early summer in Italy and, when the breeze blew from the land as it did today, it brought with it the stifling Saharan dust.

From outside, Melissa heard someone cough. Crossing to the opening, she was surprised to see Canidius hovering behind a large potted palm. He looked deeply troubled, but he said nothing. Instead, he beckoned for Melissa to join him on the shaded veranda.

Once she was outside he began a hushed conversation. "I do not know if you are aware, but we are watched constantly. There are spy holes in the walls, cleverly disguised in the paintings."

Melissa frowned. She had often had that feeling of being watched when she was alone in her room, but dismissed it. "I thought it was my imagination playing tricks on me."

Canidius shook his head. "It is not. I have heard you are a vigilant woman and I would encourage you to continue to take care. They see everything, but most understand little if it is said in Latin. Only the queen and the eunuch speak it." He sat down on the edge of the pot in a position that gave him a good view over the gardens, but hid him from prying eyes. "We are safer talking here where we can see if anyone approaches."

Melissa took up a position on a small stone bench next to the pot and stared out into the gardens. To most passers-by she appeared to be alone. She spoke quietly. "I did not expect to see you so soon."

"I felt a similar ruse to yours was advisable to keep our hosts guessing. The occupants of this palace are experts at saying one thing and meaning another. Oddly they do not credit their guests with the same capabilities for deception." He grinned. "And this way I can send for you at another time and enjoy your company again!"

Melissa could not help but giggle slightly before the seriousness of the situation returned. "How is Mark Antony?" she asked.

Canidius sighed. "He is lost to utter despair. He believes that Cleopatra is responsible for his defeat at Actium and that she wishes him dead. I can say nothing to allay his fears, as I believe him to be right. He is nothing more than a shell of the man he once was."

"What can I do to help?" Melissa offered.

"I do not know. I told him you were here and that you wished to see him, but he reacted poorly to the news.

He threw a wine glass at my head and forbade me ever to speak to you." Canidius watched for her reaction and saw one of despair. "It is the one order he has ever given me that I have chosen not to obey. I am curious to know why he would dismiss the one woman whose counsel he valued so highly."

Melissa closed her eyes tightly as she fought back her emotions. "Who told you that?"

"Why, our mutual friend, Ventidius. He told me how much Mark Antony trusted your advice. And now you have come in the hour of his greatest need. I believe you are a sign from the gods that we may yet prevail, but he will not hear of it. He called you a liar and a whore who has betrayed him. Why would he say that?"

Melissa swallowed hard. She considered herself a good judge of character, but feared her desperation might be pushing her to trust this stranger too quickly. Canidius was her only link to Mark Antony at this time, but she could only tell him a small part of the truth.

Slowly she opened her eyes. "I am not alone. My husband is here with me. Mark Antony almost killed him. He feels betrayed because I married another man. It is why he will not see me." She held her breath waiting for his reply.

Out of the corner of her eye, she saw Canidius smile. "It appears Ventidius was correct in something else he told me. He said that he had never known any man to love a woman with such passion as the general felt for you."

"Ventidius was correct in most things," Melissa replied wistfully as she thought about her good friend. "I miss him a great deal."

"As he missed you," Canidius replied softly.

Melissa was quiet for some time before asking

Canidius about her friend's death. "What happened to him? Is it true he was poisoned?"

A noise somewhere in the distance made Canidius glance about him suddenly. He had to stay vigilant, and continued to scan the gardens as he replied, "I cannot say for certain. I choose to believe his death was natural, but there were rumours. It was said that Mark Antony was jealous of his successes in Parthia and that he ordered his murder, but I do not believe it. Ventidius was Mark Antony's eyes and ears in Rome. He sent regular reports to us of Octavian's actions. Mark Antony would never have disposed of such a valuable asset in such a casual manner."

"What of Octavian? Would he stoop that low?" Melissa asked the question even though she already knew the answer.

Canidius shrugged. "Perhaps, though he would not soil his own hands on such a task. He has men who do his dirty work for him these days."

"He has always had those." Melissa shuddered slightly as she remembered her treatment at the hands of Salvidienus Rufus, one of Octavian's closest friends.

Canidius reached out and briefly placed his hand over Melissa's. "My apologies, lady, I forgot you were tortured by one of his men."

Melissa gasped in surprise. "Is there anything Ventidius did not tell you?"

His response was gentle. "I have no details. I only know it was the reason Mark Antony faked your death and sent you away. Ventidius did not tell me where you went, or how to reach you, which was a disappointment to many of us. At one time Plancus and I discussed the possibility of sending men to seek you out, but that was long ago, before Plancus turned traitor. He too believed you were the only person who could make Mark Antony see sense."

She shook her head slightly. "I wish that I could, but I fear it is too late. My influence has waned, along with Mark Antony's popularity, whereas Octavian is in his ascendency. His victory at Actium has sealed the fate of us all. It is only a matter of time before the young Caesar comes to call."

There was a groan of despair from Canidius. "It need not have been so. I know that, if the general had led the legions himself, they would have remained loyal. They felt he had deserted them, leaving a lesser man at their head — and all for that woman." He released her hand and looked down at his feet. "I am ashamed to say I was not up to the task assigned to me."

It was Melissa's turn to provide some comfort. "You are not to blame for their actions. Mark Antony was once hailed as the next Alexander the Great. He certainly had the capability to emulate the greatest general the world has ever known, but he dallied when he should have been decisive. It is ironic that he should lose his men in the same mountains that spawned Alexander's conquering armies."

Canidius nodded slowly. "Even the Larks would not remain true to our cause. Their loyalty was no match for Octavian's bribery. And it is a bribe offered with money he does not have. He cannot hope to pay them without Cleopatra's treasury, which is something he has not yet taken control of." The Larks, or Fifth Alaudae, were Mark Antony's favourite legion. They had been with him for over twenty years, ever since he had served under Caesar in Gaul. Octavian had tried to buy their loyalty once before at the battle of Forum Gallorum, but to no avail. However, the temptation of food, clothing and hard cash had been too great for even this half-starved legion of stalwarts following the debacle at Actium.

Melissa laughed lightly. "Caesars have always been gamblers. This one has cast his dice as well as his uncle ever did. Octavian is shrewd and patient. He has always known that to meet Mark Antony head-on is as to commit suicide but, if he chips away, slowly undermining Antony's support, his chances are greatly increased. Even now, when he sees victory in his grasp, he will not hurry. He will bide his time, allowing the panic of his victims to grow. The Roman governor of Syria will be the next to declare for Octavian, which is no surprise, as he is the nephew of your old compatriot, Plancus. And when Judea turns, it will bring him the greatest prize of all. Herod will kiss the feet of any man willing to stand against Cleopatra."

"I agree with your assessment. Herod has wanted Cleopatra dead for many years and often lobbied for her removal, whilst I naively took her side." Canidius shook his head in disgust. "I thought him a madman. Now I wonder if he was not the sanest one among us, seeing through her from the start." He sighed. "I have been such a fool."

"You are no fool and you are a good judge of character, for Herod is as mad as they come." Melissa knew from reading Plutarch that Canidius had once been an ally of Cleopatra, defending her when others tried to persuade Mark Antony to distance himself. She had to know what had changed. "Canidius, may I ask where you stand regarding our sovereign host?"

Canidius' back straightened. "I no longer have any

love for her royal highness. It is true I was once her ardent supporter, for she charmed me, as she does every man who spends time in her company. She also made certain financial arrangements that were to my advantage."

Melissa nodded. She knew of a decree signed by Cleopatra that had survived to modern times which gave Canidius land and preferential taxation rights in perpetuity.

"Looking back, there were always tell-tale signs of her true nature, yet I believed her affections for the general to be genuine. I turned a blind eye to any peculiarities for his sake. That is something I can no longer do. When Octavian first declared war, we should have attacked. We were ready to, and yet . . ." he paused, ". . . how did you put it? We dallied. If we had launched a full assault on Italian soil nothing could have stopped us, not even the considerable leadership skills of Marcus Agrippa! We would have brought Octavian to his knees in weeks, but the queen persuaded Mark Antony to remain in Greece, insisting it was necessary to wait until the other client kings could join our cause. I soon realised she wanted them to pay her homage. I began to see that she cared nothing for Mark Antony, only for herself, seeking to turn him into her puppet. The way she treats him is a disgrace." Canidius' new found disgust for Cleopatra was apparent. "Mad or not, Herod was right, as was Plancus, and every other good man who turned. We should have forced the general to see sense, but her hold over him has always been so strong. I have no idea why he could not see what was slipping from his grasp when the rest of us did."

"Perhaps he did see it and chose to do nothing," Melissa replied with sadness.

Canidius frowned. "Why?"

"Love maybe, or guilt. The price of betraying her may have been simply too high for him to consider. Above all else, I know Mark Antony to be loyal to a fault. Perhaps it was his loyalty, to her and to his children, which drove him to continue down his chosen path."

"My loyalty is to Mark Antony," Canidius scoffed. "It was for him and him alone that I risked my life to return to Alexandria. If I thought there was some way to extricate him from her grasp, I would do it, regardless of the cost, though I fear it is too late to attempt it."

"How did he take the news that his legions are gone?" Melissa murmured.

"Surprisingly well . . ." he paused, ". . . no, make that alarmingly well. I expected him to shout and rave, swearing curses on every man and their families, yet he did not. He remained oddly calm and a little dismissive of Octavian's success saying . . ." he put on a deeper voice, ". . . that boy has only ever won a battle when the victory was handed to him by a better man." His voice returned to normal. "It was as if he already knew the outcome. He seemed more distressed by your presence at the end of the causeway."

Melissa sighed and brushed some sand off the seat beside her. She had told Mark Antony on the *Antonia* that he would lose the legions, although at the time she thought he had not been paying attention. Obviously he had listened, meaning Canidius' news was of no surprise to him at all.

Like father, like son, she thought. Both the Antony's had a tendency to focus on trivial issues, while allowing the important ones to pass them by. Mark Antony was too busy concentrating on what she was doing on the causeway, rather than dealing with the fact he had lost his entire army.

They sat in silence as each thought about their situation. Melissa was despairing of the man on whom she had pinned her hopes for survival. Even though she had read as much in history, she had refused to believe Mark Antony would ever have given up, believing the accounts to be nothing more than products of Octavian's propaganda machine. It seemed now that the reports were true. Canidius meanwhile, was trying to formulate a plan for his single-handed defence of the city. If Mark Antony was in no fit state to lead, the task fell wholly to him, but he had few options, and even fewer troops with which to mount any sort of resistance. He needed a miracle to bring Mark Antony to his senses and to bring his general and Melissa together. He could only pray the gods would see their way to providing one soon.

Suddenly, Melissa grabbed his hand. "What if I go to him?"

Canidius shook his head. "I do not think it possible. You said yourself, you no longer hold his interest in the way you once did. In fact, he forbade me to ever speak to you. If he knew I was here, I fear he would most likely banish me. What use would I be then?"

"None," Melissa agreed sadly. "We will have to wait and bide our time. Perhaps the loneliness of his solitude will persuade him to come to us."

"Perhaps, in time," he agreed, even though he knew time was something they had precious little of.

One of the slaves from the kitchens walked past with a basket of cut herbs, prompting Canidius to take his leave. He slipped away as quietly as he had arrived, leaving Melissa alone on the veranda. She remained there for a few moments longer before rising and going inside.

She was surprised to see her husband lying on the bed.

"Making new friends, I see." He scowled at her when he spoke.

Melissa tried to smile disarmingly. She could tell from his tone he was annoyed with her for speaking to a Roman. "That was Canidius Crassus. He's one of Mark Antony's generals."

"I know who he is," Anthony replied through gritted teeth. "I can read just as bloody well as you can."

She chose to ignore the sarcasm. "He could be a valuable ally. You should have said hello."

"No thanks. I'd prefer to keep anyone that close to Mark Antony at arm's length," he sneered with disdain.

"Anyone other than Cleopatra, you mean," Melissa snapped back. Anthony's attitude towards this whole situation was beginning to get on her nerves. How dare he tell her who to talk to, when he was busy making small talk with the queen at every opportunity?

Anthony sat up suddenly, making Melissa jump. Between the speed of his movement and the black look on his face, he reminded her of the other man bearing the name of 'Antony'. In fact, the resemblance was uncanny, and distinctly unnerving.

He glared up at her.

"Do you really think I enjoy spending so much time with that woman?" he hissed. "I told you, I do it to stay in her good books. One of us has to!"

"Well, if Canidius can get me an audience with Mark Antony you won't have to cosy up to her any more, will you?" Melissa added a touch of her own sarcasm as her impatience with her churlish husband grew.

He stood up suddenly. "That's not going to happen. Cleopatra's the one with the power around here and she's the one we need to keep sweet. I'm warning you, Liss, if you go anywhere near that washed-up old drunk, I will not be responsible for my actions."

Pushing past her, he stormed out through the open windows and into the gardens, leaving Melissa staring after him.

Chapter 8

Mark Antony stood aboard the *Selene* marvelling at the wondrous images before him. Of course, he had seen a portrait of similar clarity before, inside the locket hanging around his neck, but that tiny image was nothing compared to these. They showed Melissa with a group of children, Melissa on her own, Melissa with *him*. That was one image Mark Antony did not dwell on. The thought of the woman he loved being in the arms of his son still sickened him.

All of the images were held against a cork backing with some form of netting over it. The structure allowed the net to be stretched to put items in behind. A rather useful invention, he thought, though not as advanced an item as he expected the future to have produced. Not that he really knew what to expect on that count, nor did he particularly want to. It was a future he could play no part in, and one that no longer held any interest for him.

These pictures were the only link he had to a family he knew nothing about. His fingers ran over the photos, pausing on one. It was of three children: a girl and two boys. The girl looked around the right age to be his daughter, depending on whether time had passed at the same rate for Melissa as it had for him. The boys had such similar colouring, with their dark hair and dark eyes that they had to be related to the girl. Perhaps they were her brothers, or, more precisely, her half-brothers. If so, they must be *his* children – offspring of the usurper who shared his face. Of course, that would make them his grandsons. He shook his head to clear his thoughts, which had the makings of a Greek tragedy about them. He could not afford to dwell on matters that could never be of importance to him.

He looked around at the rest of the ransacked cabin. He had opened every locker, emptying out the clothing and books onto the bed and floor. The books were unusual in comparison with those he was familiar with, being so tightly bound at one edge that the pages held together without any visible fastening. And there were other, more fascinating items than these. He found plates that bounced and glasses that did not smash when thrown to the floor. And then there was the food, some of which he recognised – rice, salt, oil, garlic, dried peppers – and some he did not, but assumed it to be edible as it was in the same cupboards. Melissa's love of organisation meant it could have no other purpose, though he could not imagine why anyone would want to eat the thin, hard sticks that were crunchy, brittle and tasteless. As pasta would not be introduced to Italy for another 900 years, spaghetti was unknown to the Roman world. Therefore, Mark Antony had no idea you were meant to boil it prior to eating it.

Of more interest was the amber liquid in the odd-looking glass flask. Its stopper had been easy to remove, with a nice, familiar popping sound. The smell that greeted his nostrils was somewhat earthy; the strong sensation of burning in the back of his throat when swallowing it, a little disconcerting. Recognising it immediately as some form of strong liquor, Mark Antony decided this bottle of twenty-year-old single malt whisky would accompany him back to the Timoneum to be properly tested.

His attention returned to the photos. Of all of the items the future had delivered on this boat, these were the most damning and had to be removed, if for no other reason than to protect Melissa. Despite giving orders that this craft was off-limits to every person within the palace complex, he had no doubt that one of Cleopatra's minions would find a way to sneak aboard her now she was moored behind the Timoneum. He considered putting the pictures into one of the little cupboards that seemed to be everywhere and covering them with clothing, but he feared it would not be good enough. The photos had to be destroyed, or Melissa would need to answer some very awkward questions at some point.

He reached into the netting and began pulling them free, his fingers fumbling with the task at first. A number became damaged, but he was careful to gather all the pieces together into a single pile until only one remained: the picture of the three children. As he pulled it free, a corner ripped off and fell to the floor. Retrieving it, he placed it on the pile with the photo on top. As he stared at the image one last time, he found he could not dispose of it without knowing for certain who these children were and what relationship they were to him. Folding it in half, he tucked it into his belt, and then picked up the remainder of the pictures, and the whisky, which he would personally make sure he disposed of. If anyone from the palace did try to board the *Selene*, he had done his best to make sure there would be nothing of interest for them to find.

Regardless of his poor attempt to convince himself that he hated Melissa, his sense of loyalty to the woman who had once stolen his heart left him with an unwitting desire to protect her at any cost.

Chapter 9

Anthony Marcus' anger continued to grow as he stomped through the gardens. For too long he had harboured a grudge against a man he barely knew. He had always tried to deny his jealousy, pushing the feelings aside and excusing what Melissa had done on her previous journeys into the past as purely down to survival. It had been relatively easy when he believed there was no chance of his wife and his father ever meeting again, but now his hatred bubbled beneath his outwardly nonchalant manner. Knowing the man he loathed was less than a few hundred metres away only made it worse. The time had come to face his nemesis.

He could not understand why Melissa was so keen to see Mark Antony again, especially after she had watched her husband being beaten half to death by the man. It seemed to Anthony that she had lost her senses. Mark Antony was a vicious and dangerous thug – a man to be avoided at all costs – and Anthony Marcus was determined that his wife should stay away from her former lover, whatever it took.

There were no guards on the causeway. No one tried to hinder his progress in any way as he strode up to the door of the Timoneum and forced it open with a great shove. He expected someone to stop him inside, a slave perhaps, but there was no one in sight.

He walked from room to room, his footsteps echoing loudly in the bare spaces. This was not the Timoneum described by the ancient sources. It was a grand building with marble floors and frescoed walls, not some simple hermit hut, but it was certainly empty. The rooms lacked furniture of any sort, and it lacked people. A building of this size needed an army of slaves to keep it running, but there were none. It felt to Anthony that he was the only person there.

Eventually, he found a room with some basic furniture - a bed, a wardrobe, side tables, and a couch. The windows looked out over the harbour, just as they had in every other room in the building, but this was the first set that was open. On the couch, which was positioned in front of the windows, sat Mark Antony. He was slumped slightly to one side, wine glass in hand, the dregs tipping onto the arm of the couch. He made no effort to move at the sound of Anthony's footsteps.

Anthony stepped forwards more quietly than when he initially entered. Assuming his father to be drunk and asleep, his plan was to drag the older man from the couch and vent his frustrations before the man could call for help. Beating a drunk was not a particularly chivalrous action, but Anthony did not feel particularly chivalrous. All he felt was hatred for this man who had left him for dead only a few weeks earlier. If the tables were turned, he felt sure Mark Antony would have no compunction in repeating his actions from their last encounter. Anthony had no intention of giving him the chance.

As he moved closer, he glanced out of the window. What he saw stopped him in his tracks. The windows opened onto a small jetty, alongside which was moored the *Selene*.

Anthony had assumed his yacht had been sunk at Actium, but seeing her here in Alexandria made him forget his reason for coming to the Timoneum. It was as if the Fates were offering him a chance to escape, even though it was only the smallest of chances. He had no idea how he would get her out of the harbour unseen, but at least he had found a form of transport he was familiar with, provided she was still seaworthy. All he could think about now was getting to the *Selene*.

He tiptoed around Mark Antony's unmoving form without giving him a second glance. He put one foot through the window and stepped down onto the jetty.

It was as far as he got before he felt the coldness of a blade at his throat.

"Planning a trip?" a deep voice growled in his ear. The stench of alcohol that accompanied the voice was almost overwhelming, but Anthony remembered some of the stories his estate manager, Henry, had told him. Henry had been with Melissa on her last foray into the past and had spent some of his time with Mark Antony, whom he had described as far more dangerous when drunk as when sober.

Anthony gulped. He had underestimated his opponent yet again. The dagger pressed harder against his jugular. If he made any sudden movement it would to cut deep into his skin. He would bleed out in minutes.

"No" he croaked in a near whisper. "I came to find you."

He felt the blade moving slowly. He swallowed again, expecting it to be his last act. His thoughts flew immediately to Melissa and how his last words to her had been words of anger. He had been a fool, but it was too late to apologise.

The blade moved away suddenly. Slowly Anthony turned around to see his father standing over him.

"It appears you have found me or, to be more precise, I have found you," Mark Antony waved the dagger in a sideways motion, signalling that he wanted his son back inside the building.

Anthony glanced back at the *Selene*. He was half tempted to make a run for it, but there was nowhere to go, even if he could make it as far as the boat.

"Do-o not try it, boy," Mark Antony hissed as if reading his mind. There was the slightest hint of a slur in his voice, but not enough to make Anthony feel he had much of a chance to surprise this experienced warrior.

Slowly, he stepped back through the windows and into the room. He remained perfectly still, eyeing his father nervously. It felt as if he was looking at his future self, or at least one version of the man he could become. Mark Antony was older and more haggard, with a nicely developing paunch where his abs should have been. His hair was greying, as was his unkempt beard, but there was a wicked twinkle in his eyes, which said he was still capable of making mischief. Anthony felt sure he could take the older man if the moment was right, but he needed to choose his moment carefully.

He jerked his head towards the open window and the yacht outside. "Thank you for not sinking her," he finally said, with as much civility as he could muster.

Mark Antony too was sizing up his son. Anthony was the image of the man he himself had been ten years earlier; strong, athletic, thinner. Although it was no surprise that Melissa preferred the younger model to the old and battle-worn one, it did not lessen the jealousy coursing through him at the mere thought of her in these younger arms. He did not want to talk. He wanted to fight.

"You did not come here for that boat," he snapped, barely holding his temper in check. "State your true business, or be gone."

Anthony's temper began to bubble again. He had never liked being told what to do, especially by a man he had no respect for, but he was determined not to be goaded into a fight until he was ready for it. Mark Antony was armed and, even if he was drunk, extremely dangerous.

"I am here to talk about Lissa," was Anthony's eventual answer.

"Your slut, you mean." Mark Antony spat the words out as he walked over to a side table. On it sat a flask of wine, some glasses, and the now empty bottle of Anthony's very expensive whisky.

Anthony clenched his fist in anger. It seemed there was nothing that belonged to him that this man was not determined to take. He was desperate to lash out, but he forced himself to take a breath. Despite the difficulty, he remained calm. "My wife is no slut. I demand you stay away from her."

"What makes you think I would want to associate with a lying whore?" Mark Antony's jealousy had risen to the surface as soon as Anthony had referred to Melissa as his wife. His fist tightened around one of the glasses on the table as he tried to remain civil to his love rival.

"She tried to contact you, sending messages via Canidius Crassus." Anthony stated the facts only and without emotion, but his words were stilted as he delivered them.

Mark Antony shrugged and picked up the glass and the whisky bottle, tipping it up to pour from it. When the glass remained empty, he held the bottle up to eye level.

Realising it had been drained, he discarded it and picked up a wine flask instead, pouring a large glassful.

"She may have sent messages. I have not replied."

"Will you?"

The response was a little too eager and Mark Antony knew it. It meant his son feared what outcome a reunion between his father and his wife could bring, but why he would think that was unknown.

Downing the glass of wine, he slowly wiped his lips on the back of his hand. "What business is it of yours what I do, my young Oedipus?"

Anthony paused in surprise at the reference to Oedipus, a character from Greek literature who had fallen in love with his mother. As Melissa had raised him until he was four, she could have been seen by some as his adoptive mother. Melissa had always sworn she had never mentioned his parentage to anyone, but he was now wondering if Mark Antony knew who he really was. Had she told Mark Antony the truth or had he simply guessed the familial link between them? If so, did that put him and Melissa in even more danger?

"I am her husband. I have rights," Anthony finally replied, guardedly.

He said it with so much caution, it made Mark Antony laugh.

"Her husband! Ha!" He pointed at his son and vocalised the fears the younger man had been suppressing for his entire marriage. "Look at yourself. You are nothing more than a substitute - someone she settled for when her choices ran thin."

"She did not settle for me, she chose me," Anthony defended himself. "She chose me over you."

Mark Antony stared at his son coldly. "If you really

believed that, you would not be here."

Both men knew that statement to be true. Despite all of Melissa's assurances to the contrary, Anthony had always doubted that he was the man she chose. He had always wondered whether Melissa would have stayed with his father if there had been a way to do it without changing history.

On their last night together, Melissa had told Mark Antony she loved him and that she did not want to leave him. As Mark Antony saw it, Melissa had chosen him. He had forced her to leave to save her life. She had, as he saw it, merely settled for a similar man.

Each glared at the other in silence for a few moments, considering their options. One knew his position was weak and becoming weaker by the second, the other suspected his chances were improving. Both were filled with the desire to fight for the woman they both loved.

"I want your word you will not see her," Anthony demanded.

"Why should I agree to such a demand, when you see my woman every day?"

Anthony frowned in confusion. "Huh," he muttered, unsure who his father was talking about.

"Oh, I have heard how you walk with her, and fawn over her. I ask you, how long will it be before you have her in your bed, Oedipus?"

Anthony grimaced at the suggestion, realising at last which woman was being referred to. He was keeping Cleopatra at arm's length at present, but he knew that to get the freedoms he really wanted he would need to get much closer to her. Despite his promises to Melissa to the contrary, he knew he would sleep with Egypt's queen eventually, and it did not bother him in the slightest. He would do it willingly, if it provided him with a way to gain his wife's freedom, and he would most likely enjoy it. However, extra-marital affairs were not best discussed with a jealous husband. And there was the reference to Oedipus again, except this time in relation to Cleopatra, who was technically Anthony's stepmother. He was becoming more concerned that Mark Antony either knew, or at least suspected, the truth of his parentage.

"I want your word you will not see Lissa," he repeated slowly, unwilling to be drawn into any other discussion.

"What if I refuse?" Mark Antony calmed himself. From the moment he had first laid eyes on his son in the bay of Actium, he had believed he had lost Melissa to this younger version of himself. Now he had seen firsthand his son's insecurity, he had reason to doubt his earlier convictions. He could no longer afford for this situation to be driven by his emotions. He needed to retain control and allow his opponent to be the one to lose his composure.

Calmly, he put the empty glass down on the table, but did not let go of it.

"What if I choose to enjoy the feel of your wife's thighs around my waist?" he replied coolly, smiling smugly as he waited for an answer.

Something in that smile made Anthony snap. "I will make sure that never happens," he hissed, slamming a fist into the open palm of his other hand in an open gesture of aggression. He had thrown down the gauntlet.

And Mark Antony willingly picked it up.

"You do not have the balls to try," the older man murmured, tensing his body in preparation for the attack he knew would come. His grip tightened around the glass.

And then, he waited.

Anthony leapt forwards, but his attack was dodged

with ease. As he sprawled across the floor, he heard the splintering of glass as his father threw it at him. Instinctively, his arms went up to protect his head. It had missed, narrowly, hitting the wall above him. The shards fell, scattering around his hands. He could not avoid them as he pushed himself up and one small piece sliced into his palm.

He reached for a larger chunk to use as a weapon. As he rose from the floor, Mark Antony lunged, knocking him back down. The glass shard flew from his hand as he grappled with his assailant, each of them landing hard blows on the other.

Father and son struggled together, rolling to and fro across the floor until Anthony finally gained the upper hand with a hard punch to the solar plexus, winding his opponent. As Mark Antony gasped for breath, his son pinned him to the floor and slammed his fist hard into Mark Antony's kidneys, followed by another punch to the jaw.

Anthony was about to deliver a further punch when he caught sight of the locket which had slid up towards Mark Antony's throat in the struggle. It made him pause in disbelief. He recognised it immediately as the one he had given to Melissa before her last trip into the past. She had told him Octavian's agent had stolen it, but here it was, hanging around his father's neck. Melissa must have given it to him – yet another lie she had told.

The disbelief quickly turned to anger, but Anthony's momentary hesitation was to be his undoing. Before he had the chance to land another blow, he felt his body being wrenched backwards by another pair of hands, these belonging to Canidius Crassus, who now held Anthony's arms behind his back too tightly for him to escape.

"Attacking the general is punishable by death, you insolent shit," Canidius barked.

Anthony struggled to free himself, but the Roman had too good a hold.

"Who do you think you are?" Canidius demanded as he pulled Anthony up onto his feet.

Mark Antony rose to his knees slowly. "Hold him, Canidius," he gasped, still winded from Anthony's last punch.

Anthony knew he was in trouble. He could not hope to fight them both and win. Survival instinct cut in.

"I am Lissa's husband," he shouted, answering Canidius' question.

Canidius looked towards his general in time to see him lining up for an attack. This was a fight he did not want to be in the middle of, so he swung his body around and flung his captive in the direction of the couch.

Mark Antony pulled up short, narrowly avoiding punching Canidius in the side.

"Out of my way, Canidius," he ordered. He went to push past, but Canidius positioned himself between the two men.

"I cannot let you do this." Canidius put his hand against Mark Antony's chest to stop him. He began to turn towards Anthony as he spoke. "Lissa will never forgive you if you hurt her hus . . ."

His words tailed off as he saw Anthony's face for the first time. He did a double take, looking from one man to the other in confusion. At a quick glance he could barely tell them apart.

Mark Antony tried to pass him again, jolting him back into action. This time he grabbed his general's arms, holding him back.

"Go!" he shouted at Anthony. "Leave, before I change my mind."

Anthony hesitated for a split second, considering the same attack his father had planned when their situations were reversed a moment earlier. He wanted to use the advantage, but common sense told him he would come off worse. Canidius intended to stop the fight, nothing more. If he was forced to choose between the two opponents, Canidius would choose his commander and friend. He would not side with an interloper.

Anthony gave him a brief nod of thanks and then withdrew, running from the room as fast as his legs would carry him.

"Coward!" Mark Antony bellowed after the fleeing Anthony, as he shook Canidius off. "Lissa is twice the man you are!"

He waited a moment to see if Anthony would return to face him. When the fleeing footsteps had completely faded, he turned on Canidius.

"What did you do that for? I had him!"

Canidius was still struggling to understand what he had witnessed. He sat down on the end of the bed. "I do not understand. He looked just like you."

When the only answer he received was a shrug, he tried again. "I thought Lissa was your lover, but she married a man who looks exactly like you."

"I am aware of the similarities," was the eventual reply, as Mark Antony turned away and walked over to the side table. He placed both hands on it as he tried to calm himself.

"But I do not understand how this can be? Is he your cousin? Or a brother perhaps – one you had no knowledge of?" Canidius asked as he tried to make sense of the situation.

Mark Antony stared at the wall, his rage subsiding. Canidius had remained loyal when every other officer had deserted him. He deserved an explanation, but to tell the truth might prove too much even for Canidius. Mark Antony decided it best to limit the explanation to the biological facts rather than listing the esoteric ones.

Slowly, Mark Antony turned around. "I am surprised Lissa did not explain this during the conversation you swore to me you would not have," he remarked with sarcasm.

When Canidius had the decency to look embarrassed at defying his orders, Mark Antony gave him the answer he craved. "You see, my good friend, Lissa's husband . . ." he waved his hand in the direction of the door Anthony had fled through, ". . . is my son."

"Your son?" Canidius shook his head in disbelief. "That man is far too old to be your son."

Mark Antony sighed. He turned back to the table and poured two glasses of wine as he considered how to respond. Picking up both glasses, he walked over to the bed and offered one to his bemused officer. "I was much younger when he was born, and he has had a surprising life. It has aged him somewhat prematurely."

"I would say so." Canidius took the glass, gulping at its contents. He looked troubled by the revelation, but appeared to accept what had been said.

Mark Antony took a mouthful of wine from his own glass as he considered his next move. When Ventidius had first told him that the woman he had trusted above all others was married to his son, he refused to believe it. To him the entire notion seemed farcical and yet, from the moment he had first glimpsed Anthony through the mists at Actium, he knew it to be the truth. It was a betrayal he could not excuse. How Melissa could have acted in such a callous way as to marry the boy she had herself raised was beyond him. A part of him wanted to make her suffer in the same way he had: by losing the person she loved the most.

And yet when the moment came and he stood over his opponent's unconscious form on that boat, he found he could not bring himself to murder the son he had previously neglected. Over the years, the guilt of his decision to disown the boy at birth had gnawed at him and he had vowed to make amends in any way he could. When Cleopatra presented him with his illegitimate twins, he refused to make the same mistake again and acknowledged them. It went some way to assuage his guilt at abandoning his first-born son all those years before. Rather than tipping Anthony overboard, he threw him into the hold of the *Antonia* and left him there to rot, not knowing that Cleopatra would intercede and provide aid. Mark Antony could have cheerfully throttled her for doing that, but it was her flagship after all. She could do what she wanted and he could not stop her.

In the end, he accepted that Melissa had made her decision long ago as to which man she wanted. He had let her go because it had been the right thing to do, or so he had thought. He told himself that he wanted nothing more to do with Melissa. His head told him that to stay away was still the right thing, but it was not what his heart wanted. His heart wanted her back at any cost, and Anthony's blatant display of desperation gave him reason to hope he might have a chance to reverse their fortunes.

"Arrange for Lissa to visit your rooms in a few days' time. I will see her there," he suddenly decided.

Canidius was becoming even more confused. "I do

not understand. You said not two hours ago that you would never see her again."

Mark Antony shrugged again. "Have I not told you many times always to keep your opponents uncertain of your motives? The thought of my meeting with her scares him." He pointed towards the doorway that Anthony had fled through. "I want to know why that is, and the best way to find out is to do exactly what he fears most." He ran his hand over his chin a couple of times. "And get a barber in here. It is time to lose this beard."

Canidius had asked for a miracle, and the gods had answered, although the manner of its delivery was unusual, to say the least.

Chapter 10

Melissa approached the door of Canidius' upstairs suite with her escort of two Roman soldiers. It was the first time she had seen Roman troops inside the palace, but she felt secure in their presence. These were Canidius' hand-picked men, so far more trustworthy than any of the Egyptians she had so far encountered.

They passed another Roman standing in front of a fresco of a jackal-headed god. Melissa had seen this picture in many places in the palace. It seemed to be a recurrent theme, although it seemed odd to her that the Ptolemies would have chosen to portray one of the Egyptian funerary deities so prominently within this palace. The image seemed out of place amongst the wonderful scenes from Greek mythology adorning most of the walls and the impressive Roman floor mosaics. As Cleopatra had been the first of the Ptolemaic pharaohs to fully embrace Egyptian culture, perhaps whichever of her predecessors had chosen the image had no idea what it represented.

Egyptian culture had never particularly interested Melissa. She had always found the tombs too gaudy, the language overly complex, and the climate too hot to stomach for long enough to go on a dig in the country. Melissa preferred the classical cultures of Greece and

Rome – the birthplaces of modern civilization – with their structured languages, philosophy and law. Anthony, on the other hand, had more than a passing interest in Egyptology and had travelled to Cairo, Luxor and Abydos on many occasions. She made a mental note to ask him about the image, if he ever calmed down enough to hold a civilized conversation that was.

In the past week her husband had managed little more than the occasional grunt. To her utter dismay, he had seemed only too pleased to be called to an audience with Cleopatra earlier that morning and had left her without a word. It felt as if he was spending more time with the queen than with her, and she resented it.

A few paces further, and they reached the door to Canidius' suite. One legionary kicked the door with his foot and Canidius duly opened it, a beaming smile on his face. He quickly ushered her inside, ordering both men to stay outside the door, but to notify him if anyone approached. The soldiers were to ensure Melissa's discussion with their commander was not interrupted.

She smiled at her host as soon as he closed the door. "I am very happy to see you again, Canidius, and so soon. What news do you have for me?"

Canidius shook his head. "It is not news that I bring you, lady. It is something better."

When he looked over her shoulder her, Melissa realised they were not alone.

She held her breath. Slowly she turned, her heart beating hard in her chest. In a second doorway stood a clean-shaven Mark Antony, arms folded, with a grim look on his face. He backed into the other room and disappeared.

Melissa felt light-headed. Just knowing he was in

the same suite of rooms gave her reason to hope he was willing to listen, but she was unsure whether to follow him or not. She looked back at Canidius for guidance.

"Have no fear, Lissa," he said confidently, "I can assure you that you are perfectly safe. You may say whatever you wish to each other here without fear of being overheard." He raised his hand and gestured for her to follow Mark Antony. "You are to talk alone. My presence is not welcome."

Taking a deep breath, she walked forwards and through the other door into Canidius' simply furnished bedroom. Directly in front of her was a large bed. Against the far wall was a tall cupboard, a table and one chair. To reach the chair, she would have to pass between the bed and Mark Antony who was standing at the window, staring out across the harbour. She decided not to risk getting too close to him until she had assessed his mood.

She walked forwards and sat down on the end of the bed, coughing lightly to make her presence known. When Mark Antony neither spoke nor turned towards her, she feared that this meeting would be as unproductive as their last.

One of them had to break the deadlock.

"How are you?" she began.

She waited for some time. Eventually Mark Antony replied, though when he did his response was heavy with sarcasm.

"Let me think . . ."

There was a pause.

". . . I am disgraced . . ."

Another pause.

". . . My army has been bought . . ."

And another.

". . . Whilst much of my navy takes instruction from the fishes at Actium on how best to swim."

He turned his head just far enough to see where she had chosen to sit, but still did not turn to face her.

"How do you think I am?"

"I was merely trying to make conversation," Melissa replied apologetically.

At last he turned. "Is this what we have been reduced to? Idle discussions which are of no interest to either party? Perhaps you would like to debate the predicted height of the Nile flood, or ask my advice on how to keep the sand out of your clothing? Believe me, it is a skill you will need to learn, and quickly." Still, the sarcasm was there, but now she could hear his bitterness as well.

"If that is what pleases you, I am happy to discuss it," Melissa replied quietly, smoothing the creases out of the section of her dress that was lying across her thighs. She needed a distraction to prevent her giving a sharp retort. She might have been willing to argue with her husband, but she knew better than to cross Mark Antony when he was in a black mood. She had made that mistake before and had suffered dearly for it. He could snap her neck in a heartbeat if he chose to.

"Oh no, do not do that!" He glared as he pointed at her. "Do not play subservient. There is nothing on this earth I detest more than you playing the submissive woman."

"What do you expect me to do?" Melissa asked, raising her head to stare at him.

"Fight back. Argue with me. Annoy me. It is what you do best and what I . . ." he stopped himself. He wanted to say 'love', but did not dare. ". . . It is what I have come to expect from those I who give good counsel." He grumbled the last phrase, his words barely audible.

"Is that all you want from me? Counsel?" Melissa could not hide the surprise in her voice. Was that really what he expected from her? The last time they met he had made it plain he no longer trusted her. He had also told her he knew the truth about her alleged visions. It made any conversation on that matter difficult, but she decided it was probably best to humour him.

"You do not deserve to hear my counsel," she scoffed.

"And yet you will no doubt give it!" His sarcasm was now tinged with sadness.

"I will," she said decidedly, ignoring the sarcasm, "but are you willing to listen to what I have to say?"

Mark Antony's fixed his stare on Melissa. What he really wanted to do was to push her down on the bed and force her to remember the passions they once felt, but now was not the time. He needed answers, and he needed her to remain oblivious to his feelings until he was sure himself what they were. He swallowed hard and nodded slowly.

She shook her head in dismay. "You have made a mess of things. For too long you have listened to the words of a woman who has only had her own interests at heart. You have ignored the words of wiser advisors – men like Ahenobarbus, Canidius, Herod. You turned your back on friends and allowed your allies to be destroyed. You have snatched defeat from the jaws of victory and all because you doubted yourself and trusted her."

She paused as she watched him close his eyes and wondered if she was being too hard on him. She decided not. He had asked for her advice and she was going to give it. "Octavian is coming. He has gambled everything on the contents of Egypt's treasury and he will not be stopped until he holds it firmly in his grasp. You could have beaten him if you had only attacked sooner. Instead we will all suffer for your inaction."

He opened his eyes and shrugged. "Perhaps I would have attacked, if you had been here to tell me to do it, but you were not. I had to rely on my gut rather than your knowledge of what you regard as history." He began pacing about the room in front of the window in an effort to control his nerves. "I managed the best I could under the circumstances, but the past is of no matter. What does matter is whether my foolhardy actions have changed anything? I must hear it. Do we still travel the path your history speaks of, or are we equals for the first time, traversing some new road unknown to either of us?"

Melissa hesitated, unsure how to deliver the bad news. She had no need to.

He stopped pacing and stood in front of her. Crossing his arms, he answered his own question.

"I will take that as 'no'."

She nodded her agreement and his shoulders drooped. He had hoped that Melissa's history had recorded a different outcome to the engagement at Actium, but it appeared not. They were still on the same path, as always, with him hurtling towards an unknown future, of which Melissa alone was aware.

Melissa stared at the pitiful man in front of her. The arrogant alpha-male she had once known was gone, replaced by a tired shell of a man.

"Why did you hesitate? Why not attack a year ago?" she asked gently.

He turned and sat down on the bed beside her. "I had my reasons. Did your books not tell you why I did it?"

She shook her head. "They say you were under a powerful spell cast by an eastern temptress. That is all."

He laughed. There was a long pause, during which a glimmer of the old Mark Antony reappeared. He half-turned towards her with that familiar look of mischief in his eyes as he asked his next question. "Let us see how well you really know me." He poked her in the shoulder. "Why do you think I did it?"

Melissa thought for a moment. It was a question she had often asked herself and had been the subject of her doctorate. "I believe you waited because of what happened in Parthia. You marched at the head of an army that made all of Asia quake, yet still you pushed ahead too far and too fast. In your haste to reach your goal, you over-extended your resources and spread yourself too thinly. When the attack came, you could not adequately defend yourself. You lost too many good men on that campaign. I believe it made you cautious."

He stared at her. Whether or not Melissa could see his future, he was in no doubt that she knew him almost as well as he knew himself. He was no longer sure who she was or what it was she felt for him. He was too proud to ask what her feelings were, and too scared to hear the response.

"It did," he said simply and turned away again.

Melissa could not contain her curiosity. "What happened to the brave soldier I once knew who lived alongside his men, sharing their hardships and caring nothing for the trappings of wealth?"

He looked towards the floor and, placing his hands on the bed on either side of himself, gave a half-laugh.

"You know every detail of my battle plans yet this is the question you do not know the answer to?" He raised his head to stare across the room, but she could see a wistful look on his face as he remembered fonder times.

"The man you speak of lost the person dearest to him. The person he trusted most to support him when others offered only criticism. Others tried, but none could ever take her place." He continued to stare ahead.

"I am sorry," Melissa soothed. "I know Fulvia meant a great deal to you." Fulvia, Mark Antony's third wife, had died following the debacle at Perugia, where she and her brother-in-law, Lucius, had been the instigators of a rebellion. Octavian had crushed the rather short-lived revolt with ease, leaving Mark Antony in a precarious position. He turned on Fulvia, blaming her entirely for the catastrophe. His most staunch supporter was abandoned cruelly in Athens where she was left to pine for her lost love. She died there, broken-hearted.

Melissa reached out, daring to place her hand over Mark Antony's, but her touch proved too much for him.

"NOT FULVIA!" he exploded, wrenching his hand away from hers. "I LOST YOU!"

Melissa jumped backwards in surprise as he shot off the bed and returned to standing by the window, his back towards her. Unseen by Melissa, he cradled the hand she had touched as if it had been burnt. For so long he had yearned to feel her skin brush against his. Now it had, he found he could not contain the emotions flooding through him. That simple gesture of kindness had stripped him of the false hatred he had been trying to foster. His head reeled as he tried to regain some control. He wanted, no, he needed to feel her arms around him, offering what little comfort she could to a man who had lost all hope. All he had to do was reach out and force her to be his, as he had so many times before, but he did not dare. He could not afford to let his guard slip any further. He was too proud to let her see how lost he was. He had to regain control of his feelings. He took a deep breath and returned to the conversation concerning his leadership skills.

"After Philippi I became overconfident in my abilities. I thought I could not be beaten. I marched forwards in haste, and I failed to guard my rear." He glanced behind him and laughed. "You warned me about that once before, if you remember?"

Melissa smiled. "I do - at Forum Gallorum. I told you to watch your rear and you did not. Hirtius was able to force your retreat because of that error."

He nodded and walked over to the chair. He felt more in control by putting a little distance between them. Sitting down he leant forwards, placing his forearms on his knees. His mood sobered again.

"I made the wrong decisions so many times. My arrogance led my men to defeat, and to the unnecessary deaths of so many. At every turn I was outwitted. By the time I returned from Syria, I was tired of war and the folly of power. I no longer wanted it." His voice dropped briefly as he muttered, "I did not know what I wanted."

Looking down at the floor, he began rubbing his hands together. "In the end I came to doubt myself. I trusted the bad advice of others over my own instincts."

"The Mark Antony I knew always listened to the opinions of his officers," Melissa interjected in a soft voice, unwilling to anger him again, "and he was more than capable of telling the best advice from the worst."

"I rather thought that was what you did for me," he quipped.

"All I did was to give you confidence to trust your judgement. I never asked you to believe in me, only to believe in yourself."

"And all she ever did was criticise," he muttered

absent-mindedly as he thought of his last few months with Cleopatra. He sat back suddenly. "You say I trusted the advice of the wrong woman, yet she was the only one I had. You were not there to guide me. You were safely tucked away in another land, with another man. You were with my son." The bitterness had returned.

"And your daughter," Melissa countered. "Do not forget we too have a child."

"Do we?" Mark Antony's stare burned into Melissa. When she did not answer, his tone sharpened again. "I have only your word for that, and I have come to see your word means little."

"I have never lied to you," Melissa defended herself.

"Perhaps not, but you cannot deny you have always been somewhat selective with the truth."

"She is your child," she insisted.

"If that is true, tell me why my son would choose to raise her as his?"

"For the same reason Vitruvius raised your child as his. He loved the boy's mother and in time he grew to love the child as if it was his own. It is the same with your son. Antonius, or Anthony as he is now known, has learnt to love your daughter . . ." Melissa paused and swallowed hard before finishing, ". . . because he loves me."

Mark Antony stood up and walked back to the window, choosing to look out of it again, rather than at Melissa.

"And you love him." It was as much a statement as a question.

Melissa hesitated before replying. The answer was yes, but she found it difficult to admit to a man she knew she once had some feelings for, although she was unsure how deeply they still ran.

"I do," she forced herself to say.

Her hesitation was slight, but it was enough for him to pick up on and enough to give him a glimmer of hope once again. "Yet you beg to see me. Why?" His head turned slightly in anticipation of the answer.

Having just said she had never lied to him, Melissa could not afford to start. She had to be honest and trust he still believed in that honesty. As she spoke, she stood up and walked over to stand behind him.

"I have never been as afraid as I am here in Alexandria. You make me feel safe – you always have. Even when I thought I hated you, I still felt safer with you than I did with any other, including Vitruvius. I need you."

Nervously she placed her hand on his arm, fearing he would shrug it off again, but this time he did not. He had buried his feelings deep enough to allow her touch this time.

"You should look to your husband for security, not to me," he replied turning his attention to the window once more.

She could hear a slight playfulness in his tone. He was toying with her and she knew it, but it gave her a chance. If she could make him believe she needed him, he might yet help her.

She played along. "Your son is generous and kind, but he is not strong." She moved closer and leant her face against his muscular back. It made him jump slightly, but he did not move away. "He is not you," she murmured.

"If he is an Antonius, he has more strength than you give him credit for," he said softly.

"As does his father," she whispered, sliding her hand around his waist. It was a risky move, but she felt a sudden need to hold him as she had so often in the past. She had always found his presence comforting, from the first moment they had met. Mark Antony was strong, vibrant and confident to a fault. He always seemed one step ahead of the opposition and she had seen his mere presence change a situation for the better. Mark Antony had always been a force to be reckoned with.

For the first time since her arrival in Alexandria, Melissa felt safe. Cleopatra may have been the queen of Egypt and the most powerful woman alive, but even she would know better than to try to separate this man from something he valued.

Absent-mindedly, he placed his hand over hers and lifted it to his lips, kissing the back of it gently before returning it to its former position. "No Lissa, my strength left me a long time ago. I am a lost soul who must surrender to the inevitable. There is little chance for me. You know it, as well as I."

Melissa could not counter that statement, and he knew it. He had gambled once too often, and this time he had lost. Only time would tell how long he had left, unless, of course, he could prise that piece of knowledge from the woman standing behind him: not an easy task for any man to attempt.

They stood together for some time without moving or speaking. Mark Antony closed his eyes once more, simply enjoying the moment. It felt natural to him – being held by the woman he had long wished he had made his wife.

Melissa was the first to speak. "What do you intend to do now?"

He sighed. "I have sent word to Octavian. I will leave Egypt, if he will agree to stay away. I have proposed my return to Athens to become a private citizen. I have offered to renounce my position and powers, conditional on Cleopatra retaining her rights to her kingdom. I am willing to do this to keep those I hold dear safe. I expect to hear the answer in a day or so."

Unconscious of her actions, Melissa's grip tightened around his waist. "There will be no answer. You are too much of a threat to him alive. All he cares about is her money. He will stop at nothing to get it."

"Then we are undone." He sighed and patted her hand. "Cicero once said that only a man with the strength to crush me would be able to bring an end to the bloody civil war Rome had embarked upon. I took it as a personal insult that he felt me so dangerous I had to be removed, but now I see it was a backhanded compliment. He knew I am the only man strong enough, and stubborn enough, to stand firm against the tide of change." He laughed half-heartedly. "That old goat always gets to have the last word, despite my best efforts to silence him. Will I never be free from his infernal nagging?"

Melissa simply squeezed him a little tighter, knowing it was a rhetorical question and he did not expect an answer. After his death, Mark Antony had had Cicero's severed head and hands nailed to the door of the Senate House.

In return he lifted her hand to his lips once more. "I hear Agrippa has been sent to Rome to quell some recent unrest. It gives us a little time to prepare. The whelp never moves without Agrippa to wipe his arse."

"Not this time," Melissa sighed. "Octavian will not wait. He knows Agrippa has too much respect for you and would argue for clemency. He would no doubt give a compelling argument for Octavian to accept your offer and our young Caesar cannot afford to give any ground on this matter."

"Then I can no longer prevent the inevitable from

happening. Octavian wants my head – and he shall have it." He laughed. "I will make him wait until Agrippa returns. It will annoy him all the more to have to justify his actions to his underlings." He seriously doubted that Octavian would have the nerve to face him without the backing of his second-in-command. Marcus Agrippa had impressed Mark Antony from their first encounter. Young and a little naive, he had nonetheless stood by his principles and proven himself to be a man of honour, a rarity in the dying days of the Republic. Agrippa had long been a worthy adversary and was perhaps the only man Mark Antony would admit could beat him.

Melissa nuzzled against his back until she felt him relax slightly. She still needed his patronage if she was to save herself and her reckless husband. She pressed on. "What if there was an injustice you could prevent? Would the man who once stood up to Caesar to save me, stand up to the queen of Egypt to save his son?"

"I may, if it was in my interest," he said, his curiosity aroused by the possibility of what Melissa would offer to save her husband.

Melissa took a deep breath and began. "Cleopatra has taken an unhealthy interest in him. I fear she may use him to hurt us both. You have the ability to prevent this."

Mark Antony's head jerked slightly in surprise. "I thought he loved you? If so, how can you believe he will succumb to her charms?"

"He is your son in every way. What do you think he will do?" she replied sharply, giving away her fears.

Mark Antony laughed out loud at what Melissa had said. He turned to face her once again, taking hold of both her hands. "Oh, I know what he will do. He will fuck her and he will enjoy doing it. Cleopatra has a talent for taking a man to new highs, or lows, depending on your opinion of the situation. She will have him until he serves his purpose, at which point she will discard him for a far younger man." He sighed again. "I should know – I am the far older man he will replace."

There were tears forming in Melissa's eyes. "She will take him from me, and enrage your jealousy, so you will kill him."

He shook his head. "No, Lissa, her plans are never that simple. I believe she will have far more devious intentions for that boy, and for us."

"Please," Melissa begged, "he does not deserve to die because of our mistakes. He deserves a chance to live – just as he did when he was born. If you have ever loved me, I beg you to save your son. I will do anything you ask in return, but you must send him away from Alexandria immediately."

Behind Melissa's tears Mark Antony saw a look he had rarely seen in her: fear. It told him they had no time left. Octavian was not waiting for Agrippa's return from Rome. The young pretender was already on the way and that gave him greater cause for concern for Melissa's safety.

Octavian knew of Melissa's existence and had his suspicions about the part she played in Caesar's assassination. If he found out that she was in Alexandria, she would be almost as great a prize as the Egyptian treasury. If Cleopatra had any inkling of this, she would find a way to mention Melissa's presence. Cleopatra hated Melissa because of the feelings her husband had for his former mistress. Mark Antony may have loved his Egyptian wife in the same way as he had loved all his wives, but his heart truly belonged to one woman – the one who had given him the locket which even now hung around his neck.

Once again it seemed the Fates were determined to deny him his heart's desire. As much as he wanted to renew their relationship, all Mark Antony could think of in that moment was the danger Melissa would be in if she were to remain close to him. How Cleopatra would laugh as she watched her rival being dragged away to face one of Octavian's skilled torturers. As he imagined the horrendous torments Melissa would be made to endure, Mark Antony felt a new sensation building deep inside his stomach: panic. To lose the love of his life once more would be more than he could bear. It would destroy him. He would sooner die than ever lose her again.

He could not bear to let Melissa see him in such turmoil. He felt suddenly powerless to help the woman who was the real love of his life. He knew he had to leave.

Pushing her away suddenly, he walked swiftly towards the door.

Melissa ran after him. "Please do not leave me," she begged, reaching for his hand once more. "Please help me."

He paused briefly on the threshold. "How do you expect me to help you when I can no longer help myself?" he replied bitterly, without giving her a second glance.

With that, he was gone.

Chapter 11

"Move the ships," Anthony Marcus murmured, as he pored over the detailed map laid out before him.

"Precisely!" Cleopatra nodded as she replied. "I will not waste time setting up new shipyards on the Red Sea. I will simply move the plentiful supply of ships I already have to a different waterway."

She stood next to him, on one side of a large table containing a map of the Mediterranean, North Africa and the Middle East. It reminded Anthony of the kinds of maps he had seen in movies being used to follow the progress of battles. It had a reasonable representation of the coastline, for the time, and notations of major settlements along the Nile, but little else in terms of topographical detail.

"If the ancestors of my people could move the mountains of stone they needed to build the pyramids, from here . . ." Cleopatra began pointing at the site of the stone quarries on the map, ". . . to here, I am certain their descendants can move a few hulks of wood, flax and bitumen across this short expanse here." She pointed to the edge of the Sinai Peninsula, roughly where the Suez Canal would be built many centuries later.

Anthony nodded. He already knew what her grand plan was, but tried to look astonished all the same. "I hear your proposal, but I do not understand how it can be done."

"I have a great number of Lebanese cedars in storage. Each is kept whole until it is required." Cleopatra stopped, waiting to see if her latest house guest really was as clever as she hoped he was.

"Ah, I see," he replied after a few moments. "You intend to use them as rollers. Strip the ships bare to reduce the weight and then haul the hulls across the sand on the trunks."

"Exactly," she said triumphantly. "If Octavian sends the famed Marcus Agrippa to Alexandria to destroy my fleet, there will be no fleet left for him to find."

"What then? Surely it would be quicker to make your escape on a trader already berthed in the Red Sea. Why take your own ships?"

"You think I plan to escape?" she replied, with more than a touch of incredulity. "And do what? Throw myself on the mercy of Indian traders who will strip my wealth bare in months as they treble the price of everything I require? No, Anthony, I do not intend to run like some worthless coward. I intend to fight."

Antony dialled up his acting skills, putting a look of complete bafflement on his face. "You have me at a loss, your majesty. I do not see how you can fight if your navy is in a different ocean to the opposing force."

"My fleet will not remain there long." She took a step to the left and tapped the map at the Straits of Gibraltar. "It will be brought here beyond the Pillars of Hercules."

Anthony looked across to his left, feigning disbelief. "I thought the Pillars served as a warning to mariners to travel no farther – they say that there is nothing but empty seas beyond them to the edge of the world."

Cleopatra laughed. "Tales told by old women to frighten little children. Is that what you are, Anthony - a frightened little child?"

"I am no more a child than you are an old woman," he replied with a wink. He looked back at the map and spent a few moments pretending to study it.

She leant across him to point in the other direction. Her hand moved across to the Red Sea again where she began tracing a line along the coast. "I intend to sail through the Red Sea, beyond Ethiopia and onward south." The map ran out, but she continued to trace her line, in a crude arc representing where she believed the southern coast of Africa to be, until she ran out of table. "At some point the land must end. South will again become north. My fleet will circle Africa, re-enter the Mediterranean through the Pillars, and take Octavian by surprise." Her finger moved back to the Straits of Gibraltar.

"It is ambitious, to say the least," Anthony nodded and did his best to look impressed.

"And what is a queen if she is not ambitious?"

Anthony smiled politely. He knew she was correct in her assumptions about the African coast, but he also knew she would never be able to prove her theory. Even if Cleopatra's fleet could circumnavigate Africa it would take so long that, by the time the ships reached Gibraltar, Octavian would already have returned to Rome with the contents of her treasury in hand.

"What do your advisers think?" he asked rather than answering her question.

Her eyes narrowed. "My so-called advisers are little more than women and sheep fearing the wrath of Rome, while my most trusted general has taken leave of his senses, locking himself away in his Timoneum to mourn the loss of his dignity. They all lack the balls . . ." She paused for a moment, savouring the unintentional joke, ".

. . some quite literally. They would rather suck Octavian's cock than stand firm on their own account."

Many of the senior court officials were eunuchs and most favoured handing Mark Antony over to Octavian in the hope of negotiating a truce. So far, Cleopatra had refused to betray the father of her children. Octavian had declared war on her, not her husband. She knew only too well that surrendering Mark Antony would not help her situation in the slightest. And why should she surrender him while he was of use to her cause? Even if he was wallowing in self-pity, the mere mention of Mark Antony could still send a shiver of fear through many of her enemies. She needed to trade on his name for as long as she could.

She shook her head. "I am queen. I must be the one to protect my sovereign lands by any means available. I am the only one with the stomach for the fight."

She paused again, eyeing Anthony with suspicion as he returned his attention to the map. In all their encounters, she had failed to read him successfully and today was no exception. Her plans for his entrapment had so far failed dismally.

When her guards reported her newest house guest was haggling with the merchants in the market even though he had no money to spend, she gave him a small allowance of a few sesterces, thinking he would try to bribe someone to help him get out of the city, but instead he bought her a gift of a silk scarf laced with spun gold thread − a present for her approaching birthday. It was a mere trifle in comparison with the luxuries a queen was used to, but it was worth considerably more than his meagre allowance should have covered. Anthony Marcus had proven to be both agile in mind and body, as well as being a shrewd negotiator. She found herself planning shopping trips to the market to watch him at work, getting the better of some of Alexandria's most successful tradesmen. She would travel in a covered litter, with Anthony happily trotting along behind with the rest of her retinue.

The more loyalty, or flattery, as his obstreperous wife called it, that Anthony showed to Cleopatra, the more rewards Egypt's queen bestowed on him. She could afford to be generous to her protégé, whose company she greatly enjoyed. This man was so very different to the simpering individuals of her court. She looked forward to posing problems to his questioning mind rather than listening to the usual droning of the sycophants she had to deal with. Soon, he was travelling the city without a guard, moving freely between the palace and the gymnasium. She knew roughly how long each trip would take and did not find it overly suspicious if he was a few minutes adrift of her estimation. In fact, it was this unpredictability that added to her fascination with him. She had even begun to coax from him a few words of his own language, having him teach her everyday items: a glass, a chair, a table. It was all part of her plan to understand him better and, more importantly, to know what he was saying when he spoke to his sullen and temperamental wife.

"Well?" she finally asked. "What do you think?"

"I think it is a daring plan, but one that is worth the effort provided there is enough depth of water to take the draught of your keels. Many of the ships I have seen in the harbour are quite large."

"I will take only the smaller, faster vessels, those which are easiest to handle and have greater speed. I learnt from our experience at Actium that it is not size which is the most important factor in any engagement.

Agrippa outflanked us because his vessels had greater manoeuvrability. As for the depth of the water beneath the keel, I am more than confident in my map-makers' abilities to guide us safely to open water."

Her eyes flicked briefly to an open cabinet on the other side of the table in which Anthony saw a large pile of scrolls. He surmised that among them were nautical maps detailing offshore hazards such as shallows, reefs and shifting sandbanks. Such maps detailing the area directly outside the harbour would be useful to his plan to sail the *Selene* to safety. He looked away, not wishing to appear too interested in the cupboard or its contents.

"And your wretched wife, what will she have to say?" Cleopatra almost spat the words out in disgust. She blamed Melissa for Mark Antony's latest bout of erratic behaviour. It gave her another reason to hate the seer.

"I dare say she will say it is outlandish and doomed to failure, but of course I will ask her opinion." Anthony bowed slightly. It was becoming harder not to wince every time Melissa was mentioned by the queen and the easiest way not to show his growing concern was to hide his face from her prying eyes.

"I will return with an answer within the hour, your majesty, for I find myself wanting to return at the earliest opportunity." He threw her another wink to make her believe he was desperate to be at her side, when all he really wanted was a chance to look at some of those maps.

As he withdrew, Cleopatra found herself blushing at his flattery. It had been many years since a man had worked so hard to impress her. The last one to try had been the one she called husband: Mark Antony. The more time Cleopatra spent in the presence of this younger version, the more she understood why Melissa had married him. He was strong and handsome, with an agile mind, unlike his double, who was now suffering from the ravages of age, excess and self-doubt. This man would be a joy to have in her bed and she found herself becoming increasingly frustrated at his flirtatious remarks, which never seemed to turn into any sort of action.

Chapter 12

Anthony strolled nonchalantly through the corridors of the palace. Few people questioned his presence in the hallways these days, or the fact that he no longer had a visible guard in tow. His presence was regarded by most as unremarkable and few challenged him. Some feared him because they knew he was the queen's latest distraction and so not a man to cross, whereas others mistakenly thought he was Mark Antony.

On his first very first outing in the market, Anthony convinced the silk merchants to take a risk on selling him a scarf at less than market value in return for a promise of future trading opportunities with the palace. Anthony used his father's name and face to his advantage for the first time. According to Plutarch, Mark Antony was reputed to have followed Cleopatra's litter around the town. Historians attributed his behaviour to the besotted general's need to follow his lover wherever she went, but what they would never know was that Mark Antony had never been to the markets in her presence, although his younger doppelganger had. Anthony may not have heeded all of Melissa's warnings, but he always bore in mind her key instruction: never to do anything to alter their recorded version of history. When Mark Antony chose to prolong his disappearance into his Timoneum with enough wine to drown an entire legion, Anthony decided to take his father's place to help preserve history as he remembered it. Gaining the queen's trust also made it far easier for him to scout the town, committing every turn and alley to memory as he went. It was not an easy task. Even in ancient times, Alexandria covered some four miles from east to west. It was a lot of ground to cover before the summer arrived, along with Octavian's troops. He had to find a way out of the city before then, and he was determined not to fail.

Unfortunately, by gaining the trust of Egypt's queen, Anthony was losing the trust of his wife. Melissa had disliked Cleopatra from the first moment she had met her many years earlier, believing her to be spoilt and petulant. The queen's fascination with her husband did little to improve Melissa's opinion of Egypt's most renowned Pharaoh. She did not trust her hostess in the slightest, and the more Anthony became a part of the queen's inner circle, the less she trusted him. All she saw was an easily-corrupted man becoming ever-deeper in thrall to a notorious femme fatale. And even he had to admit, it was a fall he was rather interested in taking.

Cleopatra had fascinated him ever since he first met her as a child. He remembered little about his humble beginnings in the backstreets of Rome, but he did remember the morning his drab and uneventful life was disrupted by a colourful woman, dripping with jewels, and her retinue of equally colourful servants. Everything about this woman was bright and grand and exciting. As an adult, he soon learnt who this colourful visitor had been. Knowing he had been so close to the most spectacular woman to have ever lived only fuelled his interest in her further. Egyptology had been his first passion, even though his godfather had pushed him into studying Roman archaeology. It was only in recent years that he had been able to indulge his fascinations, attending digs in many parts of the country. And now he was here in the presence of the most famous woman in all of history, and she was displaying more than a passing interest in him. As a man with a reputation for bedding any woman he wanted, he was more than a little curious to see just how far he could get with the infamous seductress − provided there was a way to manage it without his wife finding out.

And then there was Mark Antony to consider. Anthony realised he was walking a dangerous tightrope between the queen, his wife and the man who had been lover to both. All Melissa ever talked about was ways to encourage her Roman beau to rejoin palace life. She seemed obsessed with the thought of having him close, whilst Anthony was more than happy for his father to remain in his Timoneum for the rest of his days.

Anthony hated his father for so many reasons. Mark Antony had abandoned his mother as soon as she became pregnant. When she died, he refused to acknowledge his newborn son. Had it not been for their guard, Vitruvius, adopting him, Anthony would have had no place in Roman society and would most probably have died on a cold mosaic floor before he was even a day old. And finally, when he had fallen in love with a beautiful woman, his notorious father had stolen her away. Anthony may have been the man Melissa had married, but he still harboured doubts that he was the one she truly loved.

Her apparent fascination with the man living across the harbour did nothing to allay his fears. He had spent many years keeping these fears hidden beneath his outwardly easy-going facade. The proximity of his rival meant that facade was slipping more and more every day. If he ever found out Melissa had been in the presence of his father, regardless of the circumstance, he swore he would make both parties regret it.

"Well? What's she up to?" Melissa asked as Anthony sauntered into their rooms.

"You already know that. She plans to transport her ships across the desert." He sat down on the couch and pulled some dates out of bowl on the table to the side of it. "I'll give it an hour or so and then go and tell her it'll be a worthy cause."

Panic spread across Melissa's face. "How does lying help us? She'll skin you alive for that!" She began pacing to and fro.

"No, she won't. I'll warn her that the Nabateans will send men looking to stop her and she should be prepared to defend herself."

"Then you're going to change history."

"Not if I fail to mention the size of the Nabatean forces. She thinks they are a joke – little more than a flea on a camel's arse in comparison with the Egyptian army."

"Nice analogy," Melissa said with some sarcasm. "So, you won't tell her the expedition will be ripped to shreds and the boats burned?"

"Nope," he said through a mouthful of date. "She has no idea the Nabateans are being reinforced by their old enemy. Let's keep it that way."

Following Actium, Malachus, the king of Nabatea, had made peace with Herod and could now call on his new-found Judean ally for assistance. As both men hated Cleopatra, they would be mutually determined to thwart every attempt she made to improve her situation. A Nabatean army in league with experienced Jewish fighters would significantly alter the balance of power in the region. Cleopatra was going to underestimate her opponents yet again.

"I don't like it," Melissa frowned.

Anthony groaned. "You don't like anything I do. You need to lighten up and make the most of this luxury while we can. I am in complete control of Cleopatra and of our situation."

"I doubt that!" Melissa scoffed. "I still think we'd be better off if I talk to Canidius again. If he can persuade Mark Antony . . ."

"DON'T YOU FUCKING DARE!" Anthony exploded. He stood up menacingly and began pointing at Melissa in a threatening manner. "So far, we are alive, thanks to me. We're well cared for, thanks to me. We're not prisoners, thanks to me. We don't need his help and even if we did, you're not lying on your back to get it!"

There it was again – the jealousy that Melissa was once Mark Antony's mistress. It never seemed to be far from Anthony's thoughts these days. More and more it felt as if the spirit of one 'Antony' inhabited the body of the other. Both men were a hit with women, both took risks, both had the foulest tempers, and both were obsessively jealous of the other.

Melissa was incensed at this latest outburst, but did not try to defend herself. She had given up doing so weeks earlier and decided instead to point out something more obvious.

"I don't think there'll be any need for me to lie back and do my duty because that's what she expects from you."

Anthony shot Melissa a warning glare, but she was in full flow. "I've seen the way she looks you up and down. When are you gonna realise she's playing a game you can't win? She won't stop until she's stripped you naked and had you on her throne room floor for all to see – another good man ruined by that manipulative harpy!"

"Yeah, well, what's sauce for the goose, Liss . . ." he tailed off as he wandered towards the window, leaving the old saying unfinished. He did not need to complete it. Melissa knew exactly what he was insinuating.

"You're actually thinking of sleeping with her, aren't you?" She whispered the words in disbelief.

He folded his arms and shrugged as he stared stubbornly out of the window. "Why shouldn't I? If that's what it takes to keep us alive one more day, then maybe I should. It worked for you. Of course, I'll have to put a bit more into my performance than you did to be convincing. I mean, I do have to 'rise' to the occasion, though it shouldn't be too difficult. She's a good-looking woman, and powerful with it. They say that's a big turn-on, but having never fucked royalty before, I really wouldn't know."

"You have a choice – I didn't. I did what I had to." Melissa was almost in tears, but they were tears of rage, not despair.

He turned and glared at her. "Really? Do you expect me to believe you just lay there and let him screw you night after night? Don't push your luck, Liss. You're on thin ground already."

That was the final straw.

She snapped. "How dare you say such a thing to me? For years I put up with your sluts – paid or otherwise. You've slept your way across half of Europe and I said nothing. Damn it Anthony, you'd sleep with anything that has a pulse."

"And why is that? What would make any sane woman put up with such an unfaithful bastard of a husband? I'll tell you what – guilt. You felt guilty for every lie you've ever told me about your time with *him*. You loved having the power your knowledge brought, and you loved *him*." He shook his head in bitter disappointment. "All these years you said you were in love with a drunken, womanising, philanderer – turns out it wasn't the one you married."

"I never loved him . . ." Melissa began, but she was cut off as Anthony delivered his most damning statement yet.

"Then why give him your locket?"

For a moment, Melissa was completely thrown off guard. Her eyes widened in surprise.

"What?"

"The locket I gave you. You told me it was stolen, but he has it. You gave it to him."

Melissa's heart was racing. For years she had maintained her story that the locket had been stolen, which it had. She never thought she would have to explain that Agrippa had returned it, or that she had willingly placed it in Ventidius' care.

She had to try to salvage something of the situation. "I didn't give it to him. I gave it to Ventidius and put the name of my attacker inside to be opened at the most appropriate moment. I had no idea he would give the locket to Mark Antony as well as that name."

"Bullshit!" Anthony slammed his hand against the wall in frustration at his wife's dishonesty. "You knew damned well he'd hand it over. You probably banked on it. Something to remember you by! And it worked. He has an unhealthy fixation on his own daughter-in-law!"

Melissa was a little scared at this outburst, but she could not help rolling her eyes in disbelief. "Don't be ridiculous."

"I'm being ridiculous, am I? Then why is he still wearing it?"

Melissa paused. She actually had no idea why Mark Antony was wearing it. "I don't know, I didn't ask him," she replied honestly.

"Then you admit you've seen him."

When Melissa said nothing, Anthony shook his head in disgust. He buried his clenched fists in his armpits. If he did not do something to consciously control himself, he feared what he might do. He had never hit a woman, but in that moment he was sorely tempted.

"I knew it. When?" He waited for a reply.

Melissa slipped past him and sat down in defeat on the end of the bed. "We talked at Actium for some time before I was brought to you ... and I saw him again a few days ago, here in the palace."

"I told that bastard to steer clear, but he came anyway." Anthony muttered under his breath. He stared at the floor for a moment, regaining his composure. When he spoke again, he was calm and cold.

"Did you fuck him?"

Melissa looked horrified. "No!" she exclaimed.

"Did you want to?"

Melissa glared at her husband. "That is possibly the most insulting thing you have ever asked me."

"You haven't denied it."

She got up to leave. "There's no point talking to you when you're like this," she stated bitterly.

She took a step towards the door, but Anthony was too quick for her and grabbed her upper arm tightly.

"For fuck's sake Liss, answer me. Are you screwing my father?" he hissed and shook her slightly, his composure faltering again.

"No, I'm not," Melissa croaked, her voice turning hoarse as she struggled to pull away. His grip was hurting her. For the first time in her life she felt truly scared of her gentle, loving husband. "I love you. I always have."

"Really? Then tell me this. What's the fascination with him? All you do is go on and on about how he will help save us, when all I've ever seen is the havoc he leaves in his wake. You were a mess the last time you came home, but still you defend him and you won't tell me why."

Melissa finally extricated her arm from his grasp. She retreated to the other side of the bed and sat facing the wall. "You wouldn't hear me if I tried, because you never have. You're too jealous to listen to anything I have to say. You always have been."

She sat quietly for a moment, too scared to look at him. "I *know* him. He's not the man history has portrayed, well, not totally. He's a good man, with principles. He's honest and loyal to his friends and family and we qualify as both of those. He's not our enemy and I know he will help us, given time."

Anthony grunted. "We could both be dead by the time he crawls out of his pit and decides to lend a hand. We can't wait that long."

Melissa said nothing.

Anthony watched her for a moment as she rubbed the red mark on her arm left by his hand. His anger began to subside, and he felt a pang of guilt, knowing he had hurt her. It was something he had vowed to never do.

Walking over to the bed, he sat down next to his wife and pushed her hair away from her face gently in an attempt at reconciliation.

He spoke softly. "Tell me he means nothing to you. Tell me you would be happy to watch Mark Antony rot in hell if it meant we could leave here, together, today."

Melissa opened her mouth to speak, but she could not say the words her husband wanted to hear. She knew she had feelings for both men and she found she could not say what one wanted to hear if it meant betraying the other. She turned her head away as the tears began to fill her eyes.

"I thought as much." Anthony spat the words in disgust and pulled away again. "You can't, can you? You can't say it because you don't know yourself which of us you are in love with."

His voice faltered. Anthony was confident to the point of arrogance, but he had never quite felt the confidence he needed to step out of his father's shadow. In his own time, he could hide the fact that he had such an illustrious relation, but here in the past he could not dodge the connection. He had spent his life so far playing second fiddle to a maestro. He was desperate to prove himself to be at least his father's equal.

"If you want to know if I'm going to screw Cleopatra, I'll tell you. We both know I could. Hell, I could screw every woman in this palace if I wanted and you can't stop me." Years of anger and resentment at his wife's affair were finally being released and the bitterness showed as Anthony struggled to force his words out. "But I don't want to have to work my way along the corridor from one bed to the next because I know I'm better than that. I'm better than . . ." he paused for a moment, uncertain whether to make the comparison aloud.

"Him?" Melissa finished his sentence. "Is that what

you want to say? That you're a better man than your father?"

He gave a slight nod.

Melissa turned her head and stared at him. His head was down and his eyes were closed. For all their similarities, Anthony Marcus was a far better man than Mark Antony would ever be. Both men shared the same failings: arrogance; hot-headedness; self-doubt. They also shared the same qualities: honour; determination; loyalty. And yet, Anthony had a far greater sense of conscience than his father had ever displayed. He was often guilty of doing the wrong thing, but always for what he believed to be the right reasons.

She took a deep breath and softened her reply. "Of course you are a better man. You may be just as emotionally stunted as he is at times, but you are a better man. Vitruvius raised you well."

Slowly, Anthony raised his head to stare at his wife. The anger had vanished and she noticed he looked afraid. Melissa's sudden praise brought Anthony to his senses, at least for the moment. He loved his wife and he was terrified of losing her. In his time with Cleopatra he had learnt one fact – that the queen hated his wife. He had to make Melissa understand how much danger she was in and that, in his opinion, Mark Antony was powerless to do anything to save her.

"Liss, Cleopatra is the most powerful woman alive. I don't know what you did to piss her off, but she wants to hurt you, badly. I've seen it in her eyes and heard it in her voice. She never makes any attempt to hide it and it scares the shit out of me. That's why I'm trying so hard to keep on her good side. If I thought that in return for spending one night in her bed, I could get you safely out of here then I'd do it, even if it means losing you forever. You are all I care about. The more I schmooze, the more she gives me and every minute I spend outside these walls is another chance for me to find a way out of this hell. I'd sacrifice my life if I could get you away from here before Octavian arrives. His men will never lay their hands on you again."

Melissa swallowed hard and raised her hand to her husband's cheek. "What if there is no way out?"

He placed his hand over hers. "Trust me, Liss. I will find a way, whatever it takes. Hell, I'd do a deal with the devil himself if he said he could save you."

"But I don't want to go without you," she whimpered.

Anthony doubted that both of them would make it out alive, but he would not say it aloud. He smiled weakly. "For once in your life, Liss, please trust me."

"I do trust you. I just don't trust her," she whispered as she edged closer, resting her head against his chest.

As Anthony gathered his wife in his arms, he heard a scraping sound. It was faint, but it reminded him of a badly-fitting drawer being shut. It was not the first time he had heard it. Having watched far too many old movies, he had wondered if there was a spy hole hidden somewhere. Despite his best efforts to find one, he had so far found no secret panels in any of the walls. Regardless of his failure to find the means, he still felt certain they were being watched and, although he knew the guards could not understand English, he worried that someone else might, if given enough time to study it. Cleopatra had a talent for learning languages and had begun asking him to tell her the English words for meaningless objects: a book; a table; a door. Part of the English language was derived from Latin. It would not take her long to begin to pick out words with similarities and begin to follow some of their conversations.

He knew Cleopatra's net was closing about him, and was beginning to feel very much out of his depth, but he could not afford to stop. He had no one he could turn to for advice – no ally to call on for help. He had to get closer to the queen, despite the danger, if for no other reason than to keep an eye on everything she was up to.

Chapter 13

"I want her HEAD!"

Cleopatra screamed the words aloud and threw another glass at the wall of the Timoneum. It smashed, the shards tinkling as they fell to the floor.

"Your bitch of a seer will die for this! She has lied to me for the last time!"

Mark Antony said nothing as she grabbed yet another glass from the tray and hurled it across the room. He had not had a drink in days. His head was pounding and his hands shook. The last thing he needed was a hysterical woman screaming at him. He remained seated on the couch without flinching as each piece of tableware met its sorry end. He had been in this situation many times before and had learnt from bitter experience that it was better to duck and keep your opinion to yourself, unless specifically asked to give it.

"She knew that weevil, Malachus, would destroy *my* ships to gain favour with Octavian and his new henchman, Herod. She knew this would happen, yet she did nothing to warn me. She will suffer this time, and you will not stop me."

She glared at him, pointing in his direction. "Say something, you drunken halfwit!"

Mark Antony slumped back against the cushions. "Why? You are saying more than enough for both of us."

She put her hands on her hips and pouted. "I will drag her here, to this very room. I will cut out her tongue and shove it down her throat." She was desperate to get a reaction from him, but he knew better than to allow her the satisfaction of knowing she was right.

He shrugged. "If that is what you want to do, then do it." He closed his eyes in an attempt to halt the hammering in his temples.

The last glass flew past his head and hit the opposite wall.

"AAARGH," she screamed in sheer frustration. She reached for another glass, only to realise they were all gone. She paused, looking for something else to throw. Eventually she turned back to face him. "Speak to me, damn you!" she spat sarcastically.

Slowly, he opened his eyes and focussed on Cleopatra. "What is it you wish to hear - my sympathies, or my advice?"

Cleopatra folded her arms in front of her and pouted again. "Both, if you can be bothered to give them."

He nodded slowly. "Then tell me exactly what Lissa said to you."

"I do not speak to *her*," she sneered.

"Then who gave you the information that your plan was sound?"

After a few moments she replied. "He did – the husband."

Mark Antony frowned. "Perhaps the information was lost in the telling. What did he say exactly?"

"That the plan was bold and worthy of exploration."

"And did he offer any warning?"

Cleopatra glared at him with murderous intent, but remained silent. She knew exactly what she had been told.

Anthony said the Nabateans would make efforts to thwart her plan. She also knew she had dismissed his warning out of hand.

"Did you ask him to describe the outcome?"

"I did not need to," she hissed. "The Nabateans have no army worthy of concern."

"Yet Herod does and it appears he has been making friends at our expense." He closed his eyes and put his hand to the bridge of his nose, gripping it as he fought back the sudden wave of nausea that washed over him. Taking a deep breath, he exhaled slowly, fighting the urge to retch. Eventually, with his composure regained, Mark Antony opened his eyes once more.

"Did the husband say that Malachus would stop you?"

Cleopatra looked away. "He said they would try to stop me from reaching the Red Sea," she muttered. "I doubted his sincerity."

Mark Antony sighed. "Then by my reckoning, neither Lissa, nor the husband lied – they simply answered the questions you asked of them." He stood up, immediately regretting it as the dull throbbing in his head spiked to a searing pain. He wanted to drop back onto the couch, but he could not afford to allow her to see how ill he felt.

He forced himself to walk over to her. Placing his hands on her upper arms, he bent his head to look into her half-hidden face. "As an invested member of the College of Augurs, I can say with some certainty that the art of divination lies not so much in what is said as what is not. Any seer will only give the most basic of facts, leaving you to decide what remains for yourself. They do not venture pertinent information unless it is directly asked for, no matter how useful it could be."

Slowly, Cleopatra turned her head to look him in the eye. "Are you suggesting this is my fault?"

He shook his head quickly, and then wished he had not. He was far too sober to be so foolhardy as to suggest anything of the sort. "Not in the slightest. We all tend to hear only what we want to. Time and again I would hear of the glorious battle I would fight, yet I would not hear the warning to watch my flank, and I would be soundly beaten because of it."

She looked away again, sullenly, but Mark Antony ploughed on. "For years your simpering minions have encouraged you to believe you are an all-powerful god. You are not. You are flesh and blood the same as any of us – and any one of us can be guilty of . . ." he chose the next phrase carefully ". . . a misunderstanding."

Cleopatra's mood softened slightly. Anthony Marcus had tried to warn her, but she had ignored him. She was at least partly culpable in the disaster that had befallen her navy, but she still did not like it.

She returned her gaze to her husband. There was something different about him today. He looked more youthful than he had of late, and there was a glimmer of the old Mark Antony about him: the strategic genius.

"When did you become so insightful?" she murmured.

He looked thoughtful for a second. "I am uncertain of the exact moment, but I believe it may have been around the time I ran out of wine."

She tilted her head in a quizzical manner. "Why not simply order more to be brought?"

He grinned. "I did. Canidius told me he would wait on me no longer. If I wanted it, I would have to get it myself. As I am too stubborn to do that, I had little option but to sober up."

Cleopatra smiled. Take away the booze and the man she had once fought so hard to seduce was still there after all. It gave her hope that the future was not yet lost. They might yet prevail, with or without the seer's help.

Her smile faded as she thought back to her reason for coming to the Timoneum. Melissa would pay, and soon.

"The witch must be punished. She will learn Egypt is less forgiving than Rome." Her eyes narrowed. "Though I do not think I will kill her. My gratification would be short-lived and I wish my revenge to last a very long time. What would you suggest I do?"

Mark Antony stepped back and rubbed his clean-shaven chin shakily. He was walking a thin and dangerous line between keeping Cleopatra happy, and keeping Melissa alive. His response had to be very carefully considered.

"Find a way to embarrass her. Lissa fears humiliation more than anything. That is how you hurt her."

Cleopatra frowned as her mind raced through the possibilities. Slowly, an idea began to form.

"I believe I know exactly how to wipe that smug smile off her deceitful face. I will take that which she holds dearest from her." She prodded him in the chest. "And you will play your part. Swear it."

He dutifully lifted her hand to his lips and kissed the back of it. "As you command, so shall it be."

She stepped away with a look of satisfaction spreading over her face. "Then I will leave you. Arrangements must be made for the impending celebrations." She left, humming to herself as she plotted an unconventional revenge on her rival.

Mark Antony's hands shook as he collapsed onto the couch. He was sweating profusely and his stomach was cramping from where he was badly in need of a drink.

Canidius stepped in through the window from the jetty outside where he had been concealed. He had hidden there the moment Cleopatra was spotted crossing the jetty.

Mark Antony looked up at him. "Did you hear that?"

Canidius nodded grimly. "Yes, I heard it. What do you think she will do?"

Mark Antony wiped the sweat from his brow. "I do not know, but I must find out. Send word to Eros to come to me tonight. She will not think it odd for me to summon him. He will act as our eyes and ears. We must be vigilant and prepare for every eventuality."

He lurched forwards suddenly, his stomach cramping once more.

Canidius rushed to kneel at his side. "What do you need?" he asked, concern spreading across his face.

"I need a drink," Mark Antony gasped as the pain in his stomach subsided. Becoming a drunk had been relatively easy, becoming sober was proving more of a challenge.

Canidius nodded. "I will bring you more wine." He went to rise, but Mark Antony grabbed his wrist, with surprising strength.

"No," he gurgled. "Get me a physician."

Chapter 14

"You have got to be kidding me!"

Melissa glared at her husband. He stood before her in the same garb worn by many Egyptian men – a kilt and an open silk robe. His eyes were so heavy with kohl liner, she barely recognised him. His body glistened from the fragrant oils that had been carefully massaged into him. Around his neck hung a large golden ankh; the Egyptian symbol of life. He looked like any other courtier in Cleopatra's grand palace. It made Melissa feel sick.

Anthony shrugged. "I had to agree, Liss. She's been in a foul mood since she heard the Nabateans burnt her fleet. She wanted your head."

"Then you should have let her have it."

"Don't be ridiculous," he replied through gritted teeth. I don't see why you're so het up. It's just a couple of rounds of wrestling. She wants a demonstration of the skills I've been learning at the gymnasium. I think it's a test of my loyalty."

"You'll be naked!" Melissa exclaimed.

"Well, duh. It's Greek wrestling." His sarcasm only made matters worse.

"She'll be watching!" Melissa shrieked in the high-pitched way that only a woman can, grating on the nerves of any man having to listen to it.

Anthony's patience ran out. "And so will half of Alexandria," he snapped. "This isn't a small dinner for a few carefully-chosen guests. This is a celebration."

"You're to be the evening entertainment," Melissa gasped as she sat down on the bed.

Anthony stared at his wife for a moment. These days, it felt as if they spent more time arguing than anything else. Melissa had always been stubborn, and he had always been headstrong. Being cooped up together in a small space for most of the day did nothing to help. The stress of the situation was getting to them and, rather than pulling together, they were drifting ever further apart.

He gave a shrug and tried his best to remain calm. "If I'd said no, we'd be in serious shit by now."

Melissa's eyes were filling with tears. "Well I'm damned if I'm going to watch you parade your wares in front of that trollop. I won't be a part of it."

He folded his arms in front of him. "Oh, believe me, you will. She was most insistent you attend."

Melissa pouted defiantly. "Why should I?"

Anthony turned his eyes to the ceiling and let out a groan of frustration. "Work it out for fuck's sake, Liss. What day is it? The date that is, not the day of the week."

"Day after the Ides of January . . ." Melissa tailed off as she realised the significance. In the Roman calendar, the Ides of January fell on the 13th. January 14th was historically recorded as Mark Antony's birthday.

"And the penny drops at last." Anthony's sarcasm had returned.

"Oh," she whispered.

The full extent of Cleopatra's revenge was becoming clear to Melissa. The wrestling was only the start. The queen intended to make her squirm in humiliation throughout the evening as the queen lavished attention on both her 'Antonys'.

She swallowed hard. "Oh god, Anthony, she's going to try to humiliate me."

"Us, dear, she's going to try to humiliate us. This is payback for not giving adequate warning of the loss of her fleet. I say we take the hit and play her game, rather than you throwing a paddy meaning we're in jail by morning . . . or worse."

Melissa slumped in defeat. "I don't want to go," she whimpered.

"Tough," Anthony replied sharply. He threw a parcel wrapped in linen and tied with a fancy woven cord at her. "I'm guessing that's your dress. It was outside the door."

Melissa loosened the cord enough to rip it off the wrapping, and opened the parcel, dreading it being some awful Egyptian costume. Instead, she was surprised to find a stola: the dress worn by Roman matrons. It was made from the finest green silk, probably woven in India and shipped across the Red Sea, before being tailored by a talented Alexandrian seamstress. This was too expensive a garment to have come from Cleopatra, who, Melissa felt, would prefer to see her in sackcloth. As she lifted the dress by its shoulders, a small drawstring bag fell out onto the floor with a metallic clunk.

Anthony bent over to pick it up. The contents were heavy. He pulled open the drawstring and removed a large gold bangle in the shape of a coiled snake.

"Wow," he sounded genuinely impressed. "She can't be planning anything too bad or she wouldn't have sent you this. Get changed, or we'll be late. I'll wait out there." He dropped the bracelet and its bag on the bed and wandered out into the gardens. He needed some air, before he said something he would, no doubt, regret.

It was then Melissa noticed the slip of papyrus peeking out of the opening of the bag. She pulled it out and read the short message on it. It said simply:

> *An item appropriate for a woman of your standing*

She recognised the handwriting immediately. The dress and the bangle were from Mark Antony. There had been no contact between them since that day in Canidius' suite, but he must know she was being forced to attend his birthday celebrations. Was that good or bad? Was he part of the plan to embarrass her, or was he prepared to be her protector once more?

Perhaps Anthony was right, and she was over-reacting. There was only one way to find out. She had to go to the banquet, and hope for the best.

"Woo hoo!" Anthony whistled, visibly shocked at his wife's appearance when she walked out into the garden some ten minutes later.

"I've done this before," she muttered, twisting her hands together nervously.

"You look so . . ." he paused, searching for the words to express how beautiful she looked in the shimmering material, which clung delicately to her petite frame, flattering her natural curves. He knew how self-conscious she was, and how uncomfortable she always felt receiving compliments, but standing there with her hair pinned and combed into loose waves about her face, she looked simply stunning.

A nervous smile played on Melissa's lips. It was not often she left her spirited husband speechless.

"Roman!" He blurted out suddenly.

Melissa frowned, unsure whether to feel complimented or insulted, and was about to say so, when a voice behind her made her jump.

"Good evening to you both."

The voice was that of Canidius, but no sooner had Melissa recognised him than he was gone, hurrying in the direction of the banqueting hall, brightly lighting the farthest end of the rose garden. Melissa realised Anthony had been unintentionally distracted by Canidius' sudden appearance during his compliment, but the moment was ruined nonetheless.

"Let's get this over with, shall we?" she muttered, gathering up her skirt to make it easier to hurry after Canidius.

The closer they got to the hall, the louder became the cacophony that was an Egyptian celebration. Melissa became more anxious with every step towards what she envisaged to be her impending doom. Anthony knew from her silence that she was nervous and, when she stumbled on the bottom step up to the hall, he grabbed her hand and pulled her to one side briefly.

"Whatever happens tonight, remember I love you. I always will." He reached behind her to a bush and broke something off it. Then, reaching up to the pin holding the dress at her shoulder, he tucked a delicate bloom behind it. It was a small, blue flower; unassuming in nature and unlikely to draw attention, but it was a thoughtful gesture. He kissed her forehead gently before turning back towards the steps. In return, she squeezed his hand as they climbed into the unknown.

Neither of them spotted the man, hidden in the shadows, watching their every move with interest.

Chapter 15

Melissa had experienced her fair share of Roman meals. She had even been to one lavish banquet. She had never seen opulence on the scale exhibited by Cleopatra's court.

This was a spectacle that bombarded all the senses at once. The hall itself was draped in a rainbow of the finest Indian silks, each of which fluttered on the gentle evening breeze. The air was heavy with the scent of the sea, mixed with the heady aromas of cinnamon and cardamom. Rose petals and lilies were strewn in heaps around the floor, adding to the sensory bombardment. Bronze couches, inlaid with ivory and glass were adorned with animal hides. Melissa recognised the skins of lions, leopards, zebras, gazelles; enough pelts to embarrass even the most successful modern big game hunters. Musicians played, and dancers danced, while jugglers, magicians and story tellers circulated, titillating the guests with their exploits.

And then there was the food.

Honeyed dates with walnuts, sea urchins, doormice, stuffed lambs' kidneys, soft boiled eggs in a pine nut sauce, olives, dates, figs and a type of pate on crisp pastry slices were amongst the initial trays proffered by the slaves.

Silver salvers were then brought forth, containing a variety of fish and shellfish: mullet, tuna, sturgeon, eels, whole lobsters, clams, mussels. A menagerie of wild fowl came out next including geese, ducks, cranes and imported peacocks, the latter with their tail feathers beautifully displayed in full fans.

There was an unpleasant looking squishy substance in one dish that was held out to Anthony by one of their neighbours. As he went to take a piece, Melissa grabbed his wrist and whispered, "I wouldn't – I think that's a sow's vulva!"

He paused momentarily, while he contemplated whether to be bold or not. Then he took a piece anyway.

"When in Rome!" he said with a shrug, slipping the prized delicacy into his mouth.

Melissa gagged. "What's it taste like?"

He pulled a bit of a face. "Tastes like chicken."

"Really?"

Anthony pulled a face that said it clearly did not taste anything like chicken.

"I can't begin to tell you how revolting that was," he said through gritted teeth, politely raising his hand to the man holding the dish to turn down the kind offer of more.

The slaves then delivered a hundred gold plated platters on which lay suckling pigs, their bellies stuffed with a variety of exotic delicacies such as oysters, scallops, finches and thrushes to name but a few. Anthony laughed, describing it as 'the ultimate surf 'n' turf' as he dived in. Melissa simply scowled at him whilst picking at a salad.

"What are these?" she asked, picking up an odd-looking stone from a small tray on a table to the side of their couch.

Anthony took it gently from her hand and replaced it on the tray. "I could be wrong, but I think they are the stones from the fruit of mandrake plants."

"Aren't they poisonous?" Melissa asked, wiping her hand surreptitiously on the zebra skin she was sitting on.

He grinned, knowing that for once he had more knowledge on a subject than his wife.

"Yes, they are, but more importantly those stones are believed to have a narcotic effect, if sniffed. The ancient Egyptians used them as an aphrodisiac, and Cleopatra is one to uphold tradition!"

Melissa shuddered. She felt as if everything in this palace was designed to encourage its occupants to indulge in a life of sin. It was a shock to a woman more in tune with the refined attitudes of Republican Rome. There, sin was readily available to men of all ranks, but less so for women. Melissa regarded herself as a virtuous Roman matron, a part she had played for many years under Caesar and found it impossible to indulge in this unabashed hedonism in the same way as her husband. It was yet another trait he shared with his father: not knowing when enough was enough.

Anthony laughed at her reaction as he accepted yet another glass of wine. As the slave moved onwards, his eye caught that of their host. Cleopatra lay on one of a pair of couches set on a raised platform at the far end of the hall. She was dripping in pearls, strung from her neck, her wrists, even from her hair. They were sown into her dress and on her slippers. As the pearls caught in the light of the dozen candelabra surrounding her, she almost seemed to glow in an ethereal manner. He raised his glass slightly in acknowledgement to her and she gave the slightest nod in return, before shifting her gaze elsewhere.

The other couch remained empty while its intended occupant circulated. Mark Antony moved around the room from couch to couch, socialising with all his guests in turn. His pattern was erratic. To begin with, he moved from one to another in a seemingly methodical manner, and then randomly flitted across the room to another grouping. It seemed as if he were deliberately avoiding Melissa and Anthony, not that Melissa minded. She had no wish to be party to a confrontation between her husband and his father, which would inevitably turn nasty. It was an event Cleopatra would, no doubt, enjoy, which made Melissa all the more keen to avert it.

Melissa sat quietly during the meal, choosing to limit her conversation with their neighbours, whom Anthony appeared to know. They were, in fact, the importers of fine silks from whom Anthony had bought the scarf in the market some weeks earlier. He had persuaded Cleopatra to invite them: part of his promise to get them further trade from the palace. The man appeared extremely grateful for his sudden rise in status, and his wife was dumbstruck at what she was witnessing. Melissa was more than a little miffed to find out that Anthony had been buying presents for the queen. She made a few snippy comments on the subject, which he ignored, so she gave up. It was not the best time, or place, to start an argument.

Melissa could not help but watch Mark Antony in his wanderings. She may have seen a different side to him in private, but outwardly he was still the same vibrant personality he had always been. Wherever he went, the room seemed to come alive with laughter. He always had been the life and soul of the party. Facing certain defeat had made little impact on that.

He turned around suddenly and, for a moment, their eyes met. Despite the jovial air he portrayed for his audience, Melissa could see no emotion in his eyes whatsoever. The wicked twinkle that she remembered so fondly was gone, replaced by two dark, empty pools. The old Mark Antony was firmly buried beneath his new shell of indifference. And then Melissa saw something more in his face – misery. For the briefest moment she was looking at the most unhappy man she had ever seen.

He looked away towards the queen and lifted his glass to her as if giving a signal. She returned the salute with her own glass before taking a sip of the wine. Slowly, she stood up. Then, with a single clap of her hands, she brought the room to order. Silence fell as all eyes turned to the queen.

"Friends. We are gathered here to celebrate the birth of our great general. He is a man who has provided for our people, defended our borders and brought us peace for many years. He may have been born Roman, but his heart belongs to Alexandria. This is where he calls home and where his loyalties will forever lie. We are his people and he is our protector. Let us gives thanks for another year past, and a new year to come in the life of Mark Antony: the hero of Philippi!"

Mark Antony politely turned to all sides to acknowledge his guests. Everyone applauded and a few people began to echo a call of 'speech'. He raised his arms in the air until the room fell silent again.

Melissa felt her pulse quicken. Mark Antony was not the greatest orator, but he was passionate in everything he did or said. It had always been a pleasure to hear him speak.

He drew a breath and began.

"Our queen is most gracious with her praise for a humble soldier. I, myself, do not feel my efforts are worthy of such high estimation. I have only ever done that which has been asked of me, and I have done it willingly. When

I was a young and naive man, I would often wonder what the future held for me. Now I have more years behind me than are left ahead, I find the future no longer holds my interest." He stared directly at Melissa briefly. "It is the present that interests me now. Tonight my friends, I find the most pressing thought on my mind is . . ." he paused, surveying the whole room with the most serious of expressions, before laughing heartily and turning to face the queen ". . . when will the promised entertainments begin?"

He sat down on the end of the nearest couch and pulled one of the female dancers into his lap, blatantly fondling her as she wriggled on his knee.

Melissa found herself thinking *Was that it? Was that his great speech? Is that all he has to say? Was it even worth him bothering?* Her disappointment was beyond belief. She watched another slave pouring more wine into his glass. *Was this really what he had become - a washed up old lecher, too sodden to articulate his feelings properly?* But then, Mark Antony had always been fond of a drink, and a woman, or two, and all at the same time. She felt deflated. Despite all the evidence that had presented itself, she had always held on to the belief that the man she had grown to admire was still inside the one she had become acquainted with since Actium. For the first time, she doubted that to be the case. Worse still, it meant Anthony was right that their only remaining chance for survival lay with Cleopatra. For Melissa, that meant there was no chance at all. She wanted to cry, but she did not want to give the queen the satisfaction of seeing her depressed.

Worse still was to come. She had completely forgotten that her husband was due to provide the evening's entertainment. With a second clap of her hands, Cleopatra gave the signal to her chosen wrestlers. Anthony immediately rose and began to remove his robe.

"Please don't," Melissa whimpered.

"No choice, love. I do this or else ..."

"Or else what?" Melissa asked.

He did not answer. He merely winked, dropping his kilt onto the couch before striding out into the centre of the floor to meet his equally naked opponent.

With the wrestling underway, Canidius slipped quietly round behind the couches towards Melissa. He had been careful to avoid her or her husband, knowing everything they did would come under the scrutiny of the queen. Now the entertainment was in full swing, he had his chance to make contact. As he moved in, he kept an eye on Cleopatra, who paid very little attention to anyone beyond the two naked men grappling in the centre of the floor.

His gaze moved to Mark Antony, sitting over on the far side of the room. Their eyes met briefly; long enough for Canidius to receive his instruction. Concealed in the palm of his hand was a small phial. He quickly tipped its contents into Melissa's half-empty wine glass. There was a slight fizzing, which went unnoticed by all bar him. As soon as it stopped, he picked up the glass, swirled its contents slightly to ensure a thorough mix, and moved to sit next to Melissa.

Handing her the glass, he spoke quietly.

"She wants your husband." He nodded towards the queen. "Drink up, I'll get us more wine." He caught the attention of a passing slave, who waited patiently until Melissa had downed her drink before refilling the glass.

"I know she does," Melissa replied, before taking a further gulp from the newly-filled glass.

"She always gets what she wants, in the end," Canidius said, with a sigh of relief, content that Melissa had drunk the wine so quickly. He felt uncomfortable that he had drugged his newest acquaintance, but he had managed it without incident. Very soon he believed Melissa would fall asleep and be saved from the spectacle that was to follow.

The news of Cleopatra's somewhat public revenge on the seer for her apparently poor predictions had reached Mark Antony that afternoon. Once he had vented his anger on an unsuspecting chair, he had ordered Canidius to administer a sleeping draft to Melissa as soon as was practicable. She would pass out and Cleopatra's scheming would be foiled, for a few days at least. It was a ploy designed to buy Mark Antony time. Cleopatra's callous planning had finally made him take action, but he needed time to make proper arrangements for Melissa's safety.

"Sh ... she will not get *him*," Melissa slurred slightly.

Canidius did his best to ignore it. The draught was working far faster than he expected. He shook his head. "I fear your confidence is misplaced. She has the better bargaining position."

"What do you *mean* by that?" She spun her head to look directly at Canidius, but did so a little too fast and her vision blurred in front of her.

"I *mean* she has you. He does what is asked of him, or you die." He pointed towards the wrestlers. "She already has him performing like a trained ape. It will not stop there. I have seen stronger men than your husband writhe across that floor to the delight of her majesty." He was of course referring to the general, Plancus, who painted himself blue and wriggled like an eel for the queen's amusement.

Melissa made a strange gurgling noise in her throat and lifted her hand to her mouth.

Canidius glanced sideways. "It is the truth, Lissa. It will start here tonight. Your husband will win this match, as is arranged. And to the victor, go the spoils."

"Spoils?" Melissa gulped. She felt both hot and a little faint.

He pointed to the dancers hovering around the edge of the room. "Those are the spoils. His final performance tonight will be with them, while you are made to watch."

"He will not do that," she murmured as she tried to focus. Her vision had doubled.

"You do not believe that any more than I do. The Ptolemies have always had a reputation for Dionysian revelry. This one is no exception." Canidius glanced at Cleopatra, who was still watching the wrestling intently. "Enough wine and a man will do anything, especially with a dagger held to his wife's throat. He will do as he is told, for fear of the consequences."

"I feel sick." Melissa replied, but she was not being metaphorical. A wave of nausea had washed over her quite suddenly. She felt her throat tighten, her stomach spasm, and then her mouth fill with a warm bile-tasting liquid. She put her hand to her mouth, but she could not stop the flow. She leant over the side of the couch and vomited into a half-empty bowl of dates.

The room went deathly silent as everyone turned to look at her. She hardly noticed as she retched again. Some of the onlookers were shocked, some were disgusted, but almost all had a look of terror about them. This was not the first time they had seen someone in such a state at a court dinner. Poisoning had long been rife in the halls of the Ptolemaic pharaohs, and Cleopatra was known to have an unhealthy fascination with toxicology.

A moment later and Anthony had extricated himself from the grasp of his opponent and was kneeling at her side. He looked on in terror as he tried to help his ailing wife. "Liss," he soothed. "I'm here."

Canidius too had a look of panic on his face. He was told the powder was designed to knock Melissa out, but she seemed to be having a bad reaction to it. He searched the room for Mark Antony, who had moved on to yet another couch. As the two men made eye contact, Mark Antony gave the briefest nod. He appeared unflustered by the development and his nod was an instruction for Canidius to continue as arranged.

Anthony was beside himself with worry. He turned to the queen and pleaded to be dismissed. "Your Majesty, my wife is unwell. May I take her to our room?"

"No, you may not," Cleopatra snapped. As Anthony stared at her in horror, she added, "If she must go, have one of the slaves take her. You will continue your performance."

Canidius could see Anthony was going to protest further, which was unwise. "I will take her," he said quietly, placing his hand on Anthony's arm.

Anthony tried to pull away, but Canidius' grip tightened sharply. He was supposed to say nothing, but he had to prevent Anthony from provoking the queen. "Your wife is in danger. I gave her a draught to turn her stomach, nothing more. It gives her an excuse to leave." He told the lie with such conviction he very nearly believed it himself.

Anthony stared in disbelief. Knowing how much Cleopatra hated his wife, Canidius' words rang true. If

Melissa was in danger, then she had to leave. He knew he had to trust this Roman, even though he barely knew him. He reluctantly nodded his agreement. "If it pleases your majesty, I would have this man take her," he said loudly.

Cleopatra glared at both men for a moment and then relented with a nod.

Canidius turned to Melissa. She looked so pale he could not be sure if she would make it. "Can you walk?" he asked, standing up.

"I . . . err . . . yes." Melissa stood up slowly and smiled weakly at her husband. "A little too much sun today, I think."

"I will finish this and come to you," Anthony whispered, but Canidius shot him a warning look.

"You will do as you are told, for all our sakes. Keep the queen happy and all will be well. Anger her further and your wife will pay dearly for your actions. Lissa has my protection. No harm will come to her." He wrapped an arm around Melissa and supported her as they began to walk through the room.

"Looks like someone is incapable of holding her drink," Mark Antony boomed with a laugh as Canidius guided Melissa out of the hall. "That one always was a lightweight where wine was concerned."

Anthony glared at his father. His fists clenched tightly at his sides. He wanted to beat that smug smile off the older man's face but, as he took a step forwards, Cleopatra clapped her hands together once again.

"Continue," she ordered.

Anthony glared at her, but did as he was told and resumed the match. Regardless of Canidius' warning he intended to throw the remaining rounds and be sent away in disgust.

Or so he thought.

No matter what he tried, Anthony could not lose. Every half-hearted throw seemed to gain him points. If he was caught in a hold and tried to yield the move, a foul would be declared and they would have to start again. He quickly realised that the rule book had been thrown away and, whatever he did, he was destined to win. He found himself becoming increasingly frustrated at the constant stalemate, and changed tactics to aim for a quick and decisive victory. He channelled his anger into the remaining rounds and soon had his opponent begging for mercy.

As Cleopatra stood up to declare Anthony the victor, Mark Antony stepped forwards and strode across the room towards his son.

"An impressive display from one unaccustomed to our provincial ways," he boomed and slapped Anthony hard on the back. As his son turned to glare at him, Mark Antony thrust his robe into his hands and pointed to an empty couch.

"Sit down," he growled menacingly, before turning his attention to Cleopatra. "You always did have a good eye for talent, my dear," he called, with a laugh.

She glared at her husband, leaving him in no doubt that she was displeased with his interference in her plans for the evening, but she made no comment.

He grinned and winked at her, knowing she was allowing him to take the lead rather than causing a scene that might reflect badly on her. It was his birthday celebration after all, not hers.

"And what of this newcomer to our court? What shall I give him as reward for his considerable efforts?" Mark Antony walked over and sat down next to his son. "More dancing, I think." He laughed heartily as the musicians resumed at his signal.

Once the dancers were again in full flow, he leant closer to the younger Anthony, who was adjusting his robe.

"I have eyes and ears all over this palace. I know you have encouraged the queen's attentions in the hope of gaining certain privileges. I do not know what game you think you are playing, but I will give you a piece of advice, my son. If it is your intention to eat at Cleopatra's table, you must learn to sample every dish on offer with relish." He gave a slight nod to the dancers.

Anthony looked at his father in surprise, both at the comment and the fact that he might have just acknowledged his parentage. "Are you telling me to join in with the dancing?" he asked casually, even though he knew that was not the intention.

Mark Antony roared with laughter again and, by use of hand signals, encouraged Anthony to pretend to share the joke. Whilst Anthony reluctantly joined in, he shot a glance at Cleopatra, who appeared to be extremely nervous that the two of them were talking and apparently enjoying each other's company. His eyes travelled around the rest of the room and he noticed many guests retiring to quiet corners, taking some of the dancers with them.

Mark Antony leant on his son's shoulder in order to speak more quietly. "She expects you to have whoever is left while she watches. She likes to watch, and then she likes to fuck. She intended for your wife to witness this shameless depravity, with you playing the leading role. I could not allow that. I ordered Canidius to remove Melissa by any means possible. I assure you she will be quite safe in his company. The queen must settle for a private performance." He waved his arm in a wide gesture towards the floor.

Anthony flinched, not at what he was expected to do, but at what he thought he had heard his father call his wife. "You may think drugging Lissa was in her best interests, but I do not. I am going to see to her."

"Melissa will not hear of your indiscretions from me . . ." he saw Anthony flinch this time, " . . . and yes, you heard me correctly. I know that is her real name, I know where and when she comes from, and I know you are Antonius, my eldest son, though I must say you have aged poorly for a sixteen-year-old boy."

Anthony said nothing. He tried to get up, but Mark Antony held his shoulder with an iron grip, forcing him to stay in his seat. "You cannot leave. Cleopatra has her sights set on you, and she will have you one way or another. If I were you, I would aim to fuck her on your terms rather than hers. Would you want to do it with a dagger at your wife's throat?"

Anthony ignored the question. "If I am your son, then Cleopatra is my step-mother. I consider it immoral to do as you suggest," he replied quietly.

"Morality means nothing in this land, where brother marries sister as a matter of course. Considering the woman who once sang your lullabies now shares your bed, I would not have thought it too much of a wrench on your sensibilities, either. And anyway, you know as well as I do that a hard cock lessens your conscience."

Mark Antony smiled across at Cleopatra and raised his glass to her, but she looked away, not wanting to acknowledge she was watching them so intently. "My power here is not without limits. I can intervene in your affairs only so long as our queen allows. Nod once if you understand what I am saying." He never took his eyes off Cleopatra while he spoke.

Anthony gave a brief nod to show he understood.

"If you value your life, and that of your wife, you will continue to humour her royal highness to the best of your abilities. If you refuse and try to leave, Melissa will not live to see the morning, and I will lose a good officer in the process, for Canidius will not give her up without a fight. One way or another, you will be well and truly fucked. It is my suggestion that you be a man, get it up, and get on with it."

Anthony had always known Cleopatra's intentions towards him were less than honourable. He had been using it to his advantage thus far, but it appeared his hand was about to be forced. He gave another nod and reached for his wine glass, which had been refilled at some point during their conversation. As he raised it to his lips, Mark Antony made one last stunning statement.

"You should curtail how much you drink. The wine contains the tears of the poppy." He meant it was laced with opium. "It is designed to lessen your resistance and encourage your erection. If you intend to make my 'wife', as you call her, wait to feel the breadth of your cock within, then drink shallow. Exhaust yourself with the dancers and leave nothing to satisfy her. Otherwise drink deep and reap your rewards for they will be plentiful, though you would be wise to remember that everything has a price, and for you that price will be to sacrifice your wife. Whatever your choice, know this – I am not done with you. We will talk again, and soon."

He sat back and spoke louder, so the queen could hear his words. This time there was a distinct bitterness to them. "Yes, this palace has many pleasures, my boy. The young and talented man will be offered them in abundance until he has had his fill, while those past their prime are left to chew on the scraps."

He stood up and walked towards Cleopatra's couch, intercepting a slave and relieving them of a full flask of un-drugged wine destined solely for her glass. As he approached, she languidly lifted her hand for him to kiss, and he faithfully obliged.

"Bed him well, my love," he whispered. His eyes narrowed as he spoke, hinting that the thought of her being with another man was causing him great pain, but that he knew he was powerless to prevent it.

Cleopatra simply smiled in return, her face a mask of indifference. Mark Antony had lived in the palace long enough to know which flask of wine was which. His deliberate choice of her flask meant that he was planning on drinking himself into unconsciousness yet again. In the past, he would have opted to drink the wine laced with opium and participate fully in the orgy for many hours, before whisking her off to the privacy of their bed, where they would indulge in some of the most interesting entertainments imaginable. In those days, he could have maintained his performance all night and the following day. The handsome, virile man he had once been was fast turning into a lacklustre, bloated sot, but she still felt a pang of frustration when he turned and walked away. She had been aiming to have both of the men named 'Antony' in her bed that night. One might have the stamina of youth, but the other had the benefits of experience that only age can bring. Together, they could have provided her with the most exceptional delights imaginable, but it was not to be. She could only hope the younger one alone would not disappoint her.

Her attentions returned to the man still seated to her left, who now appeared mesmerised by the twisting bodies dancing before him. He reminded her so much of the man Mark Antony had been in his prime – intelligent, witty, handsome, muscular, well-endowed.

She gave a nod to the musicians, who changed the tempo. The dancing slowed and became more overtly sexual. The men's hands no longer brushed sensuously over scantily-clad flesh, they openly groped breasts and tweaked nipples through the sheer fabrics. The women began removing the loincloths of the men, releasing their erections which they proceeded to stroke and tease. Within moments they were all engaging in a variety of sexual acts, in couples, threesomes or alone. Anthony was left in no doubt he was witnessing his first orgy.

One of the women knelt between his legs and opened his robe. Within seconds her lips were around him, but he made no effort to stop her. He had heard Mark Antony's warning and knew what he had to do. Having meaningless sex with strangers held no concerns for him. Having sex with Egypt's queen was another matter entirely. Once he crossed that line, there was no going back. He was determined to make her wait until Octavian was literally knocking on the door. As long as he kept Cleopatra at arm's length, he could keep Melissa alive. He knew that, even before it had been confirmed for him by his father.

And what of his father? Were his intentions truly honourable, or was it nothing more than an attempt to throw his son off guard long enough to steal Melissa away?

He had been careful to only take small mouthfuls of the drugged wine, measuring the affect the opium had on him. He could feel the relaxing effects at work on his mind, and his attempts to keep his arousal in check were failing dismally.

The girl on her knees backed away slowly and, taking one of his hands in hers, tried to pull him to his feet. To her surprise, he pulled back on her arm and did not get up. This was the first time he had been asked to participate in an orgy. Even though the possibilities intrigued him, he was still unsure of where it would take him. He was watching the whole group carefully, checking the activities of the other pairings, some of which were all-male. He had no intention of getting into a situation he was not fully prepared for. He would join in with the girls as instructed, but that was as far as he was prepared to go.

He had failed to notice that Cleopatra had walked round behind him. Seeing what she believed to be doubt, she bent to whisper in his ear, making him jump.

"Why do you hesitate? I can see you want to join them. Why resist? Fuck one. Fuck two." She pointed over towards a muscular male slave carrying more wine. "Fuck him for all I care. They are my gift to you, in return for your outstanding performance this evening. Give in to your lust, Anthony. Enjoy yourself. Enjoy them."

When the girl tugged on Anthony's hand again, he rose and allowed her to lead him into the midst of the writhing bodies in front of him. Cleopatra watched with delight as the women removed his robe and drew him into their orgy, believing her plans for his fall into disgrace were almost complete.

Chapter 16

Mark Antony left the dining suite at a pace, storming through the empty halls. He was heading for the guest wing, and for Melissa.

He had lied to Canidius about the contents of the phial, knowing that his most trusted officer was too principled go along with his true intentions. He did not want Melissa asleep. He wanted her briefly incapacitated with a quick and volatile illness that would force Cleopatra to allow her to leave the banquet. The physician had assured him she would recover within minutes of being taken to her room. However, if this prediction proved incorrect, the physician would barely live long enough to regret his mistake.

He had to speak to Melissa, to hear her deny she loved him. Ever since their last encounter, he had agonised over his feelings for her. Did he love her? Did she love him? Too much had passed between them for him to simply walk away with nothing more than the suspicions he had gleaned from that last conversation. He had to know whether there was any hope of regaining her love. She was everything to him. She was the reason he had sobered up.

There were many thoughts buzzing in his mind. He knew the other Anthony was up to something. He could tell his son was deliberately flattering Cleopatra, but he did not know if it was purely for personal gain, or as a means of deception. If it was the latter, it was a dangerous game to play with a woman so well-versed in the art of the double-cross. It was a game he himself had once played, and lost. As yet, he had no idea what his son's character was. Did they share more than looks and the liking for a drink? Was the younger man as able a tactician as he himself had once been? Would he agree to participate in the evening's entertainments, or would he display a greater moral fibre and refuse, regardless of the consequences? Even if he was his father's son and willingly took part, there was no way of knowing how long the younger Anthony's stamina would last without the aid of the drugged wine. Time was of the essence, and Mark Antony had little of it to waste.

Once he arrived outside the door to the guest suite, his need for haste left him. There were no guards, which seemed most unlike Cleopatra, but perhaps she really was so enamoured with her new beau that she had relaxed security. Either that or she felt that, given enough rope, her latest 'guests' would find a way to hang themselves. If so, Mark Antony could be playing right into her trap, but he no longer cared what she was up to.

He had come there purely with the intention of talking to Melissa but, as he stared down at the handles, he wondered if it was such a good idea. Their initial reunion had not gone well. In a fit of jealousy, he had beaten her husband to a pulp before her very eyes. And the last time they met he blatantly refused her request for help. His behaviour so far had done nothing to improve relations between them.

He had so many questions he needed to ask. How old was his daughter now? Did she like the horse he gave her? Who were the boys in the pictures he found aboard the small boat? Were they his grandchildren? What were their names? And, of course, there was the most important question of all. Which man did she prefer - the son she had married, or the father she left behind? He really had no idea where to start. For all he knew, she might refuse to hear him out. All he knew was that he had to try.

He put his hand on one of the handles and pushed the door open. Once inside he closed it quietly behind him with nothing more than the lightest click. There were no lamps or candles burning in this room and no sign of Melissa or Canidius. There were rooms to the left and right. The door to the left was wide open. The one to the right was slightly ajar. Knowing Melissa's habit for closing doors, he concluded she was more likely in the room to the right.

As he took a step towards it, he heard a dagger being pulled slowly from its sheath. He stepped sideways until he was bathed in a shaft of moonlight coming in through the window.

Canidius stepped from the shadows by the other door, re-sheathing his weapon. "I was unsure if it was you or the husband in this darkness," he whispered. "Where is he, anyway?"

Mark Antony ignored the question, preferring to ask one of his own. "How is she?" He nodded towards the partially closed doorway.

Canidius folded his arms. He knew he had been lied to and was not best pleased, but now was not the time to call his commander on the issue. "She has a headache comparable with one of your worst hangovers and is a little shaky on her feet. Otherwise, I believe she will be well, with a good night's sleep."

Mark Antony nodded. "I will watch over her until he returns. If he does not delight his audience, Cleopatra will have no concerns in running you through to wreak vengeance on his wife. I do believe she will think twice before slaying me."

Canidius nodded. "I concur. Nonetheless, I wish you a quiet night." He pressed the dagger into his commander's hand before leaving the suite as quietly as Mark Antony had entered it.

With his officer gone, Mark Antony's nerves returned. Melissa was only feet away from him, but he did not know how his presence would be received. Taking a deep breath, he headed over to the bedroom door and nervously pushed it open.

Stepping inside, he returned the door to the same position as it had been. A single oil lamp sputtered in a recess high on the wall, giving most of its light to the ceiling and leaving much of the room in shadow.

Melissa was sitting on the edge of the bed with her head in her hands and her back towards him. The window was slightly open. She was still feeling the effects of the drug she had been given and needed fresh air, despite the sudden deluge which had begun only moments earlier. The hammering of the heavy droplets on the ground outside made her head hurt, but she could not be bothered to get up to shut out the noise. She had removed her dress and was now wearing a simple dressing gown. Her dark hair tumbled down her back, free from the pins and combs that had held it back earlier in the evening. She looked so lost and alone sitting there that it made Mark Antony pause. She looked exactly the same as she had the first night they had spent together so many years before.

She sat quietly for a few moments before speaking.

When she did, she spoke in English. "You joined in, didn't you?"

Having no idea what she said, Mark Antony said nothing.

"Oh boy! If you can't even speak to me it must be bad."

Slowly, Melissa turned around, expecting to confront her unfaithful husband. Her gown was open, revealing a glimpse of bare breast before she realised her mistake.

"Shit!" she exclaimed and quickly turned away again, making her head spin, but she was able to pull her gown tightly around her, tying it with the belt. She reverted to Latin immediately.

"What do you want at this hour?"

As soon as he saw her face, Mark Antony could tell she had been crying. Anger welled in him, but he forced it away, along with his desperate urge to comfort her.

"Only to talk," he replied nervously. "There are things I must know – that I should have asked before."

"Can it not wait until the morning? I am unwell and …"

"No, it cannot." He cut her off harshly, but immediately regretted it. "The w-w-wine," he stammered, displaying his nervousness. "It gives me the confidence to ask …" He stopped talking and fumbled in the folds of his toga for the piece of shiny paper he had found on the *Selene*. He looked at it again, before holding it out at arm's length.

Melissa turned to face him again, curious at what made him so uncharacteristically shy. As she did, she was presented with the photograph of her children that Mark Antony had torn from the board on the *Selene*.

"Is this my daughter?" he finished in a rush. He moved his arm slightly, encouraging her to take the photo, but to his surprise she did not.

"Yes," she whispered before collapsing backwards onto the bed. "Your daughter and your grandsons," she wailed as her grief at their loss overtook her again.

Watching Melissa give in to her pain was too much for him to bear. Dropping onto the bed beside her, Mark Antony gathered his former lover tenderly in his arms and held her head to his chest while she sobbed.

Anthony lay back on the empty couch exhausted, his arm across his eyes. His head spun from the effects of the wine, but now it also had to struggle with the memory of his actions. He had participated in the orgy and all under the watchful eye of the greatest seductress in history. His fall into debauchery had begun.

Cleopatra smiled knowingly. Her victim was at his most vulnerable and she fully intended to strike. She watched the rise and fall of his chest as he struggled to regain his breath. His muscles, glistening with oil, seemed to ripple in the fading candle light. He was tired, flagging from his physical exertions with two women, but his performance was not over. Her time had come.

She stood quietly, not wanting to disturb her tired guest. With a mere jerk of her head, the remaining participants received their instructions to leave, slipping away as silently as they had first arrived. She moved across the floor like a cat stalking its prey, her eyes never leaving their goal until she reached Anthony's prone form. She sat at his hip and placed her hand on his chest.

He raised his arm slightly to see which girl had come to tease him and was surprised to see it was the queen herself. He tried to sit up, but Cleopatra pushed him back onto the couch and began stroking his chest.

"Your stamina does you credit, but you need rest. I want you to feel relaxed," she oozed. Her hand moved swiftly downwards, finding his softened penis. "Perhaps not that relaxed," she added with a slight laugh and tightened her grip.

Anthony shot forward, grabbing her wrist and pulling it away from his manhood.

"Your majesty, I am truly flattered, but I cannot."

"You say that, but you will be surprised what you can manage, given the correct encouragement."

"Please, your majesty. Do not ask me to do this."

Cleopatra was taken aback. She was unused to people saying no to her. "You do not find me attractive?"

"You know I do. Have I not told you that you are the most beautiful woman I have ever met?"

"Then why do you not wish to satisfy me as you did those lesser women."

"You are the wife of another man, a great man deserving of my respect. It is a boundary I cannot cross." He did not dare to tell her she was, in fact, his step-mother. Not that it would have mattered to Cleopatra. As his father had already reminded him, the Ptolemies practised incest. She would hardly have raised so much as a quizzical eyebrow at a step-relation.

"I see." Cleopatra frowned as she mulled over his words. She could not understand his deference to a man he barely knew. "Your loyalty does you credit. It is a pity my husband did not show the same restraint when he bedded your wife."

Anthony winced slightly. The knowledge that Melissa and Mark Antony had once been lovers gnawed a little deeper on each occasion that it was mentioned. Cleopatra's offer was tempting, but his infidelity was not going to stretch to the queen, not tonight.

"She was not my wife at that time." The statement was only partly true, but he wanted the subject closed. He let go of Cleopatra's wrist and got off the couch, grabbing his clothes in the process. "You are my queen and to deny your request is difficult, but I regret I cannot do this. Please do not ask it of me."

Cleopatra was smiling when he turned to look at her. She could tell he was struggling with his sensibilities. It was apparent he was interested in her offer from the protrusion now visible beneath his kilt. All he needed was a gentle nudge and he would be hers, but not tonight. Patience shown now would pay dividends later. She would make him come to her and that would make her victory far sweeter.

"I understand. I wish you good night."

Anthony walked calmly from the room, fully expecting to be dragged back at any moment and forced into having sex, though she would not have to do much forcing, considering he had drunk a little too much wine for his own good. He had toyed with too many women in his youth not to know how much she wanted him, and he was intrigued to find out if she really was the famed lover portrayed by history.

He was playing a dangerous game with Cleopatra. Bedding the queen of Egypt might well improve his chances of survival but, in doing so, he knew he would lose the love of the woman who meant the world to him. Melissa was the main reason he had walked away from this opportunity. Their situation was not that desperate – at least, not yet. The day would come when he would have no choice but to bend this royal strumpet over a couch, but it would not be today. When he did eventually give in to her sexual demands, he would ensure she was so desperate to have him that she would agree to almost anything in return for his attentions.

Once he had made it back to his suite, he decided he would sleep in the other room. As desperate as he was to check on the health of his wife, he had not had an opportunity to wash. To get into bed with Melissa in his current state, covered in the bodily fluids of two other women, would only cause an argument he was not prepared to have.

His decision meant he would never know she was in their bedroom with another man.

Chapter 17

"Would you like some more wine? Sipping it seems to help stem your tears." Mark Antony reached for the flask at his feet, but Melissa refused him.

"No, thank you," Melissa sniffed. "It helps, though I am feeling a little light headed."

"I am sorry, he murmured honestly. "I did not mean to intoxicate you. Would you like me to open the window again? I believe the rain is easing."

Melissa shook her head. "No, the noise is unbearable. I never realised it could rain so hard."

"Welcome to Alexandria; the city where everything is done to excess, including the weather!" There was more than a slight hint of sarcasm in his tone.

Melissa stifled another sob, this time at the thought of the excesses her husband might be indulging in at that very moment.

Mark Antony grunted in frustration and filled Melissa's glass anyway. He pushed it towards her lips, until she reluctantly took a sip.

"I cannot bear to see you in such distress. Were he not my son, I would have him whipped for the pain he has caused you."

"It is not his fault. As you say, he is your son, which means he is not only blessed with your looks, he is also cursed with your vices. We call it 'a chip off the old block', the chip referring to the child being …"

Mark Antony held up his hand. "You do not need to explain. I understand the analogy." He smiled. "I like it. I feel it is rather apt."

"Rather too apt," Melissa grumbled. "You both seem to be a little too enamoured with Caesar's Egyptian whore for my liking."

"Now, now, Lissa. It is not polite to call your hostess a whore, especially not one who is as good as my wife."

"Is she your wife?"

He grinned. "That depends on your perception of events. Egyptian custom decrees that, if a man lives with a woman, it is enough to make her his wife. In this way, Cleopatra believes us to be married. I have never uttered the words that would make our union legally binding in Roman law, and so I believe that we are not. You know as well as I do that I cannot marry a foreigner. I would forfeit my rights in Roman society." He winked at her.

Melissa frowned. "I do not understand why you had any kind of relationship with her in the first place. You did not appear interested when we first met her in Rome?"

"Why would I, when I had a far more challenging prospect to mount me each night? You were more than enough for a simple soldier." He laughed as Melissa scowled at him, before offering her a proper answer.

"To begin with, it was the money. I will not deny it. Egypt's wealth has always eclipsed that of Rome. I desperately needed the funds. When I summoned Cleopatra to Tarsus, I wanted an explanation for her failure to answer my call for aid at Philippi. The ships she promised never arrived. The troops she sent by land were easily subverted by Cassius. The woman had to be called to account for these failures, but that was not my primary objective. It was my intention to give her an ultimatum. Either she gave me the money I needed, or I would strip Egypt of its wealth by force. She offered me a third option, which proved most beneficial to us both."

"You mean you sold the future of Rome in order to bed your first queen."

"Not true, Lissa." He frowned. "I had already had the queen of Cappadocia by then. Screwing royalty is easy for a man hailed as the new Dionysus."

Melissa raised her eyes to the ceiling. "Oh, forgive me. I stand corrected. I forgot the city of Ephesus proclaimed you a living god. Only a living goddess would be good enough to satisfy your ambition."

Mark Antony merely smiled, despite the sarcasm he could hear in Melissa's voice. If she was trying to goad him into an argument, she had failed. No longer as volatile as he had been in his youth, he remained calm as he gave his reply.

"Do you know what it is like? To have rich and powerful people throw themselves at you? I was the hero of Philippi, the new Alexander, saviour of the Roman Republic, the avenger of Caesar. Cities and Kings fell to their knees to honour the greatest Roman general still alive. If one or two chose to offer their wives for my entertainment, it would have been rude of me to say no."

Melissa shot him her most disapproving glare.

In the past, that look would have been enough to raise his blood pressure and make him yell at her, but no longer. This time he merely shrugged. "That kind of adoration changes you."

"All power corrupts," Melissa interjected.

He sighed. "By that measure, my corruption must be absolute."

She said nothing, merely raising her eyebrow, so he continued.

"The power is intoxicating. You feel invincible, when in reality you are nothing more than a man, and a man with a considerable list of creditors at that. I knew this only too well. Cleopatra's arrival on that golden barge only helped to confirm my belief that Egypt offered a ready supply of funds and a solution to all my financial problems. In return, she wanted very little - Cyprus, a few rivals removed, nothing of consequence."

"One of the 'rivals' she had you remove was her sister, Arsinoe. She was a child to whom Caesar had shown clemency. Surely she posed no real threat?"

"That 'child' was by then eighteen. She was both an adult and a princess of Egypt with men loyal to her cause. A faction within the priests at Ephesus was aiding the flow of information to and from her followers. It was possible those priests may have eventually been persuaded to assist her to escape to rejoin her renegades who had already declared her the true queen of Egypt. She could easily have mounted a challenge for the Egyptian throne. You yourself told Caesar – war in Egypt is bad for Rome. I could not afford to take that chance. What price was one girl's life in return for access to the wealth of Egypt?"

"Cheap, I suppose." Melissa had to admit Mark Antony's logic was sound. It was what had happened next that interested her. "Why come here?"

"I came to Alexandria to seal our arrangement. It is a beautiful city, with many distractions to entertain a battle-weary soldier. Cleopatra felt a week or two would help to rejuvenate my fighting spirit, and I am too polite to refuse such a generous offer."

"You stayed a year!" Melissa exclaimed

He nodded his agreement that the duration of the stay was excessive. "I admit I became overly distracted, but once you have lived in this city a while, you will understand. It offers freedoms you cannot hope to experience in Rome, and excesses to tempt the most pious of men. If the mighty Caesar fell victim to the many delights Alexandria has to offer, what chance did I have?"

Melissa shrugged. It was a question she could not answer. In the months since she had been there, she had watched her husband fall victim to Alexandrian excess. If she heard Anthony tell her to 'lighten up and live a little' one more time, she would throttle him.

Mark Antony was still in full flow. "I was a man who was as high on success as he was desperate with grief for the loss of a loved one. Alexandria gave me a chance to forget my sadness. I had destroyed Brutus and Cassius, but that was never my agenda. I fought hard for peace in Rome after Caesar's death – you know that. All I wanted was to live in happiness and security with you. Octavian forced my hand on that island in Bononia, making me commit to leading his war and to murdering good men whom I respected. And then that slimy piece of shit he called friend took you from me. The sight of your bruised and broken body haunted me for years. Cleopatra made me forget."

"And what of your wife and children in Rome - had you no concerns for them or for their feelings?"

"Fulvia was more than used to my dalliances, and at that stage Cleopatra was nothing more than an idle dalliance. By this stage in our marriage I could have who

I liked provided she could keep my name and her status as the wife of the most powerful man in Rome. I answered her summons purely to sort out that blasted mess she and Lucius got themselves into in Perugia."

"You could have prevented their capitulation. You could have ordered Ventidius to go to their aid, or even Pollio. Both were within easy reach."

"I did give the order . . ." he paused, eyeing her with curiosity, ". . . but it appears those orders were ignored. It seems a lemur whispered other instructions to Ventidius many years before."

Melissa blushed slightly. It was no lemur, or ghost, who had told Ventidius not to go to Fulvia's aid. It was her. She ignored his remark. "Fulvia loved you and you abandoned her. You broke her heart."

He waved his hand in the air dismissively. "Fulvia had no heart. All she ever wanted was power. She slept her way up the political tree: Clodius, Curio, me. She would have tried her luck with Caesar if she thought she could have got away with it."

"But Cleopatra beat her to it."

"Indeed." He nodded. "Cleopatra is a woman cut from the same cloth as my dear, departed wife. She knows what she wants and the best way to get it. Allowing me to hide from my responsibilities in Alexandria gave our queen another Roman general on hand to use as she saw fit . . ." he paused and gave a large sigh ". . . though even I must admit that I have never been used so pleasurably in my entire life."

"What about Octavia? You married her after Fulvia died."

Mark Antony looked wistfully into the distance for some time before answering.

"Octavian's sister is beautiful, intelligent, kind and loyal to a fault. She is a woman of good standing and high morals, but you cannot escape the fact that she is, and always will be, his sister."

"And she was your wife. She argued for leniency towards you until the very last. They dragged her in tears from your house when you divorced her. She will never forgive her brother for what he has done to you."

Mark Antony shook his head. "You are wrong. She will soon be married off to the next poor sap whose genius Octavian needs. Agrippa, no doubt will be the next in her bed."

It was Melissa's turn to shake her head. "She will not remarry. She will love you and only you until the day she dies, as did Fulvia."

He had the decency to look embarrassed. "I had no idea."

"You have this effect on people," Melissa added. Without thinking, she was admitting that she too still had feelings for him. She blushed when she realised her mistake and turned away.

Antony studied her reactions. At last, he was certain that she was not entirely lost to him. He sat close beside her and took her hand in his.

"I have done many things in my life that I am not proud of. Octavia was one of those and I am sorry for it, and yet I had no choice. She reminded me too much of someone that I will love until the day I die." He placed Melissa's hand over the locket still hanging around his neck beneath his tunic. "I could not give Octavia my heart without betraying your memory."

Melissa turned her head and found herself staring into his dark brown eyes. She was so used to seeing them full of mischief, but tonight they only smouldered with passion.

"You were all I ever wanted, Lissa. You were so different from every other woman I had ever met: intelligent, witty, kind, beautiful. I waited too long to tell you my true feelings. When I finally found the courage, our happiness was short-lived. You were snatched from me in the cruellest of ways. Even watching that bastard Salvidienus choke gave me little comfort. I thought you gone from me forever, yet you have returned. I cannot bear the thought of losing you once more. I will not let any man take you from me again."

She knew he would try to kiss her. Her head was telling her to stop him, but her heart ached to be held by him one more time. The thought of her husband fawning over Cleopatra only helped to dull her resistance further. Here was a man who knew what it was like to lose everything he held dear. Here was a man who could understand the pain she felt at never seeing her children again. He would show her the love and attention she craved. As his head moved towards hers, she simply closed her eyes and waited for the inevitable to happen.

His lips brushed against hers, gently at first, but with the pressure mounting. He took her hands and placed them around his neck before wrapping his arms around her, crushing her body into his. The second his tongue began probing through her lips and she made no attempt to resist, he knew he had her. Whether she had married his son or not was irrelevant. Her body was his to command.

Lowering her onto the mattress, Mark Antony stood up and ripped the clothes from his back, throwing them carelessly to the floor. His hands moved swiftly to Melissa's legs, lifting her ankles high in the air and kissing the soles of her feet before pushing her legs wide apart and positioning himself between them. It appeared the gods had answered his prayers at last. He would have Melissa again before he died, not once but many times.

A noise outside distracted him. It was so slight he almost missed it, but years of army training had honed his hearing. His guard was up and as solid as his erection. He turned his head and listened again.

"What is it?" Melissa whispered in sudden confusion, but he shook his head indicating the need for quiet.

There was a clicking sound which they both heard. Mark Antony recognised it immediately as the main door of the apartment closing. Melissa's expression turned from confusion to panic and she struggled to sit up, pulling her legs out of his hands. He moved silently to the bedroom door. Opening it a fraction further, he peered through the gap where he could see a man moving in the outer chamber. His heart fell as soon as he realised it was his son.

He pushed the door closed again and returned to the bed. Sitting next to her once more, he gave Melissa an ultimatum. "Antonius is outside. I can dispose of him and we can be together, or I can leave. The choice has to be yours, but you must be quick to make it."

Melissa hesitated, torn between her duty to her husband and her desire for the man at her side.

Desperate for an answer, Mark Antony tried, somewhat tactlessly, to influence her choice. "I promise his death will be painless."

Melissa pulled away from her would-be-lover in disgust. "He is your son. Taking his wife is one thing, but how could you even think of taking his life?"

Mark Antony had his answer, though it was not the

one he wanted. He knew from the late hour that Anthony had taken part in the orgy. As much as he was bursting to tell Melissa of her husband's infidelity, he did not. He had foolishly told Anthony that she would not hear of his misdemeanours from him, and these days all he had left of his honour was his word.

Planting a swift kiss in the palm of Melissa's hand he rose and gathered his clothes.

"This is not the end, my love," he whispered as he struggled back into his under tunic. Throwing his toga over his shoulder, he walked across to the far wall and began searching behind the curtains.

"What are you doing?" she whispered.

"Have no fear, he will not see me." He blew her a kiss. "Until the next time," he whispered before pulling the curtains away and disappearing behind them.

"Don't be a bloody fool!" Melissa muttered to herself as she went over to the curtains. She could not believe a man in his fifties was behaving like a naughty teenager. He could not possibly be thinking of hiding behind the curtains all night. Nothing had happened. All they had done was talk – at least that was what she planned on telling Anthony.

When Melissa reached the wall and pulled the curtains back all she saw was a wall painting of that same jackal-headed Egyptian god she had seen in the corridors.

Mark Antony had vanished.

Chapter 18

Moving swiftly through the dark passage between the walls, Mark Antony headed for the royal apartments. After so many years living in the palace, he knew these walkways well. Criss-crossing the main hall, these short corridors ran between some of the suites; small spaces used over many centuries to spy on visiting dignitaries.

He could easily have walked through the main door of the royal apartments, but he did not want his arrival to be announced. Instead, he slipped behind a column and entered the longest of the private passages. From his entry point in the main hall, it ran alongside the current quarters of the senior court advisors – another group Cleopatra liked to watch closely. Reaching a junction, he had one of two choices. He could either go straight ahead towards the harbour, retracing the route taken by the queen on the night of her first meeting with Caesar, or he could take the turn and enter Cleopatra's bedchamber. He took the turn and slipped through the secret doorway into the room, closing the panel quietly behind him.

Cleopatra sat quietly at her dressing table applying a cream to her neck. She did not hear him enter, nor did she know he was watching her so intently. As her well-practised strokes moved across her cheeks, he thought back to the day she had first come to him in Tarsus, when she travelled up the river Cygnus on her golden barge. She had been an awe-inspiring sight back then, and the years had in no way diminished her appearance. She had never been what could be described as a beauty in the classical sense, but she had a presence that caught the attention of every man in her company. Caesar had noticed it. His generals had noticed it. He had noticed it. They had spent many happy years together and, in that time, she had made him forget his anguish at losing the love of his life: Melissa.

When he marched his army to Parthia, his world turned upside down. The terrain was far harsher than he had anticipated. His supply train and siege engines were too slow and cumbersome to keep up with the fighting forces. He pressed on with his troops, leaving the rest to follow on behind. When the enemy attack came, it was against the support train, not the army, completely destroying it, leaving his legions exposed and surrounded in hostile territory. The retreat was humiliating; with his forces harried for the entire twenty-seven-day march back to Armenia. Through attack and starvation, he lost twenty-five thousand men – over a third of his army. A further eight thousand were lost on the harsh march to Syria through the bitter winter snows and sub-zero temperatures.

His defeat was so complete, it had made him re-examine each of his past successes. What had been the difference? Why did he now fail where once he had succeeded? There was only one conclusion he could reach. He needed Melissa. Whether she could foretell his future or not was unimportant. Without her, he was nothing: a fact that had been the cause of many colourful disagreements between himself and Cleopatra over the intervening years. Melissa's appearance at Actium only helped to widen that breach to the point where he and the mother of his youngest three children now lived apart.

Mark Antony knew that the only power he held in Alexandria was that which Cleopatra allowed him to have. Melissa was within his grasp, but she was far too vulnerable here in the palace while he was in the Timoneum. He had to return, if he was to watch over his true love. To do that, he had to convince Cleopatra to allow him back into the royal quarters and he knew exactly how to do that.

He shifted his position and spoke quietly.

"How was the entertainment?"

Cleopatra jumped slightly, but regained her composure in an instant.

"Enjoyable," she replied coyly, as she placed the lid on the pot.

"What of your new charge? How did he perform?" he asked, sounding as uninterested as he could.

She turned slowly. "He rose to the occasion admirably. His stamina is exceptional." She was trying to provoke a reaction.

Mark Antony refused to be drawn. He walked over to the open window. "How many did he have?"

There was a slight twitch at the corner of Cleopatra's mouth, but nothing more than that to show her irritation at his apparent lack of interest.

"He had two of the girls, but both many times. It seems to be the preferred way amongst men who share the name 'Antony'."

He stared out of the window and breathed in the warm, salty air as he listened to the gently lapping of the waves against the harbour wall. "And the boys – what of them?"

he continued, without looking at her.

Her answer was given in a tone almost as sultry as the night air. "He showed no interest in male attentions, though with the right encouragement, I am sure he will partake of all the pleasures offered to him."

Mark Antony knew now was the moment to give her what she wanted – a jealous lover. He turned around, a pained expression in his eyes. "How did he perform for you?"

Cleopatra's face hardened. "That is of no concern to you," she snapped suddenly.

He knew from her tone that the evening had not gone entirely as planned. Her intention to seduce the younger Anthony had so far failed. Perhaps his son had more substance than he had first thought, and perhaps the loyalty the man felt towards his wife would win the day. This was something Mark Antony could understand. A woman like Melissa commanded loyalty.

He smiled triumphantly as he walked towards the door, as if pleased she had failed. "You must be tired. I will leave you," he said, with a joyous lilt in his tone.

As he reached the door and began turning the handle, Cleopatra called after him.

"Wait. It has been many months since you last shared my bed, husband. Would you not like to stay? It is your birthday, after all."

He smiled to himself. He knew the best way into any woman's bed was to offer to withdraw. Playing it cool always seemed to get better results than attempting to force the issue. He had learnt that from years spent pursuing Melissa. Cleopatra might think herself a great seductress but, when it came down to it, she fell for the same tricks as any other woman. He let go of the door handle and slowly turned around.

He might have been older, a little fatter, and less lucid after a few drinks but, when it mattered, Mark Antony was still a force to be reckoned with.

And he could still get a good-looking woman to jump into bed with him at the drop of a hat.

Chapter 19

Night rolled into day far too swiftly. As the sun rose, Mark Antony knew the time for love was over – the time had come to get some much-needed answers. He cradled Cleopatra in the crook of his arm, stroking her back gently as he began to probe subtly for information.

"You have not told my why you are so interested in my younger twin."

"He intrigues me," she murmured. "He wants me, yet he resists."

"What makes you so sure?" He kissed the top of her head gently.

She stretched against him seductively. "I have been able to arouse him without difficulty, and with his wife watching. The wine should have made it easy to entice him last night, but he eluded me."

He stopped stoking her arm. "He did not drink much. I told him it was drugged."

She lifted her head. "Why would you do that?"

His answer was laced with both sarcasm and jealousy. "Do you really think I would walk up to him and say, 'here is my wife – fuck her as I have fucked yours'? If you do, you do not know me as well as you think."

Cleopatra pondered his reply, sensing the jealousy in his tone. "What I do not understand is why he does not simply give in as better men have? Caesar was a far greater challenge and I had him on the first night."

"I made you wait," he countered.

She laughed lightly. "I believe I was the one who made you wait."

Mark Antony said nothing. He merely raised an eyebrow and waited for an explanation, which she willingly gave.

"I knew your reputation well. Women of all ranks were throwing themselves at the hero of Philippi. You only had to snap your fingers and one would lie on her back and allow you to rut with her. I needed you to want me above every one of those women." She shifted her body over his, rubbing herself against him in an attempt to arouse him again. "I calculated the number of days I could keep you at bay – long enough to keep you yearning, but not so long that your eye would wander. I could not afford for you to reach satisfaction with a lesser woman."

He rolled sideways shifting her back onto the bed. "And you were more than worth the wait. But tell me, why is it so important that you have *him*?"

Cleopatra looked confused momentarily. She was not used to having him turn down an offer of sex. She answered the question. "Your looks and personality are so similar I find myself interested in what other similarities you share."

"A fair point," he agreed with a nod, "but I do not believe that is all you are interested in."

At once, Cleopatra realised she had misjudged him. For too long, Mark Antony had been a slow-witted drunk, but once again she saw the sharp, intelligent schemer she had first come to admire. There was no point in making a denial he would see straight through.

"You are correct. My interest is in vengeance on the seer. I want her to feel the agony of losing that which she holds dear, before she loses her life."

"In all our years together, you have never told me why that is so important. What has she ever done to you?" he asked, with apparently genuine interest.

To Cleopatra, it seemed he finally wanted to know why she hated Melissa. At last she had made progress in her efforts to undermine the only woman she had ever envied. For once, she dropped her guard, eager to please her lover.

"Do you remember the first time we met?"

He nodded again. "You were regal . . . and I was naked."

She smiled at him. "Indeed. That day, your seer told the most wicked of lies. She told me Caesar would murder my son."

He did his best to sound surprised that this was the only reason for her dislike. "And you want her to suffer for that? A lie told fourteen years ago?"

"She did not say Caesar would die," Cleopatra added. "She could have prevented this, but she said nothing."

Mark Antony did not bother to point out her mistake. He knew that Melissa had indeed told Caesar of his impending doom, but that her warning had been ignored.

"Ah, so this is all because of Caesar. It has nothing to do with me and the affection I once had for her?"

Cleopatra remained calm, but her eyes betrayed her true feelings. Her jealousy for what Mark Antony had shared with Melissa bubbled too close to the surface not to be seen. Her tone hardened along with her stare.

"You say affection as if it was nothing of consequence, but I say it is a love you have always felt. Your stubborn loyalty to her memory has come between us too often for me to believe otherwise. You wish to have her again."

He laughed in the way the old Mark Antony used to laugh – as if he was wholeheartedly enjoying a joke. "You say I loved her, I say not. Once I might have felt . . ." he paused, appearing to consider his phrasing carefully, just as he had been rehearsing all night, ". . . a fascination for something that I could not have. Caesar forbade it. I took her because it was forbidden. I gained great pleasure from the experience, but she no longer holds my interest. From the moment I saw your new *pet*, I knew Lissa had duped me as she had Caesar." He stopped laughing and allowed a hint of bitterness to creep into his tone. "For years I held on to the thought I meant something to her. I never have. I was nothing more than a replacement for *him*."

"Then why does this still hold a place next to your heart?" Cleopatra tapped the locket which hung around Mark Antony's neck.

"Habit," he replied dismissively. "I have worn it for so long I simply forgot it was there." He wrapped his hand around the locket and ripped it from his neck, snapping the chain. It had been snapped many times before and he knew it could be mended later.

Cleopatra gasped with delight as he leant over her and dropped it carelessly onto the floor. Foolishly, she believed that to have removed it with such force could only mean he had given up on his longing for the seer at last.

He ran a finger lightly across the top of her breast, following the line of the sheet.

"You have not answered my question. What are your intentions for my younger twin?"

"I have not yet decided," she sighed and lay back against the pillows, ensuring the sheet fell away, exposing her bare breasts.

Mark Antony took his cue. "That is most unlike you. You usually know exactly what you want from a man." He bent his head forwards, allowing his mouth to engulf one nipple as he sucked gently.

"I had thought to kill him and send his body to Octavian," she moaned, enjoying the renewed attention.

He paused and looked up at her face. "Or you could kill me and keep him. I am sure that you have considered a younger man could be more beneficial, in certain areas."

Cleopatra smiled and nodded slightly as she moved her hand to the back of his head to make him continue. "It had occurred to me, but only as a last resort."

To her surprise, he pulled away. "Really? I would have thought that was high on your list of options. First get rid of the old sot and hold a very public funeral – maybe let your priests mummify me and send me back to Rome to be put on display. You could quietly accept Octavian's rule and allow him to believe you were happy to be free of me – the man who 'forced' you to fight a war you did not want. Many months would pass, a year perhaps, and then your rumourmongers would begin to weave their web of lies."

Cleopatra was again confused. She had not known Mark Antony to talk so much and act so little for many a year. She was more used to a direct sexual advance these days, and not a particularly gentle one. She frowned. "What rumours do you speak of?"

It was his turn to lie back against the pillows as he toyed with her again, feigning further lack of interest. "I should imagine a sighting or two to start with, nothing more than the odd glimpse out of the corner of an eye. A citizen of some standing, preferably a Roman, would claim to have seen my ghost – or lemur, as I call it. Gradually, the appearances become more frequent. Perhaps this lemur would even speak. Its message would be plain." He raised his hands in the air for effect, as if giving prayers to a deity. "Mark Antony is Osiris reincarnate. Isis has again raised her husband from the dead." His arms dropped once more. "The repercussions would ripple across the Mediterranean. Every person from here to Armenia would hear of your demonstrable life-giving powers. Once they had seen me appear before them, other rulers would flock to your side with their warriors; most through fear of your unearthly power, some purely because they would welcome another chance to wipe the smile off Octavian's smug, childlike face. You may even win over part of the senate as your army scourged the land on its relentless march north. All would tremble at your feet and at the feet of the impressive army you would by then command. Put a reincarnated Mark Antony at the head of such a tremendous force and even Marcus Agrippa would turn tail and run."

Cleopatra rolled onto her side and propped her head on her arm. This morning was reminiscent of the early days they spent together at Tarsus, when they had sealed their alliance through tough negotiations made from the confines of their bed. It made her realise how much she had longed for this Mark Antony to resurface – a man as driven by his thirst for power and control as she was. He was her true equal and the man she found the most stimulating.

"I admit it is an interesting proposal," she replied, "though I feel it has one fatal flaw."

"Which is?" He looked suitably bemused.

"The young pretender does not have your military skill or tactical flare. I would need both to turn such a plan into a success. Your double would most likely be slaughtered during his first engagement. Better to hide you and sacrifice him to ensure our victory."

Mark Antony grinned. "Aha, we substitute the imposter for me when the moment is right – his death to secure our lives. Is that your suggestion?"

Cleopatra nodded. "It is, but until then I will have my fun at his expense and you will not stop me." She prodded him in the chest.

"You still plan to have him even though he has denied you thus far?" Mark Antony's eyes narrowed.

"I intend to have him *because* he has denied me. No man has ever refused my demands. He must learn his place." She pouted. "And I want that bitch to watch helplessly as I steal another lover from her bed. A parting gift, before I send her onwards to her new master. One of those flesh merchants who sells girls on the streets would provide a good home, if you have no objections."

Mark Antony was angered by the thought of Melissa being forced into prostitution, but he did not let it show. Instead he smiled wickedly. "I have none whatsoever, my love, provided obedience is all you want from this younger man. A minor tryst I will allow, if you swear it is purely for your amusement. If it was his love you wanted, I would slit his throat and be done with him."

When she nodded again he continued, "Then we have reached an accord. As for the seer, I want her spirit broken as she once broke mine. If I can watch the ruination of the bastard who shares my face as well, then I say the sooner the better. For too long I have played her fool."

He rolled onto his side and resumed stroking her arm. "In fact, I may have a way to speed his demise."

"How so? What information do you hold?" Her eyes

flashed with excitement, but he could not tell if it was from the thought of revenge on Melissa or of bedding the young stud that so closely resembled him in his prime.

He waited a few moments before answering her. "His hatred of me is almost as strong as yours is for her. The best way for you to bed him, is to inflame his jealousy. If he believes I am screwing his wife, he will be yours."

Cleopatra's face hardened. "I thought you wanted nothing more to do with her," she snapped, unable to hide her disgust.

"I do not," he lied convincingly, "he merely has to *believe* I have had his wife and he will be yours to command. Allow his suspicions to fester. Let it be known she has been seen in my company. When his jealousy reaches its peak, you may strike. You will have him, whilst she will serve the good men of Alexandria for years to come."

"Or we could offer her up to Octavian as the last of Caesar's assassins."

He shook his head. "She was not involved," he lied, "even if she said nothing to prevent it." He smiled again, as if he had suddenly thought of a way to implicate Melissa in Caesar's murder. "I am sure we can make her sound as guilty as either Brutus or Cassius. Octavian will not know any different. We must not reveal our hand too soon, though. She is our greatest bargaining point and must be kept in reserve, should all else fail. The more she feels I can be trusted, the greater her eventual fall. I will speak with her and listen to her pleas for mercy. I may even walk with her in the gardens, to inflame her husband's jealousy." He winked. "I will make her think I have feelings for her and all the while I will tease the information we need from her lips. We will know everything she sees and she will not suspect a thing, for she will believe I love her. It will destroy her to know she has been taken for a fool, and it will make our victory all the sweeter to watch."

Cleopatra felt elated. The first part of her plan to destroy Caesar's witch had fallen into place: she had regained her husband's love.

She placed her hand on the back of Mark Antony's neck. "On that day we will both have the satisfaction we seek." She leant forwards and kissed him firmly.

Mark Antony's plans were also falling into place. He had gone some of the way to regaining Cleopatra's trust by offering up his love rival. Melissa would be so hurt by the loss of her husband, she would fall willingly into his arms. His son would be dispatched by the queen, allowing him to keep Melissa with him for the rest of his life. All he had left to decide was whether he could live with his conscience for plotting the murder of his eldest son.

He pulled away slightly. "Indeed, we will," he murmured. "You may take her lover from her, but I will take everything else."

Rolling Cleopatra onto her back, he finally slid his body over hers. He closed his eyes as he thrust into her.

And he imagined she was Melissa.

It was early afternoon before Cleopatra woke. She had fallen asleep in her husband's arms following their night and morning.

Mark Antony was gone, which did not surprise her. In the old days he would often slip out of bed before her to plan some grand romantic gesture – a sumptuous breakfast, a fishing trip, or simply to cut a flower for her pillow, like he had today.

She smiled to herself as she looked at the bloom, wondering if he had ever done this for his other wives. Her mind wandered once more to Melissa. How she loathed the woman now a guest in her palace. Although she barely knew her, Cleopatra had always envied Caesar's witch for the influence she held over two of the most powerful men ever to have lived. Both danced to the tune the seer set and, whilst Caesar had been easily persuaded to listen to a different melody, Mark Antony was too besotted to break free. He had belonged to that woman long before he had enjoyed the love of a queen, and, despite the considerable advantages of his present match, he always yearned for the one who got away.

Or so she had thought, up until that very morning when he ripped the harlot's necklace from his throat. That wretched piece of metal had been the cause of so much heartbreak. Over the years, Cleopatra had succeeded in separating him from almost everything that reminded him of his former life, everything that made him Roman, at least. His wives, his houses, his titles and his men were all gone. Only that locket remained as the final connection to the past. It was the one item he had refused to discard. Now it lay on the floor of her suite, abandoned in a moment of clarity.

She leant over the bed, eager to find the trinket and learn what secrets it held. She rummaged through the pile of sheets and clothing discarded by them both, but found nothing. She slipped onto the floor and thrust her arm about beneath the bed, thinking it had been knocked further under, but to no avail.

Like Mark Antony, the locket was gone.

Chapter 20

The heat in Alexandria made exercising in the middle of the day inadvisable. Anthony had not been at the gymnasium that morning, making sure instead that he remained in their suite in order to lavish attention on his wife. It was something he always did when he had been up to no good and guilt got the better of him. And he had good reason to feel guilty for his behaviour of the previous night: Anthony was no saint, but participation in an orgy was a new low, even for him.

Usually, Melissa would see straight through his efforts and know he was covering something up, but her untimely sickness the evening before had disturbed her intuition. It had also given him a genuine excuse to stay at home. By lunchtime though, she had had enough and told him to go out and let her sleep. He had no idea that she too was struggling with her own demons and needed some peace and quiet to think about her latest encounter with Mark Antony.

Anthony wandered through the markets of Alexandria casually on his way to the gym, barely paying attention to any of the stall holders. As he walked, he thought about the previous evening's events, wondering what his father was planning. He knew to expect another confrontation, but not what it would entail or when it would come. He had found the whole conversation confusing, to say the least. Despite their mutual hatred, it felt almost as if his father was offering some form of assistance, just when it was most needed. Could Melissa have been right after all? Did he have an unexpected ally he could rely on? After much deliberation, Anthony decided it was little more than wishful thinking on his part and dismissed the idea.

When he arrived at the gymnasium, he found it almost deserted. Those with any sense were having lunch or enjoying a good massage. Only a few men were there and all of them were simply engaged in stretching exercises before their afternoon's programme began in earnest.

Anthony went to the changing area. Before he had a chance to undress, a man coughed behind him. He spun around to see Canidius.

"We have never been formally introduced," the Roman said, offering his arm in a gesture of friendship.

Anthony smiled politely as he clasped the Roman's wrist. "You are Publius Canidius Crassus."

"I am indeed. I am glad to meet with you under happier circumstances. How was your wife this morning?"

"Well, thank you. I am grateful that you removed her from the banquet while the evening was still young."

Canidius smiled. "I imagine so. I have been at many such gatherings, and I know only too well the pleasures that are on offer, though I do not believe your wife would have found it as enjoyable as the rest of us."

Anthony shook his head. "She would not, and I thank you for your quick thinking."

"I was pleased to be of service, though I was merely the vessel by which her escape was facilitated. It was not my plan and I can take no credit for it."

Anthony gave no reaction. He knew only too well

that Mark Antony was the one responsible for Melissa's removal from the banquet, but he had no intention of acknowledging it.

Canidius pressed on. "The general bid me deliver another message, if I were to see you here."

"What is it?" Anthony replied, suddenly wary. He glanced around, looking for some sign that Cleopatra's men were about. He had become used to their tactics and knew they would be in the shadows, barely visible. Little did he know they had already been dealt with by the ever-vigilant Canidius. Anthony was, for once, very much alone.

Canidius leant closer and spoke quietly. "I am to tell you that your father sends you his best regards." He stepped back.

Anthony could not hide the look of shock on his face. He could not believe that Mark Antony had admitted his parentage to any other man, Roman or not.

Canidius turned away and bent over, as if to retrieve his belongings in the wall niche, but paused as if remembering something else. "There is more. He wanted you to have something."

Unseen by Anthony, Canidius' hand was closing around the hilt of his sword.

Bemused, Anthony fell for the ruse. "What?" he asked, leaning forwards.

Canidius straightened up, ensuring the sword was concealed by his body. He turned his head to gauge the distance between himself and his unsuspecting victim.

"This," he said.

For Anthony, the next few moments passed in slow motion. Although he saw Canidius swing his arm, he failed to anticipate the blow or make any attempt to block it. He only felt the searing pain as Canidius slammed the hilt of the sword into his cheek.

He went down immediately, hard, reeling, but still vaguely aware of what was happening. As he floundered on his hands and knees, he turned his head slowly upwards in time to see the second blow coming.

That blow knocked him out.

"Is he secure?"

Mark Antony was pacing around one of the empty rooms in the Timoneum, waiting for Canidius to finish tying his son to a low backed chair. Anthony remained unconscious and slumped forwards, his ankles already secured against the front legs of the seat.

Canidius ensured his wrists were bound together and then tied to the back before he answered. "As well as I can tie him."

He stood up and pushed Anthony in the chest until his captive was sitting up straighter, his head lolling backwards. "Are you sure you want to do this?" he asked.

"I have no choice," Mark Antony murmured. He paused to pick up a bucket before walking around to face Anthony's prone form. As he swung the bucket to his side, Canidius jumped backwards to avoid being soaked.

The water hit Anthony full in the face. The shock of it woke him immediately. He shook his head and tried to move, turning his head frantically from side to side as he tried to assess his situation. He saw Canidius walking toward an open window.

"Why have you done this?" he shouted. "I demand to know why I am here."

His attention was drawn by the sound of the empty bucket dropping on the floor. Anthony felt his pulse increase as he slowly looked around to see his father standing before him, looking somewhat triumphant.

"You are not in a position to demand anything, except mercy," Mark Antony said menacingly. He pulled a stool forwards and sat down opposite his soaking prisoner. He cracked the knuckles of one hand with the other.

"I hear you frequent our gymnasium on a regular basis. I would have thought you would be kept safely locked in the palace zoo, along with the queen's other pets."

Anthony glared at his father defiantly as he strained against his bonds. "I am no one's pet," he snapped back, unwilling to show the fear he really felt.

"Really? How then do you explain your freedoms, when your wife is little more than an inmate in a prison, albeit a luxurious one?"

"I have given Cleopatra no reason to doubt me. I have proved that I am her loyal subject. My freedoms are a result of that loyalty."

Mark Antony roared with laughter. "Do you hear him, Canidius? He dares call her by name rather than her title. Most men would die for such impudence."

Canidius turned and smiled briefly to acknowledge the remark, but said nothing. He quickly returned his attention to the window where he kept watch for any palace guards coming across the causeway. It would take them a while to work out where Cleopatra's favourite house guest was but, when they did, he expected them to come in force.

"And he speaks of loyalty in a place where the word means nothing. He is either confused or a fool. Which do you think it is, Canidius?"

"I am no fool," Anthony hissed.

Mark Antony returned his attention to his son. "No, you are an Antonius, and that is a far worse thing to be."

For some time, the two men stared at each other. Eventually, Mark Antony barked another question. "Why are you really here?"

"I do not know, ask him." Anthony jerked his head in Canidius' direction. "He is the one who dragged me here."

To his surprise, Mark Antony smiled. "I would learn to control that temper if I were you, my son. This is not your world and you do not understand its rules. If you were any other man, I would have killed you merely for looking at the woman I love, but your filial relationship to me keeps you alive, for now."

Anthony's eyes narrowed. "Which woman are you referring to – my wife or yours?"

Again, he watched his father smile. "He may be more astute than we gave him credit for, Canidius," Mark Antony said in a raised voice, and then, more quietly, he added, "perhaps I mean both."

Anthony strained again, but could not loosen the ropes. "What do you intend to do? Kill me so you can have both our wives in your bed?"

"Or perhaps I was wrong, and he is a bigger fool than I believed him to be." Mark Antony shouted again. He shook his head and sighed as he lowered his voice once more. "If I wanted you dead, Canidius would not have hit you with the hilt of his gladius - he would have used the point. As for your wife, it is my intention to offer her my protection, for she is in grave need of it."

"Protection?" Anthony scoffed. "Is that what you call it? I call it seduction."

Mark Antony pointed at his son as if chastising a small child. "You would be well advised to listen for once. Cleopatra intends to harm her. I am the only one who can keep her safe."

Anthony knew his father to be correct in his assessment of the situation, but he remained defiant. "And who keeps her safe from you? Who will stop you from 'taking' my wife?"

Mark Antony merely smiled.

Again, Anthony strained against the ropes. "If you touch her, I swear I will kill you."

"I would like to see you try," Mark Antony replied, goading his prisoner yet again.

"How dare you, you bastard!" Anthony's wrists were sore, but he did not give up his struggle.

From the window, Canidius made a tutting noise, announcing his disapproval of the way the situation was being handled. Mark Antony acknowledged his officer grudgingly with a nod and another sigh.

He turned his attention back to Anthony and pointed at himself. "How dare I? Those are strong words coming from a man tied to a chair!"

Anthony glared, but said nothing.

"Vitruvius would be proud of your determination in this matter, but not for the rest of your behaviour. He was no lover of Caesar's Egyptian whore, as he used to call her, but he would have cautioned you to take greater care when deciding who to call friend and who to make an enemy in a place like this. He would also have told you that, on occasion, those lines become blurred, though you would no doubt choose to ignore him as you now choose to ignore me."

Anthony swallowed hard as he remembered his godfather. Vitruvius, or Victor, as he knew him, had taken Anthony in when he was a few hours old. He was the only father Anthony had ever known. Victor had often despaired at his godson's wayward behaviour, grumbling that he would one day turn into his father, knowing that ultimately the genetic makeup was simply too strong to deny. He knew his godson to be Mark Antony's son in every way, but he tried hard to instil some sense of right and wrong in his charge. He had always drilled into Anthony the need to assess every situation before rushing headlong to disaster, though Anthony usually paid little attention. For once, Anthony decided it was best to heed that advice.

"What is it you want from me?" he asked, more calmly.

"That is better. If you maintain this new-found civility, perhaps we can get down to business." Mark Antony stood up and began to pace slowly up and down. "Why did you appear through the mists at Actium? Was it by design or an accident, as your wife insists?"

"Why do you have her necklace?" Anthony shot back as he twisted his arms again, more subtly in the hope the move would not be spotted, but he failed.

"You are not in a position to be asking questions. Answer those which you are asked, and I will release you. If not, you will remain here for many hours, straining to free yourself. Your wrists will become raw long before I grow tired of watching you struggle."

Anthony's wrists were already raw. As his brawn was failing him, he had to use his brain. He stopped his struggling and answered the question. "It was by accident. We did not mean to come here."

"And what of your two children - are they safe in your time, or were they abandoned somewhere when I boarded your craft?"

"They were not with us," Anthony replied, noting the specific reference to the number of children. "Did Lissa tell you we have two boys?" he asked.

Mark Antony pulled a battered piece of paper from his tunic. "I have this." He waved the photo in Anthony's face. "Three are shown. The girl is my daughter and the other two my grandsons, though I know the youngest of them to be dead. Lissa is vague on the details of the accident that took him. That is unlike her. I would have expected her to be clear on every detail of his fate."

Anthony looked down at the floor as the terrible memory of Jack's death flooded back. He had been the one who found his little boy's body, almost slashed in two, beside the Rubicon. It was an image that would haunt him for the rest of his life. He could not bring himself to speak of it to anyone, preferring to drink the memory of it away.

"You lied to her. There was no accident, was there?"

Mark Antony's perception surprised Anthony. For a man reported to be a washed-up drunk by this point in his life, his father appeared surprisingly sharp. He nodded his agreement. "It is my belief that someone struck him down, with a sword, most likely a gladius, meaning it was someone from your time rather than mine. His injuries were too severe for our physician to save him. I invented the story of the accident to protect Lissa from the truth." He looked away as he muttered, "I failed her."

"I know what that feels like, Mark Antony sighed. "I too failed to protect her once. Because of me, she was tortured, raped and left for dead. I have never forgiven myself. It is not a mistake that I intend to repeat. I will not allow her to face that kind of danger again."

Anthony raised his head and stared at his father. "Nor will I."

Mark Antony studied the face of the man in front of him. He could see his son's hatred for him, but there was also pain, partly at the loss of the child and partly from the thought of losing Melissa. He found he could empathise with his son for the first time since they had met. Perhaps they could find common ground after all.

"We can agree on one matter, at least. I tell you, Cleopatra will only keep Lissa alive while it suits her purpose. What are you prepared to sacrifice to keep your wife from harm?"

"Whatever it takes."

"Your life?"

Anthony's back straightened. "If I have to, then yes. Would you?"

"Without hesitation."

The two men stared at each other for some time weighing each other up. Suddenly, Mark Antony produced a small knife and walked around behind his prisoner. Anthony's heart pounded in his chest, fearing his throat was about to be slit. He closed his eyes and waited, but nothing happened. Eventually, Mark Antony spoke again.

"As much as it pains me to admit, we each need the other. Cleopatra wants Lissa to suffer, and greatly. I do not want that, and neither do you. Together we may prevail, if we can learn to trust each other. Can you do that?"

Anthony thought for a few moments. He did not trust his father a jot, but it was the only way out of his present situation. "I am willing to try, if you are."

To Anthony's surprise, his father reached down and cut the rope holding his wrists. "Good. We move forward together."

"How do you intend we proceed?" Anthony asked as he rubbed his wrists.

"You must gain Cleopatra's full confidence, something I believe you had already planned to do. Your behaviour

– playing to her vanity, agreeing to her games – it reeks of a level of cunning I have only previously known in one other man."

"Who?"

Mark Antony merely raised an eyebrow.

"Ah," Antony smiled knowingly. His father was talking about himself, of course.

"We must know what the queen's plans are and how she intends to execute them."

"I agree. I have been trying for months to do this, but surely you are better-placed than I am to learn what they are."

"Cleopatra is a woman driven by a need to control everyone and everything around her. She does not like to fail, and she is jealous . . ." he pulled the locket out from under his tunic, taking care not to break its newly-repaired chain. He showed it to Anthony briefly before returning it beneath the material, ". . . of this. She has often tried to take it, though I could never allow it. We both know its contents are too dangerous to fall into the hands of another."

"If you knew it to be so dangerous, why keep it? Why not destroy it?"

"Who can say why any of us act in the ways we do? Perhaps sentimentality drove me to keep this trinket, or perhaps having it allowed me to retain a modicum of control over my destiny – a small reminder of the man I once was. What I do know is this piece of gold has been the cause of many an argument over the years. Cleopatra loathes the very sight of it and, by association, she loathes its previous owner. Lissa's very presence here gnaws at her. It worries her that your wife may succeed where others have failed in reconciling me with Rome. She believes

Lissa's influence over me to be greater than hers."

"And is it?" Anthony's fascination with how much Melissa meant to his father drove him to ask, even though he was unsure if he really wanted to hear the answer.

Mark Antony pondered his response for some moments. Melissa always counselled caution in everything, but he was still a risk-taker. She also told him that Anthony was very much like him in every regard. Whilst the truth could further inflame his son's anger towards him, to lie would destroy the fledgling relationship he needed to build. They did not have to like each other, but some level of mutual respect had to develop if they were to succeed in saving Melissa. In any case, their situation was so dire that there was no point in keeping anything back. He decided to tell his son the whole truth and hope for the best. If the younger man was even half the man Mark Antony hoped he was, the gamble would pay off.

"Cleopatra is correct in her assumption. Once, she demanded I strip Herod of his lands. I refused her, yet if Lissa had asked for such a gift I would have delivered it, and more. If your wife asked me to travel into the underworld and confront Dis herself, I would do it, and willingly too. I would do anything she asked of me. Yet your wife asks for nothing, save for me to spare your life. It is a request I will honour so long as it is within my power to do so."

Anthony was relieved that his death was not imminent, but also embarrassed by his father's declaration. It was one of genuine love, and it was uncomfortable to hear. At the same time, it gave him some comfort that he might at last have found an ally in his efforts to escape. It was not an alliance he would have chosen, but adversity makes for strange bedfellows.

"You think our arrival has given Cleopatra reason to doubt your sincerity?" he finally asked, avoiding the more difficult elements of his father's speech.

Mark Antony shrugged. "Who knows what any woman thinks, or why? Their minds are a like a whirlpool in the ocean – best left alone and only entered at your peril."

Anthony nodded. "You're not wrong there," he murmured absent-mindedly in English as he thought back to past experiences.

Mark Antony smiled and nodded too. He did not have to understand the words – Anthony's facial gestures said it all.

He slammed his hand down on Anthony's shoulder, jolting his son back to the present. "Our queen will stop at nothing to destroy Lissa, or any man who cares for her. That leaves us both in a precarious position."

"What do you suggest we do?"

"Cleopatra's over-confidence is her sole weakness. She is only vulnerable when she believes she is winning. To keep Egypt's sovereign ruler off-guard, we must give her exactly what it is she wants."

"Which is?" Anthony asked the question, but he already knew the answer.

"You. To save your wife, you must fuck mine."

"That prospect holds no interest for me," Anthony lied unconvincingly.

Mark Antony laughed. "Do not try to fool me, boy. You are more than interested."

"What makes you say that?"

"I would be."

"Fair point," Anthony conceded. He had known from their first meeting aboard the *Antonia* that bedding

Cleopatra was a distinct possibility. It did not concern him, provided it gave him what he wanted. And yet he also knew that it was a line he could not cross without losing Melissa.

"I have always known that sex was the price for the freedoms I have been granted, but I have been deliberate in my efforts to frustrate her thus far. I hoped I could get Lissa safely out of the palace if I bartered my body for her freedom."

"Cleopatra will never allow Lissa to leave this palace."

"Then it does not matter whether I fuck her or not, not if there is no way for me to get Lissa out of this city."

"You have a way." Mark Antony smiled. "You have me."

"You expect me to simply hand her over without any concerns for your intentions towards her?"

"You have no choice."

"Yes, I do. I can refuse Cleopatra, and your offer, and remain loyal to my wife."

"Then you will die far sooner than I expected." Mark Antony shook his head. "I have already warned you Cleopatra is not a woman who takes no for an answer. You have refused her at least once that I know of. The next time she offers herself to you, I advise you to say yes. If you do not, she will kill Lissa before your eyes and then have you anyway, as a slave, if nothing else. There will be nothing I can do to prevent it."

Anthony admitted defeat gracefully. "I will do it if I have to, to save Lissa's life, and for no other reason."

His father smiled knowingly. "You make it sound like a chore. Believe me it will not be too much of a hardship."

"Oh, I have a feeling it will be very hard," Anthony replied with a wink.

For a moment, Mark Antony simply stared at his son, and then he roared with laughter at the joke. "Indeed, it will – hard and longstanding. So, are you up for it?"

Anthony looked down at his crutch, "Not yet," he joked again.

Both laughed, sharing a moment of bonding – father and son united in their liking for coarse humour.

"Lissa would be frowning at us if she were here," Mark Antony said, as the laughter subsided. "She finds such base references immature."

"She does," Anthony agreed, as he considered how alike he and his father were. He was beginning to understand that his wife and the man standing before him had shared more than a bed: they had shared a life together. Melissa knew both men equally well. She knew their strengths and failings, how they would both use humour to detract from a serious situation and how they both would love her until the day they died. For a moment, it no longer mattered which of them she would choose, only which of them would live the longest to claim his prize. Anthony knew his father was destined to die on the Kalends of Sextilis: the first of August by the modern-day calendar. There was every possibility a liaison with Cleopatra would bring his own date with death sooner than that.

He became more serious. There was a question he had to know the answer to before he embarked on his mission. "I have to know. Have you already had her?"

Mark Antony made a point of being deliberately obtuse. "Your wife?"

Anthony nodded slowly.

"I had her years ago, boy, as well you know." When Anthony failed to react, Mark Antony sighed, knowing he would not be able to goad his son any longer. It seemed the ability to bury their emotions was another trait they shared.

He stared directly into his son's eyes. "I swear to you on the life of my youngest child, I have not had sexual relations with your wife since your arrival here. I give you my word I will neither force myself upon her, nor will I encourage her attentions in any way."

"You mean this?"

"It is the truth. Listen to it well, for it is a rarity to hear such a thing spoken within the walls of this palace."

Anthony studied his father's face. He could sense no hint of deception from him. "I believe you," he finally said.

"Then I believe we have reached an accord. I will ensure your wife has a way out of this city, and in return, you will keep watch over mine." He extended his arm, offering Anthony a chance to seal their agreement.

"I may lose Lissa if I do this," Anthony replied warily. "She will never forgive me."

"Oh, you would be surprised at what she will be willing to forgive, given enough time and patience." Mark Antony smiled to himself as he remembered some of the appalling behaviour he had managed to get away with over the years he had spent with Melissa in Rome. He had tried to kill her on at least two occasions and forced her to perform degrading sexual acts with other women, purely to amuse him. He had been forgiven, eventually, though he knew this was a little too much information to share in the present circumstances.

"It will be dangerous. If Cleopatra even so much as suspects we are working together, you will not last the night. She will spin the wickedest of lies to ensnare you, but you must see through them. You must convince her of your absolute hatred towards me, and of your disgust that your wife had feelings for another man. You must do all this while staying focused on the only issue that matters, and that is saving Lissa. Can you do that without allowing your true emotions to cloud your judgement?"

Anthony nodded, even though he had his suspicions he was being played in some way. He clasped his father's wrist to seal the deal.

Mark Antony grinned and pulled his son to his feet. He leant forwards and wrapped his other arm around Anthony's back, patting him on the shoulder. "You and I are much the same in every way. If you stay off the wine, and away from loose women, you may do well for yourself."

He pulled away and took hold of Anthony's chin, inspecting the red mark on his cheek. "Now get yourself back to the palace. If you are asked, say you came here to confront me about my intentions towards your wife. Say, I was disinclined to respond. We fought. It will explain the rather handsome bruise you are developing. And remember, Lissa must never hear a word of any of this. She would not approve."

Anthony left, with merely a nod to Canidius, who still felt a little guilty at having knocked out the son of his general, but an order was an order. He would do it again if he had to.

"What do think?" Mark Antony asked Canidius.

"I think he has a chance at gaining Cleopatra's trust, although I am still unsure what you intend the outcome of this to be."

"I have not yet decided that myself. Cleopatra intends to harm Lissa and I will never allow that. I need a suitable distraction, if I am to get her safely out of the palace. He is more than suitable."

"I assumed you wanted Lissa for yourself."

"I do, but Lissa is loyal to him. If I am ever to convince her that her loyalty is misplaced, he must disgrace himself most publicly."

Mark Antony paused as he poured himself a glass of wine before laying out his dilemma for Canidius. "I love Lissa with a passion I have never before known. I swore to kill her husband, if I ever had the chance.

"Then why seek his help? Why not simply kill him?"

"Because I will not be responsible for the death of my son, and he is undoubtedly my son. He shares my looks, as well as my arrogance. He could not be the product of anyone else's loins."

He stared wistfully into the glass as his mind whirred with every possible permutation of the options before him. "I abandoned the boy because it was the best choice for me. I did not care what happened to him, believing he would die. I never expected Vitruvius to claim him, or that he would grow into such a wonderful child. The more time I spent with him, the more I came to regret my decision. And then he was gone." He waved his hand in the air randomly. "Vanished, like that. I have long wished for a chance to make amends for my poor judgement and now I have that chance to redeem myself in his eyes. Lissa asked that I save him and, for that reason, I must – if I can, even if it means losing her forever."

"Then why not tell him this?"

"We need an ally in the palace."

"I thought we had one."

"We need another – one with Cleopatra's ear. She has set her sights on him and you know she will not be easily swayed from a decision. Remember how she schemed to have Plancus paint himself and writhe like an eel before her?"

Canidius nodded. "I do, though I do not think he needed much persuasion."

Mark Antony pointed at the doorway. "My point is she wants that boy. She will not stop until he is ruined. He may as well be useful while he is at it."

"It is a dangerous game you have asked him to play. Do you think he can defend himself, should the need arise?"

"The boy certainly can wrestle, and he has proved a reasonable adversary in a fist fight, but I wonder how he is with a sword?"

"How do you expect to find out?" Canidius asked nervously.

Mark Antony winked as a broad grin spread across his face. Again, he pointed at the door. "Tell him the old man wishes it."

Canidius rolled his eyes to the ceiling, knowing he would have to do it. He ran out of the room, chasing after Anthony, reaching him on the far end of the causeway that joined the Timoneum to the rest of the palace complex.

"You there, wait," he shouted after Anthony.

Anthony half-turned around and acknowledged Canidius warily. "What can I do for you, Canidius?"

"I am hoping there is something I can do for you. Call it an apology for that." He pointed to Anthony's face. "Your wrestling skills are excellent, but you will need more ways to defend yourself in this nest of vipers. How are you with a sword?"

Anthony's jaw set as he remembered the one time he had held a Roman gladius in his hands. "I killed a man once," he replied sombrely.

"And how was it?"

Anthony's silence said it all.

Canidius put his hand on Anthony's shoulder and leant closer. "Your first is always the hardest. It will get easier in time."

He patted Anthony's shoulder and moved away again. "The old man says you must learn to defend yourself adequately, and I must be the one to teach you. Your lessons begin the day after tomorrow. Be at the gymnasium early and we can avoid the worst of the heat."

Chapter 21

Two days later, Anthony entered the gymnasium, ready for his first training session. He found Canidius limbering up in one of the courtyards. Despite being a little older than Anthony, Canidius was in exceptional shape, which was no surprise considering he was a serving general in the Roman army. It made facing him a daunting prospect, even in a training arena.

Canidius acknowledged Anthony's arrival by throwing him a wooden gladius. "We will start with the training swords until you have the basics."

So much for pleasantries, Anthony thought. He half raised the sword and stood in front of his opponent, unsure what to do.

"Get on with it! Attack me!" Canidius barked. His sword hung loosely in his hand at his side.

Anthony raised the sword in front of him and lunged. Canidius stepped to the side, tapping Anthony on the back with his sword as he shot past.

Anthony stumbled, but regained his footing. He turned to face Canidius, who looked serious.

"Again," Canidius shouted.

They repeated the moves a few more times, Anthony varying his attacks each time, but with little effect. Eventually he stopped and bent over, hands on his knees, puffing from the exertion. He was sweating profusely, whereas Canidius looked as fresh as he did when Anthony first arrived.

"Shall I tell you what your mistake is?" Canidius asked as he walked towards his student.

Anthony straightened up. "Which one?" he asked.

Canidius laughed. "You share the old man's sense of humour, I see!" He threw his practice sword from one hand to the other, gauging its weight. "You slash at everything." He raised his arm over his head and brought it round in a large circular motion. "It gives you no power, little control and your aim, well, I have not actually seen you aim as yet, but it will come in time."

Anthony crossed his arms and waited for the demonstration to begin.

"You must learn to thrust like this." Canidius gave a short, sharp stab into the air. "The thrust is controlled. It is powerful. It will penetrate your opponent with devastating results, whereas to slash ..." He brought the sword around in a loop again "... will do less damage by comparison."

"It could take a man's arm off," Anthony countered, trying to sound like he knew what he was talking about.

Canidius stopped swinging his sword and smiled politely. "Indeed, you could, but you are far more likely to strike a glancing blow or miss entirely. It also takes longer to complete the manoeuvre, exposing the entire right side of your body. A slash has its place, but it is the thrust that must be mastered. It needs to become the mainstay of your attack. The thrust comes from the body like a punch does." He stabbed the air again "Whereas to slash only uses the power of the arm."

"What if you get the blade stuck in the other person?" Anthony asked, recalling the day he killed the assassin who had been chasing Melissa.

Canidius walked around to stand next to Anthony. He raised the sword for another demonstration. "First you stab," he stabbed the air, "then twist." He twisted his wrist. "You will loosen the flesh's hold on the blade, as well as maximising the damage you cause."

"Nice," Anthony said with sarcasm, which was lost on Canidius, who only frowned.

"It is not meant to be nice. It is meant to save your life. Now, try again. You must learn to fight before I die of old age. You will be no use to anyone if you do not master this before Octavian arrives."

The sparring continued all morning, with few breaks. Anthony was fit, but he was flagging by the time the sun reached its midday peak and Canidius called a halt to the session.

"That is enough for today. You learn fast. The old man will be pleased with your progress thus far."

"How do you get away with calling him that?"

Canidius looked inquiringly at Anthony as the pair headed into the changing room.

"You call Mark Antony the 'old man'. It surprises me he allows it."

"I would not dare, were it not his suggestion. He does not think it wise to announce his interest in you too widely. And he is adamant that no one in the palace ever hears of your filial relationship to him. It would be dangerous for you if Cleopatra knew the truth of your parentage, or that the two of you had made an alliance."

"I had worked that one out for myself. Our queen is manipulative, untrustworthy and, in all honesty, a danger to be near."

"You are a better judge of character than I gave you credit for."

Anthony shrugged and pulled off his sweaty tunic.

"She has held the throne for twenty years. She has not managed that through being nice. Where I come from, there is a saying - I would not trust her any further than I could throw her – and, believe me, I would not dare to pick her up!"

Canidius thought about Anthony's words for a moment, before removing his own tunic. "I understand the analogy, yet not your behaviour. If you know her to be so untrustworthy, why make such an effort to be in her good graces?"

Anthony waved his arm, gesturing towards the gymnasium. "Why, for this, of course. Pandering to her majesty's vanity gives me many freedoms I would otherwise be without. I need those freedoms to learn about my surroundings."

Canidius nodded in agreement as the pair headed into the baths. "She has granted you far more than most." He fell silent as they mingled with the other bathers.

Once they reached the Caldarium, or hot room, and were again alone, Canidius reopened the conversation. "The queen's interest in you is intriguing," he mused.

Anthony, sitting opposite his sparring partner, laughed loudly. "It is definitely that, but I am not stupid. I know she wants more from me than sex, although I have not yet worked out what it is. I did think she might want to substitute me for Mark Antony, but I believe he is too valuable a bargaining chip to remove. She certainly believes me more malleable than he is, for now, at least, and I know she will dispose of me if my actions do not please her."

"Then you must ensure you do please her, and often. The old man needs you in her confidence if his plan is to succeed. He must know what the queen is up to."

"And what is *that plan*?" Anthony asked with suspicion.

Canidius frowned again. He was unsure what 'that plan' was. Even if he knew, he would not betray his general's confidence to any man.

"It is best that you do not know," he replied simply. "Your ignorance may help keep you alive should the queen's interest in you diminish. Torture loosens every tongue eventually, and Alexandria is home to some of the most skilled torturers I have ever encountered."

Anthony gulped. He did not want to contemplate any sort of torture, so he changed the subject. "Canidius, there is a question I must ask."

"Name it. I will answer if I can."

"Why did you come back? Octavian must have offered you a small fortune to switch sides. You could have been living a comfortable life in Rome."

Canidius paused for some time while he thought back to the discussions he had with Octavian in Macedonia. "I already have wealth and position here in Egypt. Octavian could not improve on that, but I do believe a consulship was mentioned if I was prepared to return to the nest of vipers our fair city has become. Believe me, there are far less dangerous snakes in the palace reptile farm than there are in Rome. The Senate pander to Octavian now but, if they get so much as a hint that he will fail to subdue Egypt, they will rip our young Caesar apart faster than a pack of wolves chasing down a stag."

Canidius sighed and gave a half-laugh. "If I wanted, I could take my belongings and leave even now. Mark Antony has grown more than accustomed to those close to him wanting to save their own skins." He shook his head. "Yet I cannot betray him. I swore an oath, and my word means more to me than any amount of money or position. I returned to Alexandria to stand at my general's side. There was no other reason."

"Why? What is so special about him to engender such loyalty? All I see is a man past his prime and a little worse for drink."

"Ah, but it was not always so. Mark Antony is the hero of Philippi: a military genius. I have watched him turn certain defeat into victory time after time. I have seen him mediate peace treaties between the most hostile adversaries and end up with a better deal for Rome than for either of the concerned parties. I have stood by in awe as he has faced certain death and come out unscathed. He has laughed with me, fought with me, bled for me. If I asked it, he would give his life to save mine and I tell you I will do the same for him. Spend a little time around him. Listen to him. Learn from him. You may yet see the man I have come to admire, and not just a man who slept with your wife."

Anthony's eye twitched at the mention of Melissa's relationship with his father. "And has he?" he inquired.

Canidius shook his head. "I would not tell you even if I knew. I have witnessed the damage palace gossip, most of it untrue, can do to marriages." He pointed across to Anthony. "Believe almost nothing in this land: Cleopatra's retinue will unearth your deepest fears and turn them into reality. They will twist your mind until you come to doubt yourself. Eventually, they will influence your every action until you will have to choose whether to fight to retain your free will, or to simply give in and become another of the queen's slaves."

"Is that what happened to him? Did he just give in?"

"Who? Mark Antony?"

Anthony nodded.

Again, Canidius shook his head. "It is not that simple. If you make a decision in your life, good or bad, it affects few people – yourself, your family, perhaps your friends. If *he* makes a decision, it affects thousands. Only when you are faced with that much responsibility will you understand how difficult it is to make those choices."

"You could say the same of Cleopatra," Anthony countered. "She has an entire country to consider as her family. Its people are all her children, and they all live or die as a result of her actions. She must do what she thinks best for them."

Canidius shrugged. "It is my belief that it is best to be honest with your family. Only then do you develop trust. Our queen does not have the trust of her people. She has their devotion, which is different."

"How so?"

"Devotion is far more dangerous!" He raised his hand. "Let us forget Cleopatra for one moment. When are you going to tell Lissa the truth about your son's death?"

Anthony shook his head. "It would break her heart. I cannot do that to her."

"Better to break her heart than to lose her trust. Secrets have a way of being discovered. You will regret it if you are not the one to tell her."

Anthony frowned. "You think my father will tell her?"

"No, I think you have agreed to embark on a dangerous mission, the outcome of which is uncertain. I always ensure my house is in order before I take on such a task. I advise you to do the same.

Canidius patted Anthony on the shoulder as he passed him, a farewell gesture, meaning he did not want Anthony to follow him. "Let us meet every third day.

We can continue your training, and you can pass on any intelligence you have gleaned." He climbed the steps and headed for the door.

Anthony turned and called after him. "What if I find out something that cannot wait three days?"

"For you to try to contact me could prove dangerous," Canidius mused, rubbing his chin. "If there is an urgent matter, lay a single rose on the bench outside your window at dusk. I will come to you."

Anthony smiled. "Sub rosa," he murmured, half to himself, as he thought about the name of his home back in Italy.

Canidius nodded. "Exactly, though this rose will not need to be hung to keep our secrets."

Chapter 22

Mark Antony read the note again. Written in Cleopatra's hand, it was quite clear in its intentions.

It said simply:

Entertain your seer tonight

"So it begins," he murmured to himself and then, louder to Canidius, he said, "Short and to the point, I see."

"What point? Canidius asked. He had decidedly missed it.

"Cleopatra will wait no longer for her prize and will make her move on our boy tonight. She demands I openly occupy Lissa to give her the opportunity. I would say I am expected to wine her, dine her and then return her to her room at a most inappropriate moment. I have no doubt that our queen intends to mount the husband whilst his wife looks on."

Canidius shook his head. He was an honourable man and his conscience was getting the better of him. "I thought we had agreed to help your son save Lissa."

"We have, and I will honour that agreement in time. For now, we must find out what Cleopatra is up to. I needed to get a man inside, so to speak, and you will recall he was more than willing to volunteer."

"I do not like this," Canidius grumbled. "You already have a man inside the palace."

Mark Antony waved his hand nonchalantly. "Eros has his uses, but they are limited. He will pass on what little he is allowed to hear, but she knows he is loyal to me and no longer trusts him the way she once did. Besides, he is not adept in understanding the nuance of the phrasing. My boy will do better."

"What makes you so sure of that?"

Mark Antony had a look of amazement on his face as he replied. "He is an Antonius. It is in his blood to be a devious bastard."

Canidius folded his arms whilst he carefully considered his response. With the possible exception of the man in front of him, no male member of the Antonii could be described as devious. Most bordered on the incompetent – a bankrupt father, a corrupt uncle in exile, two brothers with questionable military careers - and, so far, Canidius had seen little promise from any of Mark Antony's younger male children here in Egypt either. Each lived in his own cosseted world and appeared lacking in basic common sense.

Canidius decided it was best not to mention any of this and plumped for a less inflammatory reply. "You hardly know him. He may be a disappointment."

Mark Antony drew himself up to his full height, taking in a deep breath. "I know Lissa," he replied decidedly. "She has faith in him and that is good enough for me. He will do exactly what is expected, if for no other reason than to satisfy his own curiosity."

He tore the papyrus into pieces as he spoke. "Send word to Lissa to formally request her company. I will entertain her because it suits me to keep to my side of the arrangement with Cleopatra."

"I will do as you have asked," Canidius replied

pointedly, "when you tell me whose *'side'* we are on?"

The answer came as a solitary word, delivered without emotion.

"Mine."

Chapter 23

Melissa had no idea where she was. She lost track of her direction in all of the twists and turns they had taken. Hidden away behind the curtains of a hired litter, she could see very little, but her instructions were clear: she was not to make any attempt to speak or to look outside, unless instructed by Canidius. The one time she did try to open the curtains slightly Canidius slapped her hand away with an accusatory grunt from outside.

She knew they were in still in the city, but had no idea how far they had travelled from the palace. For all she knew, they had gone around in a large circle and were right back where they started. In fact, they very nearly were. Canidius had to ensure none of Cleopatra's minions followed them and had taken so many turns and doubled back so many times, there was little chance even he would be able to retrace his steps.

The litter stopped with a jolt. Canidius drew the curtain back hurriedly and pointed to a small gate in a wall.

"Quickly," he whispered, and Melissa dutifully jumped out as he dismissed the litter.

She found herself in the corner of a small courtyard. Its high walls kept the worst of the sun at bay and provided much needed shade for a variety of pots filled with aromatic herbs. Directly opposite her were three steps leading up to a rather unassuming doorway.

"Back door," Canidius said, almost apologetically. "Mark Antony will join us shortly. He will arrive via a different route."

Melissa was in no doubt that Mark Antony would make a far grander entrance through the front door. Although he was more than capable of subterfuge, she believed the once cunning fox was now too accustomed to the pomp of royal living to use such techniques. She sat on the bottom step, believing they would be left in the courtyard until his arrival had been announced.

As they waited for the door to open, the slightest noise from the alley made Canidius jump. Wearing only a plain tunic and bereft of his sword, in order to blend in with the average Alexandrians, he felt naked and defenceless. The dagger in his belt did little to allay his fears. His military training told him the unfamiliar byways of Alexandria were no place to be wandering unarmed and with an attractive woman in tow. Pimps and thieves were known to operate in these quiet streets by night. Their scouts could well be operating during the day, waiting to spot an easy victim that took a wrong turn and ended up trapped down a dead end. This small courtyard, with no cover and a bolted door at his back, certainly felt like a dead end. He moved back to the gate, taking up the only defensive position there was: behind it.

After a few minutes the gate opened again and a hooded figure slid inside.

Melissa gasped, her eyes widening in fright.

Canidius tensed. He drew the dagger and had it at the figure's ribs in an instant, jabbing slightly until the figure raised his arms in submission.

A familiar voice boomed out from beneath the hood.

"There was a time when I would have had that dagger out of your hand and in your throat before you had chance to draw breath, my friend."

Canidius relaxed immediately. "I expected you to come that way." He pointed to the door behind Melissa with the dagger, before tucking it back in his belt.

"As did I," Melissa echoed the sentiment as she rose from her seated position, her heart still pounding in her chest.

"Change of plan," Mark Antony replied nonchalantly, dropping his hood. "I decided it better to follow your lead, but my litter bearers lost you some time ago. Using legionaries for duties they are unaccustomed to is never a good idea."

"That is why I hired professionals," Canidius said with a wry smile. "At least I know we have not been followed by the palace guard – not if you lost me."

Mark Antony gave a brief nod. "Indeed." He pointed at the door. "Shall we? Sosigines abhors tardiness in his guests."

"*The* Sosigines? Astronomer to the court of the Ptolemies and the man responsible for giving Caesar the calendar we now use?" Melissa exclaimed.

Mark Antony grinned. "I am pleased you have heard of him. It is good to know a man of such talents has made an appearance in your history books."

Melissa looked nervously at Canidius for any sign that he had picked up on the reference Mark Antony had made. He had, but he seemed to be taking it all in his stride.

"I was told earlier," he said with a shrug, in answer to Melissa's unspoken question.

When he had first been told the full story, Canidius

believed his commanding officer had completely lost his mind but, the more he thought about it, the more the story rang true. Ventidius had spent many hours regaling tales of the sudden appearance (and disappearance) of this woman, of how it was impossible to find her, and of how she would always come to Mark Antony in his most desperate hour of need. He had detailed Melissa's uncannily accurate predictions and advised that she should be given assistance if she ever appeared again. It also explained how a man in his early fifties could have a son so close to his own age. Canidius decided to follow his commander's lead and go along with this crazy suggestion, wherever it took them. Whatever happened, it was a better option than throwing in with either the deceitful queen of Egypt, or the manipulative young Caesar-in-waiting.

Melissa glared at Mark Antony. "Is there anyone you have not told?"

He put his hand to his chin as he pretended to think. "Ah, yes," he announced suddenly, "I did not tell that street vendor two roads over. I will remember to do so, on the return journey."

Melissa scowled, but he ignored her, turning her around and nudging her up the steps to the door. He leant around her and rapped twice, then twice more after a short pause.

As they waited for an answer, he whispered in her ear, "I would trust Canidius with my life, as should you. He had to know the truth if he is to lay down his life to get you home."

"Home!" Melissa gasped. She tried to turn around, but he grabbed both her arms to stop her. This was not the time for an emotional debate.

Mark Antony was trying to keep his options open. So far, he had sent word to Octavian that he would retire to Greece, if it meant Cleopatra could keep her throne. He had agreed to help Cleopatra destroy Melissa and use her husband – his son – to dupe Octavian. He had told that same son he would help save Melissa from Cleopatra. Now, he planned to convince Melissa that he intended to send her home. It was no wonder Canidius was unsure whose side they were actually on.

The truth of the matter was, he had yet to decide himself. He needed to be in possession of all the facts. As much as he wanted Melissa, he knew the longer she stayed, the more danger she was in. Cleopatra, driven by jealousy, wanted her rival dead. He could only protect her so long as he was alive and he knew his Egyptian lover well enough to know that her primary concern was her throne. If his death allowed Cleopatra to secure her position, she would not hesitate to give him up. At that point, Melissa too would die. And then there was the husband: his eldest son. He might yet be the answer to every problem, if he could be persuaded to take his father's place as regent to the queen. Mark Antony knew he could easily persuade the younger man into sacrificing himself to save his wife, but something was nagging at his conscience and preventing him from doing it. Melissa always told him to be a better man and to do the right thing, and the right thing was to let her, and his son, go. He had done this twice before, each time for the greater good of Rome. Could he do it again for the greater good of a family he had never even met? He had to know if sending her home was even a possibility before deciding which course to follow. He could not afford to let his heart rule his head, not yet.

At that moment, they heard the grating sound of the bolts on the door being slid back. The door was opened by a frail, elderly Egyptian, but this man was no slave. He wore an expensive embroidered tunic and his eyes were heavy with kohl.

"Welcome, welcome," he said with genuine jollity. "It is so nice to see all of you, please do come in."

Melissa and her Roman escorts entered the astronomer's home via a narrow corridor next to the kitchen.

"I apologise for bringing you this way," Sosigenes said to Melissa as they passed by the kitchens, "General Antony was most insistent that your visit be kept secret. Imagine my surprise when he told me I would be entertaining Caesar's infamous seer. I was sorry not to make your acquaintance when I visited Rome. I have always wanted to discover how you can know . . ."

The old man kept talking as they entered a larger room in the main house. Melissa gasped at the sight before her. Every wall was covered from floor to ceiling with shelves laden with scrolls and bound tablets. It was the last thing she expected to see in a house in this period in time, and it instantly reminded her of her own library in her villa in Italy. She stifled a small sob. For the first time since her arrival in Alexandria, she was in a place that made her feel at ease.

Sosigenes clasped his hands in front of him and nodded knowingly. "Every true scientist appreciates a good library, though I admit I was a little surprised to hear that a seer was a lover of the written word." He looked up at the shelves with pride. "Mine is an outstanding personal collection. One of the perks of being astronomer to the house of Ptolemy was to have my pick of the many texts that were superfluous to the collection of the library – duplicates and the like, many courtesy of our generous benefactor here." He gave a nod of appreciation to Mark Antony, who had gifted the library at Pergamum to Cleopatra's collection some years earlier.

Mark Antony merely gave a nonchalant wave of his hand in reply as he headed towards a side table with a wine flask and glasses on it.

The astronomer returned his attention to Melissa. "I have a complete history of Egypt's pharaohs, Upper and Lower Kingdoms, of course, all five books of the Jewish Torah, the Babylonian epic of Gilgamesh, the works of Sophocles, Plato and Homer, every play entered in the Dionysia festivals in Athens and, naturally, a great number of maps of both the skies and of the world as we know it today, though I am sure you will tell me there is more to be discovered."

Melissa merely smiled as she sat down on a sofa. She had no intention of saying anything that would confirm those suspicions.

Sosigenes studied her face for a moment and then smiled himself. "I knew it," he said emphatically. "The world we know is but a portion of that which exists. There must be many more cultures we have yet to encounter."

Melissa tried not to react, still hoping to keep her knowledge of geography under wraps, but the old man simply laughed.

"My dear, there is far more to be learnt from what you do not say than from what you do. It is always the case in any situation. Had Caesar realised this, he would most probably have lived a little longer."

At last Melissa spoke. "Perhaps he did know. He was not a well man. His seizures were increasing with age. Perhaps he had simply had enough."

Sosigines rocked with laughter. "Oh, what a delight! Here is a woman who is unafraid to speak her mind or to debate such sensitive issues as the health of a tyrant. I can see why you are so enamoured with her, Mark Antony."

Mark Antony said nothing as he handed Melissa a glass. She took it graciously. He turned around and walked over to Canidius, who had taken up position by the doorway.

"Relax. There is nothing to fear in this house," he said, offering his colleague a glass.

"No, there is not," Sosigenes agreed, as he shuffled over to Canidius. "I have dismissed my servants. We are quite alone and safe from prying eyes and ears."

He prodded Canidius in the chest. "Do you know how I managed to keep my position in service to three Ptolemies? By knowing when to keep my mouth shut, that is how." Taking his elbow, Sosigenes guided the anxious Roman to another sofa.

Canidius sat down uneasily and took the wine glass he was offered. Despite the assurances of the astronomer, he found his eyes wandering to the door.

Sosigenes sat at his desk and refused the wine offered by Mark Antony. "Thank you, but at my age a little wine takes a large toll and I need to keep a clear head for my visitor." He turned his attention back to Melissa. "Now, my dear, I understand you are a little lost and need some assistance to find your path home."

Melissa looked nervously at Mark Antony, who had joined her on the couch. He squeezed her hand but said nothing.

Sosigenes was poring over a map of the Mediterranean laid out on his desk. "And where is it you call home, my dear?"

Melissa stared at Mark Antony and shook her head. She could not tell the truth. Sensing her dilemma, he gave the answer on her behalf.

"It is not so much a question of where Lissa comes from, as when."

Sosigenes raised his head slowly, fixing Mark Antony with a piercing gaze. "Are you trying to suggest this lady is not of our time?"

"I suggest nothing. I tell you it is fact."

Sosigenes' gaze shifted to Canidius. "And you can confirm this assertion?"

Canidius shrugged. "I can neither confirm nor deny it. I have been told Lissa is not of this time and that she has a gift unequalled even by the Oracle of Delphi. I have been told this by more than one man for whom I have the greatest respect. For this reason, I am willing to consider the possibility."

Sosigenes turned to Mark Antony again. "And what evidence do you provide that the lady moves through time?"

Melissa found her voice. "Perhaps I should . . ." she began, but was immediately silenced by Mark Antony's statement.

"It was told to me by Publius Ventidius Bassus, a man known for his honesty and trustworthiness, who witnessed the event more than twelve years ago. I have since had the good fortune to witness it myself – at Actium. I have the vessel she arrived on, which holds many wondrous inventions, and I have the physical evidence of a child who travelled with her. Antonius, or Anthony as she calls him, was but four years old when last I saw him. That was in the year of Caesar's death. More than thirty years separated us in age at that time. Now he is but ten years my junior."

"Nine, to be precise," Melissa said with sarcasm.

"Is that why you married him?" Mark Antony shot back.

"Please, no bickering." Sosigenes interrupted before any fight could begin. "I am a man of science and I must have the facts. I will hear from you last, my dear."

Melissa bit her lip as all eyes returned to Mark Antony. "Her predictions are too precise to be the work of any seer." He lounged back against the cushions as he began to explain his rationale. "Seers, augurs, oracles – they all peddle the same tricks. They examine the entrails of some dead animal, scare some birds and note the direction of flight, or take some powders to enable them to reach a trance-like state. They make wild claims which are interpreted by their benefactors in the way that best meets their present needs. Having held the position of augur, I can speak with some authority of how this sham works. And it is a sham . . ." he pointed at Melissa, as if telling her off for some misdemeanour, in the same way a father would a child ". . . designed to fleece the desperate. Those of us in such a position profit well from it."

"All seers are liars who have no interest save for the money they are given. Is this what you are saying?" Sosigenes folded his hands as he posed the question.

Mark Antony turned his attention to the older man. "In the main, I would say yes. Lissa is different. Her predictions are precise, not vague. She could recount Caesar's battle plans verbatim before he had set his mind to them, and mine, come to think of it."

"Anything else?"

Mark Antony stared into his wine glass for a moment. "There is an account of the battle of Forum Gallorum. It is the official record as dictated by me, except I did not give it. She did. And she gave such accuracy of events she had not witnessed, it made my blood run cold to hear."

Sosigenes finally looked at Melissa. "And how were you able to achieve this, if you did not see it in a vision?"

Melissa sighed. "I read it in a history book, that and everything I told Caesar. Mark Antony is correct in his assertions. You, Canidius, Cleopatra – all died many years before I was born."

"How many years exactly?" the astronomer asked.

Melissa paused, only to be elbowed by a less than patient Mark Antony. "Two thousand," she replied in a near whisper.

Canidius nearly choked on his wine, breaking the tension that was developing.

Unperturbed, Sosigenes continued his questioning. "I see. And we are all famous enough to be in your history books?"

Melissa nodded.

The astronomer sat back and placed his hands in his lap. "Then I believe you must tell us what history has in store for us."

"You are the man responsible for providing the world with a more accurate calendar with each year containing three hundred and sixty five and one quarter days. Even though we know it as the Julian calendar after Caesar, your name is credited as the Alexandrian astronomer who provided it."

"This much I know," Sosigenes muttered. "Tell me something I do not."

Melissa shook her head. "I cannot. It may change the course of my history if I do."

"How do you know that? It could change the course of your history if you do not. Answer me this – did Caesar follow his own path, decided by his own mind, or did he follow the one you laid out for him?"

"Which came first – the chicken or the egg?" Melissa muttered to herself in English. Hers had always been a paradox of similar scale. Was she merely witnessing history being made, or had she been responsible for charting its eventual course.

"I do not know," she finally replied, in Latin. "I have always believed the Fates would not allow me to change the course of history. Every time I tried, I failed."

Sosigenes shook his head. "If the Fates alone dictate our path, they would not grant you the right to decide what is to be told and what is best left unsaid. What will be, will be, regardless of any words you have spoken. Also, I believe you have little to lose with such a powerful benefactor at your side, unless, of course, you intend to predict his death."

Melissa stared into her wine glass, but said nothing.

"I see," Sosigenes remarked. His gaze flicked to Mark Antony, who merely shrugged.

"I already know it to be the case," he sighed as he raised his glass to his lips again.

"How?" Melissa gasped. Even Canidius sat up a little straighter.

Mark Antony swallowed his glass of wine whole. "As our host said, it is not so much what you do say as what you do not. Octavian is coming. He ignores my letters. You offer no counsel, yet beg to leave at every turn. Even a dim-witted fool could predict that outcome."

"Oh," Melissa's gaze dropped to her wine glass again.

Mark Antony placed a fingertip on her chin and gently lifted it until he was staring into her eyes. "My death is of no consequence. If Dis calls me, I will not run. I have accepted this. It cannot be changed any more for me than it could for my friend Curio, or for Caesar. You taught me this. My only concern now is for those around me. If I can save the life of one person I care for, I will die happy. We cannot benefit from silence, only from knowledge." He moved closer and whispered in her ear, "Help me to help you live."

Melissa blinked a tear away and nodded. Taking a gulp of wine, she waited for Mark Antony to sit back and then she began.

"Octavian will come once spring is in full bloom, not because he waits for Agrippa's return from Rome, but because he is content to linger in benign winter quarters, where his men are well catered for, and the dry climate is beneficial to his health."

"Herod." Mark Antony and Canidius spoke together and then grinned at each other.

"What is that fool doing?" Canidius' question was aimed at his commander, who was busy refilling his glass. "Delaying Octavian could give us time to regroup and mount an offensive. Surely Herod knows this?"

"Of course he does." Mark Antony replied with a chuckle. "Herod is not one to miss an opportunity. Why else do you think I supported his claim for kingship?"

"I assumed he paid you," Melissa threw in.

"You really think that little of me?" Mark Antony feigned surprise before continuing. "An independent Judea is vital to stability in the region. Herod knows this as well as I. He will do nothing to endanger his throne. He offers Octavian hospitality, but waits for Cleopatra's envoys to come knocking. He wants to know what price, if any, she will put on the head of my former brother-in-law." He turned back to Melissa, adding sarcastically, "and if he did offer some form of monetary gift, it would have been inappropriate for me to refuse his generosity."

Canidius shook his head at the bickering pair, wondering how they had ever maintained a loving relationship. He guided the conversation back to the Judean king. "Herod will wait a very long time. Cleopatra will never pay him a penny. She loathes him even more than Octavian."

Mark Antony shrugged. "Herod and Cleopatra are far too alike to form an alliance. It is a shame. We could do with a man of his talents."

"Herod is a homicidal maniac with a tendency to kill off members of his family!" Melissa interjected once more.

Mark Antony looked at Melissa quizzically. "How do you know so much about Herod? I thought your interest in your 'past' was restricted to Roman matters? No Roman document I am aware of gives such a detailed account of Herod or his 'tendencies'. To do so would be. . ." Mark Antony smiled as he chose his words carefully " . . . inappropriate, to say the least."

"Nicolaus of Damascus," Melissa replied softly.

"Nicolaus? The man who is tutor to my children?"

"Yes," she nodded. "When the house of Ptolemy falls, he will look for a new position. Herod will be most obliging. In return, Nicolaus will document Herod's memoirs, including a full account of Cleopatra's attempts to seduce Judea's king, although I am less certain that she was the one doing the seducing. She was, in fact, pregnant with your son at the time it is supposed to have occurred."

Mark Antony winked at her and patted her leg. "As I said, Herod and Cleopatra are very much alike. Murder and sex are never far from their minds - though not necessarily in that order."

Sosigenes raised a finger as he offered support for Mark Antony's statement. "I have witnessed many deaths in the scramble for power in the house of Ptolemy. Few of them have been attributed to natural causes."

Melissa returned to her speech. "Octavian will not wait for the return of Marcus Agrippa because he has no need to. He will come by land and sea, arriving on the borders of Egypt in the month of Julius. Any envoys sent by Cleopatra, or by you, will be entertained, though no firm answer will be given to their requests. The young Caesar has no need to broker deals. He waits to see which of you will betray the other as panic ensues."

Mark Antony laughed. "I think we all know the answer to that question."

"Whatever deal is struck, it will not be honoured. Octavian wants you dead and to see Egypt's queen paraded through the streets of Rome in chains, to be spat at and vilified by the plebeians, whose adoration you still hold. Alexandria will fall and with the death of Mark Antony comes the death of the Roman ideal of Republic. Octavian will achieve his goal."

"Which is?" Canidius asked the question.

And Mark Antony answered. "What he has wanted from the start. Sole rule of Rome and her provinces. He will no doubt be declared king in time."

"Imperator," Melissa corrected.

"Same thing," Mark Antony stated with a dismissive wave of his hand.

"It is not and you know it," Melissa replied emphatically. "Rome will not tolerate the idea of kingship."

"Then this is our chance," Canidius sat forwards as an idea came to him. "We must get word to our remaining allies that he has declared himself king. Rome will turn."

"We are surrounded, with no way to get that message out." Mark Antony reminded Canidius calmly. "Octavian bought Pinarius and his legions with the promise of gold he does not have. Pinarius was my last hope."

"Rubbish!" Melissa exclaimed. "Pinarius was never any hope. He is Octavian's cousin."

"I did not know that," Mark Antony's brow furrowed as he wondered how he had missed that particular fact. It was a careless mistake, but one that could not be rectified.

"Well, you should have," Melissa sighed, with frustration. "Yet it is irrelevant. Any Roman proclaiming himself king would be ripped to shreds by the mob. Octavian knows this and has made sure he has enough independent witnesses to say he has no desire for kingship. He is rather fond of his head being firmly above his shoulders."

"As are we all," Sosigenes tapped his hand on the table to regain everyone's attention. The conversation was getting off track. "Please continue, madam, with your 'history' lesson," he requested.

Melissa nodded. "The reign of the Ptolemies will come to a savage end. The last of the pharaohs will be tricked into a misguided surrender; Caesarion will be led like a lamb to the slaughter."

"That boy is dim. He has never has shown the astuteness of his mother, or his father, come to think of it," Sosigenes said with a sigh.

"You once told Cleopatra he would die by Caesar's hand, although you neglected to specify which Caesar would wield the knife," Mark Antony said with another wink.

Melissa ignored him. "Cleopatra will send your children to safety in Thebes, but her efforts will be wasted.

Octavian will take them hostage, thereby forcing her to submit to his demands. Broken and defeated, Egypt's queen will take her own life, leaving her beloved country to suffer at the hands of Rome for centuries to come - her riches pillaged to honour Octavian's bribes."

She turned towards Canidius. "Those who refuse him will pay the ultimate price."

Canidius nodded. When he had refused Octavian's money, he knew he had signed his own death warrant: Melissa was merely confirming the fact.

"What is the fate of the children?" Mark Antony asked. "What has Octavian planned for their demise?" He leaned forwards. Resting his elbows on his knees, he stared at the ground, dreading the worst.

Melissa did not know. Selene would eventually be married off to King Juba of Mauretania, but it was assumed both boys died in childhood. She decided to limit her account to the recorded facts. "They will be taken to Rome where they will find a most generous, if unexpected benefactor, who will raise them, as if they were her own."

Relief spread through Mark Antony and he closed his eyes to prevent any emotion from showing. "Octavia," he murmured.

Melissa nodded, though he did not see it.

"She always did have a soft spot for a hopeless cause," he said with a false laugh, but Melissa could hear him struggling to make the joke.

"She is not the only one," she said quietly. Briefly she brushed her hand against his thigh, offering him a little support.

"And what happens to you?" Sosigenes asked. He found he rather liked this unconventional woman and was interested to know her fate.

"I have no idea," she said, with honesty. "I have no role to play in history as I know it. I do not know my fate." She moved her hand to Mark Antony's back and leaned closer to him. "If I am destined to remain in Alexandria I pray the same blade that takes your life takes mine."

He knew immediately what she meant. He was destined to kill himself and was asking him to kill her first. He looked at her and gave a brief nod, though he knew in his heart he could never do it. He loved her too much ever to hurt her again.

He sat up suddenly. "It will not come to that. You have my word on it," he boomed and turned to Sosigenes. "Well, man, say what you think now you have heard her for yourself."

"I think I must hear more about how you came to the past before I pass comment," the astronomer said directly to Melissa. He could tell she did not relish a life spent under Octavian, and for that he could not blame her.

She shrugged. "There is little I can tell you that will help. There is a mist that rises over the water. It is eerily quiet before it comes, as if there is nothing else alive. You feel as if you are being watched. It is so unnerving it makes the hairs on the back of your neck stand on end."

Sosigenes nodded. "I am familiar with the feeling you describe. What else?"

"It is always hot. Then the temperature drops suddenly with the arrival of the mist, so much so you can see your breath form in front of you."

"And the smell, do not forget that," Mark Antony interjected making everyone look at him in surprise. "It smells musty, like the smell of a dirt floor in a damp hut." He glanced at Melissa. "Ventidius' description of your departure was most precise, though it was harder to spot these signs amidst the smoke from the burning hulls at Actium."

"Ah," she murmured in understanding.

The room went quiet for a few moments as Sosigenes muttered away to himself, repeating key words from the descriptions given. Suddenly, he stood up. "I believe your mists to be a physical manifestation of an emotional need," he stated emphatically.

Mark Antony agreed. "That was what the philosophers in Athens said, though their theories on the mechanics proved unsound."

Both Melissa and Canidius stared at him in disbelief.

"You already knew of this?" Canidius asked.

Mark Antony nodded.

"Then you tried to summon these mists before?" Canidius looked dumbstruck at his commander's revelation.

Again, Mark Antony nodded.

Canidius folded his arms and frowned. He looked like a father about to chastise his child. "For what purpose?" he demanded.

Mark Antony turned his gaze to Melissa, but did not speak. He did not need to.

"To find me," she whispered.

"The thought occurred to me on many occasions," Mark Antony finally said. "I set the best minds in Athens on the task. It was their belief that I wished to conjure Caesar's lemur. I allowed them to work towards this misplaced assumption."

"What was their theory? How did they suggest you try to contact Lissa, or Caesar, for that matter? If you tell me their ideas, perhaps I can identify their mistake." Sosigenes was now flitting up and down his bookshelves, pulling out scrolls to glance at their titles, before thrusting them back with disapproval. "Damn slaves – never file a thing properly," he muttered as he searched.

Mark Antony sighed. "What is the point in that? She is here through her own doing."

"I believe your intention is to send her home," Sosigines muttered, still digging through the scrolls.

"A fair point, well made," Mark Antony replied, and began to explain what little he knew. "I set the academics in Athens a challenge. Can a mist that forms over water under extraordinary circumstances act as a bridge between two people? After many months they came to me with an unexpected answer. They believed that a traumatic experience could force a person's soul to cry out silently to the gods. The gods would only answer if the suffering was great enough on both sides. Only then could the two parties be drawn together to make some kind of bond, though they felt it could only be in a non-corporeal form. They surmised the water of the river would be sucked upwards as a physical representation of the person's psyche. They went so far as to imply you could converse with it, but they would not entertain the idea that it could make a person flesh and bone, despite my encouragement to think more laterally."

"Ah, here it is," Sosigenes finally found the scroll he was looking for. He opened it, discarding the cord that had tied it onto his desk. He scanned the words it contained at speed.

"An emotional upheaval in a life has been known to cause unusual summoning activity. It is as if the soul in pain called forth and manifested what it needed to heal itself." He stopped reading and looked up. "Is that what you tried to do, General Antony?"

Mark Antony hesitated as his eyes flicked from Melissa to Canidius and back again. Eventually, he gave a nod. "Yes, though without success. The mists appeared at Leuke Kome, but Lissa did not. Not until they formed at Actium."

"Then the theory is sound," the astronomer declared, "it is merely the application that was in error. We must look to establish the differences between successful and failed transmogrifications."

"The difference of what to . . . what?" Canidius looked perplexed. "You are losing me."

Sosigines glanced at Melissa, who was deep in thought. "But not the lady, I believe."

Melissa brimmed with excitement as she spoke. "In my time, eminent scientists have theorised that space and time should be considered in relation to one another." She could barely believe she was discussing Einstein's theories with an Egyptian astronomer and two members of the Roman Senate. Picking up the discarded cord from the scroll, she pulled it taut in front of her, using it to demonstrate the theory. "It has been suggested that both can be bent, allowing two distant points to be joined." She took the two ends and put them together, forming a loop. "If the theory is sound, time briefly becomes irrelevant."

"Interesting." Sosigenes smiled in admiration. "You need two variables to meet to make this theory work." He pointed at the two ends of the cord and then looked at Mark Antony. "It is my belief your previous attempt failed because it had only one of the required variables, thus preventing Lissa's appearance. We must establish what the other was and why it was absent."

"Me!" Melissa suddenly cried. "What if I was the missing variable? The White Village, or Leuke Kome as you call it, is in Syria. I have never been there. My husband went and I was supposed to join him, but I became ill. I did not go. Perhaps a link can only be made if both parties have been in the same place, no matter when in time it was. I could not answer the call if I had never been there to receive it."

Sosigenes nodded as he considered Melissa's logic. Taking the cord from her, he repeated her earlier demonstration. "If both parties occupy the same space, for a brief moment, time becomes irrelevant. A temporary bridge is built to span the divide and join the two souls in need."

Mark Antony shook his head in disagreement. "The first time you came to me, I did not call for you. I did not know you existed."

"Someone did," Sosigenes interjected. "Both of you must tell me what happened on each of the occasions this has occurred. Be precise. Do not leave out any detail that may be important. Let us test your theory, Lissa."

Melissa thought back to the first time she had travelled to the past. "I had argued with my husband. I was sitting beside the Rubicon, thinking about Caesar and how he once made a difficult decision on the very same spot. The next day I was transported to the past, and to Caesar, on the day you and Curio arrived at his camp."

A look of realisation spread over Mark Antony's face. "Caesar told me he had been walking beside the Rubicon the night before I arrived, considering his options. He thought he saw something – an odd mist that took human form, but he dismissed it as being nothing more than his imagination. He chose to give in to the senate's demands to surrender to them. He asked the god Mercury to send him a sign if there was an alternate path for him to take. He believed you were sent to dissuade him, and it worked."

"And on the second occasion? What happened then?" Sosigenes asked, encouraging the debate to continue.

Mark Antony answered first. "I had come to the farm to look for you and was told you were dead. I was mourning your loss. I begged the gods for a chance to hold you one last time."

Melissa smiled. "I was thinking about the necklace you gave me. Vitruvius buried it and we were trying to find it, but could not. As much as I pretended it did not matter that it was lost, it upset me. It made me sad to think I would never see it, or you, again."

"And at Actium – what happened there?" Again the astronomer pushed for information, his excitement growing as each new fact added another piece to the puzzle.

"The night before the battle, I had to decide which of my forces to lead, the army or my navy." Unconsciously, Mark Antony's hand moved to the locket hanging at his neck.

Canidius recognised the movement immediately. He had seen his commander perform it so many times before, but never realised the significance until now. "You were thinking about Lissa," he stated.

"I was. I would have given anything to have heard her opinion at that time."

"And you, Lissa? Were you thinking about Mark Antony?" Canidius may have been slow to understand at the beginning, but his disciplined military mind could see the pattern developing as clearly as Sosigenes had.

Melissa fell silent and looked away. She did not want to think about what she had been doing that day.

"Lissa? Tell us please." Canidius pressed her gently to answer.

"I was thinking about my son," her voice faltered as the tears welled and her emotions took hold.

Mark Antony took her hand in his. "Do not speak of it. It is too painful for you."

Sosigenes re-entered the debate. "I insist she must answer if we are to prove our theory."

"If I say she does not have to, then she will NOT!" Mark Antony exploded. He stood up suddenly and positioned himself in front of Melissa as if protecting her. His hand rested on the hilt of the dagger tucked in his waistband menacingly.

Canidius and Sosigenes both stared at him in surprise. The Mark Antony they knew was generous, jovial and not unused to showing his affections, but they had never before witnessed him defend anyone so zealously.

From behind him, Melissa placed her hand on his arm. "I will answer," she soothed. She had seen him react in this way before, and knew the result could be dangerous if not managed carefully.

She waited until he resumed his seat. "We had moored in the bay overnight. I was thinking about my son. He died." She gave the clarification for Sosigenes, who nodded his understanding. "I blamed my husband for his loss." Her nerves got the better of her suddenly and she leant against Mark Antony for support. "I thought if he were your son, the accident would never have happened. In that moment, I wished I had stayed with you."

Canidius' expression changed to one of shock. Melissa still had no idea how her son had really died, or that Anthony was not to blame. He looked to Mark Antony who merely shook his head as he placed his arm around her trembling form. Both men knew telling her was the right thing to do, but now was not the time.

"It is as if you are joined in some way. One soul split in two halves," Sosigines mused half to himself.

"Yes," Melissa agreed excitedly. "Einstein – the man whose theory this is – also suggested that if even a speck of matter was split apart, the halves remain linked on some unseen level, no matter how great the distance between the two parts."

Sosigenes returned his attention to the scroll and was running his finger along the lines as he re-read them. "I believe there must be a fixed point, an anchor, if you will, in the same place in both times for the loop to close. It must be something tangible that can be used to form a bridge across the gap between the ages." He spoke in a very matter-of-fact way, ignoring the emotions that were building. Again, he picked up the cord to demonstrate.

Melissa swallowed hard and nodded in agreement as she watched the old man repeat her earlier actions. "Henry said the same thing once."

"Who is Henry?" Canidius asked.

Mark Antony answered for her. "An odd little man, who knew much and said little, though he was the most generous of hosts." He waved his hand in a nonchalant way, implying a lack of relevance. "He also travelled through these mists."

"Then he too had some form of anchor." Sosigenes said, with a knowing smile, realising this man must also have travelled in time.

Again Melissa nodded. "He wanted to travel to improve his knowledge and to escape an unhappy marriage. He used to paint symbols on the trees in one time and look for them to return from the other."

"And how did you return to your time on the previous two occasions?"

"It was Anthony, my Anthony that is. He was waiting by the river for me both times."

"Then I believe we have our answer," Sosigenes said calmly. "You have an anchor in both times – a man you love."

Melissa suddenly looked afraid. "But Anthony is here this time, with me. How will I get back, if he is not there for me to find?"

"This is something no one can answer. Perhaps the anchor is not necessary and merely helps speed the process. Or perhaps there is another anchor that we have not thought of. Perhaps there is something else of importance to you? Your children, say?"

"What about that fool of a farmer?" Mark Antony's eyes narrowed as he voiced his thoughts. "If he is smart enough to have used these mists before, perhaps he will come looking for you provided he knows you went missing in Actium."

"But he would be looking at Actium surely?" Canidius asked. He could now follow the logic, but also saw the flaw in its application.

"He knows what she knows, and it is that I did not remain at Actium," Mark Antony muttered. He slapped his hand on his thigh suddenly, making everyone jump. "This is it. He will know I have brought you to Alexandria, and he will search for you here. I am sure of it. Your mists will form over the sea and he will appear on the other side. All that remains is to get you and your boat back out on the water."

He spoke with such certainty, no one wanted to challenge him. The Mark Antony of old was resurfacing at last: the man Melissa admired. He was not unintelligent, he simply tended not to apply himself, not unless he was pushed or coerced into doing so. It was the worst of his character traits, and another his son shared, but he could always be relied upon to step up when the situation demanded it. Whether Anthony Marcus was capable of the same, was yet to be seen. He preferred to sidestep important issues whenever possible.

"Well. There we are," Sosigenes said, with a smile. "I suggest you pray to the gods for guidance. You have the theory of how to travel. I am sure the details of the variables will show themselves given time."

"Time is the one variable we have little of." Mark Antony's eyes fell on Melissa in search of confirmation of his statement. When Melissa nodded her agreement, he knew their remaining time together was to be short.

"Then I advise you to waste no more of it talking to me!" Sosigenes turned to Melissa. "It has been a delight to meet you, my dear. Had our circumstances been different, I believe we could have spent many hours debating your time-space theory."

"They call it space-time actually," Melissa corrected and then smiled. It seemed so odd to hear an ancient Egyptian using a phrase so similar to the one she was used to hearing in so many science fiction shows on TV.

Mark Antony took her hand as she stood up, kissing the back of it gently. "Canidius will take you back to the palace. I must speak to Sosigenes on another matter. I will see you again in a few days when we will formulate a solid plan to return you to your home."

Melissa nodded and said her goodbyes to the astronomer, thanking him for his hospitality. When Mark Antony had first brought her to this house, she dared to believe that she could get home. The knowledge that she may need some form of anchor in the other time to aim for had all but dashed her hopes, except her previous experiences in the past had taught her that there was always hope. She refused to dwell on this, knowing that she was about to face a dangerous return journey to the palace complex. As safe as she felt in Canidius' presence, she always felt far safer walking in the formidable shadow of Mark Antony.

Canidius jerked his head towards the door, crossing to it as Melissa spoke with their host. Mark Antony followed.

"Are you sure it is wise to take her back to the palace?" Canidius asked.

Mark Antony grinned. "Provided you take her to your room, and not to hers." He slapped his officer on the back. "No one will think to look for her in there."

Canidius rolled his eyes to the ceiling as he took Melissa by the arm. Sometimes his commander's ideas frustrated him, but he would follow his orders, even if it meant spending the night on a less than comfortable couch.

Once they had left, Mark Antony returned his attention to the astronomer. "Do you believe this to be real?" he asked.

Sosigenes stood with one hand on his chin as he contemplated what he had heard. "It makes no difference what I believe. You believe it and she believes it. If she is not from the future, then she is cursed with the foresight to rival Cassandra. The future she foretells is one I fear greatly. And if she is right, she cannot remain within this city. If you truly care for her, you will help her to escape. Perhaps you should even go with her."

"I cannot do that," Mark Antony replied with sadness. "My place is here."

"Why? You are Roman, not Egyptian. What loyalty should you show to a people who will sell your soul to save themselves?"

"I do not believe the Alexandrians would do that."

"We each of us have our price. You of all people know this."

Mark Antony went to answer, but Sosigenes silenced him immediately with the raising of his hand. "Your seer has something we all lack. You would do well to foster it while you still can."

"What is that?"

"Despite everything she claims to know, she still has hope. Take her and her hope, and run. Get as far from here as you can. Octavian is near. He will be at the gates before you know it." He began replacing the scrolls on the bookshelves. "Go south. Use the Nile to guide you beyond our borders. Seek refuge in Numidia, or sail for India, if you can buy a passage on a trading vessel. No sane man would want to stay in an Alexandria ruled by yet another Roman despot." He glanced in Mark Antony's direction. "No offence meant," he added.

"None taken." Mark Antony smiled disarmingly. He had more pressing concerns for Melissa's safety. "Does our queen still visit you?"

"Not often." Sosigenes paused with a scroll in mid-air, ready to be returned to its place. Slowly he dropped his arm to his side, and then replaced the scroll on the desk. "If she hears of your visit, she will come. It will arouse her curiosity to hear that your seer was in this house."

Mark Antony nodded his agreement. "Yet you agree that the queen must never hear any of what has been discussed today. She must never know that Lissa and her husband are not of this time."

Sosigenes nodded. "I do agree most wholeheartedly. Such knowledge is too dangerous for any person in Alexandria to have, especially our divine goddess."

He shuffled over to the couch and dropped wearily onto it. "There are those who believe we follow a path in life that is pre-ordained by the gods and that we must all play our part as it has been written, whether we like it or not. You may or may not be able to change your future, but I will make you a prediction. You will live long enough to see the final, desperate days of a free Egypt. I, on the other hand, will not."

"What makes you say that?" Mark Antony asked.

"I have known Cleopatra since she was a young girl and in all that time I have never lied to her. She is my queen and has earned my respect. Though I will not pass the information I have gleaned to any of the palace spies, should the queen herself come to me, I will be obliged to recount what I have heard. I am a danger to your seer's very existence."

Mark Antony shoulders drooped as he felt for the dagger in his waistband. He had known it might come to this. He had to silence Sosigenes, but the burden of yet another senseless death weighed heavily on him.

Eventually, he walked over and stood in front of the elderly astrologer. "I cannot allow that to happen."

Sosigenes sighed. "I know." He was tired, his joints ached constantly and Melissa's words had confirmed his fears that the world he knew was coming to an end. He wanted to die in service to the great dynasty of the Ptolemies, content in the knowledge that his life had meaning. He did not want to end his days a pauper, struggling beneath the yolk of Rome.

Slowly, he swung his legs up one by one and lay back against the cushions. Closing his eyes, he uttered his last words of wisdom. "I am an old man. I have lived a long and highly respected life. I am more likely to die in my sleep than be stabbed with a dagger like the one in your belt you caress so frequently."

Mark Antony let go of the dagger in surprise. Sosigenes knew what he was planning and yet he had made no effort to stop him. This behaviour made no sense to a seasoned warrior with a strong survival instinct.

On the couch, Sosigenes opened one eye. "I told you, I will not serve another Caesar; serving one was quite enough. I am done with this world. I want to see what there is waiting for me in the next."

He closed his eye again and clasped his hands tightly across his chest. "I will keep your secret, provided you get on with it before I change my mind. And take that scroll with you. There may be something of use in it. If there is, your seer will find it. She has a keen mind, that one."

Without further hesitation, Antony reached down with one hand. Covering the old man's mouth tightly with his palm, he pinched Sosigenes' nostrils with his thumb and forefinger.

"Goodbye old friend," he murmured.

As his grip tightened, the venerated astronomer passed into the afterlife with barely a struggle.

Chapter 24

Almost a month had passed since the night of the banquet. There had been no contact between Anthony and the queen in that time, so he had been a little surprised to receive her dinner invitation, handed to him by her handmaiden when he left for the gymnasium that morning. He was less surprised when Canidius then informed him of the note Mark Antony had received from the queen. In fact, he was annoyed. Even though he had agreed to go along with this plan, he still harboured doubts that his father's intentions towards his wife were completely honourable. He had suffered the occasional liaisons between the pair of former lovers in silence: accidental meetings when walking through the gardens. However, an evening spent openly in each other's company was pushing the boundaries of decent behaviour. It was only Canidius' assurances that he would be present all evening that helped Anthony to keep his suspicions in check.

A pang of guilt hit Anthony as he approached Cleopatra's private suite. His hypocrisy, it seemed, knew no bounds. He loathed the idea of his wife being in the presence of her former lover, yet here he was, expecting to spend the night in another woman's bed. He knew it would happen, even before Canidius told him it was the queen's intention. He knew he was as much a pawn in this game as he was a player but, if there was any way to stack the odds a little more in his favour, he would willingly do it. If he played hard to get, he still thought he could negotiate something in return. Canidius' parting shot was to warn him not to take anything at face value.

The doors were opened for him and he walked into the private apartments, where Cleopatra reclined on one of two couches set opposite each other. She wore a simple tunic-style dress, with an unusually large split up the side, leaving little to the imagination. She rose to a seated position as he entered, holding out her hand for him to take.

Dutifully, he walked over and bent to kiss it. His eyes fell immediately on her bare thigh, so he deliberately looked away, scanning the room. He spotted two servants, but no guards. This surprised him.

He straightened up and took a step backwards towards the vacant couch, but Cleopatra patted the seat next to her. "Here, sit by me. I promise I will not bite."

He hesitated slightly for effect. "Where are your other guests?" he asked casually.

"I wanted a private dinner to apologise for our last evening together. My behaviour was inappropriate, and I wish to make amends. I hope you will humour me." Cleopatra blushed slightly as she spoke, but it was not from true modesty. It was all part of her act.

Anthony nodded his agreement. He knew he had to humour every request made of him if his father's plan was to work. In truth, he wanted to. The wantonness of Cleopatra's court appealed to him in ways he found hard to resist. The more he experienced the sheer decadence, the more he wanted to indulge in its extravagant hedonism while he could, regardless of any promises he might have made to Melissa to the contrary. As much as he hated to admit it, he could see how his father had been so easily swayed towards the Egyptian way of life.

If Cleopatra offered herself to him tonight, he would say yes, not only because his father had ordered it, but because the chance to bed the world's most infamous seductress was simply too good an opportunity to miss. Meaningless sex meant nothing to Anthony, whose appetite for women was almost as great as his father's. Melissa knew it. She even turned a convenient 'blind eye' to his arrangement with a high-class madam back home: all the while he was paying, she knew there was nothing more to the relationship than sex. Despite this, he knew his wife would never forgive him for bedding Egypt's most notorious pharaoh, whatever the reason. Melissa loathed the very thought of Cleopatra.

The queen had waited long enough. "Sit down!" she ordered sharply, adding in a softer tone, "you are quite safe."

Anthony sat on the couch as ordered and watched as Cleopatra settled against the cushions in a relaxed pose. The servants brought food and wine. He was careful to watch for any signs that it was drugged, but saw no evidence as he was served from the same flask as the queen. Cleopatra engaged him in witty conversation and the evening passed pleasantly enough.

"Are there to be no entertainments this evening?" Anthony asked eventually. He had observed that even private dinners at the palace were usually accompanied by music. So far, the evening had been unusually quiet.

Cleopatra laughed. "There will be none tonight. I thought we could enjoy some of the intellectual pleasures this palace has to offer."

Anthony smiled politely. Now he was intrigued, although he did his best to hide it. To learn more about this stunning palace, and what went on in it, was too good an opportunity for an archaeologist to miss.

She smiled, knowingly. Her real plans for the evening were devious to say the least. First, she had to lull her victim into a false sense of security. "Let us begin with a little educational discussion Tell me what you know about my country and heritage."

Anthony puffed out his cheeks. The last thing he was expecting was to have to give a history lesson. "You are descended from Ptolemy Soter, cousin to Alexander of Macedon, the greatest warrior ever to have lived. That makes you Greek by birth."

"My blood may be Greek, but my heart is Egyptian. Never forget it!"

The way Cleopatra spat the words made Anthony realise he had opened an old wound and was on exceedingly dodgy ground. He felt suddenly nervous and needed more wine to calm his nerves. He looked around for the slaves, but they had both disappeared.

Cleopatra spotted his discomfort. It was exactly the reaction she wanted, being intent on keeping him on the defensive. She saw he was searching for a slave to pour the wine. Ever the attentive host, she pointed to the flask herself.

"Allow me," she offered, taking his glass. Turning her back on him, she added a large pinch of powder to it from a dish hidden behind the flask. She poured wine over it, swirling it around before returning the full glass to him.

Anthony gratefully accepted the wine without noticing the difference. He began again, choosing a safer topic of conversation. "Your title of Pharaoh is but one of many bestowed upon you. My personal favourite is 'Mistress of Sedge and Bee' referring to your rule over the two lands of Egypt through their respective emblems - the sedge plant for the South and the bee for the North. You are regarded by your subjects as a living god."

Cleopatra nodded her approval of his knowledge. "Speaking of gods, how well acquainted are you with the Egyptian pantheon?"

"I know some of them." Even though he had specialised in Roman archaeology, Anthony studied Egypt as a hobby and knew the mythology rather well. His display of humility was deliberate. He intended to supply her with as little information as he could.

She rose from the couch gracefully, holding out her hand.

"Come," she commanded. "We will test your knowledge."

Anthony downed the rest of his wine before he took her outstretched hand. As he stood up, his vision blurred and he stumbled slightly. He did not think he had drunk that much, but he did feel giddy. Cleopatra merely smiled and so he allowed her to lead him out of the dining area. She walked over to a section of the wall where a life-sized fresco of a jackal-headed god was framed by two thin marble columns.

"Do you know who this is?" she asked.

Anthony studied the painting for a few moments, concentrating to clear his vision. There were many jackal gods to choose from, but this particular one was present in many parts of the palace, and he had been wondering why.

"I believe this is one of the funerary gods, but to be positioned here on this wall seems unusual . . ." He thought of the Shabaka Stone in the British Museum and was certain an image of this god was carved on that stone.

"Is it Wepawet?" he finally asked.

She smiled. "I am impressed. What made you think of him?"

"I remember seeing his image before. It was linked to Horus, thus giving him strong royal connections. If my memory is correct, he is responsible for guiding the deceased on to a good path in the underworld, hence his name, which literally means 'opener of the ways'.

Cleopatra nodded. "That is his traditional duty but, in this palace, he has another role. Look closer and you may find it."

Anthony stepped closer to begin tracing the outline of the image with his fingers. Almost immediately he exclaimed with excitement, "This panel is wood, not plaster."

Cleopatra laughed. "Indeed, it is. Our god is quite literally the opener of another way."

Anthony turned and grabbed her by the shoulders, shaking her slightly. He had forgotten completely that she was a queen for a moment, but she was not concerned. He looked as excited as her eldest son, Caesarion, had the first time he had ridden a horse.

"Is it a secret door?" he asked.

She nodded and reached across him to pull on a lever almost hidden by the far column. The portrait swung backwards, revealing a hidden passage. "My father would use this as a quick way to move between his wives' beds in the night. As children, my sister and I would hide in here and spy on people, giggling at the strange ways in which they behaved when they thought they could not be seen. We learnt a great deal about the ways of adults from this passage."

"You mean you learnt about sex," Anthony countered.

"Amongst other things," she agreed coyly. "This passage brought me my throne. When my brother refused to allow me an audience with Caesar, my bodyguard brought me to him through here."

"Wrapped in a carpet," Anthony murmured, his interest growing further. If this was the way Cleopatra had got into Caesar's quarters, it meant there was a way out to the harbour. He had to explore it. "How far does it go?"

"Wherever you see the image of Wepawet you will find a door to the passages. The network can take you almost anywhere in the lower part of the palace. On the upper floors the passages are merely small galleries used for viewing the other rooms. Some lead into the gardens. This particular passage is the longest and most interesting."

Looking around him, Anthony spotted a lamp on a nearby table. He walked over and picked it up. "Shall we?" he asked with a wink, as he returned to her side.

Cleopatra beamed at him. "Why not?"

She stood aside, allowing him to go into the passage first. They walked a few paces and reached a junction. Anthony was certain the passage on the right went towards the outer walls of the palace and then into the harbour. He took a step towards it, but Cleopatra steered him to the left. *Another time*, he thought.

After a few more paces, Cleopatra put her hand on Anthony's arm and he stopped. She raised her fingers to her lips before putting her hand up to a wooden panel at head height. Carefully, she slid the panel to the side to reveal a small hole. A shaft of light pierced the darkness. Cleopatra put her eye up to the hole and peered through before stepping aside for Anthony to look. Inside were the two girls whom Anthony had slept with. One was sitting on the bed with her legs spread wide open. The other knelt between them fondling the first girl's breasts. As Anthony watched, the kneeling girl buried her face between her partner's thighs. When the girl on the bed began to groan and squirm, Cleopatra forced the panel shut before him.

"I was enjoying that," he said with honesty, as she brushed past him, moving swiftly down the passage.

"It is nothing you have not already seen," she called over her shoulder. "Let us see who else we can find."

The pair moved along the passage, looking through a variety of spy holes to see what the occupants were up to. In many cases there was a sexual act of some sort in progress. Cleopatra allowed Anthony to watch just long enough to titillate him, before dragging him to the next room. Frequently, the passage would open onto a corridor in the palace which they would have to cross to find the next entrance to the network. As she had described, each entrance was behind another image of Wepawet. As they roamed, Anthony tried hard to visualise where they were, but there were too many twists and turns to keep track.

They continued in their journey for some time, giggling at some of the sights they saw and marvelling at others, like two naughty children. At one point they came across Diomedes. The secretary was hunched over a desk mumbling away to himself. Anthony could make out a few less than pleasant phrases he muttered about the queen and her growing list of demands.

Again, Anthony felt the brush of Cleopatra's hand on his arm. He stepped away and she closed the panel. "He is often quite rude about some of my decisions. I make notes of his misgivings to use against him later."

"That is cruel," Anthony chided.

"How else do you think I maintain my status as a divine goddess? Unlike your wife, I cannot see the future, nor do I read minds. My subjects must believe I am all-seeing, all- knowing. This is how I keep up appearances."

Anthony laughed, prompting Cleopatra to step in close to put her fingers to his lips to silence him. Her touch was as light as a feather, just as it had been the first night on the flagship. She drew her fingers downwards across his chin and then his throat. It was an act designed to tease an already aroused man, and he knew it. She was trying to tempt him into breaking his word, and she was winning, although it had never really been a fair fight. She was a woman worthy of bedding. He enjoyed her company, whether they were locked in a heated philosophical debate, or engaging in childish pastimes as they were now. Cleopatra indulged him, spoilt him and flirted with him audaciously. She was the one woman he was supposed to resist, which made her the one woman he wanted, even before he agreed to give in to her advances. He closed his eyes and fought his urge to pull her into his arms and kiss her.

She brushed past him again, ensuring her hand dragged across his chest. "There is more," she gushed, trotting away from him into the darkness. She knew her behaviour was having the desired effect, as was the drug she had administered to his wine. Soon, he would succumb to his desires. She had made sure he would be unable to resist and her revenge on the seer would be complete. She had been patient. Now, that patience would be rewarded.

Anthony followed obediently, wondering how much more of this voyeurism he could take. He knew it was all designed to tease and arouse him, and he was now so aroused it was becoming painful to walk. When he caught up to her for the final time, she was leaning against the wall in a most seductive pose, one leg slightly bent so the split of her skirt displayed the full length of her thigh, daring him to touch it.

She pointed to a small ledge obviously designed to take a lamp and then to just above her shoulder where the next panel was. He put the lamp on the ledge. She did not move from her position, meaning he would have to lean against her to look through the hole.

He stepped forwards, pressing his body against hers and she put her hands on his sides, pulling him closer. Her perfume was intoxicating. It was not the usual rose water, but the spicy smell he associated with the oils used in the orgy. It was almost enough to make him forget any remaining loyalty to his wife, but he concentrated on peering through the spy hole.

His viewpoint was well hidden from the room's occupants by the sheer drapes that hung in front of it. There was a bright orange glow emanating from the flames of the multitude of oil lamps and candles inside. His vision was blurred by the drapes and the effects of the wine, but he recognised the room as his. He knew because he could see his clothing, carelessly strewn over the padded chaise longue at the end of the bed, whilst Melissa's was neatly folded on the box in the corner. His focus moved to the bed, where a naked man with greying dark hair stood beside it. He was about the same height and build as Anthony was himself, but this man's once muscular frame had seen better days. He bent over the bed and pulled something towards him. It was obviously a woman and Anthony held his breath as the man positioned himself between a pair of beautiful, slim legs. He could not see her face, only her long dark hair spreading out across the mattress. He swallowed hard as he heard the woman gasp with delight.

"Antony," she gasped. He watched as the legs wrapped around the man's waist. And then Anthony Marcus heard the word he dreaded more than any other, groaned with pure lust.

"Lissa!"

Anthony looked away. He had no wish to see any more. His heart was breaking. He was watching his wife make love to his father in the bed they had shared only hours before. Despite his own abominable behaviour, this betrayal was too much for him to bear. Melissa had sworn Mark Antony meant nothing to her. Mark Antony had given his word not to touch Melissa. They had both lied to him and that cut deeper than the pain of watching them together.

Cleopatra moved her hands gently on his sides. He jumped at the feel of her touch.

She spoke softly. "I am sorry that you must witness such a betrayal. I feel your pain, though I no longer share it. It is a hard lesson to learn. Mark Antony takes what he desires. The first time you see your lover with another is shocking. I have come to accept his assignations over the years. You will too, in time."

He tried to step away from her, but she held on tightly, pulling her body closer to his.

"What is it you want from me?" he croaked, already knowing the answer.

"I want nothing. I am offering you an opportunity to claim that which is rightfully yours. I decree that, if one man takes that which belongs to another, the wronged party has the right to equal recompense. He has your wife,

Anthony. I offer you his in return."

Anthony felt Cleopatra move one hand downwards in search of his already hardened shaft. He offered no resistance as she began to stroke it. Within seconds his resolve was just as hard. Anger quickly turned to passion. Slamming the body of the Egyptian queen hard against the wall of the corridor, he lifted her legs around his waist. After allowing her to guide his engorged member to the soft opening of her welcoming body, he rammed his body into hers again and again, until his frustrations were utterly spent.

Chapter 25

Melissa was sick with worry.

She had not seen Anthony since the night of her trip to Sosigenes' house. She had assumed he would be waiting in their suite, in the foulest of moods, when she returned to it the next morning, but he had not been there. Neither did he return the next day. She asked for an audience with Cleopatra to enquire where he had been taken, but her requests were refused. A week passed and she had not seen or heard from him. She tried to see Canidius, but was told he had left Alexandria. In desperation, she asked one of the servants to send word to Mark Antony. It was dangerous to make such contact, but she was out of options.

As she waited, she held a tiny scrap of linen in her hand. It contained the pressed blue flower given to her by Anthony on the night of the banquet. It was the only thing he had given her since their capture at Actium and all she had to remember him by.

The door of her suite burst open less than an hour later, but it was not Mark Antony, or even Anthony Marcus that entered. It was two of the palace guards, with instructions to take Melissa to the queen. They gave her no chance to accompany them under her own steam. Each one grabbed an arm and dragged her through the corridors to the throne room.

Cleopatra sat on her throne, stiff backed, with her crown on her head and the crook and flail in her hands. Her eyes remained focused on some point in the distance, never looking at her subjects. This appeared to be an official audience.

The guards threw Melissa to the floor in front of the throne. Terrified of what was about to happen, she did not move. She did not dare.

Cleopatra left Melissa on the floor for some time. Eventually, she barked an order.

"Rise, witch."

Slowly, Melissa rose, pushing herself up from the polished floor carefully as her sweaty palms slipped across the tesserae. She trembled as she stood before the queen, who was most imposing in her official apparel.

"What do you have to say in your defence?" Cleopatra's gaze remained fixed above Melissa's head.

Melissa had no idea what she was supposed to have done. "Majesty, I am unaware of the charge," she replied quietly.

"Lies, deception, adultery – where would you like us to start?"

Melissa noted Cleopatra's use of the plural in referring to herself. She was being tried for a crime by the pharaoh of the land. This did not bode well.

Finally, the queen looked down and, as her eyes met Melissa's, Cleopatra smiled cruelly.

"Let us start with your prophecy concerning the death of my son at the hands of Caesar. A seed planted years ago, which can never bear fruit. How could it? Caesar is dead. And what of your poor husband, left for so long to wonder about your honesty? Another poor creature you have deceived."

Cleopatra rose slowly, placing her crook and flail on an outstretched cushion that was quickly proffered. "Your worst crime was committed here, in this very palace, against us. You have lain with the man we call husband. It is a slight that cannot be forgiven. Deny your infidelity if you dare."

"I have no reason to deny it. It has not happened."

The queen and stepped down from her throne to stand eye to eye with her victim.

"More lies. You pervert the very air you breathe," she spat in reply, daring Melissa to defend herself.

Melissa retaliated under her breath, so only Egypt's monarch could hear her. "And you have perverted the destinies of the greatest men."

Cleopatra's eyes flicked to her assembled entourage, who dutifully took their cue to leave. Within moments the room emptied of all but the guards and Diomedes, who stood off to the far side of the room. Despite their distance, the queen replied in the same hushed tone employed by Melissa.

"Perverted you say? I prefer enlightened. Was it not I who enlightened Caesar, showing him the true path to immortality. Is it not I who has enlightened Mark Antony to see beyond the confines of his Roman upbringing to make him master in the East?"

Melissa heard the switch to the singular in Cleopatra's address. Now they were getting down to it, it was personal. She retaliated with facts.

"Might I remind you that Caesar is dead and Mark Antony powerless? Your 'enlightenment' brings nothing but destruction to the men beneath your influence."

"Such grandiose words from one who claims to see the future. Tell me, who was it who had the knowledge to save Caesar, yet did nothing? Who had the wisdom to make Mark Antony the greatest Roman ever to have lived yet deserted him? It was not I, but you, Lissa, who brought destruction to the men over whom she once held sway. You flatter them for your own advancement. You encourage them and give false hope of your interest, only to discard them when they have outgrown their usefulness."

"I have no interest in Mark Antony and I have not lain with him, as you put it."

"There was a witness - one who brings the complaint."

Melissa's brow furrowed. "Who?"

Cleopatra clapped her hands. From behind the curtains at the rear of her throne Mark Antony appeared, fully clad in the uniform of a Roman general. He looked like the Mark Antony of old; a powerful, virile force to be reckoned with. It was as if he was where he was meant to be.

And yet something did not fit. The face was Mark Antony's without doubt, and yet the body was that of a younger man. The leg muscles were taut beneath his tunic, the armour too loose around the waist. As he undid the strap beneath his chin and removed his helmet, the truth dawned on Melissa. The man in front of her was not Mark Antony at all. It was his son, Anthony Marcus.

He spoke.

"I have seen possibilities long hidden from me. I have seen a future of greatness ahead. I have no further use for your counsel, witch. I stand at Cleopatra's side. I heed only her good advice. Together we will face the armies of Octavian and together we will be victorious."

"Anthony! What are you doing? "Have you gone completely mad?" Melissa gasped in English. "This isn't a game. You can't take his place, if that's what you're thinking. You know damned well what's going to happen if you try. You lose."

"Yeah," he sneered, "I know what's going to happen alright – to him, not to me. I saw you together, and in our bed, of all places. She's offered me a better future here than I could ever hope for and I'm taking it. After all, I don't exactly have a lot left to lose, do I?" He stepped backward and nodded to the guards at the back of the room to come forward. Speaking in Latin again, he gave his first order as a Roman general.

"I no longer wish to look upon the face of such a barefaced liar. Take her away."

The last sight Melissa had was of her husband taking Cleopatra in a passionate embrace.

Chapter 26

Melissa was dragged to the Alexandrian jail, where she was handed over to the jailer; a disgusting man with a bad limp, one eye and few teeth.

He eyed Melissa hungrily as he bound her hands with a long piece of rope. He would have liked the opportunity to enjoy this one on her previous visit, but he had his orders, then as now. Last time, she was to be kept safe without being defiled. This time, the prisoner was to be taken directly to the cells and left for every man to enjoy. The gargantuan palace guard standing at his shoulder ensured he would follow his orders to the letter. At least he got to watch. The queen wanted him to provide her with a full description of every degrading act this prisoner was forced to endure.

He dragged Melissa down the same narrow corridor as before. Even though it was her second visit, the strong stench of sweat and human excrement still made her gag. It was only when she had passed the last of the dark, cramped cells, that Melissa realised she was being taken even further into the bowels of hell.

A small staircase at the far end of the corridor led down to a large open cell. There was little light down here. She could barely see more than a few feet in front of her as the jailer dragged her to the far end of this evil pit, but she could hear the murmurings from a number of men coming from the shadows. On the far wall was a large metal ring, to which the jailer tied the free end of the rope. Melissa realised she was to be tethered and left for sport. It was her worst nightmare.

As he turned to leave, the jailer shouted out to the inmates.

"This is a present from her majesty. Take your time lads – plenty to go around."

As a final insult, her jailer took hold of Melissa's dress at the neck and ripped a section of it downwards, exposing one breast. She shuddered as he groped her before leaving her to await her fate at the hands of the other prisoners.

Melissa pulled against the ring to which she was tied, but the rope would not give. She was trapped at the mercy of whichever of the men took her. She knew her troubles would not end there. They would all have her, one after the other, unless one dominant male decided to make her his property. Either way her options were equally bad. Memories of her rape at the hands of Salvidienus flooded back and, as terrible as that had been, it would be nothing in comparison with what she was now facing. She stifled a sob as the door to the cell clanged shut. She was alone and defenceless, facing an unknown number of men: the dregs of a society whose depravity knew no bounds.

The other prisoners stood off to begin with, each looking her up and down with hungry eyes, until one made a move. He took a step forwards, and then another, cautiously as if he was expecting the palace guard to come in and stop him. As he got closer, another moved in, and then another until the melee began. Fists flew as men clambered over each other to get to the woman roped to the wall. One was thrown sideways, landing at

Melissa's feet and cracking his skull. When he did not move, Melissa knew he was either unconscious or dead.

Melissa flattened herself against the wall, desperate to escape the bloodbath that was developing around her. A few men took serious punches and retreated, deciding it was not worth the effort – they could wait their turn after the frenzy had died down. Eventually, only two remained. One of the men had the other in a head lock. He continued to twist and squeeze until he snapped his victim's neck. He leered at Melissa as he dropped the corpse on top of the other prone figure, stepping over them both.

She cowered in the corner where she was trapped. She tried to pull away, but there was nowhere to go. To the victor go the spoils. Taking hold of her ankles, he dragged her across the floor until her arms were stretched tight above her head. He spread her legs, pinning them down with his as he knelt over her, fumbling to remove his loincloth in his hurry to claim his prize.

Behind her attacker, Melissa could hear a commotion. Suddenly, a hand appeared on the man's shoulder dragging him backwards. A second later, the glint of a blade appeared at his throat and sliced through his jugular, spraying Melissa with his blood. She screamed as the hot liquid covered her face. His body slumped on top of her, pinning her to the floor with her arms still stretched out above her head.

The corpse was pushed to one side to reveal her saviour: a wild-eyed Mark Antony. Behind him stood Canidius, his back towards the general with his own bloodied sword drawn. At the door to the cell lay the dead jailer and the palace guard.

Mark Antony took a step forwards and swung his sword at the rope restraining Melissa. Sparks flew as it hit the stonework, severing the rope with one blow. He dropped to his knees as Melissa pulled her arms down over her chest. He reached out for her, but she pulled away, shaking and covering her face with her hands. There was little he could do for her here.

He shouted to Canidius to take his sword from him. Once he had handed the weapon over, he forcefully pulled Melissa off the floor and threw her over his shoulder. He staggered to his feet, adjusting his grip on her shaking body, before exiting the cell. Canidius backed out after him, preventing any attack from the other prisoners, and then followed as Mark Antony strode through the palace grounds to the Timoneum. Bursting through the doors of one room after another, he began shouting orders, the general once more.

"I want guards outside the doors at all times - Romans, mind, not those Egyptian shits who only do the queen's bidding. Lissa's safety must be assured. Whatever is needed, she will have it."

When he reached his bedchamber, he deposited Melissa on the end of the bed. On a side table stood a ewer and basin. Pouring water into the bowl, he took it, with a small towel, over to the bed, where he proceeded to gently wash the blood from Melissa's face.

"You are safe here," he soothed as she continued to shake. "I will never let them harm you, but we must clean this mess from you. Let me do this for you, Lissa."

Mark Antony continued to work, first dipping the corner of the towel into the water, then wringing it out and finally wiping it across Melissa's skin. All the time he muttered words of comfort until his task was complete.

"Find me a tunic - a clean one if you can," he called to Canidius, as he gently began to remove the remains of Melissa's torn clothes. She put up no resistance as he undressed and re-clothed her, eventually allowing him to put her into his bed.

The sun was setting when Melissa awoke in the sumptuous bed. It was larger than the one in her room and adorned with the most luxurious red silk drapes. She sat up slowly, trying to get her bearings in her new surroundings. When she looked over towards the window, she was relieved to see a familiar figure by the window.

"Anthony, I've had this terrible dream . . ." she began in English, but as soon as the figure turned around, she knew it was not the Anthony she was hoping for.

Mark Antony crossed the room, picking up a bowl of fruit from a side table on the way. He sat on the side of the bed "You are awake. Good. You must eat something. You will need your strength. The coming days will not be easy."

Melissa politely took a peach from the bowl and immediately discarded it onto the bed. "Where are we?" she asked.

"This was once the palace of one of Cleopatra's ancestors. They each built their own, resulting in this mass of buildings here in the royal quarter. I call this one my Timoneum."

Melissa shook her head in disgust. "I thought you retired to a hut, not a grand mansion!"

"Is that what your books told you?"

She nodded.

"Then your knowledge is proved fallible yet again, although in comparison with what I am used to, I suppose it does resemble a hut. This room is adequately furnished, but you will find the rest is a little sparse, even for your tastes. I will have more furniture brought from storage to improve it for you." His mood sobered. "I can keep you safe here. There is only one way in or out. My men guard it night and day. Cleopatra has no influence here."

"What about Anthony?"

"You husband is lost to you. His head has been turned by the vices of the court, and by the promises of wealth and position. Accept it and move on. Do not give her the satisfaction of seeing how successful she has been in driving you apart."

"He . . . he let her . . . do this," she whispered.

"He did," he said in a most matter-of-fact way, before thinking better of it. As the tears welled in Melissa's eyes, he softened his tone. Taking her hand gently in his, he tried to give her some context. "I am told he thinks badly of us both. It seems he caught us in an uncompromising position."

"I do not understand. We have done nothing." Her sobbing was pitiful.

"No, we have not. And yet the queen was able to stage the most perfect of deceptions. Your husband watched as I made love to you, in your own bed. I mean who would believe I would do such a thing?" He grinned half-heartedly, but he knew Melissa would not see the irony in his remark. She was too distressed to see anything clearly.

"I . . . would . . . never . . ." she gasped in English. Her breathing was coming in desperate pants, as she fought to maintain some control. Everything she cared for was gone: her home, her children, her husband. There was nothing left, no reason to go on. Cleopatra had won. She collapsed backwards onto the bed and wailed in grief.

Mark Antony could do nothing but stare at her. He had the woman he loved within easy reach. He had removed every obstacle between them and their mutual happiness, but at what cost? Melissa was so distraught, she could not even hear his words. She was babbling in her own language, as she had done in the past when she had been upset, or ill. What she said was a mystery to him, though he knew she was suffering.

Eventually, he lay on the bed next to her. Pulling her into his arms, he rocked her gently until she fell once more into a fitful sleep.

Chapter 27

Anthony returned to his suite with a sense of trepidation. That morning, he had casually dropped a rose onto the bench, just as he had done for the past two days. He wanted some answers as to why his father had so blatantly reneged on the deal they had struck. As Canidius had not appeared at the gymnasium for nearly three weeks, he had resorted to the agreed alternative method of communication.

He had been hurt by what he had seen through the spy hole on that fateful night but, as his anger subsided, he became increasingly worried. For too long he had harboured the fear that his wife preferred his father, despite her denials. Now he believed he had proof, he needed to confront her and discover why she had continually lied to him. He knew his marriage was over this time, but he needed to hear her say it. Worryingly, Melissa was nowhere to be found to ask.

The very next morning after witnessing the debacle, Cleopatra began to hint at sending Melissa on a visit to her reptile farm. He agreed to take part in her charade in the throne room only on condition that did not happen. As disappointed as he was with his wife's actions, he did not want her sent to that evil place. Cleopatra had reluctantly agreed to send Melissa away from his sight to a place where she would be well cared for. As no one seemed to know where Melissa was, he now harboured fears that his wife was dead, and that he was, in part, responsible.

He opened the door to his suite, hoping to find Canidius, but there was no sign of the Roman. His shoulders slumped immediately, and he walked over to the window to check the bench. Once again, the rose was gone, but no visitor had come. Anthony suspected that their communication method had been discovered. Without it, he was alone, in over his head, angry and terrified.

In need of a drink, Anthony headed off to the bedroom in search of a flask of wine. He stopped on the threshold of the door, confused by the presence of three rose heads, in varying stages of decay, lying on the end of the bed. His eyes scanned the room, but he saw no evidence of anyone being there. He was certain that Canidius had never received his messages. Thinking he had but a few minutes' freedom left, he stepped into the room and headed straight for the flask on the table by the bed.

As he reached the flask, the door slammed behind him.

He froze; his heart began to pound and he felt himself begin to shake. He felt sure Cleopatra was standing behind him. She would demand answers; he had none to give. He took a deep breath. If this was to be his last moment alive, he would do so facing his executioner. He could only hope it would be quick. Straightening himself, he put his shoulders back and turned around to face his fate.

He was completely unprepared to see his father standing beside the closed door, wine glass in hand.

Mark Antony pointed the glass towards the wilting blooms. "I credited you with more intelligence than to leave yourself so exposed. I understood you wanted to talk at the appearance of the first bloom. You must learn patience."

"I expected to see Canidius ..." Anthony began, but was cut short.

"Canidius is watched, as are you. I have certain freedoms to move through this palace unseen . . . if I so choose."

"You use the passages behind Wepawet," Anthony coolly stated.

"They have their uses." Mark Antony smiled, knowingly.

Anthony folded his arms. His fear of death was slowly being replaced by cold, hard hatred for the man in front of him – the man sleeping with his wife. He had to be patient, though, if he wanted answers.

"And how do you know there is no one in there now, watching us?"

The older man shrugged in a rather non-committal manner. "The mechanisms are old and frequently jam." He grinned suddenly. "Especially when wedged from the inside. It only works on the smaller passages where there are no more than two entrances – one you wedge and the other you use to make your escape."

Stepping away from the wall, Mark Antony headed towards the bed. "Well, what was so urgent that it required the destruction of so much beauty?" He brushed the decaying flowers onto the floor and sat down, placing his empty glass at his feet.

Anthony glared at him. "Why should I trust you? Your word has meant little this far."

"Meaning?"

The reply was so casual, it made Anthony snap.

"I SAW YOU!" he shouted as he stormed around to

confront his father head-on. He pointed at the bed. "I watched you fuck my wife, and in that very bed, no less."

Mark Antony remained calm. "As much as I wish that I had, I did not fuck her, in this bed, or any other."

The comment took the wind out of Anthony's sails. His confusion apparent, all he could manage in reply was, "Huh?"

Mark Antony sighed and shook his head. "What you saw was a deception, nothing more. Cleopatra's speciality! Her greatest talent is to make the eye believe what the heart knows to be false. The man was most likely one of my own legionaries, paid handsomely to play his part."

"Who was the woman?" Anthony towered menacingly above Mark Antony, who merely smiled up at his son.

"I would say she was one of the women from the court. Cleopatra whores them out as she sees fit. They do it without question. They believe her to be a divine being to be obeyed. I believe you have witnessed some of their unwavering loyalty first hand – at the orgy."

Anthony thought back to the night of his orgy. He gulped and took a step backwards. "Some."

"In this palace of deceit, your eyes may see and your ears may hear, yet only your heart knows what is true. Canidius told you this, but you did not heed his warning." Mark Antony sighed again. "Search your heart, my son. What does it tell you? Do you really believe Lissa would allow me to take her here, between the same sheets you had spilt your sweat in? Or that I would stoop so low as to do such a wicked deed after we had sworn allegiance to each other? I may be half the man I once was, yet I still have my honour." He made no mention of the fact that he had attempted to do exactly that only a few weeks earlier. He felt it irrelevant at this juncture.

Anthony bit his lip. He had not seen either person's face. It could have been a set-up. The more he thought about it, the more he suspected that Mark Antony was right, but he was too proud to admit it.

"I do not know," he mumbled.

"Then you are a fool who does not deserve to be loved by such a beautiful creature as Lissa. Perhaps I will take her from you. Only then will you understand what an idiot you have been. You have more than had your revenge with what you have done to her."

Anthony's fists clenched tightly, his anger growing again. He had only obeyed orders. His first thought was to lash out, but was forcing himself not to. He bit his lip harder and listened, as he struggled to keep what little of his temper he had managed to regain.

"When I heard Lissa had been dragged from the throne room, I knew Cleopatra intended her harm. I have taken her to the Timoneum, where she will be safe."

"Safe? Is that what you call it?" Anthony's reply was heavy with sarcasm.

"Would you rather she was left to rot in chains in the cells of the Alexandrian jail?" Mark Antony's tone was incredulous. "Kept at the mercy of murderers, thieves and rapists, for that is where she was taken. Cleopatra will not touch her if she believes her to be my lover."

"So, she has been in your bed?" Anthony spat.

Mark Antony sighed. "Ah, so you think her a whore now?"

"TELL ME THE TRUTH!" Anthony shouted as he lost his temper again. He raised his fist, but the move was anticipated. With lightning speed, Mark Antony was on his feet. Grabbing his son's fist in mid-air, he twisted Anthony's arm downwards, turning the younger man around and pinning both arms to his sides in one move. Anthony was so surprised at the speed of the attack that he barely resisted. He struggled briefly, but quickly realised it would do him no good. He gave in, slumping forwards in defeat and begging for an answer.

"Please. I must hear the truth."

For a man who was not known for his tact, Mark Antony chose his next words carefully, using his son's real name in a low, gentle tone.

"Antonius, my son, hear my words for they are the truth. I loved Lissa with all my heart, but I have always known her feelings for me were . . ." he struggled briefly, searching for an appropriate phrase, ". . . indifferent. She told me from the very beginning that she loved another. I never imagined that he would be you, or that you would love her with as much passion as I. I would give all I own to see her smile just once, but it is not to be. I can only offer her companionship. She wants nothing more from me than that."

Anthony looked down at the floor, embarrassed by what he had done. Cleopatra had tricked him, and he had fallen for her web of expertly-crafted lies. He had become too arrogant, thinking he had the measure of the woman but, in reality, she had the measure of him.

Slowly, Mark Antony let go of his son and backed away. He reached down to his belt and pulled out a scrap of material. He held it out towards his son. "Here, I found this after I rescued her from the jail. She held it so tight it was difficult to prize it from her clenched hand." He waved the scrap of material until Anthony turned and took it. "Look inside," he added.

Nervously, Anthony opened the small piece of folded linen. Inside was a small, blue flower. It had been carefully pressed at one time, but now one petal had been torn away.

"Do you remember? You gave it to Lissa the night of the celebrations to honour my birth. You plucked it from the bush at by the stairs and placed it under her brooch." Mark Antony stared wistfully into the distance, as if he were remembering the moment fondly.

"How did you know?" Anthony began.

"I make it my business to *know*, boy," Mark Antony snapped. He had no intention of announcing that he had been watching them from the shadows that night. "And I *know* this means a great deal to Lissa, if she did not wish to be parted from it."

Anthony collapsed onto the bed and dropped his head into his hands. That flower was the only thing he had given his wife since they had arrived in Alexandria, and she had kept it with her ever since as a reminder that he loved her. He knew as soon as he saw it that she still loved him, and that he had been a fool to doubt her.

"What have I done?" he groaned. It sickened him to think how easily he had been led.

"You did what you had to, though you have allowed emotion to cloud your judgement, despite all advice to the contrary. I swore to you that I would not take your wife from you and, in that matter, I have kept my word. Cleopatra has poisoned your mind with tales of my sexual exploits, all of which were probably true, but they did not involve Lissa."

Anthony did not move and groaned again at his own stupidity.

Mark Antony stared helplessly at his despondent offspring. He was not a man known for tact in such situations, but he knew tact was what was needed. *What would Lissa do?* he thought, knowing he must find some words of comfort for his son. Now was not the time to give into melancholy. Now was the time to stay focused.

He collected the wine flask and poured another glass, offering it to his son, who took it gladly. Sitting down next to Anthony, he placed a hand firmly on his shoulder.

"We both knew it would come to this, although we did not know the depth of Cleopatra's vindictiveness. I did my best to convince her of my indifference to Lissa and that I too wished to watch Caesar's seer suffer. In that way I hoped to be able to exercise some control over her actions. My intervention in taking Lissa from the jail has shown my true hand. Cleopatra now doubts my motives, regardless of any effort I make to convince her otherwise. The burden of watching our queen must fall entirely on you. You must watch her every move, while I concentrate on the plans for your escape." He paused, waiting for a response, but continued when he got none. "We still have a chance to save Lissa, provided we continue to work together. After all, we are well ahead of schedule."

Anthony looked round at his father, his confusion apparent at the last statement.

In return, Mark Antony grinned and slapped his son hard on the back. "Lissa is already out of the palace," he boomed, but got no response to his attempt at joke.

He shook his head in disgust when Anthony winced. Instead, he poured them both more wine. "What of your relationship with our queen? How does she treat you?"

Anthony ran his hand through his hair. "I do not understand. What is it you want me to say? That we . . ."

Mark Antony laughed. "There is no need to tell me that. I know exactly what you do. I do not blame you for it, nor do I feel the same jealousies you experience. I will not deny it pains me to think of it, but I know how her mind works." He leant towards his son, nudging him with his shoulder in a jovial manner. "Tell me, when she whispers in your ear, is it words of love you hear, or words of war? When your sexual needs are utterly spent, does she curl beneath your arm with her head on your chest, or does she rise and dress herself? Does she show the same concern for your exhaustion as she does for her affairs of state?

"She is a queen. She has many responsibilities." Anthony tried to sound convincing, knowing only too well the queen felt nothing for him.

Again, Mark Antony roared with laughter. "Her fascination with you has been more short-lived than I imagined possible." He became more serious. "Has she brought my boy to bed yet?"

"What boy?"

"You must have seen him in the orgies. Young, muscular, hung like a horse, name of Eros."

Anthony nodded. Eros was present at the orgy he himself took part in.

"She likes to watch while he fucks someone, but your involvement does not end there. As gifted as he is, his preferences lie elsewhere. At some point you will be told to spread his cheeks as wide as he spreads a girl's legs."

"I will never do that!" Anthony exclaimed indignantly.

"Really?" Mark Antony's eyes widened. "With the right encouragement a man will do anything. Suppose she brings Lissa before you, with a knife to her throat? What would you do then?"

Anthony took a drink of his wine as he mulled the question over. Would he partake in a homosexual act to save Melissa's life? Would she thank him for it if he did? Would he really want to live enslaved to Cleopatra's whim as little more than a male prostitute?

"Lissa would never forgive me if I did," he eventually replied, without committing himself either way.

"Then perhaps you do have more honour than your father, who needed no such encouragement to partake in every pleasure of the flesh this palace has to offer."

"Do you prefer boys then?" Anthony asked. Homosexual behaviour was commonplace in the classical world and the historical accounts did refer to both Mark Antony and Julius Caesar having relationships with men. Melissa had always been a staunch believer that it was untrue in Mark Antony's case. Anthony wanted to prove her wrong for once.

Mark Antony shrugged. "It is less about preference, and more about availability."

"Any port in a storm," Anthony murmured.

His father looked at him quizzically, not quite sure of the analogy. "Explain, if you please?"

Anthony considered briefly how best to explain it to a Roman. "It means you take what you can get."

"As do you," Mark Antony grinned. Topping up his son's cup with more wine, he added, "Cleopatra makes as good a 'port' as any."

"Ah," Anthony replied, looking a little embarrassed. It seemed his father was far more astute than he had given him credit for.

"Do you know what she wants from you yet?"

Anthony nodded. "She means for me to impersonate you. She believes that to see the general you once were will be an encouragement for the men."

"And what have you told her you want in return?"

"I have asked for nothing, as yet. I thought it best to wait a while. If I ask too soon it will give her greater reason to doubt my motives."

"Good. Now you are thinking like an Antonius."

Anthony was unsure whether that statement was a compliment or an insult. He knew, as Canidius did, that the Antonius males were incompetent in the main. He continued. "There is more. I know her plan. She is going to hand you over to Octavian."

"Dead or alive?"

"She has not expressed her preference, but I believe she wants you dead. She intends to hide me from his sight, playing the dutiful servant until Octavian returns to Rome, at which point her role as Isis will truly come into its own as she conjures a new Mark Antony from the ether to replace her dead husband."

Mark Antony nodded. "I am to play Osiris, and you will play Horus." He sighed. "It always was a good plan, and almost perfect."

Anthony frowned. "What do you mean, almost? Did you know about this?"

His father grinned wickedly. "I made sure we discussed it at length while I still had her ear. All the Mediterranean would hear the news of my death, and many of them will mourn, whether or not Octavian allows them the privilege. For Cleopatra to produce my reincarnated self at some future date would leave her in an unimaginable position of power. Greeks, Jews, Syrians, would flock to a banner raised in my name, especially if they believe me returned from the dead. The plan was a good one, genius in fact, except for one serious flaw which I may have failed to mention."

"What is that?"

"Cleopatra thinks she can manipulate Octavian in the same ways she manipulated me and Caesar, and you. She believes that playing to his vanity will give her an edge.

It will not. She will learn to her cost that not every man wants a foreign queen to dangle off his dick. Octavian is cold and humourless. He cares nothing for her flattery, only her wealth. Whatever deal she may make for her survival, Octavian will renege on any it as soon as it suits. He will parade her in Rome as his trophy before having her strangled in the Tullianum. She will not live long enough to execute the finer details of her plan."

"Good," Anthony said bitterly.

Mark Antony feigned astonishment. "What is this? You do not wish to be master of the civilised world? You would have power beyond your wildest dreams, and if you are truly like me, I know how wild those can be."

Anthony shrugged. "I would be nothing more than a pawn in her grand game. Once I had outlived my usefulness I would be discarded."

"What makes you so sure that would be the outcome?" the older of the two asked.

"She has discarded you."

Mark Antony pouted and then nodded. "That is a fair point." He slapped his son on the shoulder. "What new plans does she have for Lissa? I am assuming she will try to retrieve her?"

"She has not said outright, but she took me on a tour of her reptile farm. I watched while she had prisoners subjected to the venom of many different snakes. It was sickening to watch them die. Some were quick, but others were terrifyingly slow and painful. The worst made a man turn red and sweat as his body became swollen. He vomited and shit himself uncontrollably until the end finally came. I fear she will send Lissa there, if she gets her hands on her again."

"I do not think she will be that generous." He thought

back to the conversation he had with Cleopatra. She wanted Melissa broken and ruined, used cruelly by as many men as was humanly possible. "Whatever plans she has for your wife will be far worse than poisoning. I fear your visit was meant as a warning of what she will do to you if you dare to cross her."

Anthony shuddered. He shook himself as he tried to put the images of the dying men from his mind.

His father let him think on the prospect for a few moments before moving the conversation on. "If I tell you I have a way to get Lissa out of the city, what then? Do you have a way to return her to your time?"

"No. I do not understand why the mists formed in Actium. I thought they only formed over the Rubicon. I need to get access to the library. I hope the answer is in there, but my requests have so far been denied."

Mark Antony shook his head. "These mists may well form in many places, but the answers you seek are not in that library." He saw a look of bafflement cross Anthony's face and so explained further. "I have looked long and hard for a way to control your mists. I set the best minds in Athens to the task, but they found nothing. Even the most learned man in Alexandria could do little more than furnish me with one scroll on the subject, which is of little use, according to your wife."

"Lissa has seen it?"

Mark Antony nodded.

"And she cannot find the solution?"

Mark Antony shook his head.

"Then there is no hope for us." Anthony exclaimed.

"There is always hope." Mark Antony said to encourage his son. "What if no one can find the solution to this puzzle? What will you do then?"

Anthony shrugged dejectedly. "I do not know."

"Not good enough. Think, boy. You have a boat, a good mind, and a very rich father. What do you do?"

Anthony downed another glass of wine as he thought the problem through. "I take Lissa and sail as far away from Egypt as possible. She has to be out of Alexandria before Octavian arrives."

"How soon will he come?"

Anthony stared at his father in disbelief. "Do you really need to ask me that?"

Mark Antony said nothing, but he shook his head. He knew only too well Octavian could not afford to delay any longer. As he was the only Roman general capable of stopping the young Caesar's relentless advance, his removal from opposition was becoming more urgent.

He downed his own wine in one go, wiping the back of his hand across his mouth. "I agree with you, my son. Lissa must be gone before Octavian arrives. If he knows she is here, it will renew his purpose, for he is a man with a long memory and has borne a grudge since I made him condemn that bastard Salvidienus. Octavian's revenge will be far from swift."

Anthony sat up straight and held out his glass, which was immediately refilled. "We cannot allow that to happen."

"Then we must continue to trust one another. We must see this through to the bitter end, whatever that may be." Mark Antony filled his own glass again, draining the last of the wine.

"I am beginning to think none of us will come out of this alive."

"Nonsense. You let me worry about the future. All you have to do is remain strong and keep our queen content.

Has she told you how she intends to make her offer to Octavian?"

"Through a man called Thyrsus. He has been courting Cleopatra for many days. They spend hours together, locked in conversation."

Mark Antony shook his head ruefully. "And we both know where that will go. You cannot allow her interest in you to pass to another so quickly. Get rid of him."

"I cannot do that. According to my history, you have him seized and whipped in a fit of jealousy."

"I am neither jealous of a man I have never met, nor in the palace to do as you suggest. If you say he must be whipped, order it."

Anthony gulped. He did not want that on his conscience.

His father huffed and grabbed him by the shoulder. "You are an Antonius: a man of my blood. You have it in you to do this. You must find the strength for two very good reasons. Cleopatra has little respect for a man who will not stand his ground. Show you are jealous of this Thyrsus, and then stand fast. Make her understand she may be mistress in this palace, but you are master in the bedroom, where it is she who must do as she is told. Do you understand?"

Anthony nodded slowly. He had an inkling of what his father was getting at, but needed more time to consider the implications. He waited a few more seconds before prompting his father to continue. "That is only one reason. What is the second?"

Mark Antony let out a laugh. "Allow your history to be changed and Lissa will kill us both, long before Octavian gets the chance."

Both men smiled and clinked glasses before finishing

their drinks. It was time for them to part before anyone realised they were in the same suite.

Mark Antony walked over to the portrait of Wepawet and opened the panel, but stopped short of leaving. He turned to face Anthony again.

"The boy I mentioned – Eros. It is thanks to him that Lissa is alive. He is Cleopatra's only failure as far as I know. He does her bidding when it comes to sexual favours, because he must, but his loyalty is to me and to me alone. He would make a good friend for you. I will see to it that he understands we are different men, with different tastes. I will instruct him to stay close to give assistance, if you are in need. It could be useful for you to have an ally within these halls, and safer than you destroying so much of the foliage that you arouse suspicion."

Anthony took a deep breath and exhaled slowly. He got up and walked over to join his father. "Thank you," he said calmly. "I appreciate your help."

Mark Antony grinned. "I know that hurt to say, but it is a sign of progress between us. At this rate, we may even learn to like each other."

He threw a small, oval stone to Anthony, who caught it with ease. "Come – I will show you how to wedge the lever to give you privacy. That way, you decide what is seen, not Cleopatra's harpies."

Chapter 28

Anthony Marcus strolled into Cleopatra's private apartments nonchalantly. He had received a summons earlier that afternoon, the first since Thyrsus' departure the week before. He had struggled with the idea of having a man flogged for some time before finally deciding to give the order. Now he had to face the consequences. As the call was to her quarters, not the state rooms, he anticipated he was going to get a chance to put his side of events. That gave him an opportunity to charm the queen, so he took his time in answering the call. He bathed and summonsed Eros to his room to give him a massage with musky, scented oils.

Despite his initial concerns, he found Mark Antony's young servant to be fine company. Good looking and muscular, Eros was naive for his age, which Anthony estimated to be around twenty. He was most definitely in awe of his master, making Anthony wonder how old he had been when he had first been used sexually. There was no age of consent in these times, but Anthony pitied this gentle soul, who had most likely been abused by many men since adolescence. To gain the protection of a man as powerful as Mark Antony must have seemed like a gift from the gods for such a young, impressionable boy.

Because of his position, Eros was able to move around the palace unchallenged and was a frequent nocturnal visitor to the Timoneum. He confirmed Melissa was living there and that she was safe. He was also able to confirm that she was not granting any sexual favours to her host: that was his job.

Whatever else Eros was good at, he was an excellent masseur and had been a blessing now that Canidius had resumed, and intensified, their training. Anthony often found himself stiff and in need of a firm pair of hands to soothe the aches away. Once his massage finished, he dressed in one of the luxurious new tunics the queen had added to his wardrobe since he became her lover. All in all, he was quite pleased with the result. He hoped it would be enough.

With a nod to the guards, Anthony pushed open the door to the queen's bedchamber, entered and closed it shut behind him. The room was brightly lit with candles and lamps, which was unusual for one of their assignations.

Cleopatra was sitting at her dressing table, the usual contents of which had been pushed to one side. It was now home to several documents that she was studying intently. He walked up behind her. Brushing her hair to one side, he bent over to kiss her neck. She pulled away.

He straightened up. "You wanted me, my lady?" he asked, a little put out at her reaction.

When she made no effort to respond, he turned back towards the bed. At the end of it was a long couch, in front of which sat a low table. On it was a flask of wine and two glasses. Anthony picked up the flask, which was nearly empty. He drained it into one of the glasses and turned back to offer it to the queen.

She now sat facing him, a glass already in her hand. Anthony glanced back at the table. There was definitely another glass there and now he noticed it had been used.

Someone had already been there, most likely telling tales of his exploits. His guard immediately went up, but he did not let it show.

Returning his attention to the queen, he repeated his question a little more formally. "What do you want with me, your majesty?"

She scowled. "We wish to know what you think it is you are doing."

She was using the royal 'we'. This meant it was an official audience, even if they were in her private quarters. He could guess why, but he looked baffled anyway.

"You ordered Thyrsus to be flogged and returned to Octavian. What gives you the right to do that?" she barked.

He shrugged. "You expect me to replace Mark Antony. I am playing the jealous husband. I doubt he would stand by and watch you flirt so openly with another man as you have with that one for the past three weeks."

"Mark Antony would have more sense than to involve himself in matters of state. He would nurse his jealousies with a generous amount of wine." She eyed the glass in his hand. "That part, at least, is something you have mastered."

"I am simply trying to live up to your expectations," he defended.

"We expect you to do as you are told."

Her retort was sharp and unfeeling. It was clear he had gone too far and was being chastised. He dropped onto the couch, slamming the glass down on the table, and waited to see what reprimand he was to receive.

"Thyrsus was the envoy of the new master of Rome. Our negotiations were at a delicate stage. If they have been ruined."

He cut her dead. "There is no negotiation. Octavian will not give you what you want."

"And now you have gained your wife's aptitude for foresight. What will you achieve next?" Cleopatra threw in sarcastically.

Anthony's blood pressure was on the rise. This woman could be just as frustrating as Melissa, always believing she was right and never listening to another point of view. The two women were far more alike than either of them would care to admit. He was beginning to see why Mark Antony had become so enamoured with her all those years ago.

He found himself less than impressed by her reference to Octavian as the new master of Rome. It sounded as if she had already given Mark Antony up as a lost cause. If this was true, Cleopatra was not the infatuated lover epitomised by Shakespeare, but a ruthless leader out to further her own ends.

"I do not need foresight to know you are being played!" He ran his hand over his head to hide his frustration. "Octavian wants your money and he wants Mark Antony dead. As I am currently the man sitting in Mark Antony's chair, that makes me somewhat nervous of my position. I gave the order to . . ."

"I am queen," she spat, momentarily dropping the formality. "I give orders. You obey them. I decide who lives and who dies, who is to be flogged and who is not."

"And am I to be flogged for trying to keep you safe?" he shot back angrily.

Knowing he was losing his composure, Cleopatra took her time to respond in order to regain hers. This 'Anthony' could be just as irritating as the other one, thinking he was her equal in all matters.

"We are yet to decide," was her eventual reply. "You will learn your place, or Ammut will make a meal of your heart." She was referring to the weighing of the heart ceremony recorded in Egyptian Books of the Dead, where the dead man's heart was weighed against his deeds in life. If his heart weighed heavy, it would be eaten by Ammut, the devourer, thus denying the dead man entry to the afterlife.

Angry at being toyed with, he pushed against the table, moving it backwards. "Damn you, woman, what is it you want from me?" he shouted.

"Obedience."

"I am a man, not a dog!"

"Really? I hear you are spending much time with young Eros. If that is true you now screw like a dog." She was hinting that Eros was Anthony's lover. "Go! Enjoy his tight arse, while I write to Octavian to beg his forgiveness for your rash actions." She turned back to her desk and her papers.

Anthony clenched his fist. "I have never done that, nor will I," he replied through gritted teeth. "I would sooner die."

"That can be arranged!" she snapped without looking at him.

Anthony fell silent, for a moment, knowing she meant it, until the realisation hit him that he no longer cared whether she did or not. He was fed up playing her games with a spoilt brat, who belittled, embarrassed and bullied people. The gambler in him knew the time had come to risk everything. One last throw of the dice, so to speak.

Fuck it, he thought, *what have I got to lose.*

"If that is your wish, do it," he said calmly, calling her bluff.

Cleopatra shoved all of the papers back on the dressing table in a fit of rage. This man might be her most favourite courtier, but he had overstepped his position. He had to be punished for having Thyrsus flogged, but how to do it without losing him? She needed Anthony, or his dead body, for her plan to succeed. The future of her country depended on it.

A hint of a smile formed on Cleopatra's lips as she considered another unconventional punishment. Anthony had often expressed a desire to travel beyond the confines of the city and now seemed an opportue moment to grant his request. The desert was one of the harshest environments known to man and to attempt to cross it was something few seasoned Egyptians would attempt in summer. An unskilled foreigner would last no more than a few hours in the searing heat. She could not afford to lose her greatest prize at such a late stage, but, by her estimation, there was little danger he would escape. Whether Anthony died in the palace by her hand, or in the desert from his own stupidity, was of little consequence and a dead body was just as easy to retrieve as a live one.

"As much as I enjoy your company, Anthony, I cannot allow your actions to go unpunished without appearing weak. I will send you away for a brief time. You have previously expressed a desire to see more of my country. Now would be an appropriate time for you to do so. Arrangements will be made tomorrow for a trip beyond the lake. Only a day or two, and I insist you take the palace guard with you for your protection. There is a price on Mark Antony's head. I would not want someone to mistake you for him and dispatch you to Octavian by accident."

Anthony could scarcely believe his luck. Once again

he had gambled and won. He wondered just how much longer his luck could last.

He gave a low whistle. "I thank you, your majesty, for your clemency. Let us hope your guards are as loyal as you believe them to be, for I have heard the amount offered is considerable."

Chapter 29

"Who was that young man I saw here last night?"

Melissa sat on the couch at the end of Mark Antony's bed, eating a fig, while he gently rubbed her feet. It was the most intimate level of contact he had managed since the love of his life had been resident in his bed. At least she had stopped crying, which meant he was making some progress. Now it seemed all she wanted to do was talk.

"He is none of your business," Mark Antony snapped back.

"Oh, then it is true," she sighed. She looked disappointed. "You do have a male lover."

Mark Antony held his hands up in despair. "Lissa, your new-found frigidity may serve your needs, but it does little for mine. I will do as I please, with whom I please, when I please. I would ask you to keep your opinions to yourself."

He seemed embarrassed. It was not something she had ever seen before and she could not stop herself from giggling.

When his eyes narrowed, she knew it was best to change the subject before his mood darkened.

"What happened to Ventidius?"

"What do you believe happened to him?" he asked, relieved at the change in direction, if somewhat surprised by it.

Melissa picked another fig out of the bowl. Her appetite was improving. He considered this another good sign.

"I believe he led a successful campaign against the Parthians, celebrated a triumph and retired with honour in Rome. I wish to know how he died."

He smiled to himself as he remembered his old friend fondly. "Ventidius was loyal to me until the last. He acted as my ears in Rome, sending me reports of Octavian's rumour mongering. Losing him was a great blow."

"Then I take it you did not kill him?"

Mark Antony was taken aback by her question. He was a man of many failings, but to be accused of murdering one of his closest friends and most loyal allies shocked him to the very core.

"You think me capable of such a wicked deed?" he asked.

Melissa shrugged. "You offered to kill my husband not so long ago."

He grinned and pinched her little toe. "Ah . . . well . . . that was different. Those were words said in the heat of passion." Cheekily, he ran his hand up her calf and onto her thigh, before she slapped it away. "I would never have done it, and I did not kill Ventidius, regardless of what your books may say to the contrary."

He became more serious. "Whispers reached me that his death may not have been natural. Poison was suggested, but there was no proof. If there had been, I would have gone to Rome and laid my suspicions in front of the Senate. I could have crushed that boy before he could do any more damage. Instead I allowed him to whisper and plot, sowing the seeds of discontent at my abhorrent behaviour. Once he read out that ridiculous document he claimed was my will, there was no way to save the situation. He could declare me an enemy of the state quicker than he could take a shit!"

Melissa frowned. "But he did not do that. Octavian's declaration of war was against Cleopatra, not you, even if you were his primary target."

"You are correct." Mark Antony rubbed his chin as he pondered the situation. "He wants – no, he *needs* me out of the way, even if he stops short of admitting it." He sighed. "I may have little love for Rome herself, but I will still uphold the principles of the Republic regardless of the lies Octavian spreads. Senatus Populusque Romanus: the Senate must be allowed to run the state for the good of the people. No single man can be in overall control." He grinned suddenly. "A man with that much power would be impossible to bribe!"

Melissa shook her head disapprovingly. "You are incorrigible at times."

"As are you," he replied, pointing a finger at her. "In that much we are equal." He gave her a cheeky wink and, for the briefest moment, Melissa saw the old Mark Antony: the vibrant chancer with a lust for life, not the depressive soul he had become.

"I am the biggest obstacle to Octavian's plans for world domination because the people of Rome *love* me, no matter what I do. That reason alone is almost justification enough to dispose of me, but he also has another problem – funding. Octavian has been making promises he could not keep for years. It started when he promised to give the people the legacy promised to them in Caesar's will, even though there was never enough money to achieve it."

"Only because you spent it!" Melissa exclaimed.

He waved his hand in the air dismissively. "Your opinion in this is subjective, and unfounded. Rome was bankrupt. I simply diverted the money that Caesar himself had stolen back into the coffers of the state."

"Where, as consul, you could realign the Republic's spending priorities to meet your own ends."

"Exactly." He stopped short, realising that Melissa's words were a thinly veiled insult. He pointed at her. "Do not twist my words, Lissa. I may be old, and a drunk, but I am no fool."

She nodded, apparently acknowledging defeat, but the smile on her lips told him she had won that point.

"Remember this," he chided, "you could have prevented all of this, had you only told me that boy would lay claim to his inheritance. I could have warned my dim-witted siblings to take more care in their dealings with him, had you been a little more forthcoming with your information." When Octavian first arrived in Rome, his claim to be Caesar's heir had been ratified by both the Praetor responsible for recording wills, and the Tribune serving as his assistant. The two men concerned were none other than Gaius and Lucius Antonius, Mark Antony's younger brothers.

She had the decency to look sympathetic. "I could, but I could hardly tell you your brothers were both idiots. You would have ripped my head off for even thinking it in those days. You had to come to that conclusion of your own accord."

Mark Antony frowned, knowing she was right yet again. Neither of his brothers had ever shown so much as a flicker of genius. They had both been easily led by a shrewd opponent.

Melissa took another fig. "What I have never understood is why you ever let him become so powerful in the first place."

"I did not see what he would become. He had us all fooled."

"Brutus knew," she said quietly, "even before the Pedian law condemned him, he knew." Octavian's first act as consul in 43 B.C. had been to force Pedius, his co-consul, to pass a law that set up a special tribunal to try each of Caesar's assassins for their crimes. It was less of a tribunal and more of a witch hunt, with every man found guilty and sentenced, in absentia.

Mark Antony shrugged. "Then he should have said something."

"I believe he did. He tried to warn you all that Octavian was the one with dreams of following Caesar, yet you all failed to listen to him. Brutus told Cicero to put aside his hatred for you and support you to remove Octavian before he could become too powerful, but even Cicero believed the boy to be little more than a harmless child."

"Ah yes, what was it Cicero said? The boy should be lauded, applauded and cast aside. Look where that suggestion got him," he stared wistfully into the distance, remembering fondly the demise of his old nemesis.

Melissa gave a loud tut of disapproval. "Dead, with his hands and head nailed to the senate house door. While we are on that subject, which one of you proscribed him? Was it really Octavian's idea, or did he succumb to pressure from you?" After the treaty of Bononia had been agreed, Mark Antony, Octavian and Lepidus drew up an initial list of seventeen names of men whom they deemed to be their enemies. These men were to be eradicated, their wealth and property confiscated by a process known as proscription. It was a quick and effective way to remove political opponents, settle scores, and to generate a significant amount of cash in the process.

"Me?" Mark Antony laughed heartily. "No, Lissa. I gave up my uncle, a man who was both rich, and of very little use."

She pointed an accusatory finger. "And only because you knew that your mother would intercede. She would never allow her brother to be taken away in such a cruel manner."

He grinned again, allowing the familiar twinkle of wickedness to flicker in his eyes. "You never met my mother. She was a most formidable force, and a woman who always got her way. Cleopatra is a mere novice in comparison with her ability for diplomacy!"

"Sheer bloody-mindedness more like," Melissa muttered in English.

He did not wait for the translation into Latin. He knew Melissa well enough to know that it would be less than complimentary. He returned the conversation to the proscriptions instead, referring to Octavian again. "Cicero's demise was all the idea of the 'child genius'. That was when I first realised what a nasty little arse he was. You know, he really is so very little and so very vain. He has special soles put on his shoes to make him taller."

When Melissa frowned, he knew she was not in the mood for joking and carried on in a more serious vein. "Octavian's vindictiveness towards the old goat knew no bounds, and yet it was me that took the blame for it. Everyone assumed it was my hatred of Cicero that led to his death, yet I had more to gain from him living. My brother was still alive at that time. Allowing Octavian to name Cicero signed Gaius' death warrant." Gaius Antonius had been a prisoner of Brutus for many months at the time of the agreement made at Bononia. When news of Cicero's murder reached him, Brutus executed Gaius in retaliation.

"Perhaps Octavian was scared that Gaius was in a position to reconcile you to Brutus, thus leaving him out in the cold. You and Brutus were friends, after all."

He shook his head. "Never friends, though I would say we had a mutual respect for each other. He had the name to garner the respect of the Senate, but no balls to do what was needed. I had power, but lacked support because of the inferiority of my status. I would have considered an alliance with him if one had been offered, not only because he held my brother, but because he was an honourable man. That made him a rarity in Rome, and someone to be respected. Together, we could have achieved greatness."

Melissa nodded her understanding. She too had found Brutus to be a good and honest man. He had helped her when no one else would, and she had always been grateful for that.

They sat for some time in silence, while Mark Antony pondered the past mistakes that he had made. Eventually, he pushed her feet away and rose from the couch. He walked over to the side table where a flask of wine sat, and poured two glasses. Walking back to the couch he gave one glass to Melissa before wandering over to the open window, where he stood breathing in the salty evening breeze.

He resumed the conversation. "Declaring war on Cleopatra was a masterstroke. Octavian is fighting an immoral foreigner who has seduced the people's hero with witchcraft. He has legitimacy to steal her lands and treasury, all under the guise of saving me from myself. It is a work of pure genius."

"The success of Octavian's entire campaign rests on his securing the treasury of the Ptolemies. Without it, he will meet a very sticky end at the hands of the very men he promises to pay."

"We can but hope," he muttered, knowing that his wish was nothing more than an idle fantasy.

Melissa sighed. "From the moment war was declared on Cleopatra, your destinies were entwined. That is the reason you did not heed Herod's warnings to send her away from Actium. You knew your only choice was to stand together, or die alone."

He raised the hand holding the glass and pointed it towards Melissa, acknowledging her statement. "Precisely. If she abandoned me, it would leave me vulnerable and exposed." He adopted a whining tone. "*The great Mark Antony, cast off by a woman* – that is what they would say, and laugh whilst doing so. If I abandoned her, it would do untold damage to my reputation." Again, the same tone. "*If that wastrel Mark Antony will turn against the mother of his infant children, he will turn against anyone.*" He sighed as he wandered back to the couch. "Together we had a chance, albeit a slim one. I allowed her too much influence, as I did with Fulvia. I held back when I should have struck forward. I bowed to her judgement while Agrippa nibbled away my power base.

"In your defence, I would say it is difficult to say no to the woman who pays the wages of twenty legions," Melissa offered.

"And the rest!" he scoffed as he sat down again. "To fund any army means a great deal more than paying its wages. There are the logistics to think of. Armies fight and they move. Men need weapons, armour, transport, clothing, quarters, bedding, food, wine. Then there are the slaves, the cooks, the blacksmiths, the barbers, the whores. The list is endless. Damn woman even paid for the sponges they wipe their arses with! Men have been declared bankrupt for far less than I owe to Cleopatra, myself included." Mark Antony had accepted bankruptcy at the age of ten as he was unable to pay off the debts he inherited on his father's death.

"And still the dent in Egypt's finances is minimal. How does she manage it?" Melissa murmured.

"She has a shrewd mind, and an endless supply of eunuchs. Fat little fucks they are, with their heads so far up her arse, she need never again walk unaided." He downed his wine. It seemed bitterness brought out his need for alcohol. "They *hate* me. They cannot bear the thought of a real man, with both his balls intact, acting as adviser to a living deity. Or the even worse thought, that *I* could possibly be considered her equal."

"No, you were never her equal," Melissa soothed, but he misunderstood her meaning.

"Even you see it. She is a goddess, and I am nothing." He looked away suddenly, not wanting Melissa to see the bitterness in his face, even if she could hear it in his voice.

"You are Roman – she is not," Melissa countered forcefully, determined to change his attitude. "You will always be her superior. She knew that from the first moment she came to Tarsus. She was nothing more than a merchant, peddling her wares in the hope that you were looking to buy, and you bought the lot. You allowed her to hold power over you, although there were moments when the real you shone out."

Slowly, he turned to face her again. She could see the wicked twinkle in his eyes once more. He was teasing her now, daring her to flatter him. "Name one?"

"Herod. You stood firm in your refusal to remove him from your circle. You allowed him to keep his lands, even though she demanded they be given to her."

"And what a good decision that proved to be," he muttered.

"You cannot blame him for his desertion, not after you personally helped Ahenobarbus to leave Actium, and many others since. Herod is a survivor. He will kiss the backside of any man if it means staying in Rome's good books. He fears the sound of Roman boots in the streets of Jerusalem, far more than he fears the well-paid flunkies of this court and, believe me, he is right to do so."

"Why? What do you know?" He sat up straight, suddenly showing more interest.

"Nothing." Melissa looked away, embarrassed at her near slip.

"Liar! Tell me or I will put you out on your ear." He grasped one of her ankles suddenly, and a little too tightly. It took her by surprise.

"Do you really think you can threaten me into telling you what the future holds?" she asked as she wriggled to free herself from his grip.

He sighed and let go. "No, but you could at least humour me. Would it hurt to allow me to believe I am still a man to be scared of?"

Melissa frowned. She of all people knew the dangers of mentioning future events, but there seemed little point in keeping secrets, not now that he knew the truth of where her knowledge came from. "Herod is what we term a night watchman. It means his rule is a temporary arrangement. There will be a Roman governor installed soon enough and Judea will be made to tow the line, as does every other province. A hundred years from now, the Jews will revolt against Roman rule. The response will be devastating. The great temple of Jerusalem will be reduced to rubble. Only a single wall will remain to serve as a reminder to others not to displease Rome. The rebels will flee to Masada, where they will remain under siege."

"Sensible. I have seen that place. Even I would think twice before attacking such a heavily-fortified bastion."

"Yes. So well-fortified that nothing will get in . . . or out."

Mark Antony thought for a moment before the brevity of her words hit him.

"That is not so sensible," he remarked, understanding that the people of Masada would starve long before the Roman army would relent. "I recall such a siege in another land. The commander sent the women and children out, hoping they would be shown leniency. None was given." He closed his eyes, remembering the siege of Alesia in Gaul. "I still hear the cries of those women, wailing helplessly as their children starved to death before their eyes. Some smothered their offspring themselves to end their suffering."

He shook himself to lift the melancholy that was descending. "Now that Herod has switched sides, there is no one left with command of an army capable of putting up even a half- decent fight. Octavian's net is closing fast. War will come to Egypt, and it is a war I cannot win."

"Nor should you try," she sighed.

"Then what should I do?"

She scrambled along the couch. Taking her hands in his, she squeezed them tightly.

"You should run," she begged.

He shook his head. "I have never run from anything in my life."

Melissa raised an eyebrow. It was a gesture that said *really?* As a young man, Mark Antony ran away from his growing debts, to Greece. He then joined the army to avoid another scandal. After being ousted from Rome, he withdrew his forces across the Alps when the siege of Mutina failed. He ran back to Syria, and Cleopatra, when his Parthian campaign became a disaster. Running was something he had become rather adept at.

He slouched back into the couch, pouting like a naughty schoolboy.

"I cannot run," he grumbled. "I have nowhere left to go."

Chapter 30

The trip began well. Anthony sailed south across Lake Mareotis, accompanied by four of Cleopatra's personal guard. Once across, they followed a tributary snaking through the farmland until they reached the expansive sands of the Sahara. They rode on until they reached a small encampment by a lone palm tree, which turned out to be a caravan of traders who had stopped for the night.

Anthony was allowed to dismount and talk to them for some time. They had never met anyone from the palace before and appeared somewhat in awe of him. They even offered to share their evening meal of some kind of stew, bread and dried dates, which the guards encouraged, producing a wineskin each as their contribution to the festivities. The food was a little salty, encouraging Anthony to drink more than his share as the wine was passed around. He failed to notice that no one else was drinking it, or how quickly it was affecting him. By the time the guards insisted they return to the palace, he was feeling decidedly drunk as he climbed back on his horse and waved his goodbyes to his hosts.

He had no memory of falling from the horse, nor did he remember ending up face down in the sand dune, but that was where he awoke the next morning. Slowly, he raised his throbbing head to stare at a scorpion, sitting about an arm's length from his head. Neither moved for some time; each one afraid of the other. Eventually, the scorpion scuttled away across the warming sands, leaving Anthony very much alone.

His mouth felt as dry as sandpaper. Pushing himself up into a sitting position, he surveyed his surroundings – nothing but sand in every direction. Not a good start. Looking behind him, he spotted one of the wineskins near the top of the dune. Turning over onto all fours, he scrambled up the sand to retrieve it. He removed the stopper and drained the last few drops of wine from it. It tasted bitter and grainy, and made his tongue tingle. He spat it out immediately, realising the dregs were thick with some form of opiate.

"Fucking bitch," Anthony cursed in English as he discarded the empty wineskin. He knew Cleopatra had ordered him to be drugged and abandoned, his punishment for having Thyrsus flogged.

The sun was quite low in the sky, but it was already warm. A deep breath gave nothing but hot, stifling air, with no hint of the salty tang he was used to by the shore in the palace. He had no idea where he was, how far it was back to the city, or even which direction to go in. His situation was dire, to say the least. Clambering to the top of the dune did little to help. All there was to see was sand, in every direction.

Looking back down to where he had first woken up, he could see a trail stretching in two directions, left by his guards after deserting him. One way would lead him back to the palace and the other back to the caravan, if it was still there. They had probably moved on at dawn and could be miles away by now. If he followed them, he might never catch up with them. He thought back to his sailing experience. If you were out at sea and your instruments failed, you had to navigate using the stars. As it was day, there was only one star available to him: the sun. Knowing it rises in the east, Anthony put it to his right, meaning he should be facing north. One trail went roughly in that direction, so that was the one he decided to follow. He set out at a steady pace, trying not to overexert himself in the heat.

He had plenty of time to think on his actions as he trudged over the dunes. Melissa had definitely been wrong in her approach to their situation. She wanted to act as she had in Rome, but this was not Rome and Roman sensibilities meant nothing to Cleopatra or her decadent court of vipers. To survive here, you had to play by Alexandria's more depraved rules. Melissa's brain was simply not wired to understand that, whereas his was.

His biggest mistake had been allowing his overconfidence to cloud his judgement. He had grossly underestimated Cleopatra and her vindictiveness. He would not make that mistake again.

As queen, Cleopatra was used to getting her way without question. From the outset Anthony had known this. He had met her type before – the spoilt little rich girl expecting everyone to be at her beck and call. He had played her games for months, fooling himself into thinking he was in control. Her manipulation of him had been so clever, it left him bitter and angry when he realised the truth.

His pace slowed with the increase in heat as the sun rose. He had no idea what the time was but, as the sun was still on his right, he assumed he was still heading north. Little did he know that his guards had been very clever when leaving the trail, running it round in a great loop. It meant that he was actually going back in the direction of the encampment. It was a fact he realised as soon as he reached the crest of the next dune. Below him he could see a large flat area next to a solitary palm. Heading off in the distance was the wider trail left by the caravan as it moved off that morning.

Anthony sat down in the sand, dismayed that he had walked so far, only to be back where he started. He knew the tributary was somewhere nearby. He had to try to find it, knowing it would eventually lead him to Alexandria and safety.

And still the relentless sun blazed down on his back.

Anthony stumbled along as the sun reached its peak. His mouth was dry and parched, his stride erratic. He had removed his tunic to use as a cover for his head and neck, but it left the remainder of his body exposed to its searing rays. The backs of his legs stung where the skin was tightening in the merciless heat. Even the soles of his feet felt hot from the sand slipping into his sandals. Despite the agony he felt, he knew he had to go on.

He fell as he slid down the next dune, rolling onwards to the bottom. He cried out in pain as the harsh sand scraped across his blistering flesh. He lay where he was for some time, unable to bring himself to continue. *Was this to be his end? Was this where he would die?*

He knew he had to keep going. *One more dune and I'll see the ocean*, he thought. He tried to push himself up, but his legs began to shake and collapsed back onto the sand. Arm- over-arm he crawled up to the top of the next dune, hoping that, when he reached its peak, the vivid blue sky would reach down to meet the equally vivid green Mediterranean. Instead, he was greeted by nothing but sand. His throat tightened and his torso shook as he waited for the tears to fall, but none came. It was as if there was no moisture left to spare in his body. *Was this what the Fates had in store for him?*

And still the relentless sun blazed down on his back.

He laid his head on his folded arms and closed his eyes, deciding he would rest for a few moments before continuing. His thoughts drifted to his home, to his children, to his wife. He loved them all, and he missed them. He would give anything just to see them one more time.

He needed a miracle, if such a thing existed.

The Fates have a way of bending all things to their will, and they were not done with Anthony Marcus just yet. His miracle was delivered shortly after he passed out. It came on horseback, in the uniform of a Roman general, and carrying a full skin of water.

Canidius had been looking for Anthony ever since Eros had delivered the news that the palace guard had returned from their expedition without their charge. Having the odd friend of his own amongst the female servants, Canidius was quickly able to establish the direction the guards had come from, and then retraced their route south in search of his wayward sparring partner.

Turning Anthony onto his back, he was relieved to hear his patient groan. Removing the bung from the water, he carefully dribbled some along his fingers and between Anthony's swollen lips. Gradually Anthony began to move his jaw, encouraging Canidius to dribble a little more until Anthony's eyes fluttered open.

"More," he croaked, in English, but Canidius understood what he meant.

"Careful, lad," he chided gently. "Too much can be as

bad for you as none at all. Can you sit?"

Anthony nodded and, with Canidius' assistance, he sat up, immediately grabbing his pounding forehead.

"It is the heat – like having a man hammer on your skull," Canidius informed him in a matter-of-fact way. "It will pass in time. Here, drink a little more if you can, slowly mind, or you will bring it back out." He handed Anthony the water. Dutifully, Anthony sipped at it, fighting his urge to gulp it down.

"What were you thinking?" Canidius asked, "Coming out here with her henchmen? It was utter madness."

Anthony nodded. "I know that – now," he whispered hoarsely.

"You would have died, had it not been for your father receiving word that you were missing."

Anthony winced, but said nothing. Yet another reason to be grateful to the man he hated.

"I have made enquiries. Cleopatra is angry with you, though it appears she may not want you dead, merely scared senseless. I only hope whatever you did to her was worth it."

In the distance, the sky was darkening to a deep red. "Is it so late in the day that the sun is setting already? Anthony croaked.

"No, my friend, it is barely an hour past noon," Canidius replied, inspecting Anthony's sunburn.

"Then what is that in the western sky?"

"You are looking to the south, not the west," Canidius corrected as his eyes followed Anthony's finger pointing out in front of them. Concern quickly spread across his face.

"That is the khamsin – the fifty day wind. It frequently invades at this time of year, bringing with it sand storms and unbearable heat."

"I do not like the sound of that," Anthony muttered.

"Nor should you! The khamsin has been known to claim the lives of babies, small animals and the sick. We must outrun it back to the city."

"Back to the palace I suppose?" Anthony queried, with some trepidation.

Canidius nodded sorrowfully. "I have my orders, though it pains me to follow them. Can you ride?"

What Anthony wanted was for Canidius to take him to the Timoneum and to Melissa, but that would mean his agreement with Mark Antony would become public. If that happened, he knew they would all be dead by nightfall. He had to go back to the palace and continue to trust his father. He nodded again. "I think so," he gasped.

With help, he clambered onto the back of Canidius' horse and the pair began the painful ride back to the city.

As the khamsin began to blow, the pair rode in through the Western Gate of Alexandria. Word spread through the streets faster than they could ride, meaning a welcome party was waiting for them as they entered the courtyard outside the palace. Despite the sandstorm, Cleopatra stood atop the steps to the palace as they approached.

Anthony slid from the back of Canidius' horse, landing in a heap at the foot of the steps. He groaned in agony and rolled over onto his back.

"I bring a gift from Mark Antony – something your guards mislaid, your majesty. He says to tell you that you must take better care of your guests," Canidius barked sarcastically. "This one is burnt and blistered, but alive nonetheless."

Canidius could no longer be bothered to make a show of loyalty towards Cleopatra, sneering at the queen in utter contempt of her actions. He did not dismount, and his hand remained on the hilt of his gladius. It gave a clear signal of his intent to defend himself if it became necessary, even though he knew she would not dare to challenge him while he acted in Mark Antony's name.

Cleopatra glared at him for a few moments before giving a curt nod. "He wandered away from his escort, disorientated by the heat, I believe. It will not happen again. We thank you for his safe return."

Canidius scowled, but returned the nod as he pulled on the reins of his horse to turn it. He rode at speed out of the courtyard without a backwards glance. He needed to get out of there before he changed his mind and defied his orders again, retrieving Anthony for his own safety.

With the sound of hoof beats ringing in his ears, Anthony opened his eyes and stared up at the queen who descended the steps through the dust now swirling in the courtyard.

She kicked at his shoulder with her foot. "We trust you have learnt your lesson. From this moment forth you will not deviate from our wishes."

She crouched next to him, so only he could hear her final words. "You will stay in the palace and obey my commands. Overstep your boundaries again and I will ensure you are left so far out in that desert that you will never be found, not even by a skilful tracker like Canidius."

Anthony could barely move, his skin felt so tight from the exposure to the sun, but he managed to nod his agreement.

He knew he was her slave now, as his father had been before him.

Chapter 31

As spring marched forwards, the days grew longer and the temperature rose steadily. Cleopatra continued her attempts at negotiation with Octavian in secret, as did Mark Antony. Both hoped they could secure a better deal, but in different ways. Cleopatra looked to secure her future and that of her legacy. Officially, Octavian replied that he would make no decision on her future until she disbanded her armies and renounced her throne. Privately, he sent word that, if she arranged Mark Antony's death, he would pardon her and leave her kingdom and its succession intact. Mark Antony merely tried to agree terms to save his family. He offered to take his own life on more than one occasion, and even sent his son, Antyllus, to his enemy with a substantial amount of money. Octavian kept the cash, sending the boy back. On each occasion, he left Mark Antony's proposals unanswered.

Mark Antony was fast running out of options. From the outset he had done his utmost to ensure he had plenty of opportunities open to him. His preference had always been to win Melissa back. Whist she enjoyed his company, she frustrated every attempt he made to renew a more intimate relationship. When he promised to send her home, he fully intended to go with her, but trying to leave the city was no longer an option. Octavian's troops were far too close and Mark Antony's profile was too recognisable, especially with a large bounty on his head. Every man had his price, and most would sell their souls for the money Octavian had offered. They would be caught far too quickly, and he would be forced to watch helplessly as Melissa was tortured and executed, before he too died a merciless death.

As for the agreement he had made with her husband – his son – this too looked in jeopardy. The fool had got himself abandoned in the desert without transport or water. Had it not been for Canidius' timely rescue, he would have perished. Since then, he barely left the palace for fear of the consequences. Communication had become impossible without Anthony's trips to the gymnasium, further intensifying Mark Antony's paranoia that his son was lost to them. Having spent nearly fourteen years in the queen's company, Mark Antony understood her favoured modus operandi, how she would allow men to think themselves her equals, before encouraging them to reveal their darkest secrets to her, secrets she could then use and force them to submit to her will. He himself had fallen into her trap, and it appeared his eldest child might have done the same. Melissa's description of her husband as a chip off the old block appeared more apt by the day. If true, it meant Cleopatra had decided to keep her young Horus, leaving her older lover to play Osiris to the bitter end. She would send Octavian's forces direct to the Timoneum. It would be overrun in minutes and he would be forced to watch helplessly as Melissa was tortured and executed, before he too died a merciless death.

There was, of course, his plan to substitute the younger Anthony in his place. It was well conceived and had a relatively good chance of success. To follow it through would mean betraying the woman he truly loved, as well as his estranged son. He would be forced to watch helplessly from the sidelines as Melissa was tortured and executed, although this time he would watch his son die a merciless death; he himself would be alive at least. For him, this had never been a serious consideration. He had once vowed that he would sooner die than let Melissa suffer. That was still the case.

Every option Mark Antony explored brought him to the same conclusion. Melissa would die and he was powerless to prevent it. It was as if the Fates were trying to tell him how it would end, regardless of any attempt he made to alter the course. In his lowest moments, he began to understand the frustrations Melissa must have felt for years, knowing the outcome but being unable to affect any change.

He could not afford to lose control of the situation. He needed to get back to basics. Melissa's safety was what mattered to him, but it would be better if she was kept in the dark about his intentions. That way she could not raise any objections to his plans for her, or her wretched husband, who was a wild card that needed reining in, and quickly. The stories Eros had recounted gave serious cause for concern. Anthony and the queen appeared to be closer than ever, having formed a new dining club: the Synapothanoumenoi, or the society for those who would be partners in death His wayward son had a part to play, if Mark Antony's plans were to be successful but, if the younger man could not follow orders, he would quickly find himself surplus to requirements.

Cleopatra was the unknown quantity, as always. Whatever her current scheme, the outcome would only be good for one person: her. In the days before age, alcohol and apathy derailed him, Mark Antony had been the queen's equal in all things. Could he be that man again? Only time would tell.

And time was running out.

Cleopatra proposed a joint coming of age ceremony for her co-regent and son, Caesarion, and Mark Antony's eldest acknowledged son, Antyllus, proclaiming them as future leaders, should anything happen to their respective parents. The move was one designed to boost the morale of the troops and the people of Alexandria. Despite Melissa's warnings not to go through with it, Mark Antony agreed to the spectacle. He had little choice. He needed to see firsthand what was going on within the main palace and ensure Melissa's husband kept his head.

Anthony, meanwhile, hoped to use the occasion to get into the Timoneum and board the *Selene*. Having spent the weeks since the debacle in the desert appearing contrite, he needed to do something. If he had any chance of using his yacht to escape, he had to know what state she was in. He had not bargained on four contubernia of Roman legionaries being stationed between him and his objective, placed there to secure Melissa's safety. Even though they mistook him for their general, the centurion in charge would not allow Anthony access. General Antony had given clear orders to deny everyone access, including the general himself: only Canidius could gain access to the Timoneum or dismiss the men. Anthony recognised this as a smart move by his father, preventing him from any type of subterfuge to gain access to his wife. He was forced to abandon his plan and instead used the passage network to locate the paths to the harbour and then sneak into the map room, where he inspected as many of the available documents as he could.

After the ceremony ended, a more relaxed Mark Antony returned to the Timoneum with Canidius. Cleopatra had been nothing but polite, insisting that she was only using the younger Anthony for entertainment, until such time as his dead body could be delivered to Octavian. Mark Antony duly accepted her explanation, but he did not believe a word of it. She was a woman renowned for hedging her bets and this occasion was no different. Her plans were changing, meaning he was losing ground with her. That door was closing, but it could be reopened given the right circumstance.

He was unsurprised to hear that 'he' had already returned to the Timoneum earlier in the day. Apparently, 'he' had shown particular interest in getting on the boat captured at Actium.

"He thinks he can use it to escape," Mark Antony muttered to Canidius as they walked along the wharf where the *Selene* was moored.

"Then you must remove the temptation. Sink her and be done with it," Canidius replied emphatically.

Mark Antony scratched his chin as he considered the possibility. "Perhaps that is not the best idea. This attempt proves he still intends to find a way out of here, and most probably with his wife."

"Does this mean your son is still working to your plan?"

"No, I believe he is working to his own plan." Mark Antony shrugged. "It is of no consequence. The fool can be managed, but he may have something in this idea to use the boat. Since we saw Sosigenes, Lissa has spoken at length of her 'sign of the roses' bridge." He meant the Einstein-Rosen bridge, but had misunderstood what Melissa called it and instead replaced its correct name with something that made more sense to him. "They arrived in Actium on board this ship. Lissa thinks it could be the anchor to which Sosigenes referred."

"We should ask him," Canidius suggested innocently.

Something in the cold, emotionless stare of his general made Canidius realise that Sosigenes was no longer available to answer any questions.

"Or not," he muttered to himself as he wondered briefly who else his commander was prepared to silence to protect the seer's true identity.

After staring at the *Selene* for a few more minutes, Mark Antony gave his order.

"The boat has a part to play in this, of that I am sure. Arrange for its removal from Alexandria and have it hidden nearby. We may yet need it, if our other options fail."

Chapter 32

Summer came to Alexandria all too quickly as Octavian edged closer. Having enjoyed their sojourn with Herod, his refreshed and resupplied army took the border town of Pelusium with ease. Rumours reached Alexandria that Cleopatra had ordered the garrison's commander to surrender without a fight. Afraid that Mark Antony might believe her capable of such a deception, she ordered the murder of the man's family to deflect suspicion and to send a message to the citizens that surrender was no longer an option, for any of them.

Mark Antony had no time to worry about rumours of betrayal. He was already marching 200 miles to Paraetorium, determined to win back the once-loyal legions marching in from Cyrenaica. He had finally decided to fight and was determined to mount a defence of the city with whatever forces he could muster.

Cleopatra decided she needed to explore other options. Splitting the contents of her vast treasury, she sent Caesarion out on his first solo command. He went south towards Koptos with a personal bodyguard and a large portion of the loot. Her intention was for her son to secure an escape route across the Red Sea to India. His tutor, Rhodon, went with him as adviser. This would prove to be a fatal mistake. Little did Cleopatra know that Octavian had already offered far more to the tutor than she would ever consider. Rhodon waited until they were well away from Alexandria and then led the party straight into an ambush. Octavian had claimed his first Egyptian prize. He fully intended to kill the young pharaoh, but not immediately. He wanted to see the look on Cleopatra's face when he personally told her that her son's life was in his hands.

A dejected Mark Antony returned to the Timoneum two days before the Kalends of Sextilis - the 30th of July by modern calendars. His mission to retrieve his African legions had failed and they were now camped a few miles outside the Western Gate. Octavian's fleet formed a blockade to the north, beyond the harbour walls, ensuring that no one could leave the city by sea. To the south, beyond Lake Mareotis, lay nothing but the blistering sands of the Sahara and, to the east, Octavian's men marched steadily onwards. Alexandria was surrounded.

That evening, his conduct was particularly morose as he and Melissa sat together on the edge of the jetty at the back of the Timoneum, eating a bowl of olives and watching day turn swiftly to night. The heat inside was stifling and, as darkness fell, there was a cooling breeze murmuring across the water.

They sat there for some time. She was trying hard to convince him that all was not yet lost. He was to ride out and confront Octavian's troops the next day, while they made camp at the hippodrome, just beyond the Canopic Gate. He knew he had to do as she said, but he felt it was pointless.

"Tomorrow I die. It is a sobering thought," he muttered. He flicked an olive stone into the water and watched it sink into the dark waters below.

Melissa kept trying to bolster his mood. "What if I say you will live? That you will face Octavian's cavalry and that you will be victorious?"

He shook his head and flicked another stone. "I am touched by your confidence, but the once-great Mark Antony is gone. He is nothing more than a drunken and debauched failure."

Melissa looked at him with sadness. In all the years she had known him, Mark Antony had suffered from bouts of depression. In the past, she had always proved capable of bringing him out of his dark moods. She had little time left to nurse his ego and the quickest way she knew to give him confidence was to give him what he wanted: her. She sighed, knowing the outcome was inevitable, but no longer seeming to care. They had already survived some of their worst moments by taking strength from each other's love. She had accepted the loss of her children and her husband. There was nothing left to gain by keeping this man at arm's length. Within two days Mark Antony would be dead. What little protection she currently had would die along with him, as would she.

With a new-found purpose, she gave in to the feelings she had felt on the night of his birthday celebrations some seven months earlier. "I disagree. He is still the intelligent, charming genius I came to love. He merely needs reminding of it."

Melissa's hands encircled his neck as she leaned across to kiss him. The touch of her lips was electric and reminded him instantly of every night he had spent in her arms and of the confidence her warmth instilled. She believed in him. She always had. He always felt that he could achieve anything with her by his side. He wanted to have her again, as he had every night since he brought her to his bed, but he had made a promise not to touch her, so he pushed her away. He stood up slowly, his shoulders hunched.

"I want nothing more than to throw you on that bed in there and make you mine again, yet I find I cannot. You are the wife of my son. I swore an oath to him that I would not take you." He turned and walked back inside.

Melissa scrambled to her feet and ran after him. Taking hold of his arm, she turned him back to face her. Melissa was unused to this man turning down an offer of sex. "I doubt your son felt any pang of guilt when he bedded your wife time and time again. Why should you hold faith with a man who fails to show you the same loyalty?"

Mark Antony drew himself up to his full height as his pride shone through. "To keep my word to him is the last act of decency I can ever hope to perform. Do not make me break that oath."

Melissa twisted her mouth as she thought on his words. "And what if you are not the one doing the taking? It will not break any oath if I were to take you first." She dropped to her knees and quickly lifted his tunic.

The second her lips touched his tip, Mark Antony's good intentions to keep to his word vanished. With a groan, he reached for the table to steady himself. While her tongue danced along the full length of his hardening shaft, he began to plan the remainder of the night. He looked around at the notched candle he had lit earlier. There were six notches left: six hours until dawn. He never slept well before a battle, which gave him six hours in which to engage in a variety of acts to heighten their sexual pleasure. They would drink wine laced with the intoxicating powders known to release inhibitions. They would massage each other with the same exotic fragranced oils used in the palace orgies – the ones designed to stimulate desire and the ones used to maintain erections. There was more than enough time to indulge his every wish.

He looked down at the woman on her knees in front of him. Her head was tilted upwards, her large dark eyes wide open and staring into his. She winked cheekily as her tongue continued to tease him so exquisitely, just as her presence in his bed had already teased him for so many weeks. To have her so close, but not touch her, had taken him to the very limit of his resolve. Tonight his patience was being rewarded. Now she too would be teased until she whimpered from sheer frustration. Only then, as she screamed his name aloud, would he allow her the release she so desperately craved, but her torment would not stop there. He would take her again and again, forwards and backwards, on her back and on her knees, in his lap and against the wall. He would pound her until her legs buckled beneath her weight and she collapsed sobbing into his arms.

Mark Antony had six hours to live out his favourite fantasy: that Melissa was truly his.

The sun had not fully risen over the eastern Mediterranean as Mark Antony laced his boots. A tray laden with fruit, nuts and sweetened pastries sat on the same side table he had been standing beside six hours earlier when Melissa first took him in her mouth. In the time that had elapsed since that moment, their bodies had remained entwined. He could not bear to be separated from her, or she from him. Even now, as he prepared to leave, there was hardly any distance between them, but even a mere arm's length felt like a mile.

He walked to the table and picked at the contents of the tray, choosing to stare out of the window rather than staring at the naked body lying behind him. She made far too tempting a target, even though he had no time to spare.

When he heard the sheet rustle, he knew she was awake.

"Is it time?" she murmured.

He chose a large fig from the tray and turned around. Melissa was sitting up in bed with the sheet tantalizingly pulled up across her chest. With a grin he threw the fig at her, aiming high knowing that she could not hold the sheet and catch the fruit. She reached up, allowing the sheet to slip and display her smooth breasts. With a coy smile, Melissa placed one hand on the sheet, but Mark Antony shook his head.

"Allow me to feast my eyes on you one last time, Lissa. Let this be a final vision to warm my heart before I walk into the arms of Dis."

"You will not die today," Melissa scolded, already knowing the outcome of the skirmish ahead.

"Not if I have you to return to," he replied with a laugh. "Although another night like the last may finish me off." His expression became more sombre. "Say you will wait for me as you are now?"

"I might like to bathe and dress."

"No. I fear for your safety beyond this room. I can no longer afford to spare more than one legionary to guard you. You must stay here. Swear it."

"If it pleases you, I will stay."

"And if it pleases me, will you again stiffen my resolve with your skilful tongue?" He winked and gripped his groin.

Melissa tried to look disapproving of his coarseness, but failed dismally. "I will, if it pleases you," she agreed, with a laugh.

"Then eat heartily and rest, lady. I expect to see a wide smile on all your lips when I return."

His last remark went too far. Melissa threw a pillow at his head, which he dodged, before leaving the room humming to himself.

Chapter 33

The military engagement went as Melissa foretold. Mark Antony's cavalry took Octavian by surprise and, whilst they were quick to respond to the challenge, they were beaten back with ease. He made one last attempt to buy off the approaching army by pinning leaflets to the arrows, offering 6000 sesterces to any man who would defect. Not a man accepted.

The jubilant general returned to the palace with one of his men who had performed exceptionally. He strode straight into the throne room to report his successful defence of the city to its ruler. The queen rewarded the legionary with a golden helmet and breastplate. The grateful soldier accepted the praises heaped on him, along with his reward, and then promptly defected to Octavian.

Mark Antony issued a challenge to his nemesis. No more men needed to die. Octavian only had to agree to meet him in single combat: a fight to the death between the two rivals to settle the matter. He told him to send a reply to the palace before the night was out.

Cleopatra ordered a banquet to be prepared immediately to celebrate the victory. Mark Antony agreed to participate, partly to see what effect his sudden presence in the palace would have on his lookalike, and partly to wait for Octavian's response, even though he knew there would be none. Melissa had said as much.

It did not help that Eros was becoming more suspicious of the other Anthony's behaviour, fearing his increasing closeness to the queen was detrimental to the interloper's wellbeing. Anthony Marcus was key to every plan Mark Antony had, whether it was to help the man escape or to turn him into a sacrificial lamb. Before he could decide which plan he was going to initiate, the general had to know if his eldest offspring had truly switched camp. He only needed to look his son in the eye and he would know, but his youthful doppelganger was noticeably absent from the proceedings. Anthony had been asked by the queen not to attend. It appeared Cleopatra did not want the two men in the same room at the same time.

His thoughts drifted back to the woman waiting for him in his bed. How he longed to spend what was left of his pitiful his life in her arms. For so many years he had suffered the ignominy of his birth; a wastrel of a father; a stepfather branded a traitor; a mentor who sidelined him; a country that abandoned him. Melissa had seen through all of that. She had seen someone greater than his critics could ever appreciate. She had seen a man deserving of respect; a man deserving of love. She believed in him and that belief made him want to be the man he once was. She trusted him, but the fear that he might betray that trust was almost as suffocating as the humidity of the summer night.

When he found he could take the farce of Cleopatra's spectacle no longer, he signalled to Canidius his intention to leave. With barely a word to anyone, the two Romans slipped away from the proceedings into the silence of the central columned hallway.

It was here that they were accosted by a man hiding in the shadows. It was Anthony Marcus, and he looked decidedly worried.

"General Antony, I need to speak to you."

Mark Antony politely acknowledged his presence with a tilt of his head, but kept talking with Canidius. The pair walked past him and continued down the corridor.

Anthony fell in step behind them and tried again. "It is most important that we speak."

Mark Antony waved his hand, but still walked on.

In desperation, Anthony put his hand on Mark Antony's shoulder. "Please, father . . ." he began, but never finished.

"Not here," Mark Antony hissed over his shoulder. He carried on walking, but Canidius stopped and turned to face Anthony. He put his hand forcefully onto the younger man's chest, pushing him back.

"Look angry – as if you have been dismissed. Walk in the opposite direction and find another path to the far end of the rose garden. We will wait there. And remember, it is not only the servants that have both eyes and ears." He pushed Anthony away quite forcefully, but Anthony understood it was merely for show.

Following Canidius' instructions, he returned to his suite. He blew out the oil lamps, pushed the pillows into the bed to make it look like he was lying in it and slipped behind the curtains in search of the image of Wepawet. Once he found it, he pulled the lever and slipped into the secret passages. He knew them well now, having spent many nights exploring. He emerged behind a rose trellis, only a few feet behind Canidius and Mark Antony. He coughed to attract their attention.

When they walked towards him, Mark Antony made no effort to hide his anger at his son's earlier behaviour. He grabbed Anthony by the neck of his tunic and slammed him against a statue.

"What is so urgent you would risk all our lives to speak to me in public?" he spat. Behind them, Canidius drew his sword and stood watch.

"You have to leave, tonight." Anthony gasped the words, winded by the ferocity of the attack. "I want you to take Lissa and go. Put as much distance between this palace and her as you can."

Mark Antony tightened his grip, lifting his victim slightly until he was balanced on tiptoes. "You are asking me to desert my men and for what – to run away with a younger woman, purely to flatter my vanity?"

"It would not be the first time," Anthony gargled. His eyes displayed their usual glare of contempt.

Mark Antony had his answer. Anthony Marcus was still loyal to his wife.

"Well said, boy." He smiled as he released his victim. "And yet still I do not understand. Again, I ask you – why must we leave in such haste when I am on the brink of such a momentous victory?"

Anthony did a double take at what had been said. Even Canidius looked around at his commander. A momentous victory was most certainly not on the cards and all three men knew it.

"Is that what my wife told you?" Anthony asked, unable to hide the incredulity in his voice.

Mark Antony shook his head slowly. "Lissa said nothing, though her silence has a tendency to inspire the optimist in me."

Anthony eyed his father cautiously, not wanting to find himself on the end of another attack. "I did what you asked. I got as close to the queen as was possible and she has given me with the full details of her plan. Cleopatra has made a deal with Octavian. She intends to give you both to him, sending men to the Timoneum to retrieve Lissa once she has received word that you have joined the field of battle in the morning. Lissa is to be the prize jewel in the queen's bargaining strategy. You are to meet with an untimely end before the battle commences." He looked away, clearly disgusted by his own actions. "She told me everything because I allowed her to think it pleases me to have my wife handed over to that bastard."

Mark Antony was not surprised. He knew that at some point Cleopatra would look to take Melissa from his protection. All he was left wondering was which 'Antony' was really to be sacrificed.

He patted his son on the shoulder. "You have done well to learn this. I can see the pain it has caused you. I ask you again – why me? Why not leave with her yourself? I can arrange for horses to be waiting for you at the west gate."

Anthony shook his head in sadness. "This is your world and I cannot protect her in it. I have no knowledge of the area or experience of living in the desert. The one trip I have taken beyond the city limits proved that to me. The queen would find us too quickly. You are the best chance she has for survival. I am begging you – take her away. She must be gone before dawn."

Mark Antony nodded. "I agree with you, on all counts. You would not last a day out there in the desert. For this to work, I will need you to distract Cleopatra. Can you do this?"

"I will do whatever it takes, if you promise to take Lissa tonight."

"You make it sound as if you are giving me your wife to be well fucked!" Mark Antony teased.

Anthony lashed out, but Mark Antony easily caught his clenched fist. This time, he pushed against his victim's arm until the younger man buckled and fell to his knees.

Anthony glared up at his father defiantly, until he saw the older man wink at him. He realised he was being deliberately goaded as a test of his resolve. He swallowed his anger, along with what was left of his pride. "If that is what it takes to save her life, then yes, I give her to you, along with my blessing. You say you love her – prove it. Do what you will, but take her from this city."

Mark Antony changed his grip on Anthony's fist and pulled his son to his feet. "And what of you my son – what will you do in return for such a favour?"

"In the morning I will take your place at the head of the army and give you enough time to escape. Once all is lost, I will return here and take my own life. No one will ever know that it is my body and not yours in the palace. A dead man tells no tales. Octavian will not look for you." Anthony took a deep breath, exhaling slowly as he thought about the enormity of what he had just proposed. "I am willing to do this in return for the life of the woman we both love."

Mark Antony pondered his options. Ever since that fateful day in Sosigenes' house he had all but given up hope of leaving the city with Melissa. Now a chance had presented itself, it was almost too good to miss. "It will be done as you have asked. Lissa will be gone in the morning before Cleopatra's men come to call. Octavian will never lay his hands on her." He grasped his son's wrist to seal the agreement. "Go back to the palace and wait on the queen. You must do your best work tonight, if this ruse is to be a success."

"Now it sounds like you are the one giving your wife to be well fucked," Anthony replied, deliberate in his use of his father's phrase. He waited for a reaction.

Mark Antony shrugged. "I do not need to give her to you. You have already fucked her many times and I do not find myself consumed by the same jealousies you feel. I view sex and love by my Roman standards, not by yours. It matters little to me where or in whom you stick your erection. All that matters is that you keep Cleopatra's mind off her scheming for one more night."

Anthony nodded his agreement. "I understand," he said calmly.

There was nothing more to say. He turned and gripped Canidius' wrist in a gesture of friendship, before walking towards the palace.

When he was out of earshot Canidius began to speak. "If you are to leave with Lissa in the morning, it changes . . ."

"It changes nothing." Mark Antony cut him dead. "We continue with the arrangements, as planned."

"What about him?" Canidius jerked his head towards Anthony's retreating back.

"He is not your concern. When the time comes, I will deal with him."

Chapter 34

Cleopatra handed three small scrolls to her maid, Charmion, and ordered her to send them to their intended recipients with all haste.

The first was to go to the admiral of her fleet, giving instructions for how she wanted the fleet deployed in the morning. It also gave details of how he was to signal his surrender and fall in line with the enemy's fleet.

The second was for Octavian, telling him that she had agreed to his terms. She would not participate in the battle. Instead she would retire to her Mausoleum, where she would remain in safety. The army would deliver Mark Antony to him in the morning, leaving the once-feared general trussed up like a game bird. Once Mark Antony was safely delivered into Octavian's hands, the young Caesar was to come to the Mausoleum, where Cleopatra would renounce her throne and hand the administration of her country and wealth over to him. Octavian would escort her to a port on the Red Sea, where she would be reunited with her children, the children who were currently under his 'protection', having been intercepted on their way to the temple at Thebes. From the Red Sea, she would leave Egypt forever, with a considerable allowance from the country's treasury to ensure her personal comfort. It had been an easy agreement to strike: words on a page, nothing more. It was also an agreement she had no intention of keeping.

Word had been sent to her from Upper Egypt that the people there remained loyal. They were ready to rise up and fight for their pharaoh – all she had to do was ask. And she would ask when the time was right, but that time had not yet come. The queen of Egypt would leave Alexandria quietly, as planned. She foolishly believed Caesarion was still at large with half of the treasury at his disposal. Once reunited, mother and son would raise a new army of mercenaries. She would seek out men capable of training her loyal subjects to fight the Roman military machine and win.

It was unfortunate that she had been forced to sacrifice the father of her children to secure her arrangement with Octavian, but it was a situation she could use to her advantage. Not only had she agreed to hand over her long-time ally, she had also agreed to ensure his complete humiliation. Octavian did not want Mark Antony defeated, he wanted him broken. There could be no chance of his most formidable enemy ever rallying men to fight again. Mark Antony's corpse would central to Octavian's triumph, paraded through the streets of Rome like any other fallen leader.

Of course, what Octavian did not know was that there was more than one 'Antony' in Alexandria. As soon as Mark Antony's corpse was on display in Rome, Cleopatra intended to carry out her plan for the younger Anthony to rise from the dead.

Except even those plans had now changed. Later that night, a heavily sedated Anthony Marcus would be taken from his room and shipped to the front lines, east of Alexandria. He was to be trussed up and left there.

Word had reached Cleopatra that her latest conquest had been consorting with Canidius in the gymnasium. The two men were planning to rescue the seer and escape with her to Cyrene. Neither man could be trusted any longer. Or at least, that is what she had been told by the man to whom the third scroll was addressed: Mark Antony.

All these months she had barely heard from him. She had not seen him since the night before she had first sent Anthony Marcus into the desert, when they had last taken wine together. She feared him lost to her, despite their agreement to destroy the seer and her fool of a husband. Despite her fears, she had continued with the plan, hoping against all hope that all would be well. How her heart lifted on receipt of her husband's note only that morning. His instructions were to have his doppelganger delivered to the front and left there – incapacitated, but alive. Mark Antony would follow with the seer, whereupon he would slice into the younger man's side, leaving a gaping wound that would eventually prove fatal. Next to him, Octavian's troops would discover the body of the woman known as Caesar's witch. The seer would be dispatched, though not before she had witnessed the demise of her deceitful husband.

She felt relieved that the final plans were in place as she retired to her bed chamber. This would be her last night in her own bed for some time and she looked forward to climbing into the crisp, fresh cotton sheets. It was a shame she would be there alone, but Mark Antony had been clear. It was too dangerous for there to be any reunion until after Octavian had left Egypt.

The guards pushed open the chamber door enough for her to enter. She bade them goodnight and allowed the door to close, leaving the room in darkness. She removed her own robes, not something she usually did, but Charmion had other duties to perform. Naked, she walked towards the bed. It was only when she was standing at the side of it that she realised someone was already in it.

Anthony Marcus.

"How did you get in unseen?" she snapped.

"The usual opening of the ways," he replied cheekily. "That is why you pointed the passages out to me, was it not?" He pulled the sheet back to allow her to climb in next to him, but she remained standing where she was.

"I did not expect you to you use them tonight. Not when I gave instructions that you were to remain in your rooms." Her tone was cold and untrusting.

It would take all his skill to get her to believe him. He swung his legs round and sat on the edge of the bed in front of her. Reaching out he grabbed her buttocks and pulled her towards him. He ran his tongue across her belly. "I thought you understood that I do not like to be told what to do."

"Neither do I." She tried to pull away, but Anthony was too fast for her. He grabbed her and threw her onto the bed, rolling on top of her. She struggled against him, forcing him to hold her arms above her head to keep her still. He grazed his teeth down her neck.

"How dare you defile me without permission? Do this and I will have your head for it."

"You forget, my queen, I have heard that threat many times before. And even if you mean it this time, I strongly suggest you wait until afterwards. It would be a shame to waste such a solid erection, when I know how much you enjoy it." He shifted his weight, so she could feel him pressing into her thigh.

Cleopatra struggled again, but it was only for show. Both Antony's were skilful lovers, but this one's tenderness was something she had taken great pleasure from, on the rare occasions she allowed him to love her in that way. To enjoy him one last time was an opportunity too good to miss. It made no difference to her which room he was taken from.

"I will agree to your terms . . ." she sighed, feigning disinterest, ". . . on the condition you take me the way you used to take your wife."

Anthony paused. That was the last thing he wanted to do. He could close his eyes and pretend he was with Melissa, he had been doing that for months, but the thought was too painful in that moment. Only minutes before, he had told his father to take his wife from the city, without any opportunity to say his goodbyes.

Cleopatra felt his hesitation. "Am I not worthy enough to be loved in such a way?"

He had no choice. Too many lives depended on him. Swallowing hard, he told the biggest lie of his life. "Of course you are. It is just that I never want to hear of, or see, that bitch again." His mouth covered her nipple and he began to suck it tenderly.

"I promise that after tomorrow you never will, my love," she laughed.

Anthony stifled a sob and closed his eyes tightly. As he moved his kisses downwards onto Cleopatra's stomach, her image transformed in his mind into the woman he wanted to be caressing.

Melissa.

Chapter 35

Mark Antony returned to Melissa, who was waiting in bed as promised. He looked tired and drawn in comparison with the happy warrior who had departed from her that morning.

When he sat on the edge, she snuggled up behind him.

"Today went well?" she asked, even though she knew the answer."

"It did, though I fear tomorrow will be less of a success."

She knelt up and began to massage his stiff shoulders. "What if we leave tonight? We could travel west under the guise of common peasants."

He shook his head. "To the west lies nothing but hundreds of miles of desert. It would be a hard existence, even if we could pass my treacherous legions stationed out there."

"We would be alive," she countered.

"We would have nothing."

"We would have each other. It would be enough."

He half turned to look at her. "And when Octavian finds us, what then?"

"Octavian may never find us," she shrugged.

He wagged his finger at her, chiding her gently. "You say *may* which means you do not know. It is not what is meant to be, is it?"

Melissa shook her head sadly.

"Then we cannot risk it," he sighed. "Besides, I cannot leave your husband here to die."

She pulled back and folded her arms indignantly. "He deserves it. He has been screwing your wife!"

"And I have been screwing his, or had you forgotten last night and how often we did it!" He turned and pulled her around to sit beside him. Staring straight into her eyes, he used her real name with tenderness. "Melissa, my love, would you really leave Anthony here, knowing he would die?"

Melissa paused, and Mark Antony could see the tears forming in her eyes. He knew she still loved his son, regardless of the passionate night they had just spent together. He had his answer, regardless of what words came out of her mouth.

"If it means saving you, then yes," she said defiantly, though not convincingly.

He shook his head, knowing the time had come to tell her the truth – and all of it. Placing the palm of his hand against her cheek, he began.

"How I wish that our lives were different and that we could leave this place together, yet I know we cannot. I am not Mark Antony, farm peasant. I am Mark Antony, general of the Roman Army; the hero of Philippi. I need the feel of a sword in my hand and men at my command. I cannot give you what it is you seek – a life of peace on a little farm. I never could.

"Your husband – my son – has been following orders I myself have given. I put him in Cleopatra's bed, telling him the only way to keep you alive was to do the queen's bidding. I did it because I believed his betrayal of his marriage vows would bring you to me. I hoped to make you love me and forget him, but it was not to be. To watch you mourn his loss has been almost too much for me to bear. My selfishness ruined your marriage, Lissa. I took him from you out of spite and I am ashamed of myself for it."

Melissa turned away. Her head was reeling at the news she had been given that Anthony had been duped into believing the only way to save his wife was to betray her. She had unjustly blamed him for everything that had gone wrong between them.

Or had she? Anthony had been intent on currying favour with the queen long before his father's return from the desert. Melissa doubted Anthony had needed much persuasion to agree to his father's suggestion.

Mark Antony brushed a finger down her cheek, drying a tear. "Lissa, I am sorry for my lack of judgement. For so many years I convinced myself I could make you love me, but I have been a fool for far too long. We do not belong together – we never did. I can never hope to make amends for what I have taken from you. My son gave me his blessing to leave here with you, if I guarantee your safety. That is love in its truest form. He has told me to abandon him to his fate, yet I cannot do it. I may have deserted him at birth, but I will not desert him again. Destiny waits, and I will run from her no longer. Tomorrow, I will return to the palace, and you and he will leave here, together. It is as it should be."

Melissa closed her eyes. Before she met him, she had believed history's version of Mark Antony's character: an arrogant, drunken wastrel worthy of pity, but not of respect. Then she met him and believed history to be right in every way. The longer she spent with him, the more she saw a different man. She had watched an arrogant soldier develop into a considerate leader of men. Hard living was replaced by hard negotiation. He could be cruel at times, but, when he put his mind to it, his generosity knew no bounds. He had been down on many occasions, but he had always clawed his way back up. This time he was finished, and he knew it, but he was still looking for a way to salvage something from the situation for her.

And now, when he should have been at his most despondent, she was seeing another side of his character. Here was a man showing no concern for himself, only for that of those around him. This was the kind and decent man she always believed him to be. This was the man who had earned her respect.

Whether he planned to ruin her husband out of spite or love did not matter. Whether Anthony had been following orders or indulging his fantasies did not matter. There was nothing to be gained at such a late stage by punishing either man for his misguided actions. Mark Antony would be dead within twenty-four hours. For all she knew, so would her husband, and so would she. For one last night, she would live a Roman life, with Roman morals, and Roman appetites.

"Then we will have one last night together." She pushed her hand into his lap, but Mark Antony grabbed her wrist, pulling it away.

"We will, but not this way," he murmured. "I remember another night, when I was more attentive to your needs. Your enjoyment was beyond anything I had ever before experienced or have ever experienced since. For once in my life I felt as if you loved me. It would please me if you would love me again in that way."

He turned his head to face hers and she nodded. Her hand reached up to his cheek and as the tears flowed from her eyes, she kissed him tenderly. His arms encircled her, but without the usual crushing that followed. Slowly he laid her back on the bed, before standing up to remove his clothing, tossing it carelessly onto the floor. Pulling the sheet away he stared down at Melissa's naked body for some time as he slowly aroused himself. Then, lifting her ankle to his lips, he began to kiss his way along her leg, telling her with each kiss how much he loved her.

By the time he finally entered her, she was in no doubt that she had always been the love of his life.

For one last night at least, she would let him believe that he was hers.

Chapter 36

As dawn broke, Mark Antony and Canidius watched Cleopatra's personal guard slip away from the army's encampment just outside the Canopic gate. They knew the men were on their way to report back to their mistress that 'Mark Antony' had been left tethered inside his command tent, as requested.

They waited until the guards were out of sight and then slipped inside the tent. They found Anthony Marcus slumped on the ground against a tent pole, his wrists tied behind him to the post. Unsure whether he was alive or not, Mark Antony dropped onto his knees beside him to check that he was still breathing. As he did, Anthony groaned and shifted his legs.

"He is alive," Mark Antony muttered, shaking Anthony as he dragged him up into a sitting position.

"But drugged, I think," Canidius replied, as he cut through the rope.

"Indeed." Mark Antony slapped his son around the face a few times to wake him.

Slowly Anthony nodded to show that he was conscious. "I'm OK," he mumbled in English.

"I gather that means you are still with us," Mark Antony looked grim as he stared at his son. He remembered a time when Melissa had been taken ill. Her delirium had made her revert to her own native tongue, leaving him guessing what was being said. He could only hope this was a minor lapse on the younger man's part and not something more serious.

"Latin or Greek, if you can, lad, or we cannot understand you," Canidius interjected. He handed Anthony a cup of water before returning to the entrance of the tent to stand guard.

"My apologies," Anthony managed. He gulped at the water.

Mark Antony allowed himself a wry smile. "Where is my cavalry?" he asked. He had not seen any horses outside.

"They are gone. They have deserted." Anthony shook his head and blinked a few times, trying to clear the last of the sleeping draft from his system. He seemed genuinely stunned to be alive.

Mark Antony shook his head in disbelief. "I do not believe it. These were my best men. They would never desert me."

"They did not desert you – they deserted me," Anthony replied, with more coherence. "It was all part of her plan, using me to discredit you so they would go. I may look like you, talk like you, even fuck like you, but I am not you and they knew that. I make a poor substitute for a general, and she made sure they knew it."

"It is not your fault, son. You never stood a chance. Cleopatra had no more intention of sparing you than I have of surrendering to that whiny little runt over there." Mark Antony waved in the direction of Octavian's lines. "She expects you to die here by my hand, while your wife looks on."

"Why would she think that?" Anthony was now wide awake and suddenly concerned for his own safety.

"She thinks it because I have encouraged her to ever since I first put the idea of the Osiris myth in her head. She believed you to be our sacrificial lamb."

"And am I?" Anthony asked, swallowing hard and fearing he had been duped all along.

For the briefest moment, Mark Antony paused. It was still a viable option; kill his son and tell Melissa he had been too late to save him.

He shook his head. "Do not be obtuse. If I wanted you dead, I would have run you through when I arrived. Many months ago, I gave you my word to help you. It is a promise I intend to keep."

Anthony put the cup down and rubbed his sore wrists. "I am relieved to hear it, although I will admit there have been many times when I have doubted your sincerity."

"As have I," Mark Antony winked as he held out his hand to his son.

Anthony took it and allowed his father to pull him to his feet. "There is more. Cleopatra has given the order for the fleet to attack once, though it is no more than a ruse. At the last moment, they will raise their oars and fall in line with Octavian's ships. Cleopatra has surrendered her ships."

"Why would she do that?" Mark Antony's brow furrowed. This tactic made no sense to him.

"Our queen has been in negotiation with Octavian for months. She believes they have reached an accord. She surrenders the sea in return for the lives of your children. It is my belief she will get far less than she anticipates. Her understanding of who are your children is somewhat different to that of Octavian."

Mark Antony nodded in agreement. Unlike Cleopatra, he fully understood the implications of the terminology

Anthony was referring to. "The ceremonies we held for Caesarion and Antyllus make them men in Octavian's eyes, and they will be slaughtered as such." He closed his eyes briefly as he accepted the impending death of his eldest 'official' son. His thoughts then turned to his other children in Egypt. "What hope is there for the other three? Can they be saved?"

Anthony shook his head. "It is too late. Octavian's men are already in Thebes. Alexander Helios and Cleopatra Selene will be taken to Rome and paraded in Octavian's Triumph. Octavia will rescue them from his cruelty and take them into her household where they will be safe. She will raise them, along with your other children."

"Lissa said as much and I am grateful to you for confirming it." He tilted his head quizzically. "What of Ptolemy? You made no mention of him?"

Anthony shrugged. "I do not know. It is believed he is taken to Rome with the twins. There is no official record of what happens to him."

Mark Antony frowned again as his thoughts turned to his youngest child. "He is a delicate child. The cold Roman winter will be hard on his constitution. He may succumb to a fever."

"I wish I knew his fate and could give you some comfort, yet I cannot," Anthony replied before changing the subject to one that was more important to him. "What of Lissa? Tell me she is safe and that you at least sent her away?"

Mark Antony placed a hand on his son's back and steered him towards the entrance to the tent. "She has been moved to a secure location this very morning, thanks in part to your warning. Arrangements have been made for your escape. Your boat is moored in an inlet a short distance outside the city. It is provisioned with food and water for a few days, more if you ration it carefully. Sail west towards Cyrene, before turning north. You will avoid Octavian's navy and improve your chances of reaching Crete alive. I will do what I can to give you time to get away though, with half my troops already surrendered, it will be far less than I had hoped."

Anthony shook his head. "Octavian will kill you, if you stay here."

Mark Antony smiled. "He can try." He turned his head towards his colleague. "What do you say, Canidius? Do I run like the coward Cleopatra expects people to believe I have become, or do I die a true Roman's death?"

Canidius turned away from his sentry duty to look his commander in the eye. "You will stay," he replied, "as will I."

"No, my good friend, their need is greater. Take my son and his wife to their boat as arranged. Leave this mess to me."

"If that is your wish, general, I will see it done." Despite his agreement, Canidius was less than happy at the idea of leaving Mark Antony alone in what was fast becoming hostile territory.

Anthony stepped back in defiance. "We had an agreement. You must survive to help me save Lissa. I will not leave you to face Octavian alone. Either we both go, or we both stay."

Mark Antony reached out and gripped his son's shoulder. "Allow me to be your father once before I die. You owe me this much."

"But I . . ."

Mark Antony smiled. "Our ancestors would be proud. You are a man worthy of the family name – an Antonius through and through. It is a shame to do this to one so brave."

Anthony just had time to ask, "Do what?" before his father punched him hard in the jaw.

It was the last thing he remembered before he blacked out.

Chapter 37

Mark Antony made one final stand at the head of his infantry. With his cavalry gone, it made for a forlorn sight. As the men watched the fleet up oars and surrender, they too lost their will to fight on. A loyal centurion led the fighting long enough to allow his commander to slip back to the city, before laying down his sword at the feet of the new master of Alexandria.

Storming through the hallways, Mark Antony cursed Cleopatra's name at every turn, accusing her of betraying him. It had to appear as if the world's most infamous pair of lovers were at odds with each other to the very last. Egypt's queen would need all the help she could get to maintain the ruse that she too had deserted him in his darkest hour. That had been the plan, except the plan had changed. In ordering the fleet to surrender, Cleopatra really had deserted him. Despite their differences, Mark Antony was determined to keep up appearances. Loyalty to the woman who had borne three of his children prevented him from doing otherwise. They had spent the past decade together, living, laughing, loving. Theirs had been a good life, a memorable life, but one that had run its course. There could be no escape – for either of them. Melissa had said as much, and he knew that she was right. After all, she was always right.

Eventually, he came across Eros, who was searching frantically for his master.

"Is it done?" he asked the boy. While he and Canidius had been rescuing Anthony and staging the final battle, his trusted slave had been set the most dangerous of tasks.

Eros nodded. "It is done as you asked. The mistress has left for her Mausoleum, where she will remain."

"And the tunnel?"

"An unfortunate accident – the roof was poorly supported."

What Cleopatra did not know, was that she was not the only one changing plans. Word would quickly reach Octavian of where the queen had gone. Once she had made a good show of being inside, she fully intended to sneak out of the Mausoleum, using one of the workmen's tunnels under the wall to deliver her into the waiting arms of her husband. However, her husband had arranged for the tunnel to collapse.

Mark Antony smiled to himself. The queen was caught like a rat in trap. It was what she deserved for her betrayal of him and for trying to destroy his beloved. His thoughts turned once more to Melissa and his son. He wondered if she would miss him, or if she would ever tell her children of their famous relation. He would never know the answer. He would be dead centuries before she ever found her way back to her family, if she ever did.

Octavian's men were close on his heels. The palace would soon echo to the sound of hobnailed boots marching across the polished tesserae floors. Alexandria was lost, and so was he. The time had come to bring proceedings to an end.

He gripped Eros by the shoulder. "Eros, you are free. Go now, while you still can."

Eros' eyes filled with panic. "Go? Where? There is no place for me except here." Eros had been taken as a slave at a young age. He had never known any other way of life except the one Alexandria had given him. But Alexandria was about to change, and the city's new master would be far less indulgent to her hedonistic ways.

Eros dropped to his knees and grasped Mark Antony's wrists. "Please master," he pleaded, "I would rather die here with you than out there." He pointed a quivering finger in the direction of the city.

Mark Antony looked down at his favourite servant with sadness. He watched the tears welling up in the boy's terror-filled eyes and wondered what future there could ever be for such a damaged young man, one who had been party to some of the most depraved acts any person could imagine. He knew there was no place for Eros in Octavian's new world order. Men like him would be cast out and left to fend for themselves. Being less worldly-wise than most, Eros would not last long on the streets. He would most likely be picked up by one of Alexandria's many pimps, leading to a life of cruelty and further sexual abuse. Mark Antony had dreaded that end for Melissa, so why then would he want it for someone else he had come to care for? Killing the boy was the kindest thing to do.

He nodded his agreement and helped Eros from the floor. Raising one hand gently to the boy's cheek to brush away the tears, he unsheathed his sword with the other. For a moment, he stood motionless, unable to bring himself to murder the man before him. His hand moved from Eros' cheek to the back of his neck. Pulling his head forwards, Mark Antony placed a kiss on Eros' forehead.

He stepped away and carefully placed the tip of the blade against Eros' stomach just under his left ribcage.

Eros put his hands on his master's shoulders and took a firm grip, readying himself for the blow that was to follow.

Mark Antony smiled at the boy one last time.

"Will it hurt?" Eros whispered suddenly.

The smile faded.

Mark Antony looked Eros straight in the eye.

"Yes," he said, and drove the blade home forcefully, angling it upwards to ensure it pierced Eros's heart.

Eros gasped at the pain. Shock spread across his face before he slumped forwards into his master's arms. Mark Antony caught him and laid him on the floor, stroking his hair gently while his life ebbed away. He sat for some minutes next to his slave, watching the blood pooling beneath the young man's body. He found himself thinking over some of the escapades they had shared. Placing his hand over Eros' face, he closed his slave's eyelids as he said his silent goodbye.

As he slowly rose from the floor, his thoughts turned once more to Melissa. There was nothing he could do for her now except keep her history intact and hope that Canidius managed to get her and his wayward son safely out of the city.

As much as he was loath to admit it, he was proud of the way Anthony was shaping up. He had watched this arrogant, petulant younger man develop over the past year into a patient, cunning tactician. Anthony was still a little rough at the edges, but he was now a man worthy of his family name. Only now was he worthy of the woman he was married to.

Picking up the sword, Mark Antony wiped the worst of Eros' blood from it onto his tunic. "I am tired of this life. It is time to see what awaits me in the next," he muttered.

He turned the sword around, and, placing the tip

under his lower left rib, prepared to drive it upwards into his heart. Taking one last deep breath, he pulled the sword towards him, thrusting it into his body.

At the exact same moment, something behind the curtains stirred, catching his eye: a person hiding. Their presence in the room startled him, making him pull the blade a fraction downwards and to the side. It was no longer a clean strike to the heart, guaranteed to kill instantly, but a glancing blow into his abdomen. The pain from the sword tearing through his insides was excruciating.

As Mark Antony fell beside Eros, he gasped the name of the person he had seen hiding behind the curtains.

"Ptolemy!"

Then he began to scream for someone to help him.

"Anthony, please wake up," Melissa begged as Canidius shook her husband by the shoulders.

Gradually, he began moving by himself. His eyes fluttered open.

"What? Where am I?" he muttered, as he rolled his head around groggily, trying to get his bearings.

"You're in a small house alongside the dock. Canidius brought you here. He said Mark Antony hit you."

Anthony twisted his jaw a couple of times feeling along it with his fingers. It was sore. "The old man packs a punch, I'll give him that," he said in English, as he sat up.

"What happened?" Melissa demanded.

He looked at Melissa sheepishly. "I made a deal with my father many months ago. He was supposed to get you out of here and, in return, I'd take his place. I was supposed to sacrifice my life to guarantee yours, but I'm guessing the plans have changed."

"Anthony! Why on earth would you agree to such a stupid deal?"

"Because I love you, Liss – I always have. Your safety was all that mattered to me. He had the better chance at getting you back home to the kids. I knew I couldn't do it, so I agreed to trade places with him. Keeping Cleopatra interested in me is the only talent I have. It was the only chance you had." He looked away, embarrassed by his admission.

Canidius butted in before Melissa could respond. "Whatever you have to say to each other can wait. I have to get you both out of the city and we must not delay any longer." He threw a rough old tunic at Anthony, before changing into a similar garment. Both were dirty and stank of fish.

Melissa nodded and told Anthony quickly what the plan was, as it had been explained to her. "The *Selene* is moored in an inlet not far from the city. The fisherman who lives in this house is waiting in a rowboat at the harbour entrance. He'll take us past the blockade, but he won't wait long. Canidius believes we can make it. We need to get clear of Alexandria and find the mist."

"And how do we do that? Anthony asked, stripping off the last of his Roman uniform.

"I think it finds us."

Anthony stopped dressing and stared at her. "What?"

She shrugged. "I think the mist is Einstein-Rosen bridge – a wormhole through space. I'm not sure, but it is the only option that makes sense. Somehow I'm linked to Mark Antony through some form of quantum entanglement."

"Boy, you've done one hell of a lot of thinking, haven't you?" Anthony smiled at his wife, as she blushed in response. He switched to Latin as he pulled the fishy tunic on. "You know he will die if he stays there alone." These words were not aimed at Melissa.

Canidius looked grim as he thrust a sword into Anthony's hand. "I have my orders."

Anthony grabbed his wrist. "If we go together, we could save him. It does not have to end this way. The future is not yet written."

"Anthony! What are you saying? We can't change this!" Melissa cried in English. She could not believe what he had just said.

"Be quiet and listen for once," he replied in Latin, so that Canidius could understand. "We have already changed it. Mark Antony is not coming back to the palace. He is going to hand himself over to Octavian's men. We both know what that means – a once great man dragged through the streets of Rome in Octavian's triumph. I do not want that for my father. Not after everything he has sacrificed to save you."

Melissa gasped. She had been so careful not to mention Anthony's parentage in front of anyone, including Canidius, and now he had mentioned it openly. She thought it would take some explaining but, to her surprise, there was no need.

Canidius nodded. "Spoken like a true Antonius. It is no wonder you have earned his respect in these past months,"

Melissa gasped again. "You knew!" she exclaimed, staring at Canidius.

Canidius nodded again. "Since the day I first met you, I have known who he is, as I have known that you were not of this time. I have the general's complete confidence in every matter, Lissa. I thought you knew that."

He turned his attention back to Anthony and shook his head. "You have been deceived. The general knows they will not accept his surrender and that there is no chance for him to reach that triumphal parade alive. The plebeian class would not take too well to their hero being paraded so cruelly before them, nor would the legions. There would be open revolt and Octavian's victory would be ended before it began. Mark Antony knows he would die out there in the desert today if he fought, changing all our futures. He plans to return to the palace and look to maintain the future as Lissa foretold it to Sosigenes. Arrangements were made months ago for this possibility. He will find Eros, who has sworn to help him die."

Melissa shook her head. "But he will not do it. According to our history, Eros will turn the sword on himself, leaving Mark Antony to end his own life."

Canidius looked aghast. "That is no easy feat for any man to manage." He looked at Anthony who was now measuring the length of his arm against the blade of his sword. The span of the blade of the gladius would make it difficult for a man to use enough force to drive it home as well as aiming successfully when aiming the blade at himself.

Anthony looked at Canidius and made his next statement, half from pre-existing knowledge and half from his own rough estimations. "He may miss his heart."

"Exactly," Canidius said with a nod.

"The palace it is then," Anthony said emphatically.

"Indeed," Canidius agreed. "We may have to fight to get there."

Anthony put his sword up in front of him. "Then you will get to see how good your lessons have been."

Chapter 38

Regardless of Melissa's arguments to the contrary, the three companions soon found themselves in the main palace, searching room after room in the hope of finding Mark Antony and Eros before it was too late. For reasons she could not fathom, Anthony wanted his father to live, regardless of the danger it posed to their futures. It did not help that he refused to explain his thinking to her.

They met no resistance. The few palace slaves they did come across were either hiding or fleeing in the opposite direction, many with palace treasures in their arms. For all of Cleopatra's talk of the loyalty of her people, it appeared even the most loyal of servants was terrified by the thought of another Roman occupation.

Canidius and Anthony moved cautiously from one doorway to the next, checking each room as they went. Canidius was impressed at the way his novice followed his lead, taking direction from a seasoned veteran with ease. Melissa was more difficult to control. Despite her initial resistance to the idea of finding Mark Antony, she now seemed to be in a hurry to complete their mission and had to be stopped from charging ahead into an unchecked room on more than one occasion.

Anthony was the one who found them. Eros, nearest to the door, was lying on his side in a pool of his own blood. There seemed to be so much of it, Anthony could not believe it was all from the one man. He reached down to check for a pulse, but it was too late: Eros was dead.

His eyes followed a trail of blood running across the floor away from the young man. Mark Anthony had dragged himself towards a couch, but his strength had failed him before reaching his destination. He was lying face down on the floor and he groaned in his semi-conscious state.

"In here," Anthony shouted to the others. He rushed over to his father, turning him over carefully to assess the wound, which was large and gaping. Mark Antony's hand was over the worst of it, in an attempt to hold his side together.

Defiant to the last, Mark Antony had not yet given up hope. Once his attempt at suicide failed, his survival instinct cut in. He needed to survive long enough to protect his youngest son, so that he could find a way to remove the boy from harm's way.

With his free hand, Mark Antony grabbed at Anthony's forearm with surprising determination. "Help me up," he begged.

Anthony moved around behind his father as Canidius arrived to help. Between them, they helped Mark Antony into a sitting position, leaning him against the couch. Anthony stayed beside him, supporting him so that his wound could be inspected more thoroughly.

Melissa arrived in the doorway. She gagged at the sight of Eros' blood pooling in front of her. Recovering from her initial shock, she too followed the trail of blood across the floor to where the others were. She gagged again at the sight of Canidius ramming his hand into Mark Antony's side in an attempt to hold his general's guts together.

Canidius looked straight into his commander's eyes. "This is bad," he stated plainly.

"I know," Mark Antony gasped in reply. "Find something to pack it with. We have to move."

Melissa shook herself and picked her way around the blood carefully so as not to slip over. As she walked, she ripped the left sleeve from her dress.

"Here, let me," she said. Dropping to her knees beside the three men, she folded the sleeve, forming a pad, and pressed it over the top of Canidius' hand. When she nodded to him, he slowly pulled his hand away, allowing her to apply pressure to Mark Antony's gaping wound.

She held her right arm out and jerked her head towards it. "Tear that one too," she instructed Canidius, who complied with her request to tear the other sleeve away.

"I need more – tear down the curtain," she ordered, and Canidius willingly went to work, dismantling the drapes.

Mark Antony focused on Melissa as she tended to his wound. "Once again the sight of my blood has you undressing for me, just as it did when I was wounded at Brundisium."

His skin was clammy, and his face pale, but his sense of humour had not been dulled. He winked at her and turned his head towards Anthony. "You see, son, the way to a woman's heart is not through kind words or grand gestures – you simply have to bleed for them."

"That is not funny," Melissa chided, before pressing harder on the wound, trying to stem the flow.

"Oww!" Mark Antony winced in pain. He turned his attention back to Melissa. "Your bedside manner was once more delicate, lady. Have I done something to displease you?"

Melissa glared at her patient as she heard the sound of fabric ripping somewhere behind her. "Let me think. First, you try to kill yourself out in the desert. Second, you mope around here for months doing very little, although you did find the time to put my husband in your wife's bed. And now you do this!" She shook her head. "Why would you think you have done something to displease me?" She pressed again, and again he winced.

Mark Antony turned his attention to his eldest son. "It appears I have caused your wife offence. I humbly beg your forgiveness for being the cause of such discomfort."

Melissa looked from father to son. She knew that Mark Antony was not referring to recent events. This was a dying man asking his son to forgive him for everything that had gone before.

Anthony had tears in his eyes as he responded. "A man should never judge another until he has had the chance to stand in his shoes." Although he spoke to his father, his focus was on Melissa. "You did what you had to. There is nothing to forgive."

Mark Antony was also looking at Melissa as he spoke. "I am glad to hear you say it, my son, for I have no time left to make amends."

Melissa stared at him. All she could hope to do was make his last moments more comfortable. She had to make a choice. Did she give a dying man his final wish by admitting to loving him? If she did, she might lose her husband forever. Or did she salvage her marriage and allow Mark Antony to die believing he meant nothing to her?

Canidius thrust a long section of curtain in front of Melissa, making her jump. "Here, use this," he said loudly, and then added more softly, "we have another problem."

Between them, they tilted Mark Antony forwards and Melissa wrapped the material around his midriff, tying it as best she could. "What is it?" she asked quietly, hoping not to worry her patient any further.

Mark Antony was way ahead of her in understanding the situation. "Him," he gasped as he pointed weakly across the room.

Anthony and Melissa both followed the invisible line from Mark Antony's finger to where Ptolemy was sitting on the far side of the room, hugging his knees.

"Holy fuck," Anthony swore in English. "What's he doing here? The kids were sent to Thebes last night."

"Obviously not all of them went!" Melissa shook her head in disgust. She sat back to inspect her handiwork. It was far from perfect, but the makeshift bandage was holding, for the moment at least.

Mark Antony looked at Anthony knowingly. "If Ptolemy did not go to Thebes, he cannot be taken prisoner. He will never get to Rome."

"Perhaps," Anthony muttered. He had a feeling he knew where his father's logic was heading, and he knew Melissa would not like it.

Mark Antony coughed. "Antyllus went to the Caesareum," he gasped. "Is there time to reach him?"

Melissa and Anthony exchanged a pained look. They both knew it was too late for Antyllus, but was it right to cause an already anguished father more distress? Anthony shook his head ever so slightly. It was a gesture designed to be hidden, but pain appeared to have once more sharpened the wits of Mark Antony. He knew exactly what it was they were trying to hide.

"Antyllus is already dead," he said in a resigned tone.

"Lie, Liss, please," Anthony begged in English. "He

doesn't need to know."

Melissa could not speak. She simply shook her head in response to both questions asked of her.

Mark Antony winced at another stabbing pain, this one in his heart. Closing his eyes, he asked the most painful question any father could ask, in the most Roman of ways. "How was it? Did he die well?"

Melissa sobbed, as her emotions finally took over. She still could not answer him. The pain he would feel hearing of Antyllus' murder only served to remind her of the loss of her own son.

Anthony swallowed hard. He understood how much it hurt to lose a child without the full knowledge of how it happened. He intervened. "As with Caesareon, Antyllus has been betrayed by his tutor. He murdered him for the jewel around his neck. Octavian will in turn execute the tutor for his contemptible greed."

Mark Antony laughed, immediately regretting it as pain again seared through his body. "That is a just reward for an unjust crime. Octavian has always been a righteous little runt, yet I now find I must give thanks for his unwavering loyalty to his personal moral code. That pains me almost as much as this wound."

He looked downwards at the blood, oozing out from beneath the makeshift bandage around his midriff. Even though Melissa's administrations had stemmed the worst of the flow, blood still seeped through the fabric. He knew his death would be far too long in coming. He needed to keep talking to distract himself from the excruciating pain.

"What of my remaining children? Tell me they will they do great deeds worthy of my name."

Melissa finally re-joined the conversation, having remembered another time when an injured Mark Antony chose conversation as a distraction from the pain of the surgeon's needle. She knew he wanted to keep talking and obliged him. "Octavia will be a good mother to all of them. Iullus will join the senate and Selene will become a queen herself, though not of Egypt. It is your grandsons that you should be most proud of. They will succeed where Caesar failed, becoming masters of the lands beyond the river Rhenus, and of Britannia. They will be your true legacy." She was, of course, speaking of the fearless Germanicus and his timid, stuttering brother, Claudius, both of whom would make names for themselves in very different ways – one as a successful general, the other as the fourth Roman emperor. She did not bother to mention that Mark Antony's great-grandchildren, Caligula and Nero, would both turn mad. The fates of the other boys were also best not mentioned. Octavian would eventually force Iullus to commit suicide: punishment for having an affair with his daughter, Julia. Alexander would take part in Octavian's triumph before disappearing from the historical record without a trace.

"Then I die happy," he gasped.

From somewhere behind her, Melissa heard a whimper and she remembered that Ptolemy was with them. Letting go of Mark Antony's hand, she stood up and walked over to where he was sitting. He had found two broken halves of a small wooden boat and was cradling them in his hands. She reached for him, but he pulled away from her, screaming, so she backed off until he was merely whimpering once more.

Mark Antony turned his head to see his frightened son hiding in the window opening.

"Why is he still here? He was meant to go to Thebes with the others." He coughed as blood seeped into his oesophagus from his stomach. Staring up into Anthony's eyes, he pleaded an unspoken request - *Sit me up.*

With some difficulty, Anthony raised his dying father in his arms, supporting his weight as best he could. Again, Mark Antony gasped at the sharpness of the pain in his gut, but he composed himself enough to speak to his youngest child.

"Come here, Ptolemy," he said, quite sternly. When the child refused to move, he tried again in a softer tone. "Do not be afraid. I am not angry with you. Come and let me comfort you." He smiled, with some difficulty, and reached out a shaking hand.

Nervously, Ptolemy crawled forwards towards his father. His eyes were wide in terror, his face wet with tears. Despite the risks to himself, Mark Antony gathered the boy in his arms and pulled him onto his lap. The action dislodged the bandage and blood immediately flowed again. As Melissa ripped more sections of material from her dress in order to pack his wound, Mark Antony rocked his son tenderly in his arms.

"Why do you cry, son? Is it the sight of my blood?"

Ptolemy shook his head.

"Is it that you were left alone?"

Again, Ptolemy shook his head.

"Then tell me, why is my brave little prince so distressed?"

"Alexander took my boat," Ptolemy blurted out. "He broke it. I chased him, until I lost him. I came here to wait for dinner, but the slaves never came. No one ever came."

"They left him," Melissa said gently. "He has been alone all night."

Mark Antony nodded to show he understood. He kissed the boy on the top of his head. "I am sorry,

Ptolemy. Alexander will be punished for taking your boat, as will the slaves who left you." His words were purely for reassurance. He was angry that his youngest child had been abandoned in the panic, but there was little he could do about it.

"He broke it," Ptolemy wailed again, obviously hoping to capitalise on his brother's misfortune.

Mark Antony smiled to himself. "Then his punishment will be most severe. No honey cakes for one month."

Beside his father, Anthony gulped and blinked away his own tears. It was the same punishment he would have meted out to his children. Perhaps they really did have more in common than he cared to admit, but there was more. He was also remembering his favourite childhood toy. A small wooden boat, hand-carved with much love, and given to him by the man now dying in his arms. It was the only childhood memory he had of his father.

The sound of hurried footsteps echoed in the hall outside. Canidius immediately rose and took up a defensive position by the door. Anthony motioned for Melissa to support Mark Antony. Once she was in position, he retrieved his discarded sword and took his place between Canidius and the group on the floor. For all he knew, those footsteps belonged to the first of Octavian's men, come to slaughter them all. He shook in fear, dreading the moment they were discovered, but knowing he and Canidius were the only people capable of saving their lives. As the footsteps came nearer he raised the blade higher.

"My brave son," Mark Antony murmured into Ptolemy's hair, comforting the boy, but Melissa could see his eyes were firmly fixed on Anthony. More than that, she could see his face was full of pride.

Pushing Ptolemy gently from his lap he signalled his intention to rise. Despite his wounds, he intended to stand and fight alongside his son and friend. With Melissa's help, he got off the floor, but he could not stand. Instead, Melissa helped him to sit on the couch and then placed his bloody sword in his hand. He motioned for her to hide behind the couch.

Ptolemy tried to cling to his father until Mark Antony was forced to push him aside, steering the boy towards Melissa. "Go with her. She will care for you . . ." he glanced upwards into Melissa's eyes, pleading silently for her compassion, ". . . as she has always cared for me."

At that moment, Diomedes burst in and skidded in the pool of blood beside the body of Eros. Canidius went to strike, but stopped himself in time. Diomedes stared in disgust at the mess on the floor in front of him, before turning to address Anthony, who was also lowering his sword. "My lord, her most gracious majesty, Queen Cleopatra Philopater, mistress of Sedge . . ."

"Enough! I know what her titles are. What does she want?" Anthony snapped.

"She sends word that she is alive and well and apologises for the earlier misunderstanding. You were not meant to be left behind and the soldiers responsible will be severely punished."

"If they can be found," Canidius threw in.

Diomedes ignored his remark. "She waits for you in her Mausoleum. I am to take you to her."

"Not a chance," Anthony spat in disgust. "She can rot in there alone."

The eunuch became quite insistent. "The mistress demands you come immediately. Plans have been made for your escape. A barge has been made ready to take you . . ."

Anthony grabbed the front of Diomedes' robes. "If I so much as see that bitch's bony arse again, I will take this blade and shove it . . ."

"ANTONIUS! MIND YOUR MANNERS!" Mark Antony bellowed the words with such ferocity that everyone turned to face him. "I will not allow you to sully yourself with such low name calling. That bitch you speak of is still my wife – or as good as, anyway. If anyone has earned the right to insult her, it is me, though I will not do it behind her back. I will do it to her face."

"She has not asked for you," Diomedes sneered, blissfully unaware that Cleopatra had changed the plans and that it was, in fact, the older Antony the queen expected. "She needs a strong and virile man by her side, not some washed-up drunkard."

"A washed-up drunkard I may be, but I will eviscerate you and use your entrails to rig the sails of the very barge you speak of, if you make one more remark that is not to my liking."

Mark Antony lurched forwards suddenly, in agony, and dropped his sword. Anthony quickly moved to support him, trying to hold his father upright.

"We made a vow – as in life, so shall it be in death," Mark Antony gasped. "It is a befitting end for such a pair of lost souls." He looked up at Diomedes. "You will take me to her, or we will see what other parts of the anatomy a eunuch can learn to live without."

"I doubt you will make it that far!" Diomedes scoffed. "I doubt you will make it to the shores of Lake Mareotis!"

"And why would we go there?" Melissa muttered, as she wiped the sweat from Mark Antony's face. Archaeologists had never found the Mausoleum, which was believed to be next to the Temple of Isis in the harbour. Popular belief was that it had slipped into the sea following an earthquake that levelled much of the ancient city. The lake, on the other hand, was south of the city and in the opposite direction to the believed location.

"Ha!" Mark Antony laughed, and again regretted it. "At last, I know something that you do not." He pointed at his son as the pain became too intense for him to continue. "Tell her," he wheezed.

Melissa looked up at her husband in bemusement. "The tomb's by the Temple of Isis, right?" she asked, in English.

He nodded with a look of deep concern on his face. "Yeah, but it's not the one in the harbour. It's the one at Taposiris Magna."

Melissa gasped. Taposiris Magna was at the farthest end of the lake. It was nearly thirty miles by road – too far to drag a man in Mark Antony's condition.

It was beginning to look as if history would be changed after all.

Chapter 39

Diomedes had left a heavily-guarded litter waiting outside the main entrance to the palace and, to everyone's surprise, it was still there. Canidius and Anthony half-carried, half-dragged, Mark Antony to it, dumping him rather unceremoniously inside. Melissa followed behind with Ptolemy in her arms, making sure the little boy did not get left behind for a second time.

As Anthony pulled the curtains enclosing the litter, his father grabbed his wrist with surprising strength.

"You share my face, boy. Use it, for all our sakes," Mark Antony rasped. His grasp tightened further as if giving an unspoken instruction.

Anthony nodded his understanding. The route to the lake harbour was straightforward enough – through the Gate of the Moon, heading south along the Boulevard Argeus to the Gate of the Sun – but it would no longer be safe. Octavian's main force was less than a day east of the Canopic Gate and marching steadily towards the city walls. Looters and thieves were running riot on the streets, grabbing whatever they could lay their hands on, before the Romans could grab whatever was left. A rich litter from the palace would draw attention from the worst dregs of Alexandrian society, but a rich litter guarded by Mark Antony might just receive safe passage. This was one Roman with the respect of the Alexandrian people, who had adopted him as one of their own. The son had to become the father, for the next few minutes, at least.

Pushing his own fears aside, Anthony sprang into action. Turning around, he lifted Ptolemy out of Melissa's arms and into the litter beside his father, where he would be safest. He ordered the guards to the front and rear and asked Canidius to take position next to Diomedes, who had slunk in close to the side to the litter; the eunuch did not like the way the situation was developing, but he knew where it was safest to be. Anthony grabbed Melissa by the arm and pulled her around to the other side, taking up the same position he had often walked in when he went to the markets with Cleopatra. It was his hope that, if the looters believed the queen was inside the litter, they would allow them to pass. Finally, he ordered the bearers to move forwards.

Melissa looked indignant. "What do you think you are doing?" she demanded, as she was hauled along in an unceremonious fashion.

"Becoming him." Anthony jerked his head towards the litter. "They need to believe I am him, and that he is still in control."

"Who? The guards?" Melissa asked, just as they reached the Gate of the Moon.

As they crossed the threshold of the gate, Anthony pointed out into the street with his sword and gave a one-word answer.

"Them."

Now Melissa could see the chaos for herself. Carnage littered their route. An overturned cart was being stripped of its produce by men and women alike; the cart's owner was left sitting by a wall, dazed and bleeding profusely from a gash on his head. On the other side of the street, two men were tussling over a laden sack. One pulled a knife, plunging it into his opponent before running off with his spoils. Somewhere in the distance, they could hear the sound of a woman shrieking for help. There was nothing they could do for her. They had to make their escape, if they could.

Melissa shrank back behind her husband and began to pray to every Roman and Egyptian deity she had ever heard of to grant them safe passage to that harbour.

Mark Antony survived the journey to the lake. He also survived the transfer to the small felucca commandeered by Diomedes earlier in the day. As they sailed west, the imposing walls of Taposiris Magna loomed ever larger. It was the first time Melissa had ever seen the temple complex, which easily rivalled the ones she knew of in Luxor. She barely paid it any attention though. She was too concerned for the man lying beside her to marvel at the beauty of the structure before them.

The dock at the temple was deserted. Canidius spotted an overturned cart, which they righted with the assistance of the litter bearers. It still had both wheels intact and it was far easier, and more comfortable, to use to transport a dying man. There was also room in it for Ptolemy and Melissa, who was desperately trying to apply as much pressure to Mark Antony's wound as possible. The makeshift bandage she had applied was soaked with so much blood she wondered how he was still alive.

With the bearers and guards' help, they slowly moved the cart up the slope towards the temple. Diomedes scuttled along at the head of the group, grumbling all the while about their slow progress, but he soon fell silent after some gentle persuasion from the sharp end of Canidius' gladius.

Mark Antony's pallor was ashen, his face clammy, his breathing laboured. At his insistence, he had been propped up rather than laid flat He said it was purely to give some comfort to the terrified Ptolemy, who now clung to his good side, but Melissa knew that was not the case. Every so often, he would open his eyes and scan the horizon. Death might be creeping ever closer to the man, but the general simply refused to succumb to his wound while he perceived his party to be in danger.

A short way from the dock, they reached a junction in the road. Diomedes turned along the main way towards the temple gates, but Mark Antony shouted out with a pained cry.

"Stop!"

Anthony immediately dropped the shaft he was holding and came alongside the cart. Canidius dragged Diomedes back to join them, holding the eunuch tightly by the upper arm to make sure he did not try to bolt for the safety of the sanctuary walls.

"This is where we must part," Mark Antony gasped. "My path lies to the right with the eunuch, while you must take the track left. Follow it to its end. It will lead you to the sea. Your vessel awaits you in an inlet a little farther west."

As he patted Ptolemy on the head, his words were for Anthony. "You say this one has no part to play in history. Perhaps he will have some part to play in the future, just as you once did. You will do this for me. Swear it."

Anthony paused, and then nodded his agreement. "I swear it. I will do this for you, my father."

Mark Antony reached out and gripped his arm. "He

is worthy of you, Lissa," he said loudly. "Treat him well, and always forgive his failings, for he has many."

Melissa stepped closer at the sound of her name. "How would you know that? You barely know him!" she said in surprise.

Mark Antony shook his head in disbelief. "Of course I know him. He is of my blood – my eldest and most beloved son."

Anthony felt a lump form in his throat. For so many years he had known nothing about his father. When he had learned who he was descended from, he quickly came to hate the name of Mark Antony. Now that same man was dying in front of him, he felt ashamed that he had squandered what little chance he had to get to know the complexities of his renowned father. He turned his head away, not wanting the others to see his turmoil.

"I will check that our path is safe," he muttered. He lifted Ptolemy into his arms and walked a short way down the track towards the sound of the distant waves crashing on the shore. He walked until he was well out of earshot, knowing his father would want to say a private goodbye to Melissa. For the first time in his life, he had no desire to know what was said between them.

Mark Antony turned his attention to Melissa, who was holding his wrist. She was actually checking for his pulse, which felt erratic, even to her untrained hand.

"Lissa, my love, there is no time to say the words I have long wished to say."

"There is no need to say them," she murmured, brushing her other hand across his forehead to remove the sweat from his brow. "I know."

"As do I." He held her eyes with his for a moment and then continued. "Here. You must take this. The time has come to return it to its rightful owner." He put his hand up to the clasp of the locket, but was shaking too badly to unhook it.

"Keep it, please," Melissa begged and placed her hand over his, trying to stop him releasing the clasp.

"Wearing it has given me comfort for many years, but I am no fool. It is such a beautiful piece, it could only ever have been on loan, and never be mine to keep."

Melissa sobbed, knowing he was referring not to the locket, but its owner.

In a final demonstration of strength, Mark Antony wrenched on the chain until it snapped. He pushed the locket into Melissa's hand. "We both know this cannot be allowed to fall into the wrong hands."

As their eyes met, a lifetime of shared memories flashed through their minds. She had driven him to want to be a better man, while he had driven her to distraction. He tried to kill her on more than one occasion, and she wished him dead more times than she could remember. Beyond all this, they had shared a special bond, an unlikely friendship forged out of a mutual admiration, which had slowly turned to love.

"Why am I always saying goodbye to you?" he murmured softly, breaking the silence. "This time will be the last, but I am not afraid. I know I will always be with you and, who knows, we may yet find each other in the next life." He winced again as the pain in his gut increased. "My time is short. You must go, and you must dry your tears. You know how I hate to see you cry. It is most unbecoming for a woman of your status."

Melissa wiped her face with the back of her hand and then leant forwards. Placing a delicate kiss on his cheek, she whispered tenderly into his ear. "I have always loved you, Mark Antony."

He sighed. "I told you to never lie to me," he whispered in return, "but this once I will allow it." As he pushed her away gently, he winked at her and, for one last moment, she saw in him the dashing young lieutenant she had first met so many years before in Caesar's Praetorium, on the bank of the River Rubicon.

He nodded his farewell to Canidius, who was a few paces away, holding Diomedes firmly by the arm. "You have your orders, old friend. I trust you will follow them, despite your recent tendency towards insubordination!"

Canidius nodded. He too had tears in his eyes, but he blinked them away. "It has been an honour, general." He gripped his commander's wrist, and then turned his attention to his captive.

"You get him inside that temple, you snivelling runt, or you will not live to see the sunrise." He pushed the eunuch away in disgust and turned to Melissa. "Lady, we must go," he said softly.

Then, taking Melissa gently by the elbow, Publius Canidius Crassus walked calmly down the road towards the setting sun without a backwards glance.

He knew he would never see the man he called his commander, his mentor and his friend, again.

Chapter 40

The fugitives met no resistance on their short trek to the harbour, where they stole a rowing boat and slipped away in the half-light of dusk. Anthony and Canidius took it in turns to row the short distance along the shore to where the *Selene* was moored out of sight of the Roman fleet. It was almost the exact reversal of the method Cleopatra used to enter Alexandria when she presented herself to Caesar, so many years earlier.

The rowing boat pulled alongside the *Selene* and Anthony hauled himself up the ladder at the back of the vessel. Once aboard, he threw Canidius one of the mooring ropes and they tethered the two vessels together. Once the boats were securely tied, Canidius passed Ptolemy up to Anthony. He took Melissa's hand and helped her to make the transfer between the vessels, before finally climbing the ladder himself.

As Anthony weighed anchor, he shouted to Melissa to show Canidius how to open the sail. Settling Ptolemy in the well, she began explaining to their bemused Roman colleague which of the ropes to pull on to raise the sail. Melissa returned to the well and retrieved a life jacket from the locker under the seat which she pulled over Ptolemy's head, fastening it to him. Anthony took the rudder and, within minutes, the boat began to move towards the open sea and freedom.

The winds were with them, allowing them to follow the coast to the west, just as Mark Antony had instructed. After half an hour they approached another inlet where Canidius announced his intention to leave them.

"This is where we must part. Continue along the coast towards Cyrene. With luck and Fortuna's blessing, you will reach a safe harbour in a day or so."

"Come with us," Melissa pleaded. Perhaps, she thought, she could save the life of one good man.

"No, lady, my orders were to see you safely from the city. This I have done and now I must return."

"Lissa is right, Canidius. You should come with us. There is nothing you can do back there." Anthony agreed with his wife, knowing Canidius would be executed when he was eventually caught.

He tried a little deception in an attempt to persuade the Roman. "I was told our best chance is to head north from here towards Crete. I cannot sail so far alone, but with your help we could make it. You could have a good life there."

Canidius smiled. "I thank you for your kind offer, but my answer is no. My place is by my general's side. He is the reason I risked all to reach Alexandria ahead of Octavian's army. I will never desert him."

"He is dead by now," Anthony added, as he began to adjust the sails to slow the yacht.

"I know, yet I have made my choice. I made a promise to keep you from Octavian's grasp. The best way to do that is to lead them in the opposite direction. I made my peace with Dis a long time ago, and I do not fear her. She waits for me with open arms."

He looked down at Ptolemy, still cowering in the well. "I will take the boy. I can arrange passage for him to the priests in the south, before I present myself to Octavian."

Melissa reached down and began undoing the lifejacket she had placed on Ptolemy, but to her surprise Anthony placed a hand on her wrist to stop her.

"He stays with us," he said with an unusual air of authority. It was a tone Melissa had never before heard from him. She turned her head and stared at him in disbelief, while Canidius lowered the anchor.

Anthony returned her stare with one of stubbornness. "He is my brother and as such he is my responsibility."

"Are you sure?" Canidius questioned. "Will his presence not put you in greater danger?"

"Not as much as he would endanger you. No one is looking for us, and you can ride faster without him. We are all better off this way." Anthony held out his hand. After a moment's consideration, Canidius gripped his wrist in the Roman way, agreeing to Anthony's terms. He then said a swift good bye to Melissa before climbing into the rowing boat and loosening the rope.

"Lady, I promise you this. Mark Antony will have at least one loyal Roman to mourn his passing," he called, as the rope slipped through the mooring ring.

As they watched Canidius row away, Melissa felt her throat tighten in grief. "Another good man going to a senseless death," she said hoarsely.

"We can't save them all, Liss, just this one." Anthony pointed down at the little boy cowering at his feet.

"How are we going to explain *him* back home?" she said, in a half-whisper.

"We'll worry about that *if* we get there. There's a lot of water between us and home. And every chance we won't make it," Anthony replied, in the same hushed tone. "You know damned well the kid would have died if I'd let Canidius take him."

"What if we've changed history?" Melissa asked.

"It's too late to worry about that now and, anyway, I made a promise to a dying man to save his son. There is no actual record of Ptolemy being seen in Rome with the twins, it's all supposition. For all we know, he's meant to come with us."

As he looked down at the wide-eyed little boy, Anthony saw a glimmer of his youngest son in the frightened stare. "You know, it'll be easier than you think to get away with this. I reckon I can pass him off as my love-child, which gives you an excuse to be pissed with me when we get back. We might have to change his name though to make him blend in. Ptolemy is a little unusual in the twenty-first century."

"What about his mother? What do we say about her?"

He shrugged in the same nonchalant way he always had, but this time Melissa saw something else. Briefly, she saw another man named 'Antony' reflected in the mannerisms of her husband.

"We'll say she died, maybe, or perhaps we fake a note and say she abandoned him. First things first, let's see what he thinks."

He reached down and lifted Ptolemy into his arms and spoke to him in Greek. "I told you I would give you a new boat, my son. One that Alexander cannot break."

Ptolemy looked suspicious for a moment. He looked around Melissa and across the deck towards the prow. "Is this mine?" he asked in surprise.

"It will be one day. A replacement for the one that was broken," Anthony replied, with a grin. "Do you like it?"

Ptolemy placed his forefinger on his chin as he pretended to think about his answer. Then he smiled and nodded. "It will do − thank you, father."

Looking over the boy's head, Anthony winked at Melissa, who shook her head in disbelief. The famous Anthony Marcus charm was working once again, aided somewhat by the fact that a confused and traumatised little boy still believed he was with his real father − the legendary Mark Antony.

Anthony set Ptolemy back on his feet. "You know, the *Selene* is a little low in the water. I'm hoping that means we've got a fair amount of provisions below. Let's see how many days' water we have. I'm still thinking we should head for Crete, if we can. If we do have to get back to Actium, then that's the fastest route."

"And how do we get back home?"

Anthony stared at his wife. He wanted to pull her to him and hold her. He wanted to tell her he did not care where they ended up, provided they were together. He was desperate to celebrate the fact that they were both still alive, but he did not dare do any of these things. It was still too soon. Melissa was never one to rush headlong into anything. She needed time to process the situation and consider every available option. If he was to have any chance at forgiveness for what he had done, it had to be on Melissa's terms.

He reached out and put a hand on her elbow. "Let's deal with one thing at a time, Liss. Grab me the keys while you're at it – just in case we get lucky."

Melissa nodded and opened the hatch. She stepped down into the cabin and gasped at the sight that met her.

"Er, Anthony. You'd better get down here," she called, before moving further into the cabin.

She heard his footsteps behind her, and then she heard him swear.

"Fuck me! Where the hell did this lot come from?"

One of the berths was stacked with baskets containing fresh fruit and bread, with jars of dates and olives wedged in between. On the floor were a number of flasks, some of which, on closer examination, were found to contain wine, but most contained water.

The other berth was laden with sacks of booty from the palace. In addition to piles of gold and silver tableware were bags of jewels and coins. In Roman terms it was a small fortune; to a pair of archaeologists the haul was priceless. It appeared Mark Antony's idea of provisioning covered every eventuality.

Melissa opened one bag and pulled out a handful of silver denarii, allowing them to trickle back through her fingertips. "The food will last us a good few days and then I guess we have the money to buy whatever we need after that."

As his eyes scanned the cabin, Anthony spotted a tubular leather case, which he immediately recognised as a document carrier. To his delight, it contained maps of the coastline and offshore hazards such as sandbanks and shallows. To the side, the names of major ports had been added by hand, with distances in Roman leagues noted. They were hundreds of miles, and two millennia, from home, with many Roman vessels between them and their intended destination. The odds of survival were far from favourable, but at least they had a chance, thanks to the detailed planning of a military genius.

Anthony opened one of the smaller bags and pulled out a handful of precious stones, whistling as he inspected the gems. "You do realise we are loaded. Whether we make it home or not, we will live like kings for the rest of our lives off this lot."

"Not if we have nowhere to sleep," Melissa grumbled. She had retrieved Anthony's jeans from the back of the locker and was pulling the ignition keys out of the pocket. She handed both items to Anthony. "There are three of us and no available beds.

He laughed as he took the items from her. "Is that all you're worried about? With your talent for organisation, stashing this lot should be easy."

Melissa glared at him as he stripped off his sweaty tunic and pulled on the jeans.

"Seriously," he continued, "we will get through this if we work together." He zipped up his fly and then reached for her hand. To his surprise she did not pull away. He squeezed it gently, thinking how lucky they were to be alive. Only the day before, he had thought he would never see his wife again. There was so much he needed to say, so many apologies to make when she was ready to listen, but now was not the time. For now, they had to survive.

He pushed his fears to the back of his mind and grinned as he pulled a T-shirt over his head. "You work on clearing a bunk for you two to sleep in. Tip what you can of the water into the storage tank and I'll ditch the empty amphorae over the side to lose some of the weight. I'll concentrate on getting us a little further offshore, where we'll be safe enough to drop anchor for a while. The rest can wait. OK?"

Melissa knew what he meant. There were so many painful conversations that would need to be had, but not yet. Both had done some regrettable things in order to survive this far, and these would be discussed in time. For now, it would take their combined wits to get them safely home.

For the briefest moment, Melissa's fingers curled around Anthony's. She nodded her agreement without a word, before setting to the task of clearing some space in the cabin.

Back on deck, Anthony stared at the little boy sitting in the well, calmly inspecting the strings on the life jacket. He was already thinking through what he would need to do to make the arrangements for Ptolemy to pass into twenty-first century life. Luckily, his lawyer would be able to help. The man was nearly eighty, but he had arranged new identities for both Anthony and Victor when the need had arisen some thirty five years earlier. He was a man who knew which strings to pull, which wheels to oil, and which officials to bribe. Anything was possible, if you had enough money, and they certainly had that. In fact, converting their new-found wealth into cold, hard cash without arousing too much suspicion would be considerably harder than adopting a two thousand-year-old child. Anthony had no doubt his ageing lawyer was more than up to that task as well, for a considerable cut, and no questions asked.

Of course, all these musings were moot, if they could not find a way home. Anthony thought about their children. Vicky and Alex were both well provided for and would be looked after by their godparents, but they had both suffered so much already in losing Jack. He did not want them to suffer the loss of their parents as well. It would be too much for them to bear. If there was a way home, he was determined to find it. If his father had taught him one thing, it was that an Antonius could do anything he set his mind to, provided he could be bothered to get off his backside in the first place.

He ruffled Ptolemy's hair before turning his attention back to the yacht. It was almost dark and the temperature was dropping rapidly, which surprised him. What should have been a sultry August night in the Mediterranean felt more like a cool September evening in England. He still needed to get the *Selene* far enough offshore to drop anchor safely. He had no intention of allowing the yacht to be boarded in the night by opportunist thieves. Absent-mindedly, he put the keys in the ignition and turned them. There was a brief splutter, but the engine did not fire.

Anthony stopped moving, thinking he had imagined it. When he had tried to start the engine at Actium there had been nothing more than a click as the key turned. This was more promising. He tried the key again, and again the engine spluttered, trying to turn.

He looked around him. The horizon was disappearing before his eyes, as was the shoreline behind them, all enveloped in a thin veil of mist.

Melissa's head appeared through the hatch, a look of anticipation on her face. She went to speak but he raised his hand to stop her. He closed his eyes and listened. There was barely a sound except for the gentle lapping of the water against the hull of the yacht. For some reason, the silence made the hairs on the back of his neck stand on end.

And then, the final piece to the puzzle fell into place as Ptolemy tugged on his jeans to get his attention.

"Father, there is an odd smell in this mist. It is not the usual smell of the sea. I do not like it, and I am cold. Can we go home now? Please?"

Anthony opened his eyes slowly and turned the key one last time. It seemed Fortuna herself was smiling on the Marcus family, and he winked at Melissa as the engine finally spluttered into life.

"You know, Ptolemy," he said, "I think perhaps we can."

Epilogue

"I fear I must apologise. To whom are you referring?"

Publius Canidius Crassus, general of the Roman army and loyal friend to Mark Antony, dangled like a fish from a hook in the ceiling of the Alexandrian jail. His wrists, bound by rope, were wrenched so high above his head that his toes barely touched the ground. His face was bruised and bloodied; the skin flayed from his back. And still he defiantly resisted his torturer. In fact, he could keep this up all day, if he had to.

A thin, younger man stood in front of him, arms folded. Next to him stood a brute of a man, almost a head taller than the other, with biceps as wide as a woman's thighs. The younger man gave a nod, and the brute punched Canidius in the kidneys.

Canidius wheezed, but he did not scream, despite the agony he felt. He would not give this man the pleasure of knowing how much he ached. He had no intention of giving anything away to Gaius Octavius Caesar, or Octavian as he was more commonly known.

Octavian tapped his foot impatiently. "I will ask you again. Where is the seer?"

"To which one do you refer?" Canidius gasped. "Ever since your good friend, Agrippa, banished them from Rome, we have so many. They arrive by the day, with tales of the persecution they have suffered at your self-righteous hand. Fortune-tellers set up stall on every street corner, between the pimps and the poets. Let me speak to some. I am sure I can find one to your liking."

"I do not want *any* seer. I want *the* seer. Caesar's seer – the one they called his witch."

"I have no knowledge of any witch. I was never a part of Caesar's inner circle. I never met the woman you speak of."

Octavian gave a half-laugh. "Come now, Canidius. We both know that to be untrue. She is the woman Mark Antony took from Caesar's loyal service, directly to the depravity of his bed. I believed her dead. He did well to hide her for so long." He stared at the floor for a moment, shaking his head as he tried to establish how he had been deceived for so many years. "No matter, Cleopatra promised me the slut's head and I will have it."

Canidius would have shrugged, had he been capable. All he could do was tilt his head to the side. "Cleopatra promises many things to all men. You will come to understand quite quickly – the queen promises much and delivers little."

Octavian began pacing to and fro in his frustration. "Publius Canidius Crassus. I do not believe you understand the severity of your situation. You are a traitor and will die a traitor's death. However, if a man were to admit to being led astray by witchcraft, I could be persuaded to stay the executioner's hand. I can be very generous to such a man – easily as generous as the former queen was." He paused and waved the papyrus signed by Cleopatra, granting Canidius' concessionary rights in Egypt.

Had there been even the slightest hint that the offer was genuine, it might have been tempting, but Canidius was under no such illusions. The coldness in the delivery told him all he needed to know about Octavian's insincerity. He calmly gave his reply.

"When I meet such a man, I will be sure to introduce you."

The brute sniggered and was forced to turn away to hide his grin. He knew only too well that a man of Canidius' calibre would never break. It was a complete waste of his time, although it was proving entertaining.

Octavian shot the brute a withering glare. His patience was at its limit. He could not understand why Canidius did not simply give him the information he wanted. Surely this stubborn fool could not enjoy the punishment he was receiving? He was an intelligent man. Had he taken leave of his senses?

"Do you not understand me? I am offering you clemency. There is no need to die for a woman who has deserted you."

Canidius tilted his head in the other direction to get a better look at Octavian. A pompous, preening peacock was how Mark Antony had described him. Add paranoid and puny to that list, and Canidius felt the assessment was fair.

At this point in proceedings, Octavian really should have had the upper hand, but he did not. Canidius was the one firmly in control in this interrogation, unlike his young companion who looked fit to burst. In fact, were it not for the fact Canidius was tied to the hook, it could have been argued that he was not the one being tortured at all. Mentally, Octavian was close to losing his famed control. Canidius knew it, as did the brute tasked with dealing the blows. It was time to turn the screw a little further.

Canidius sighed. "We all die at some point. It makes no difference whether it is sooner or later, though the sooner I go, the less I will have to suffer your infernal whining."

The brute laughed out loud, unable to hide his amusement any longer.

Octavian snapped. He stormed up to Canidius and in a fit of rage shoved him in the shoulder. It barely made an impression. "Tell me the whereabouts of the seer known as Lissa!" he screamed.

Canidius took a deep breath. He held it, before he slowly exhaled into Octavian's face, causing the younger man to blink and step back.

"I cannot," he said, as calmly as before.

"Cannot or will not?"

Canidius merely smiled.

Octavian nodded to the brute, who had regained his composure. He punched Canidius across the jaw again, so hard that Canidius spun around in the air.

The brute gripped his captive, stopping him from spinning and turning him back to where he started. He respected this Roman, who had demonstrated far more moral fibre than the one standing at his side.

Canidius gave a brief nod in appreciation to the brute for sparing him from giddiness. He smiled at Octavian again. He could do this all day, and he would. Not for the seer, nor for her husband, but to honour a promise made to a dying man. A man worthy of his loyalty and respect: Mark Antony.

He spat blood on the floor once again, along with a tooth.

"I fear I must apologise. To whom are you referring?"

Authors Note

After the death of Mark Antony on what we term the 1st of August, Cleopatra lasted a further eight days. In that time she did her utmost to charm Octavian, insisting that she had been controlled by Mark Antony and that without his influence, her loyalty to Rome was assured. Octavian did not care. There were no circumstances under which Cleopatra would be allowed to keep her throne. Even though Plutarch insists Octavian made every effort to save her, I cannot help but think Cleopatra's suicide proved an extremely fortuitous outcome.

After Alexandria fell, many high ranking officials were pardoned and allowed to swear fealty to Octavian, including the Roman admiral of Mark Antony's fleet. Canidius, however, remained loyal to Mark Antony to the very last and was executed for his devotion. There is no record of him being tortured as I have suggested, but I felt this was a heroic way to dispatch his character; death rather than dishonour.

Plutarch states that the children were taken to Rome and paraded in the Triumph, although only the twins, Cleopatra Selene and Alexander Helios, are specifically named. Cleopatra Selene was later married off to Juba, King of Mauretania, while Alexander Helios is never mentioned after the Triumph and may have died (or been murdered) in childhood. The lack of any mention in any ancient source, by name, of Ptolemy Philadelphus, has led some recent historians to suggest he may not have made it to Rome alive. Therefore, I have used this lack of evidence to place him on Melissa and Anthony's yacht. Who knows what the future holds for him now that he has sailed off into the sunset with new parents!

Recent research by Dr Kathleen Martinez suggests that Cleopatra's tomb was not lost to the Mediterranean, but is in fact at the temple complex at Taposiris Magna. Archaeological investigations have been undertaken, but have not provided any conclusive evidence for, or against this proposal, at the time of writing. As this location best fitted with my storyline, this is where I have placed the tomb. Wherever Cleopatra was laid to rest, Mark Antony was laid at her side. It is my personal hope that they remain there together - undiscovered and at peace.

There is no evidence of any secret passages behind images of funerary gods in the palaces of Alexandria and is pure invention on my part.

Thanks, as always, goes to Sheila Mackie for her editing and for agreeing with me that Octavian was a nasty little shit.

My endless gratitude goes to Maria Smith for her patience and for publication of this long awaited instalment of the trilogy. We have both been through so much since we began this journey, and I will forever be in her debt for sticking with me. My thoughts are with you, always.

My last words must be for Mark Antony. He has been vilified since the first historical account was penned, but did he really deserve such criticism? Personally, I do not think so and have tried to portray every known element of his character, good and bad. You may each decide for yourselves whether he is the hero or the villain.

About the Author

Linda Coleman is an author of historical fiction novels. Born in Chatham in Kent, her interest in the Roman period was sparked by a school trip to Lullingstone Roman Villa. This interest was fostered during her time at Chatham Grammar School, where she studied the Classics. After joining the Civil Service at seventeen, she has since carved out a successful career in administration in both the public and private sectors. Writing is her hobby. She now lives in Wiltshire with her husband.

Printed in Poland
by Amazon Fulfillment
Poland Sp. z o.o., Wrocław